TIME LOST

Out of Time, Book Two

C.B. Lewis

A NineStar Press Publication

Published by NineStar Press
P.O. Box 91792,
Albuquerque, New Mexico, 87199 USA.
www.ninestarpress.com

Time Lost

Printed in the USA
NineStar Edition
September, 2020

Print ISBN: 978-1-64890-086-0

Also available in eBook, ISBN: 978-1-64890-085-3

WARNING:

This book contains sexually explicit content, which is only suitable for mature readers, scenes depicting a child in danger, and the death of a minor character (both off page).

A dead intruder. A missing scientist. A terrified child.

No one wants a dramatic case first thing on a Monday morning, but that's exactly what Detective Inspector Jacob Ofori got. It should be open and shut, but scientist Tom Sanders is nowhere to be found, a dead man seems to have appeared from thin air, and the Temporal Research Institute—Sanders's company—is strangely uncooperative about assisting with the case.

Jacob's only source is TRI engineer, Kit Rafferty. He clearly wants to help, but there's only so much the man can and will tell him. As more and more impossible questions mount up, Jacob finds himself facing a reality that could change his world.

To the usual suspects—we did it :)

Chapter One

At first, everyone assumed it was a burglary.

The postman was the first on the scene. He'd arrived early in the morning to make a delivery to the house in question and found the front door wedged open. No one answered when he rang the bell, so he called the police. The two constables arrived to investigate, and they were the ones who found the body.

It escalated after that.

Not even noon, Jacob thought grimly. Hell of a way to start a Monday.

His autopod shuttled along, arcing off from the main highway. As much as he missed manual controls of old-fashioned cars and early autocars, he appreciated the driverless function of the pod because it gave him time to skim through the images from the crime scene en route.

He wouldn't get a feel for the scene until he got there, but the images let him know what he was about to walk into. There were signs of a struggle in the room where the body was found, and plenty of blood, but the rest of the house seemed undisturbed.

"Control to Delta Seven. ETA to destination?"

Jacob leaned forward and cleared the images from the display on the windscreen, bringing up his location on the map. Beyond it, he could see the country roads through the glass.

"ETA fifteen minutes, Control," he replied, then muttered under his breath, "Into the backside of nowhere."

It was half an hour beyond the miles of sprawling suburbs of the city in the middle of green fields and close to a forest. The nearest amenities had to be at least four miles from the building. He shook his head. What kind of person chose to live all the way out there anymore? It wasn't as if there were a shortage of housing in the city.

A chime indicated another image had been received.

Jacob opened it up and leaned forward, frowning.

A door, barely visible, blended into the pattern of the wall. No handle, no visible hinges.

"You seeing this, sir?" Constable Foley's voice rang through the speaker.

"I am indeed, Foley," he said, widening the image. "Is that a safe room?"

"Looks that way, sir," the constable replied. "The dust in front of it suggests a box was moved and recently. Looks like someone might be in there."

Smart girl, Jacob thought with approval.

"Any response?"

"Not yet, sir, but if they were attacked—"

"They might not be capable of replying," Jacob finished. "Keep trying." He minimised the image and looked out through the windscreen. "I have visual on you, Foley. Be with you soon."

Ahead of him, the house was visible between the trees. The red brick structure had to be at least two centuries old, but even from a distance, the modern touches were obvious. The windows were thick and secure. The roof had been replaced with faux slate.

The autopod purred to a halt beside the four other vehicles lining the gravel courtyard, and the door slid aside. Jacob stepped out and glanced at the other vehicles. He recognised the coroner's transport pod, and the standard blue-and-white-patterned squad pod, but the other two were probably the homeowner's.

Foley opened the front door to greet him.

Half his age, she hadn't been with the force long enough to be as jaded as him yet. She smiled in greeting. "Morning, sir."

He winced. "Say afternoon. It makes it a little more bearable."

She laughed. "You want a summary, sir?"

"I read up on it on the way over. Any word on the owner?"

"Thomas Sanders," Foley said, leading him toward the house. "Forty-eight. Widower with one young son. He's a well-reputed scientist and engineer. High up in some kind of historical and scientific research program in the city, the Temporal Research Institution."

"Have you been able to make contact with him?"

Foley shook her head, her sandy ponytail swinging. She offered him overalls to cover his suit. "We've tried his business and private numbers. His colleagues said he's been on a leave of absence for health reasons for several weeks. Our best bet is the safe room."

"Any sign of the son?"

"We assume he's with his father," Foley replied.

"Do we have an ID for the body yet?"

She hesitated in the hallway. "That's the strange thing, sir. We can't find anything on him. His prints aren't in the system. No DNA trace either. We still need to run facial recognition, but so far, we've got nothing."

"That's not unusual."

Foley looked at him. "There's something off about it all. I'll show you."

The house was spacious inside. The lower level was split into four rooms, all branching off from a wide, sunlit hall. Foley led him down the hall and to one of the rooms at the back, her covered boots thumping on the wooden floors.

Jacob stopped in the doorway, taking a moment, then stepped across the threshold. The crime scene team was still at work.

The room appeared to be some kind of laboratory with workbenches running along one wall. Another wall was covered in old-fashioned whiteboards with all kinds of incomprehensible text and codes marked on them in half a dozen colours. Jacob studied all of it for a moment, but whatever Sanders was working on, it was far beyond Jacob's barely adequate physics A level.

There were little machines here and there, suspended from the boards by wires. Spools of wire and gears were scattered across the floor. Several boxes had been upended from shelves and lay on their sides.

In the middle of it all, the body lay face down on the floor, a bloodied hammer close at hand.

Danni Michaels was working on the body and glanced up with a nod. "Sir."

"Cause of death?" Jacob said, keeping his eyes off the dead man's face.

"Looks like blunt force trauma," Danni replied, nudging her magnifying glasses up her nose with her knuckles. "I don't think it's a wild guess to say the weapon was that hammer. It was a single blow, landed here."

Jacob gritted his teeth and looked. The left side of the man's forehead was ruptured. His eyes were open, and he had an expression of surprise on his rigid, bloody face. He was young. Maybe thirties. Dark-haired. His eyes were dark, the pupils flared wide open, but death sometimes did that. Blood had spread in a wide, sticky pool around his body. Jacob swallowed down the familiar rising acid.

Christ, he hated the messy ones.

He glanced around the room.

A pair of slippers, several steps away from the blood pool, had left bloody prints on the polished floor. The owner must have kicked them off, and they'd ended up at least three feet from each other. Not good shoes for running, slippers. If he—men's slippers, size nine approximately—had already knocked down the man on the floor, then there had to be another assailant whom he was running from.

"Any sign of this man's accomplice?"

"Accomplice?" Foley asked.

Jacob gestured to the slippers. It was easier than looking at the body. "You don't try and run from an unconscious, nearly dead man. There was someone else here."

"We haven't seen any sign of anyone else," Foley replied. "Sorry, sir. I didn't even notice that."

He offered her a brief smile. "That's why I'm a DI, Foley." He motioned to the body. "You said there was something off?"

Foley nodded, crouching by the body. "Take a look at his right eye."

Jacob went down beside her, propping his forearms on his knees. It took him a moment, but then he saw what she was pointing out: The pupil wasn't blown. There was no iris at all.

"What the hell..." He leaned closer. "Michaels, can I borrow your magnifiers?"

She handed them over and obligingly shone the torch over the man's eyes. "Clever, isn't it?"

Jacob peered down and frowned. "A synthetic bionic eyeball? Is that even possible?"

Michaels shook her head. "I've heard of people developing them, but I've never heard of any successful trials." She squatted by the body and grinned. "I can't wait to get it out and see what it's made of."

"And there's one of those images I didn't need," Jacob murmured, peering through the magnifier again. The pupil seemed to be a focusing lens. High-quality, high-end technology. "Foley, have you checked anywhere that might carry tech this advanced?"

"We're putting together a list," she said. "But from what we're hearing back, this is off the charts, sir. No one has heard of technology like this before, or if they have, they're not telling us about it."

He straightened up. "You said this Sanders was a scientist?"

"Doctor in physics and engineering," she confirmed.

"Could he have made something like this?"

She hesitated. "From all accounts, he didn't deal in human biology or bio-artificing."

"Doesn't mean he couldn't." Jacob ran a hand over his face. "Well, if we can't find this man by standard identification, maybe we can find him by the eye he doesn't have. Danni, we need all the information you can get us as soon as possible."

"Sir," Danni said at once.

Jacob turned to Foley. "Where's Singh?"

"Still trying to get into the safe room." She jerked her head. "This way."

The safe room was up the stairs in what appeared to be a playroom. Windows lined one of the walls, the others covered in posters and drawings. Kids' toys and games were scattered all over the place. Singh was working his way along the one blank wall with a scanner.

Jacob took in the mess. "You said Sanders has a son?"

"Ben," Foley confirmed.

"About eight?"

Foley looked at him in surprise. "Seven and a half. Is this another one of those detective things?"

Jacob chuckled. "This time, it's one of those dad things."

Singh glanced over his shoulder at them, sighing in frustration. "Foley, I know you said to scan for a high intensity of fingerprints on the wall, but this whole wall is fingerprints." He nodded at Jacob. "Afternoon, sir."

"Singh." Jacob approached, studying the wall. "It's very smoothly done, isn't it?" He rubbed his short beard thoughtfully with his fingertips. "No visible buttons or latches anywhere?"

"None we could find," Foley said. "I thought it might be a pressure-point system, but seems not. We requested an expert, but they've been delayed."

"I think we need to un-delay them," Jacob said, touching his earbud to activate it. "If Sanders is wounded and inside there, we need to get him out. If not, we need confirmation, because this could be an abduction."

While they waited, Jacob had gone down to the laboratory to take another look at the whiteboards. He didn't see what it had to do with Sanders's work at the Temporal Research Institution. A quick search suggested the institution specialised in identifying historical discrepancies and confirming historical events. It could be something to do with locating old records and creating algorithms, he supposed. You would need a specialised engineer to do that.

"Sir?"

Jacob turned. "Foley?"

"The smith is here. I thought you might want to be present if he can open the door."

They headed back up the stairs to the playroom. The body had been removed in the hour before the locksmith arrived, the crime scene unit now working their way out from the house across the grounds, searching for trace evidence of the intruders.

The locksmith was already working on the wall with a scanning device.

"Apparently," Singh said, joining them, "all safe room doors come installed with a registration chip, in case the mechanism needs to be deactivated in an emergency."

"Not unlike this," Jacob observed. "Useful."

The locksmith glanced over. "It's a recent make. Give me two minutes."

In the end, he took less than thirty seconds, and the door swung outward.

Inside, there was a room big enough for a family, but only one person was there. A small tawny-haired boy shrank back into the corner of the room, his arms wrapped around his legs, his face bone-white.

Jacob motioned for the smith and the two constables to back off, and crouched a couple of feet away from the door.

"Hey," he murmured.

The boy was shivering, and tears rolled down his face from swollen, red-rimmed eyes.

Jacob took out his badge, laid it on the floor, and slid it across to the boy. "It's okay. I'm a policeman. My name's Jacob." He watched as the boy tentatively leaned forward and looked at the badge. "Are you Ben?"

The boy nodded. "Where's my dad?" His voice shook as much as he was.

"We're trying to find him now." Jacob offered a hand. "Do you want to come out? You don't need to stay in there."

"Dad told me to stay here." Ben wrapped his arms tighter around his legs. "He told me to, until he came to get me."

"I know." Jacob knelt and sat back on his heels. "We want him to come and get you, too, Ben, but right now, I think he'd want you to be safe, don't you? How about we keep you safe?"

"P-promise?"

Jacob nodded. "Promise."

Ben got unsteadily to his feet. His trousers were sodden, and there was vomit on the front of his shirt. The poor kid must have been terrified. Jacob knelt up, offering both his hands, and Ben's icy fingers wrapped around his.

"There you go," Jacob said as gently as he could, drawing Ben back out. "You're safe now."

The little boy gave a sob and stumbled forward and wrapped his arms around Jacob's neck, clinging to him. Jacob scooped him up and rose to his feet with the boy in his arms. He rubbed his hand in circles on Ben's back.

"You're okay," he murmured. "You're okay."

Chapter Two

They had bacon! Still crispy and hot too! Sometimes, once in a blue moon, a miracle happened in the staff canteen.

Kit grabbed the tongs and piled a thick layer onto his toast. Someone in the queue behind him made a sound of indignation, which Kit studiously ignored as he moved on to the eggs.

By the time construction had finished, his sandwich was a masterpiece of five perfectly balanced layers of cholesterol, slathered in brown sauce. Sometimes an engineering degree could have practical applications. He set it proudly on the table and sat down, picking up his knife and fork.

"Jesus Christ! Are you trying to build a food fort?"

"I like a filling breakfast." Kit looked up with a grin.

Dieter, the lead historian and linguist of the Temporal Research Institution, stood over him with a mug in one hand and a toasted bagel in the other. He raised a pierced eyebrow, looking at the heart attack on a plate. "How the fuck do you stay so skinny?"

Kit stabbed into the mountain of food, cutting right through it. "I need it to power my cunning little brain," he said cheerfully. "You want to join me?"

Dieter glanced around, then shrugged. "Why not? They've called everyone in here anyway. Might as well get a seat."

"They have?"

Dieter nodded distractedly as he buttered his bagel. "Whole agency, apparently." He lifted blue eyes to Kit. "Don't you check your e-mails?"

Kit swallowed a mouthful of runny egg and sausage. "I was hungry. Breakfast always comes before work." He hacked into another part of the tower. "But the whole agency? I don't think I've ever seen the whole agency together. Has that ever happened before?"

"Twice. Before your time." Dieter rose from the chair and raised his hand in greeting. Kit followed his line of sight and spotted one of the communications technicians weaving his way toward them. "This isn't the same as those situations."

He smiled up at the big blond man as he joined them and slipped into the vacant chair beside Dieter. Dieter said something in a language Kit didn't recognise, but Janos Nagy clearly did. His stern mouth crooked up at one side. As far as Kit knew, that was the closest the guy got to laughing.

"Morning, Mr. Nagy." Kit waved his fork.

Janos nodded in greeting. One of the better-looking men in the TRI, he'd caught Kit's eye on day one, but from the first day Kit had been in the building, he'd been cautioned in no uncertain terms that flirting with Janos was a fool's errand, no matter how buff he looked.

"Everyone is coming," he said to Dieter.

Kit glanced around the room. "Why do they need everyone in anyway? I mean, you guys were here last time. What were those meetings about?"

Dieter's expression gave nothing away. "Major incidents."

Janos said nothing. He picked up Dieter's coffee cup as if it were his own.

Everyone knew the two men were a couple and had been for some time, but for the life of him, Kit couldn't work them out. Janos came across as the quiet, introvert type, but Dieter was as colourful and flamboyant as they came. Opposites attracted, Kit guessed.

A big mystery hung over their history that no one talked about in the agency. The people who had joined the TRI in the last three years were all equally oblivious, and no matter who they asked, everyone said Dieter and Janos's affair was no one's business but their own.

"Major time-travel incidents? Or major 'everything is going to explode' incidents?"

Janos looked over at him. "You ask many questions for so early in morning."

"I don't usually work with people who do any interesting talking. It's all tools, cables, synchronisers, stabilisers, and stuff." Kit waved his fork at him. "Not that you do much talking anyway..."

Janos looked at Dieter, raising his eyebrows, and Dieter smacked him lightly on the chest, a smile breaking onto his lips. "Shut up."

"I said nothing." Janos widened his eyes innocently.

Dieter snorted. "Like fuck you didn't." He bit into his bagel, chewing on it thoughtfully. "If it's whole-agency business, it's probably about some system overhaul or bullshit. If it's something that'll affect everyone, they have to tell us. If it's just about a temporal jump, that's restricted to whichever team is involved."

"As long as we're not being fired," Kit declared.

"*We* will not be," Janos said. An audible slap rang out when Dieter smacked him on the thigh. Janos looked at him, offended. "What I said?"

"You were being a dick," Dieter replied and shoved the rest of the bagel into Janos's mouth. "Ignore him. They wouldn't fire us en masse."

By the time everyone filed into the dining room, Kit's tower had been reduced to a few stray beans and a smear of sauce on the plate. He swiped the sauce up with his fingertip, which he then licked clean and wiped on a napkin.

"You could lick the plate," Dieter said with a snort.

"Never in company," Kit replied virtuously. "I do have some standards."

"Everyone!" a voice called out from somewhere in the mass of people. The owner climbed on a table to make herself visible. Kit squinted at the small lady in a hijab. He'd only ever seen her in his first weeks on the job, but he'd heard of her—one of the coders who worked on level ten.

"That's Mariam Ashraf, isn't it?" He looked at Dieter inquiringly.

Dieter went pale, sitting bolt upright. "Fuck..."

Janos said something low to Dieter, his hand on Dieter's shoulder, but Dieter didn't even seem to notice. Kit looked between them and Mariam. Dieter seemed on the verge of a panic attack. That wasn't right. Definitely not good.

"Everyone!" The woman stamped her heel until silence fell. "I need your attention now. We have a code red situation."

"Shit shit shit shit..." Dieter's voice broke.

"We have received notification this morning that a temporal gateway opened close to Tom Sanders's house," the woman said, short and crisp. "It didn't open from within the TRI facilities, or at least it has not knowingly been opened *yet*. We have lost communication with Sanders and have not heard from him since the anomaly occurred."

Kit felt like the bottom had dropped out of his stomach.

Sanders wasn't just the chief of the TRI—he had handpicked Kit to work alongside him. A bloody brilliant scientist, one of the few people to have ideas even wilder than Kit's, and more importantly, he was the man who had made time travel possible. He had pioneered the system, honed it, made it work.

Kit had been both awed and terrified by him.

"What does that mean?" he asked, looking around.

One look at Dieter told him he wasn't going to get any answers. Janos had pulled his chair closer to Dieter's and had his arm around Dieter's shoulder, murmuring to him, a low, steady, repetitive thrum of words in the strange language again, and Dieter leaned into him, shivering.

"The police are currently on site," the woman continued. "We didn't have time to get someone there before the police were called, and now, we won't be able to get access until they have finished their operations. There will be questions asked, so we need to be prepared. Report to your department. Your section leaders will be notified which protocol we will be following in this situation."

People around the room started moving for the doors.

Kit got up, looking around uncertainly, then back at Dieter, who had his eyes closed, breathing hard. Sanders gone. Dieter, normally so calm and collected, having a panic attack. Janos saying more than Kit had ever heard him say before.

Something was very, very wrong.

It couldn't just be an anomaly. It couldn't just be someone going missing.

Kit took a shaky breath. His own rising alarm wouldn't help anyone. "Can I help?" he asked Janos. "I mean, is there anything I can do?"

Janos made an abortive gesture with one hand. "No," he said. "Thank you."

Heels clattered on the floor nearby, and Kit turned to see Mariam approaching. She didn't seem to notice him. He shied back, tugging at the end of his shirt, wondering what to say or do.

"Dieter," she said, approaching the table. "I'm sorry."

He glared up at her. "That was fucking tactful." His voice sounded brittle. "Couldn't have said something before? Taken us aside instead of shouting it from the fucking rooftops?"

"I realise now." She glanced up at Janos. "Get him up to my office. We'll talk there."

"You can tell me what you need me to do. I'm not fucking deaf, Mariam," Dieter snapped, rising. He reached out, gripping Janos's arm. He looked like hell. "Christ. Not again."

Kit shifted his weight from one foot to the other as Mrs. Ashraf watched the couple walk away. "I want to help," he said quietly.

She glanced at him. "Dieter?"

"Or Tom." Kit hesitated, then asked, "Do we have any idea what happened? I mean, he always kept going on about security here. Surely, he must have had something in place there..."

"I can't tell you, Rafferty." She sounded tired, and she looked worse. "You heard your orders. Report to your section leader. You'll be told what you need to know."

"Yes, ma'am."

He left his tray behind and joined the crowd working their way out of the doors. Most people headed for the lifts, but he retreated for the empty staircase to avoid the crush of people all speaking in urgent voices.

It took longer, but it meant he had time to try to even out his breathing and not let himself get worked up. They didn't know what was going on yet. Better not to think of the worst. It gave him time to put together what he knew and, more specifically, what he didn't.

The rest of his team, made up of seventeen people of all ages, had gathered already. Some of them had been with the TRI for years. Kit was their most recent arrival, and normally, that didn't make any difference: an engineer was an engineer, after all.

Now, though, they were talking and lowered their voices when he entered.

Kit made a beeline for Reggie O'Conner, one of the longest-serving members of the TRI and the oldest member of their team. Normally, he could always be counted on to be helpful. "Reg—"

"Don't ask me," Reggie said, holding up both hands. He looked drawn and grim. "I don't know anything more than the rest of you lot."

"That's a load of bull," Kit protested. "What about Dieter and Janos getting a private meeting with Ashraf?"

Reggie's pale eyes narrowed. "They are, are they?" He didn't look surprised.

"She apologised to him for telling him with everyone else. Why would it bother him?"

Reggie shook his head, the light gleaming off his slicked-back white hair. "Not my business to talk about it with anyone. If they want you to know, they'll tell you. For now, leave off."

Kit reluctantly subsided. He retreated to his workbench, looking around at the others. Some of them had clearly overheard him and were speaking in whispers. He frowned, turning back to his bench. Fair enough, they were worried, but being fenced out of their discussions reminded him they still considered him a new arrival, even after three years.

There were so many things contractually classified in the TRI.

He didn't understand all the rules when it came to time travel, but they were the only known agency that worked with it. Well, "known" was a generous way of putting it. Everyone who worked in the building had to sign a confidentiality contract, and even their customers and clients didn't realise what they were paying for.

If someone wanted to clarify a historical incident and there were no available records, they could pay the TRI to research it. The clients weren't aware the "research" involved temporal agents going back to the moment of the incident to see what had happened.

There were strict guidelines in place about what temporal agents could and couldn't do. The agency ran under a code of non-interference. Nothing could be changed or amended. No one could interfere with people, and that explained why people were on edge now.

The fact that a temporal gateway had opened, and it wasn't from in-house, was worrying.

They didn't know where the gateway came from.

They didn't know *when.*

Maybe it had happened before, in the days before he signed up. Maybe Dieter had been involved. Or maybe he was just speculating a lot about a whole lot of nothing.

Kit turned to his workstation to add some new fixtures to a new security function based on Sanders's original temporal gate design. The gates could be held open indefinitely with a sustained flow of power, but it meant people might breach the gateway from the other side. Humans were curious by nature, and a doorway hovering in the middle of nowhere just begged for someone to stick their head through to see what was on the other side.

For some time, the TRI had been reducing the portal as soon as the agents were through, but it always meant the risk of the gateway collapsing and closing.

Kit had been brought in to be a fresh set of eyes. He'd had no idea he was dealing with time travel and took it as a standard engineering problem to be solved. He'd immediately offered a dozen solutions: some the TRI engineers had thought of before, some they hadn't imagined were possible.

That day, he'd met Sanders and got himself a job in time travel.

He'd had no idea who he was dealing with when a skinny, fox-faced man hit him with a rapid-fire series of questions and problems, pushing him to think faster and harder than he ever had before. He was sure he'd made a balls-up of the whole thing, but then the man smiled, held out a hand, and he had a new job.

Sanders had given him challenges, and he'd met them every time.

Now, Sanders was gone.

No. Missing. Only missing. Not gone.

Kit picked up his magnifiers, set them on his nose, and turned on the light over the bench. He couldn't help Sanders in any other way right now, but at least he could work on the last task Sanders had assigned him, and get it as close to finished as possible by the time Sanders returned.

Sometime later, a hand tapped him on the shoulder.

Kit looked up, blinking, as Hamid Johnson's face spread across his vision. He yelped, pulling off the magnifiers, bringing his section leader's face back to its more normal proportions. "Boss?"

"Need your ears for a minute, Kit." Hamid, another long-standing member of the TRI, stood short and stocky with a square block of a beard and an equally square mass of dark curls on his head. "Everyone, you heard Mariam in the mess room. We don't have many details of what's happening, but this much I can tell you—Sanders is missing in action. He had facilities in his home where he developed new technology, but we don't know if he had developed it to the point of doing a solo jump."

"So he could have opened the gate himself?" one of the other engineers asked.

"Possible," Hamid said, hooking his thumbs through his belt, "but unlikely, given he had Ben staying at the house with him."

There were murmurs again, a ripple around the room.

"Is the lad gone too?"

Hamid grimaced, and Kit could tell he didn't want to say much more. "Mariam got a call while we were up there," he said. "Ben was still in the house. The police found him, and he's with them now. Mariam's their emergency contact, so she's headed to the police station."

"Sanders wouldn't leave him alone," Reggie said at once. A couple of people nodded in agreement. "He wouldn't have opened a gate with Ben there."

"That's the general consensus," Hamid agreed. "Some of you haven't been here through a code red, and normally, we would restrict the information as much as possible to ensure minimal damage, but the police have been involved in this situation, which means we all have to be able to answer questions, in case we're asked."

"Is that likely to happen?" Kitty McAllister inquired.

"Right now, we don't know, but best be prepared in case." Hamid gazed around at them. "I'll be talking to each of you individually, but for now, I need you to get back to your workstations and focus on your current tasks. I'll come to each of you in turn."

They nodded and moved off, but Kit hesitated, sorting through the mess of questions he had. There were no more answers to be had about Tom yet, but there were plenty of other questions. Hamid raised his eyebrows.

"Something to add?"

"I was wondering if Dieter's all right," Kit said. "He didn't look well after the meeting."

Hamid scratched the back of his neck. "Didn't realise you were friends with him."

"I'm not," Kit admitted. "I mean, we talk to each other sometimes in the canteen, but..." He frowned. "I don't know. He looked awful."

Hamid smiled briefly, but it didn't reach his eyes. "Long story. He's a lot tougher than he looks, Dieter. You've got your work to worry about and what you'll need to say if the police come calling." He reached up to pat Kit on the shoulder. "Go on. Back to work. I'll call you."

Kit returned to his workstation and stared down at the circuit laid out in front of him. He remembered Mariam Ashraf's expression, the grim look on Janos's face, and how pale Dieter had gone. He could feel the tension in the air, the edge of fear and suspicion. They were saying Sanders was only missing, but from their expressions, it was a lot more serious.

Suddenly, building a temporal keyhole didn't seem all that important.

Chapter Three

The Sanders boy had fallen asleep.

The only problem with the situation arose because he was asleep in Jacob's lap.

It made it difficult to run a team when you couldn't raise your voice above a murmur or get up from your desk. He'd left Foley and Singh to fill in the gaps in the briefing room in his absence while he went over the evidence again.

Ben hadn't been able to tell them much: His father shouted to him to hide, so he went to their secret room and closed the door. The rule was if he had to hide, he had to stay there until his father—or the police—came and told him he could come out.

Jacob hadn't pressed for answers from the terrified boy. Even with a member of social services there, it didn't feel right to push him. He'd helped Ben into a clean set of clothes, persuaded him to eat something, and wasn't at all surprised when the boy clung to him as if he were a security blanket.

Based on the photographs around the house, Sanders and his son were close and seemed happy enough. Unlikely, then, that a loving and protective father would have willingly left his child indefinitely closed up in a safe room. The fact that he'd told his son to hide seemed to support the theory it was more than a simple home invasion.

Jacob slid the images across the screen with his fingertip.

There were checks running on the TRI, but so far, they hadn't found any plausible reason for the man to be targeted. There were some pieces of scientific equipment in the house, but nothing seemed particularly valuable. Even the technology set up in the rest of the house was made up of standard, basic units. Nothing seemed to have been taken, except the man himself.

Sanders's whiteboard flicked onto the screen again, thick with codes and symbols. One of Sanders's colleagues had been called in. Perhaps they would be able to make sense of it for him, or at least point the inquiry in the right direction.

Ben shifted in his sleep, whimpering. Jacob set aside the screen to settle the child, murmuring nonsense and rubbing his back and shoulders. The boy nestled against him but didn't wake, although one small pale fist clung to Jacob's shirt.

Jacob's quill buzzed. He raised his hand and touched his earpiece. "Ofori."

"Sir, we have a Mrs. Ashraf in reception."

Sanders's colleague and also emergency contact, which would kill two birds with one stone, if she cooperated.

"Good. Have her brought up to my office."

The woman was escorted in five minutes later. Small, not much over five foot, probably close to his own age, matronly and soft-featured, with an ornately twisted veil around her head and shoulders. She stopped short in the doorway, her worried expression giving way to relief.

"He's all right?" She lowered her voice enough not to wake the boy, and Jacob guessed she had to be a mother.

"Worn out," he replied as quietly.

He motioned her closer to the seat on the opposite side of his desk, wincing when she had to lift a stack of papers off the chair. She looked for a vacant spot on his desk and ended up adding it to the most stable pile. It looked—as always—like a hurricane had swept through the office. He'd never really taken to the in-tray and out-tray, and for all that they mainly did digital reports, he still had paperwork for all occasions.

"Are you the gentleman who called?" she asked as she sat down.

He nodded. "DI Jacob Ofori. I'm sorry I couldn't give you much information on the call, but you can see I was—" He smiled crookedly. "—occupied."

The woman nodded. "Can I ask what happened?"

"The investigation is ongoing presently, so I'm afraid there's not much we can tell you." He paused for a moment as Ben moved, tucking his head under Jacob's chin. "We suspect there were intruders. At least two, possibly more. It appears Mr. Sanders fought one of them off, but we've found no trace of him or the other intruder. This young man hid in a safe room on the upper level."

Mrs. Ashraf went pale, and she clasped her hands tightly together in her lap. "Do you think the intruder abducted Tom?"

Jacob shook his head. "We can't speculate until we start putting together the evidence. We have people combing the grounds of his home, but with the lack of security hardware in the area, it's very difficult to put together a timeline at the moment."

She nodded. "You won't need to interrogate Ben, will you?"

"I don't think there's much he can tell us." Jacob tilted his head to look down at the boy to be sure he was still asleep, then back at Mrs. Ashraf. "Can you think of anyone who'd want to harm Mr. Sanders? Or any reason why he'd be targeted?"

She shook her head. "He's just a scientist."

Jacob gazed at her. "Just a scientist" made it sound simple, but people who were just scientists didn't get abducted from their homes or beat off assailants with a hammer. He slid his slate across the desk to her, showing an image of the whiteboards. "Is this his work?"

Mrs. Ashraf picked up the slate and studied it. "It looks like it, but I don't recognise these formulas. Thomas always played around with different technology and experimented on things outside of the office."

"Anything that might be financially interesting to people?"

She was very good, and if he hadn't spent more than twenty years in his job, he might not have spotted the twitch of her mouth and the way her eyes flicked down, then up again.

"He develops new hardware and software for enhanced historical research," she said after barely a split-second pause. She even met his eyes, defiant, daring him not to believe her. "Some of the facts we uncover aren't always popular with people."

"Such as?"

She shrugged. "Our institution provided the information about the Potiorek conspiracy."

He vaguely remembered the story. It had been all over the news three years before. A claim that the death of the Austrian Franz Ferdinand at the hands of a Serbian anarchist, triggering World War I, had been planned from within his own country.

The only reason it had made national news at all was because countries all over Europe kicked up a fuss about it. Some believed it, some didn't, but regardless, people thought it was worth noticing. That meant it must have been credible.

He hadn't really paid much attention at the time. Rory was still around then, and Jacob had enough going on without worrying about some old royal who'd got himself killed more than a century before.

"A lot of people weren't happy about that," he observed.

"We were talked down as a conspiracy theory," Mrs. Ashraf said, "but some people were very vocal about the institution. Do you think maybe one of them might have done this?"

It was a deft attempt at redirecting his focus away from the institution, which made him wonder what she—or they—wanted to hide.

"We'll definitely look into the possibility." He gently shook Ben's shoulder. The boy stirred drowsily, then jolted in panic at his unfamiliar surroundings. "Easy," Jacob said gently. "You're safe."

Ben looked up at him, then nodded.

"Ben?" Mrs. Ashraf rose on the other side of the desk.

"Aunt Mariam!" Ben scrambled off Jacob's lap and ran around to her, clung to her. He whispered urgently to her, no doubt telling her what had happened, and she wrapped him up in her arms.

"I know, Ben. The police are looking for him now." She looked across at Jacob. "Is it all right for me to take him home now?"

Jacob rose. "Of course. I'll come by your office tomorrow, if that's all right, so we can discuss the subject further." He smiled. "It's more convenient for you, and it should only take an hour at most."

Not a request, which made it impossible for her to make an excuse to keep him away.

She remained silent for a moment, then nodded. "I'm usually there any time after ten o'clock in the morning. Ask at the front desk, and they'll have you brought to my office." She kept her arm around Ben's shoulders. "I'll see you then."

Ben looked up timidly. "Bye," he said in a small voice.

"Bye, Ben." Jacob met Mrs. Ashraf's eyes. "You take care of him."

"Of course," she replied.

He went to the door of the office as they walked away, comforted to see the boy was in safe hands. There could be no mistaking the protective way Ashraf had wrapped herself around him.

Jacob sighed, returned to his desk, and sat down.

He pulled up all available data on the TRI and the Potiorek conspiracy, for background reading. She might have been trying to redirect his attention, but it didn't necessarily mean she was wrong. If the Potiorek conspiracy had created some enemies, it wouldn't hurt to turn over a few stones and check what might be crawling beneath.

His team awaited him in the briefing room after he'd finished putting together the additional information from Mrs. Ashraf. He stopped in briefly to see Danni and found the pathologist still working on the body. The preliminary reports had confirmed blunt-force trauma as the cause of death, but her investigation into the synthetic eye was ongoing.

"Any luck on facial recognition?" he asked as he entered the briefing room.

Several officers were going through data.

"Nothing."

Jacob paused, looking at Foley. "You mean no luck?"

She shook her head. "I mean nothing. Unless he's been going around with a paper bag over his head for his whole life, he's never been caught on camera. We tried as many variables as we could, but they were only close likenesses."

Jacob looked up at the incident screen and the image of the man currently in the morgue. His face and body gave nothing away.

"Anything interesting on him?" he asked, slipping his hands into his pockets. He found his key ring, and out of habit, his fingers started sliding each key around the ring, one by one.

"Plain shirt, trousers, underwear, and socks," Detective Constable Anton said from his desk, one of the younger members of the CID. "His jacket is some kind of synthetic. High-end. Definitely not off the rail. Possibly something high fashion, but we're running a search for ones like it. Pockets were all empty."

"Nothing special on the shoes," Detective Sergeant Temple added. Six years Jacob's junior, she'd been chasing in his wake for longer than either of them cared to recall. "Could have been bought at any standard retailer."

Jacob rocked on the balls of his feet. "So we have a one-eyed cyborg fashionista who shows up out of nowhere. He ends up fatally beaten to death by a mild-mannered scientist who works for a historical research facility."

Anton snickered. "Happy Monday, sir."

Jacob gave him a look. "Don't even start." He rubbed his forehead. "CSU is still processing the data, but looks like the second assailant may have cleaned up after himself. It would explain the empty pockets, and the lack of any other trace."

"If he abducted Sanders, wouldn't he have his hands full?" Temple asked.

"You would think," Jacob agreed. He tapped one of the images, bringing it to the front of the screen. "According to CSU, there's evidence someone scrubbed at patches of the floor quite recently." He pointed out the highlighted areas. "See what I mean?"

Anton nodded. "And it wasn't worth mopping up the blood because the body couldn't be hidden, so they left it behind."

"Exactly." Jacob brought up several more images of the shelf unit against the back wall of the room. A bloody handprint curled over the edge of one shelf. "This is where we think they caught Sanders. What happened to him after that, we have no idea. The downside of everyone using pods these days is that we've got no tire tracks left behind. Sanders could have been carried out to a pod and there wouldn't be any sign of him or it."

Sometimes, he missed the old days.

Until CSU finished processing everything, they would have to start from another angle.

Jacob looked around at his team. "Okay. Temple, I need you to start digging into the TRI. I've sent you all the extra information Mrs. Ashraf provided when she came to collect the Sanders boy, but I need you to dig deep. I don't think Sanders was just a quiet little scientist. These men targeted him for a reason, and we need to find out what."

"Would Ashraf be able to tell you?"

Jacob grimaced. "There's the problem. If Sanders is more than a scientist, she works with him. If they were working on something and keeping it hidden, I'd say it's even odds she'd want to keep a lid on it as well."

Maybe she did genuinely think it would be helpful to point him in the direction of the TRI's potential enemies, but her expression, the split-second hesitation, the calculation in her eyes, said otherwise. She was hiding something.

Until he could be sure, the team didn't need to know.

"Foley. Singh." He turned to the two constables. "We've requisitioned you for footwork on this one, since we're a couple of people short. I'll need you to start making the rounds of friends and associates to see if they point any fingers at likely enemies. Anything that raises a flag, you bring to us."

"What about the TRI?" Singh asked.

Jacob shook his head. "Leave the TRI to me. I've got an appointment there tomorrow. Anton, we need as much as you can get on Sanders's history outside of family and friends. He was about my age, so he's been doing what he does for a long time. If there's anything there, no matter how far back, we need to know about it."

"What about him downstairs?" Foley inquired, nodding toward the image of the corpse. "If we can't identify him, what do we do with him?"

Jacob scaled up the image on the board. "A man doesn't pop into existence to get his head beaten in. He came from somewhere. We just have to find out where. Could be non-UK national, so put out a call internationally. Run the DNA again. Widen the fields of the search. Go older or younger. Could be he has a close relative with similar DNA. We might get lucky." He raised his eyebrows, looking around. "Clear?"

"Yes, sir!"

Chapter Four

Sanders barely made the evening news.

Some reporter made a brief comment about the fact that he'd gone missing and the police were making inquiries. Most people wouldn't have noticed it, and that got under Kit's skin. Tom deserved more than a passing glance. By rights, they should have been shouting his name from the rooftops.

Kit scowled as the news continued as if they hadn't just glossed over him.

He wanted to rant at somebody about it, but the only people he could do that with would be other staff from the TRI, and he had a sneaking suspicion none of them would want to discuss it with him.

Not like he could ring home and talk to his mum about it, no matter how much he wanted to. What could he tell her? *Oh, hello, Mum. I'm a bit upset because my boss may have been kidnapped by someone from another time. Nothing to worry about.*

He couldn't even tell her the truth about where he worked because of confidentiality clauses slapped all over him. Or anyone else from outside the TRI either. Nothing like being stuck in a catch-22 situation: talk to someone outside and get fired, or talk to someone inside and get nothing.

So, an evening of trying not to think about it, then.

Kit snapped "Music" to switch the media unit from visual to audio. A gesture raised the volume until he could feel the bass vibrating through the floor. Every day at the TRI, he had to keep the volume frustratingly low. He'd tried putting his music on at his volume there once before, but apparently no one else appreciated club anthems from the 2010s as much as he did. Or feeling the bass, which was half the pleasure of it.

He sat on a beanbag at his coffee table, his legs crossed beneath it. The lamps at either corner illuminated the mess of wires and gears spread in front of him. It looked like a toolbox had thrown up all over the surface.

He flipped over the gearbox and reached for the screwdriver.

Technically, he didn't need to do it, but with Sanders gone, Ben would be missing him. Everyone in the TRI had met Ben at least once—a good boy, and so smart already. The last thing he needed was to be worried out of his mind, so Kit had decided to build a distraction. Okay, it might be an old-fashioned toy, and given Sanders's engineering skills, Ben probably had a crate of them. But Kit was hard-pressed to imagine any boy of Ben's age who wouldn't want to have a toy robot, even a homemade one.

He hummed along with the music as he worked. Song after song played, and once in a while, he refilled his thermal beaker from the coffee pot. The robot took shape in his hands, a delicate little biped with a shining, hand-drawn smiley face.

His eyes grew heavier with each detail he added, but it had to be finished, a present to pass on to Mariam for Ben. Had to finish. Ben needed a distraction. As soon as possible. Had to be finished. Tonight. Now.

He woke up when the television blared to life, illuminating the whole room.

Kit sat up with a startled jolt, hands scrabbling across the table. The robot stood, safe and intact in front of him, and he squinted at it. He set it carefully on its feet and pressed the control. The little figure walked across the table, and he grinned fuzzily at it.

"Full speed ahead," he said, rubbing his eyes.

Always his trouble.

He liked building things too much. Ever since he'd moved out of his mum's flat, and then away from his flatmates, he didn't have someone to give him a kick and remind him humans needed sleep. Especially when he had other stuff he didn't want to think about and hid in work instead.

He stumbled—running on caffeine fumes—into the shower and turned the spray to icy in a vague attempt to wake himself up. Not entirely successful, but got him conscious enough to pack the robot up in a retired shoebox and head for the door.

Outside, the wet gusts coming in from the coast turned the world chilly and miserable. Kit shoved the shoebox inside his coat and pulled his hood down as low as he could as he made his way toward the trams.

If anyone asked him how he got to work, he wouldn't be able to tell them. Even after stopping for a coffee from a café, the world moved around him in a haze. The caffeine had started to kick in as he plodded up the steps into the TRI lobby, yawning.

For once, unusually, the reception desk was empty. Security insisted they have it manned at all times to grant access to visitors and people who happened to forget their pass in the pocket of their other coat.

Kit peered around, frowning, and spotted Paulina Borowska in the waiting room, talking to someone.

He meandered over and tapped on the doorframe. The sun sliced in through the window of the room, glorious and bright and not good when it hit anyone right in the face. He squinted in at her. "Morning, Lina," he said. "Permission to enter?"

Paulina took one look at him and winced. Always the first to see him, she could tell when his bed had gone neglected again. For once, she didn't say anything. Instead, she gave a little jerk of her head toward the man sitting in one of the broad armchairs.

"Actually, this is good timing," she said. "You can escort DI Ofori up to see Mrs. Ashraf. She'll be in the conference room on the tenth floor."

Kit blinked at her, then looked at the man, who got up.

Tall. Broad-shouldered. Dark eyes with creases around them when he smiled. Small smile. No teeth showing. Dark skin. Dark hair with salt-and-pepper silver. Little beard. Far too good-looking for so early in the morning. Holding out a hand to shake.

Kit reached out blankly and clasped the man's hand. "Well, bugger me..."

Paulina tried to smother a shocked laugh.

Caffeine and panic hit in one fell swoop.

The man's hand closed around his, broad and warm, but Kit spotted the surprise in his eyes.

"Um." He shot an urgent look at Paulina. "Lina, did I say that out loud?"

She had one hand at her mouth and nodded once.

Kit swallowed hard, looking back at the man. Whose hand he was still holding like a bloody great tit. "Good morning!" He shook the man's hand forcefully up and down a couple of times. "I meant to say good morning."

The creases around the man's eyes deepened, and his smile showed a glimpse of even white teeth. "I'm not about to look a gift compliment in the mouth," he said as Kit pulled his hand back. He glanced at Paulina. "Do I need to sign anything else?"

"No." Paulina choked. Kit couldn't bring himself to look at her, in case she started giggling. "You're good. I'll buzz you both through to the lift."

Kit tucked the shoebox under his arm and kept his eyes ahead. The blush had accelerated past pink, heading straight for magenta, the heat radiating from his face. Never a good look with his ginger hair on top.

"This way," he said, not even pausing to check if the man was following.

It took the walk to the lift for Paulina's words sank in. DI.

Kit stared at his own reflection in the polished doors of the lift in horror.

A policeman.

He'd just said that to a policeman. Probably the policeman who had come to investigate his boss's disappearance. Of all the times to put his foot in his mouth, he'd really picked a great one. The policeman came and stood alongside him, his hands folded behind his back.

"Sorry."

The policeman's reflection glanced at him. "Pardon?"

"For what I said there." Kit shifted his feet. "Late night. Not enough coffee."

DI Ofori laughed, a pleasant, deep sound that seemed to come from the bottom of his chest. "Don't worry. I've heard a lot worse. Usually much more offensive as well."

The lift doors took forever to open, and Kit hurtled in as soon as they did, claiming the corner of the lift and hugging the shoebox against his chest with one arm and clinging to the handrail with the other.

He didn't have a problem with enclosed spaces. The potential for the suspension cables to snap—ridiculous, of course, as he'd checked them himself when no one was looking—and being aware of the exact velocity and drop that would result in sticky, squishy death unsettled him a bit more.

The policeman leaned back against one of the rails running around the walls, hands braced on it. He looked completely at ease. Kit tried to mimic his relaxed stance, wondering if his blush had faded at all. A glance at the mirrored wall assured him that no, he hadn't downgraded from a vivid shade between tomato and peach.

"So you work here, then?" Ofori said as the lift started moving.

Kit blinked, forcing his attention back to the man. He distantly remembered Hamid's warnings about what he could and couldn't say if the police asked him anything. Most of it came down to not mentioning time travel. Which, of course, was the bloody great elephant in the lift.

In a panic, he blurted out, "I didn't expect the Spanish Inquisition."

DI Ofori's eyebrows rose. "Nobody expects the Spanish Inquisition."

Kit's mouth dropped open in surprise. "What?"

The policeman's lips twitched, but he shook his head. "Never mind."

Kit hesitated. There were shows his mother had shown him when he was a kid, and he had to say something. "When you didn't even bring out the comfy chair? You call that a Spanish Inquisition?"

To his surprise and delight, the policeman actually snorted in amusement. Some people didn't appreciate the classics, but it looked like the—dammit, why did he have to be good-looking as well?—man in front of him did.

Ofori flashed a glimpse of a smile again. "Aren't you a little young to remember Monty Python?"

Kit should have paused, thought, considered his words, but he'd already made a spectacular tit of himself. He couldn't really sink any further. "Well, aren't you a little good-looking to be a police officer?"

The small smile widened. Dimples cut furrows in the man's cheeks. "Touché."

Kit couldn't help grinning. Maybe they expected him to represent the TRI, but a handsome man with dimples, broad shoulders, and knowledge of Monty Python was smiling at him. He forced his hand off the handrail and held it out. "Maybe we can try the first impression thing again. Christopher Rafferty. Kit. Most people call me Kit."

"Jacob Ofori." Ofori's hand was cool from resting on the metal rail. "Detective Inspector."

"That just means you get out of wearing a uniform, doesn't it?"

To Kit's delight, the man actually laughed again. "My superiors haven't realised that's my game." He looked up at the numbers flicking above the door. "You been working here long?"

Kit shook his head. "Coming up on three years." He could hear Hamid yelling in his ear. Keep it casual and the information minimal. No details about the role. Generic facts that could be applied to any office anywhere. "Feels like longer."

Ofori braced his hands on the rail on either side of him, all casual-like. And...yeah, Kit absolutely noticed that it drew his shirt snugly against his broad chest. "Tough job?"

Kit shrugged. "I only deal with the machines." He made a face. "Hardly last any time these days. They keep a few of us in-house to keep things patched up. Can't have business grinding to a halt because of a loose wire."

"Mm." Ofori straightened up as the lift slowed on the tenth floor. "Our stop?"

There were another five levels above it as well. The ones below ground never showed up on the public lifts as all the chambers used for temporal jumps were hidden down there, and so far, no member of the public had ever accidentally stumbled on them.

"This is us." Kit pressed his hand to the sensor panel. It scanned his fingerprints, and the door slid open.

He didn't know if he was relieved or disappointed to find Mariam already there, waiting for them. Paulina had probably called up to warn her after seeing him making a fool of himself. They'd probably expected him to spill half the TRI's secrets before they even hit the fourth floor.

"Detective Inspector." Mariam held out her hand.

"Mrs. Ashraf." Ofori took it.

Kit's eyes flicked between them, unsettled by the palpable change in the atmosphere, as if the temperature had dropped. Ofori's smile had vanished and Mariam looked as grim. They were sizing each other up, taking stock.

Secrets, Kit thought, watching them. They both knew something the other wanted to know, but weren't willing to show all their cards yet. He really didn't need to be caught up in the politics of it all.

He cleared his throat. "Mariam?"

She looked sharply at him. "Mr. Rafferty?"

He held out the shoebox. "Hamid said Ben's staying with you now. I thought he might need something to distract him."

She took the box, clearly surprised, and opened the lid. For a moment, the icy professional façade cracked enough to show a brief smile. "He'll love it," she said as she replaced the lid. "I'll give it to him later."

Kit nodded. "I'll head back down, then." He glanced at DI Ofori. "Nice to meet you, sir."

Ofori nodded, and though he didn't smile, the lines around his eyes deepened a little. "Likewise, Mr. Rafferty."

Kit backed into the still-open lift and swiped his hand over the control again, touching the console to take him down to level seven. Only three floors. Manageable without company.

As soon as the doors closed, he sagged against the rail, releasing a noisy breath.

That was not how he had expected his morning to go.

On the whole, mortal embarrassment aside, it could have been worse.

Chapter Five

Mariam Ashraf's office was neat and orderly, not a single paper out of place on her desk.

Jacob could tell from one look that no office with so many files and papers stacked in boxes by one wall was ever this tidy. It had been arranged to ensure nothing incriminating had been left lying around where some old plod could catch a glimpse of it.

Mrs. Ashraf ushered him in. The door slid closed behind him.

"Make yourself comfortable, Detective Inspector," she said.

Mrs. Ashraf circled behind the broad desk—old-fashioned and sturdy—putting her back to the wall. She set the shoebox from Rafferty on the desktop and motioned to the seat opposite her. Jacob settled into his seat, his stance informal, his expression placid.

They were in her territory and she was already on edge. He really didn't want to push her even more on the defensive.

"How's Ben?"

She folded her hands together in front of her on the desk. "Worried. We all are." Her dark eyes met his. "Do you have any news for us?"

"No good news, I'm afraid." Jacob withdrew his slate from his pocket. "We mentioned an unknown fatality at the house. We believe they were one of Mr. Sanders's attackers." He hesitated. "Would you mind taking a look, to see if you can provide a name?"

Mrs. Ashraf's lips thinned to a line, and she looked a little paler, but she nodded.

Jacob passed the slate with the image of the man's face across the desk.

Thankfully, Danni had restrained herself long enough to take the photographs before she removed the synthetic eyeball. The last time Jacob had looked in on her the night before, the man's eyelid had been peeled back from an empty, gaping socket. Disconnected wires snaked out of it like something from a horror film. Danni had laughed herself silly when Jacob threw up in one of the sinks.

Mrs. Ashraf stared at the man's face for a few moments. "I don't recognise him."

"You're sure?"

She nodded grimly. "Believe me, if I could tell you who this man was, I would." She pushed the slate across the desk to him. "You don't have anything on him?"

"Not yet, but no one springs out of thin air."

Mrs. Ashraf's eyes flicked back to the slate. "No. I suppose they don't." She sat back, rubbing her eyes with one hand. Jacob could sympathise.

He leaned forward, propping his forearms on his knees. "Mrs. Ashraf, I know this is a difficult time, but I need to ask you some questions about Mr. Sanders. We need to know as much about him and events in his life as we can, if we're to find him."

The woman lowered her hand. "Of course."

There were the standard work questions first: Sanders's role, how long he had been there, all stuff gathered from online records but needed confirmed to ensure all the data remained accurate. Nothing new there.

Personal history was more difficult.

Mariam Ashraf was listed as the next of kin on all records.

According to the available records, Sanders's father was deceased, his mother was in a care home, and he had no other living relatives, except his son. He had been married, and paperwork indicated his wife had died, but the details were hazy.

"We were informed Mr. Sanders has been signed off from work for some time." Jacob tried to keep his tone light. Any friction within the workplace could be a reason for the attack on him. "There were health grounds, I believe?"

Mrs. Ashraf glanced at the shoebox, apparently a gift for Ben. "Tom's life is divided between two things—his son and his work. He used to split his time between them, and when Tom came here, Ben would stay with his grandmother."

"Catherine Sanders." Jacob recalled the record. "She's currently in a care home, isn't she?"

Mrs. Ashraf nodded. "She had a fall less than two months ago and needed full-time care. That's where the problems started. Tom tried to maintain his usual level of work while also being a full-time father. He worked himself too hard, not sleeping, not eating well enough." She shrugged helplessly. "A wire can only be stretched so far before it gives way."

Jacob gave a sympathetic nod. "Especially as a widower."

Mrs. Ashraf was good, but once more, he caught that subtle flicker in her expression. Not much, but enough for him to know it could be an avenue worth pursuing. "I never knew his wife. He lost her when Ben was only a baby."

Jacob laced his fingers together. "Do you know what happened to her? Unfortunately, the records aren't very clear."

Mrs. Ashraf tapped her fingers on the arm of her chair, watching the tips whiten. "He didn't really talk about it," she finally said. "As far as I understand it, she went traveling. Business or something. There was an accident. She never came home." Her eyes returned to Jacob's. "Presumed dead, they said. They never found a body."

Jacob casually folded his hands across his middle. Well, wasn't that interesting? Both husband and wife disappearing without a trace. "And he never reported it to the British police?"

"If you have no information on it, I assume not." Mrs. Ashraf's expression remained unreadable. "As I said, Tom didn't talk about it, and it happened before I really knew him very well."

"Is there anyone who might know more about it?"

Her lips pressed together. "I don't see how raking up the death of his wife seven years ago can help when Tom is missing now. How can confirming how Olivia died help anything now? She's dead. He may still be alive."

Olivia, Jacob noted. First-name terms for a woman she claimed never to have met.

"We have to examine all angles," he said, "especially when there are similarities in the cases."

"Similarities?" She frowned. "She wasn't attacked in her home."

"No," Jacob agreed, "but she did disappear in suspicious circumstances."

Mrs. Ashraf rose from behind the desk and walked over to the window to gaze out on the city. "You think someone abducted Olivia?" There was a strange cadence to her voice. Jacob couldn't decide between latent shock or worry. "Do you think the same people were involved?"

He tapped the balls of his thumbs together. "It's all conjecture at the moment, but it does strike me as strangely coincidental. If you could tell me exactly what Mr. Sanders does here, whether his wife had any involvement in similar scientific engineering..."

Mrs. Ashraf said nothing for several minutes. "I don't know what his wife did, but Tom designed machines to assist us in our research." She turned from the window to face him. "He found a way of mapping out historical anomalies and patterns in the chaos. I've never seen science or engineering like it."

Jacob reached for his slate and opened up the images of Sanders's board from the house again. "So this could be developments of a similar kind?"

She returned to the desk and took the offered slate. "Knowing Tom? It could be anything."

"Would anyone want to get a hold of it?"

She scaled up the image, studying it, a frown furrowing her brow. "Unless they wanted to do similar historical research, I doubt it." She looked at him. "Tom was a scientist above everything, Detective Inspector. This could easily have been the start of an algorithm to find the best school for his son. I could have some of my technicians look at it, to see if they can work out what it is."

Jacob put on his benevolent smile. "That would be incredibly useful."

Perhaps she wanted to be helpful, but the suspicious bastard side of him didn't believe it. She wanted to know what the board said as much as he did. He doubted it had anything to do with Ben or schools. She said herself Sanders worked all the time. Whatever he'd written on the board related to his work, and she wanted it.

Mrs. Ashraf smiled in return. "If you could forward a copy, I'll pass it on to the relevant team."

"Why wait?" Jacob rose. "We could show them now. See if anything jumps out."

He saw the brief and unsurprising flare of frustration on her face.

"They may not be able to identify it at once," she said.

"All the same," Jacob countered, "it would be useful to know if this is a relevant line of inquiry, or if it can be dismissed. Perhaps call down and check? It would be best if we can whittle away the irrelevant details as soon as possible."

Her smile returned, but it didn't reach her eyes. He was pushing his luck. "If it helps," she said and reached for the phone hub.

Within five minutes, they were in the lift, on their way down.

Jacob didn't know what he expected from the technical department. Mrs. Ashraf led him along a corridor lined with glass walls, and on the other side of the glass, he could see workbenches. Some were stacked with tools, others covered in small machines in various states of repair. The largest one had a complex array of circuits and wires covering the whole surface.

The staff was nowhere to be seen, and he found out why when she led him into a conference room.

Around twenty people were seated around a long table, a mix of ages and genders, and every one of them looked around with wary expectation when he entered. Among them, he recognised one: Kit Rafferty, who raised a hand in greeting.

Jacob only nodded in response.

Of all the people in the room, Rafferty seemed the only one who didn't look sick with nervousness.

Twenty years on the force meant you were used to that reaction. It had taught him some people would be wary in the presence of the police, especially with an active investigation ongoing. He'd never seen it in a whole room of people though. There should have been no reason. After all, he was only investigating the disappearance of their colleague. No reason so many people should look uneasy at his presence, unless they had something to hide.

There was the conundrum. Did each of them have something to hide individually, or was the TRI as a whole trying to keep secrets? He was more inclined to believe the latter, and—unfortunately—they were doing a damned good job of keeping it under wraps.

Mrs. Ashraf went to the head of the table, and he stepped alongside her.

"Everyone," she said, "this is DI Jacob Ofori. He's the police officer in charge of the investigation into Tom's disappearance. He has some images from Tom's house and needs to know if they're relevant to the case. You've all worked with Tom's notes before, so we need you to have a look at them for us. Detective Inspector?"

Jacob connected his slate to the projector at one end of the room. The images lit up on the screen at the far end of the room, showing the whiteboards and the intricate display of numbers and letters. The technicians and engineers all turned to them.

Jacob watched them in turn.

From the first glance, he could tell none of them had seen the coding before. A couple of people were frowning as if they couldn't quite work out what they were looking at. Two exchanged glances and shook their heads.

Jacob's eyes flicked to Kit. Of course, Rafferty was a technician, but Jacob hadn't expected the babbling, blushing young man from the lift to be so focused. He had one hand thrust into his shaggy red hair, and he stared at the board so intently it looked like he was trying to bore a hole in it.

"Any suggestions?" Mrs. Ashraf's voice broke the silence.

"It's encoded," one man said. "Sanders sometimes did that. You'd need a key to crack it."

A woman near him nodded. "He usually only did that if he hadn't finished. In case someone tried to use whatever he'd been developing, and it went tits up."

Other voices supported this theory, and Jacob nodded as if he were listening.

One eye, however, remained on Rafferty.

Rafferty's gaze remained fixed on the board. He curled his fingers deeper into his hair, and the fingertips of his other hand drummed against his lips. He seemed to be whispering to himself, his eyebrows drawing together in a furrow.

"What about Mr. Rafferty?" Jacob finally asked.

Every head in the room turned toward the man, who didn't even notice.

The woman beside him nudged him sharply.

"Shit!" Rafferty spun around, his hair rumpled in all directions. He looked like a startled puppy caught pissing on the carpet. He glanced around warily, every eye on him. "What?"

"DI Ofori wants to know if you have any idea what we're looking at," Mrs. Ashraf's said coolly.

Rafferty blinked. "It's coded."

"We gathered that much." Jacob braced his hands on the desk. "So, Mr. Rafferty, do you know what it's about?"

Rafferty's face rapidly went red. His blue eyes darted around the table. "Um. No." He tangled his hands together. "I mean, if I had the key, I might be able to work it out. But Mr. Sanders didn't let us keep a copy of the key." He offered Jacob a wary smile. "Um. Sorry."

Jacob straightened up, releasing a drawn-out breath. It had been worth a shot at least. "Thank you for your time, ladies and gentlemen. I'll leave you to your work." He disconnected his slate and looked back at Mrs. Ashraf. "Shall we return to your office?"

She inclined her head. "Of course."

Chapter Six

As soon as the police officer and Mariam left the room, Kit bolted for the door.

The lifts were off limits anyway, since Ofori and Mariam would be using them, so he ran for the stairs. He needed something to eat. Something heavy to settle his knotting stomach. Jesus. He hadn't eaten since last night anyway, and now it was coming back to bite him. He really, really didn't want to throw up a bellyful of coffee in front of everyone.

The kitchen team was already clearing the breakfast trays away in the canteen, but he managed to snag the last sausages and some of the toast and beans. He filled a mug with tar-thick tea and spooned four heaps of sugar into it before stumbling to sit down at the nearest table.

His hand shook as he shovelled the food into his mouth, gulping it down.

The chair opposite him scraped the floor as someone pulled it out, but he didn't even lift his eyes from his plate. It helped, focusing on the eating. His heart slowed from a rapid whine to a steadier beat, and his fork clattered on the plate.

Kit buried his face in his hands.

Of course, one downside of eating quickly to stop himself feeling sick was that if he ate too quickly, he felt sick in a completely different way.

His mug slid across the table.

He peered between his fingers.

"You should drink," Sally Patil said, nudging the mug closer with her fingertips. "It'll help."

When the TRI psychiatrist offered free advice, only a foolish man ignored it. He reluctantly lowered his hands and pulled the mug toward him like a talisman. "What did I do to earn an intervention?"

Sally grinned at him. "You let the door slam closed in my face. I'm here to make you feel incredibly guilty about it." She spread her hands on her very pregnant belly. "How could you be so mean to a poor, gravid woman?"

Kit winced. "Ah. Sorry. I didn't see you."

She raised her eyebrows and pointedly looked down at her cerise kaftan and conspicuous bump. "Yes, I can see how I would be easy to miss." She looked back up at him, frowning. "What happened?"

A small, hysterical laugh bubbled up. "Oh, you know. The usual. Forgetting to go to bed. Acting like a prize tit. Lying to the police." He took a gulp of the tea, then hissed through his teeth. "Jesus, that's hot!"

Sally stared at him. "What do you mean 'lying to the police'?"

He wrapped his hands tightly around the mug to stop them shaking. "They showed us some of Sanders's work. Wanted to know what they'd found. What it meant. Hamid said we weren't to tell them anything about time travel, so I told the policeman I couldn't read it." He shuddered. "If they find out, I'll be arrested for concealing evidence, won't I? I went to university so I wouldn't end up someone's sex moppet in prison!"

Sally's eyebrows were heading toward her hairline. "I'm fairly sure you won't be locked up for saying you couldn't read something. I mean, how on earth are they going to find out?"

Kit came up short, blinking. "I hadn't thought about that bit."

She smiled. "I noticed." A soft brown hand covered his. "Just breathe."

He nodded. The relief hit him as if he'd run into a brick wall, and he started laughing helplessly, shaking his head. "I'm an idiot."

"You're an honest man asked to lie," she corrected. "There's a difference."

"Doesn't mean I'm not an idiot," he retorted. "After flirting with the policeman as well..."

Sally burst out laughing. "You *have* had a busy morning."

Kit could feel his cheeks redden, but shrugged with a grin. "What? We don't often get any good-looking specimens like that in here, and God knows I don't get out much."

"Don't let Dieter hear you say that," she cautioned.

Kit wrinkled his nose. "He wears too much makeup for my tastes."

Sally laughed, then winced as she rubbed at her back. "I wasn't talking about him." She pushed herself laboriously to her feet. "You insult Janos, and Dieter will gut you like a fish."

Kit eyed her belly warily. "Are you sure you should still be in here? You look like you're about to pop."

"Two more weeks." She patted the bump gently. "Can't wait to see my toes again." She studied him. "Are you going to be all right if I leave you? I mean, I'll still be leaving, because Bruiser is dancing on my bladder, but I'll send someone along to keep you company."

He smiled. "I'm fine. Honestly. Just embarrassed." He raised his mug in a salute. "Thank you."

Her smile returned, quick and warm. "Anytime."

He watched her waddle toward the door, then turned his attention back to his tea, still hot, but not scalding now.

Less than five minutes later, the door of the canteen opened again. Kit scraped a spoon around the inside of his mug, scooping up the sugary dregs from the bottom of the mug, but glanced up as footsteps approached his table.

"Kit." Mariam sat in the chair Sally had vacated.

"Mrs. Ashraf." He set down the mug and spoon. "Am I in trouble?"

Mariam shook her head. "Not for the time being. DI Ofori believed you when you said you couldn't read the board."

One day, Kit thought, he would have to invent a switch so he could stop himself blushing at will. "Um."

Mariam looked at him, shrewd and intent. "You know Sanders's key."

Kit shoved his mug away. "I've worked with it enough to remember it." He met her eyes, half-defiant, half-wary.

She leaned forward urgently. "What was it?"

Kit stared at her.

For the first time since his arrival at the TRI, he knew more than anyone else. He hadn't had time to break down everything on the board, but he'd seen enough to know everyone at the TRI would be interested.

"If I tell you," he said, "I want to know what happened here three years ago."

Mariam sat back. "What do you mean?"

He gave her a flat look. "You know what I mean. Something happened, and that's why this whole thing has got the whole TRI on edge. It isn't just about Tom going missing. Something happened, and everyone knows, and I'm sitting here in the dark, with no idea if I'm meant to be worrying as much as everyone else."

She drummed her fingertips on the table. "It's not that simple."

He folded his arms. "I think it is. You're expecting me to break the law and lie to the police to keep this all quiet, but you don't think I can be trusted with the whole truth? Why should I trust you with anything if you're not going to trust me?"

"Like I said, it's not that simple."

"Why?" Kit demanded angrily. "Why am I expected to lie when you won't give me the real reasons? Tom trusted me! Why doesn't anyone else?"

Mariam pinched the bridge of her nose. She looked exhausted and frustrated, and for the first time, Kit found he didn't give a damn. It was too much, to have the weight of the law pressing down on him and not knowing who was in the right. "Kit—"

"Everyone else from that time knows," he said. "They're all hiding something from me. How is that fair? I'm expected to risk my career and my reputation and even bloody prison, and all I get is 'it's not that simple'?" He shook his head. "I can't do it. Not when I know everyone is keeping something from me."

Mariam lowered her hands to rest in her lap, her expression grave. "There are reasons you haven't been told so far. I'll speak to the relevant people, and if they agree, then you can be told."

"The relevant people?" Kit huffed in disbelief. "You're the head of the TRI now Tom's missing. This is your call."

She smiled briefly. "That's where you're wrong." She got up from the table. "Like I said before, Kit, it isn't a simple situation. I'll speak to those involved, and if they agree, then you'll be told. If they don't, this is out of my hands."

He pushed his chair back too. "And until then, if the police come calling again, I don't want to be put on the spot. I'm not going to lie for you and risk everything for people who won't even tell me the truth."

She nodded gravely. "I understand."

He piled his dishes onto the tray and carried it over to the trolley. Behind him, he heard Mariam walking away. He released a shaking breath when the door closed. If anyone had told him when he left the house that morning he'd be facing down the temporary head of the TRI, he would have laughed at them.

Of course, that was before his morning went completely to hell.

His hands shivered as he pushed them through his hair.

Sometimes he wondered if it wouldn't be easier to go to work for some big engineering firm, designing new solutions to old problems.

Maybe it wouldn't involve honest-to-God time travel and the kind of advanced science that almost gave him a hard-on, but it would also be quiet and boring and, most importantly, not involve crime.

Maybe.

Ha.

As long as the TRI had the most advanced technology and state-of-the-art equipment, and as long as he got access to every piece of it, Kit would stay. He could end up with a stomach ulcer the size of Liverpool, and he would still stay.

Stupid technology.

He rubbed his eyes with the heels of his hands.

Time to get to work.

Chapter Seven

There were no leads.

Jacob was growing frustrated.

Days were ticking by, and if there ever had been a trail, it would be stone cold now. Normally, a body at a crime scene made things simpler. This time, it only seemed to complicate everything.

Their John Smith had given them nothing.

His DNA still hadn't been flagged up anywhere, no matter how they expanded the search. His face had been broadcast on the news, but there hadn't even been a single call to the hotline. Even the mysterious eye, their last hope, was proving useless.

Danni had checked it all over for some kind of registration code or maker's mark, but there were only two letters on the back: OT. Temple had gone through every possible company to try to identify them, but not one of them worked in synthetic bio-artificing.

They'd even called in the available ophthalmic specialists to examine the eye, and from the look of awed delight on the doctors' faces, Jacob didn't need to be told they'd never seen a device like it before. They babbled eagerly about the connection, the functionality, the fact that the materials used replicated the texture of an eyeball.

All very interesting, but all useless.

They could only confirm two things: John Smith's eye had been removed in infancy or childhood, judging by the scar tissue, and it would have taken a master eye surgeon to fit the eye, particularly given the intricacy of the connection to the optic nerve. Somehow, they explained, someone had managed to connect the equivalent of a tiny video camera directly into the brain.

Jacob let Temple take them back out and sank down at his desk.

Anton rapped at the door. "Coffee?"

"God, yes." Jacob rubbed his eyelids with his fingertips.

Anton returned two minutes later and handed Jacob his sturdy mug. He sat on the opposite side of the desk, his slate in his lap.

Jacob spooned sugar into the mug. "Please tell me you've got me some good news." He paused, studying Anton's expression. "Or is this cuppa here to soften the blow?"

Anton pushed his slate across the desk to him. "The TRI has the cleanest records I have ever seen for any company. No problems. No reports. No hazards. Every Health and Safety check has come back with top ratings. No dismissals. No tax evasions. No nothing."

Jacob frowned. "Nothing? At all?"

Anton shook his head. "Either this is the best place to work in the world, or the whole place is powered by robot overlords."

"Every company has something."

"That's what I thought," Anton agreed. One side of his mouth turned up. "The coffee wasn't exactly to soften the blow. You're going to need it."

"I've been there." Jacob flicked through page after page of data. "They look like any other company. How can anyone be this clean? Unless you're really good at hiding your dirty laundry, there's no way this should be possible."

"I guess that means they're hiding their dirty laundry then, eh?"

Jacob put the slate down and pulled the mug toward him. His time at the TRI hadn't been productive. He and Mrs. Ashraf had danced around each other, giving just enough information and no more. Anton's evidence supporting his theory that they were hiding something didn't help.

If the TRI weren't willing to be cooperative, he'd have to find some means to push them, and right now, he didn't have it.

A search warrant would never be granted simply because he had suspicions about organised records. So far, they only had consent to access Sanders's own computers and files, and even those hadn't contained anything useful.

"Look into the employees in detail," he said. "We need to know more about the kind of people they have on their books. There's got to be something we can use as a way in."

"On it." Anton got up. "Want me to forward everything on to you as I find it?"

Jacob hesitated. As much as he wanted to keep on top of things, it would earn him a black mark if he took work home with him, especially tonight. "Have it waiting for me in the morning. I need to be offline tonight."

Anton grinned. "Finally getting back on the horse?"

Jacob gave him a look that didn't quite rate as a glare. "My *son* is taking me to a gig. A late birthday present for last month. So no. No horse. No getting back on it." He nodded toward the door. "As you were, Anton."

Anton snorted. "One day, boss. One day."

Jacob rolled his eyes and turned his attention back to his coffee.

They'd let it lie for about six months after Rory had kicked him out, but then Temple had started suggesting people, and Anton nudged and winked more often.

After a couple of months of it, he'd threatened them both with harassment charges if they didn't quit it, and had only been half joking. When he asked why they gave a damn, they told him he tended to be more cheerful when he had someone to shag on a regular basis. Personally, he'd never really noticed a difference.

Now, they only mentioned it once every few months.

It wasn't because he didn't have time. When he'd left, Rory had said some things that were still true, and every time Jacob even thought about going for more than a drink with someone, he could hear the echo.

He downed the coffee and checked his watch.

An hour to get home, changed, and meet Luke for dinner.

He switched off the work quill, even though it made his fingers twitch to do it. They only had a few hours together, and his son was worth that. Plus, he didn't imagine they were going to get a break in a case which had already stalled in the brief three-hour window.

Anton and Foley were talking as he emerged from his office.

"That you for the night, sir?"

He nodded. "And I'll be working from home until Monday." He glanced up at the board. "Try not to solve the case until I get back."

Foley snorted. "I think the chances are between slim and none."

Jacob clasped a hand to his heart. "Well, look at that, Anton," he said with a proud sigh. "We've tarnished her with our jaded cynicism already."

Anton laughed. "That's all you, sir. I'm a ball of sunshine."

Jacob raised his eyebrows. "And on that gargantuan lie, I'm off."

Having dodged rush hour, he made it back to his flat in good time, and by the time Luke arrived, he was ready and toying with the work quill. A quick glance, he thought, to make sure things were ticking over, but one check would become an hourly check, and Luke would give him a reproachful look.

He set the quill aside when the buzzer rang.

"All set?" Luke said, beaming at him as he slid into Luke's shiny new autopod.

Jacob smiled. "Being pampered by my boy? I think it's a hardship I can cope with."

Luke laughed as he set the destination. "Still a sarcastic arse?"

"If you visited more often, you wouldn't forget."

"Likewise," Luke countered. "I've got shifts at the hospital. What's your excuse?"

"Oh, you know. The usual. Murder. Kidnapping."

"Avoiding Louise's cooking?"

Jacob met his son's eyes. For all that Luke's partner was a sweet-natured and brilliant dermatologist, her skill in the kitchen bordered on terminal. "Still that bad?"

Luke nodded with a wince. "Oh yeah. She tried to make a pie the other day. It broke the knife." He laughed and shook his head. "Thank God she's smarter and better-looking than me."

Sometimes Jacob expected there to be a distance between them, but every time Luke visited from London, they fell back into their old pattern. They always had got along, and now things were so much simpler without having to mentally censor his conversations.

They went to an elegant restaurant for a meal, and while he winced over the price of the courses and tried to go low-end, Luke ignored him and ordered the best of everything.

"I can afford it," he said. "And anyway, it's my treat for you. Let me spoil you."

Jacob reluctantly passed back the menu. "It's pricey."

"Papa." Luke folded his arms on the table, his expression grave. "I want you to listen very carefully to me: I am going to buy you the best meal you have ever had tonight, because I love you. If you don't accept this noble offering, I'll be convinced I'm an inadequate son and will spend the rest of the night crying in the gents."

Jacob managed to keep a straight face for nearly five seconds, then started laughing. "You're still a manipulative little shitbag," he said proudly.

Luke raised his glass, grinning. "I learned from the best."

Jacob shook his head. "I have no idea how I ended up with a son like you."

His son smirked at him. "Well, when a boy and a girl are young and stupid and don't use a johnnie... Do I need to go on?"

"Please don't," Jacob said, grimacing.

Luke had been twelve when Jacob gave him a very awkward talk, and his son always was a smart kid. In their few, rare arguments, Luke always threw that point back in his face: *at least I didn't accidentally make a person!*

Not that he could or would ever regret the accident of his son's birth, but it had led to some complications, especially when he had to admit—to himself, Luke's mother, and everyone else—he was actually not exactly straight.

He hesitated, hating to ruin the mood, but knowing he had to ask. "How are your grandparents?"

Luke's smile faded. He put down his glass, watching his fingertips pressing to the stem. "I saw Nana the other week. Gramp is on new medication for his heart." He reluctantly raised his eyes to meet his father's. "Papa, I know Nana would like to hear from you."

Jacob clenched his teeth, stifling the urge to demand why she ignored his letters. "I doubt that."

Luke reached over the table for his hand. "I think Gramp's health is getting worse. Nana isn't as strong as she used to be. I think..." He sighed. "I don't think they can hold on to being angry with you anymore."

Jacob looked at Luke's hand covering his. "This isn't my doing," he said quietly. "If anyone should be angry in this situation..." He shook his head. "I have tried so many times. I can't keep trying."

"Papa..."

Luke could never understand, and sometimes, Jacob couldn't understand it himself. He couldn't imagine any circumstance that would make him turn his own child away, no matter what they did.

"They're the ones that told me to go," Jacob said finally. "I've tried. They ignored me. If they want to see me, if they want to speak to me, they've had every damned letter, every Christmas card, every new address and number."

Luke sat back, frowning. "I think I can see where I get my stubbornness."

Jacob smiled briefly. "A long-standing family tradition." He picked up his wine glass. "But you didn't come all this way for us to get miserable and pissed."

"Pissed, yes," Luke said. "Miserable, not so much."

Jacob took a mouthful of the wine. "No more mentions of the family, then?"

"How about your love life?" Luke raised his eyebrows.

"No. I thought we wanted to steer away from miserable."

That earned him a smile. "Okay. Work or football it is."

"Or the food," Jacob said, nodding toward the approaching waiter.

Luke made a face. "Eh. Food's food. I'd rather eat it than talk about it. Especially if it's as good as they say."

The food turned out to be as good as they said, and whoever chose the wine had picked the perfect one for each course. By the time it came to dessert, Jacob idly wondered if he'd be showing his age if he skipped the gig and went home to lie on the couch and loosen his belt a few notches. There'd been enough to drink that he'd definitely relaxed more than usual.

"Can't help feeling you're trying to butter me up," he informed his son as they settled in the autopod for the brief ride to the venue. "Is there a nasty surprise waiting at the end of this evening?"

Luke's eyes danced. "Don't worry. No marriage or babies yet." He patted his father on the knee. "Your faith is astounding."

"I know you, kid."

Luke just laughed.

Pods thronged the parking bay of the venue, and crowds milled in the entrance of the building. Jacob let Luke take charge, steering him through the doors. Attendants scanned their wrist passes, and Luke led the way to their seats.

"A box?"

"What?"

"You booked us a box?"

"Don't forget the champagne," Luke said cheerfully. "Anyone would think I'd pissed on your shoe, the face you're making."

"Luke, you don't need to—"

"If you're going to say spend my money on my father, you can stop now." He waved Jacob over to the seat. "You get comfortable. I'll go down and get us some proper drinks, and if I find you've snuck off to try and get into the stalls, I'm calling Mum."

Jacob winced. Although he and Nicola had split up before Luke's birth, she definitely would be more than willing to come down on him like the wrath of God at any whisper that he'd upset their son. "Fine," he said, sitting down in one of the plush seats. "I'm sitting."

He took off his jacket, hung it over the back of the chair, and propped his arms on the edge of the box, looking out over the mixed crowd. A lot of people were his age and older, with grey heads scattered all around the concert hall. That wasn't a surprise when your favourite performer from your teens decided to do a one-off concert tour when you were well into your forties.

There were a few younger people as well. Probably people who had been nudged in that musical direction by their parents.

Jacob leaned forward, frowning.

A shaggy red head moved through the crowd on the stalls level.

Sod's bloody law in action, Jacob thought. Trying to keep work out of the way for a night, and one of the TRI had to show up right in front of him.

He watched as Kit Rafferty settled in a seat, talking animatedly to the older woman beside him. Out of the office, and without the stares of his colleagues focused on him, Rafferty seemed much more at ease, with the same grin he'd worn in the lift, genuine and warm.

Jacob should've ducked back, kept to the shadows of his nice private box. Work was work. It shouldn't interfere, not when Luke would be back at any minute. But if he had a member of the TRI who had talked to him willingly and who happened to be unsupervised...

He just needed to go down and casually chat to the man, and maybe, if Rafferty had had a drink or two, he might let slip something. It didn't even have to be anything big, maybe a little hint of what the TRI was really mixed up in.

All Jacob had to do was cut into the limited time he had with his son to chase his work.

He clenched his fist on the velvet-lined ledge of the box.

He could practically hear Rory saying *I told you so.*

Down below, Rafferty happened to glance up. He frowned, as if he couldn't recognise Jacob for a moment, then waved and flashed a glimpse of his bright grin.

Jacob swore under his breath but raised his own hand. Only polite, after all.

"Friend of yours?"

Shit.

He looked up at Luke, who had returned with two pints. "Someone I met the other week."

Luke peered down, and Jacob saw the look of resignation—and disappointment?—on Rafferty's face. Well, that didn't complicate matters at all, did it?

"We should go down and say hi, after," Luke decided.

"I don't think it's a good idea."

Luke settled on the other seat. "Why?"

It would be so simple to say "work," but then he might not get another chance to talk, informally, to any member of the TRI. If Anton turned anything up and they had to go in all guns blazing, then lawyers would be involved, and every conversation would be monitored. But here, he could talk to Rafferty, casual, informal, unmonitored.

Maybe he wouldn't get anything admissible in court, but he might get a starting point.

No. He was out with his son.

Work was off the table.

"I don't want to intrude."

Luke looked at him in amusement. "From the smile on his face, I think he'd be happy to let you intrude." He wiggled his eyebrows. "If you know what I mean."

To his eternal mortification, Jacob could feel himself blush. He snatched one of the pints from Luke. "Don't..." He trailed off, unable to articulate the thought of his son actively throwing him at sex. "Just don't."

Luke grinned at him. "Call this revenge for the times you knocked on my door in my teens."

Jacob glowered at him. "Little shitbag."

"Love you too, Papa."

Chapter Eight

Kit tried his best to concentrate on the music.

Not easy when the policeman he'd fibbed to four days earlier was sitting in one of the theatre's plush boxes. Things got even more difficult because he kept glancing up and catching DI Ofori watching him.

He didn't know if it was because of the lying he'd done, or because he kept looking up at the box anyway.

"Something wrong?"

Kit looked down at Jenny, his neighbour and companion for the evening. "No! Why do you say that?"

She leaned closer to call over the music. "You look like you're ready to run off."

He forced a smile and dug into his pockets for the packet of sweets he'd brought with him. "I'm fine." He held out the bag to her. "Éclair?"

For the rest of the show, he kept his eyes on the stage. It got easier when the support bands and musicians finally left and the woman he'd come to see sat down at the piano. She was as good live as everyone had told him and so different from watching a filmed performance.

By the end of the show, his hands were numb from clapping and his throat raw from cheering. He had nearly forgotten about the very good-looking policeman and his younger, equally good-looking companion up in the box. Nearly.

As the crowd started to disperse, he risked a glance up.

Yup. Still trying to pretend they weren't staring at each other.

Some things were better avoided.

He gently plucked at Jenny's sleeve. "How about we wait until the crowds clear a bit? We're not in any hurry, are we?"

She nodded gratefully, sitting back down. "I forgot how busy concerts like this get," she admitted.

He nudged her with a grin. "What was your last one? Woodstock?"

She swatted him across the back of the head. "Cheeky! I'm not that old."

He laughed, raising his hands to protect himself. "Mercy! Mercy! I meant Live Aid!"

That earned him a firm kick in the shin.

Another glance told him Ofori had left the box, which meant he would be in the first wave heading out the doors, so if they sat for another five minutes, he could be on his merry way, and there wouldn't be any question of him getting in any trouble.

By the time the crowds had cleared, Jenny already had her coat on.

"Fancy a drink before we head home?" Kit offered.

She eyed him. "If this is where you offer me warm milk, I'll thump you."

He grinned as they headed toward the lobby. "Well, I was going to say there's a pub down the road, but if that's what you want, I—"

Bugger.

DI Ofori stood in the lobby, alone. He didn't look happy to be there and glanced at his watch. Kit stopped dead halfway down the stairs which, in a sea of moving bodies, meant he immediately caught the policeman's eye.

Well, no chance of avoiding each other then.

He descended the stairs with Jenny. "Give me a minute, would you?"

She smiled. "I wanted to stop at the souvenir stall anyway."

She hurried off, and Kit turned back to face DI Ofori.

"Good show, eh?"

Ofori wedged his hands into his pockets, his expression neutral, giving nothing away. "Worth the price of entry, definitely." He shifted on his feet. "I didn't expect to see you here."

Kit raised his eyebrows. "I can't like music older than I am?"

"And television. And films."

Kit rolled his eyes. "I have taste," he said, and then his mouth disconnected itself from his brain and added, "I like things with a little age on them." And oh God, he looked Ofori up and down like a prime steak. And then his blush flared, rising like the sun. "Um."

Ofori's stern expression gave way to a flicker of a smile. "You don't go for subtle, do you?"

Kit covered his eyes with one hand. "I am *so* sorry," he mumbled. "Especially since you're here with someone. Jesus, Kit, could you be more inappropriate?"

"My son."

Kit opened a crack between two fingers. "'Scuse me?"

Ofori was smiling now, and his eyes were crinkling. "I'm here with my son. He just ran to the gents."

Kit lowered his hand. That was...unexpected, and unfortunate. Bugger. He'd thought Ofori was flirting back, but if he had a full-grown kid, maybe he'd misread. "Um. Sorry."

"Sorry?"

"I didn't realise you weren't...I mean, you're..." He trailed off uselessly, wondering if playing dead was a good option to get away.

Ofori's eyebrows rose. "A father?"

"Taken." It sounded better than "tragically het."

"I'm not."

Kit blinked at him. "Eh?"

The slow smile played around Ofori's full lips. "I'm not...taken. Single and very much not taken." He tilted his head, gazing at Kit through his black lashes. "And you, I can tell, aren't taken either."

Flustered, Kit pressed his hand to his cheek. It scorched his palm, but his heart had skipped a beat because Ofori *was* flirting with him, and even teasing him, and Jesus, it had been a good while since he'd had that.

"No. Not at all taken. Never even tried it." He breathed out noisily. "I'm sorry. My brain doesn't work well when there are good-looking people around."

Ofori's dimples appeared in his cheeks. "Do you always compliment people? Or am I just lucky?"

"Have you looked at you recently?" Kit retorted.

Ofori's teeth really were incredibly white when he smiled. And a little crooked. And good God, Kit thought, if he noticed little things like that...

"Um. I should...you know...go. Somewhere."

He had almost stepped past Ofori when the man caught his arm. Only a light touch, but enough to stop him dead in his tracks.

Ofori was looking at his hand as if it had betrayed him, then raised his eyes to Kit's. "You fancy a drink?"

A voice in Kit's head screamed, *Very bad idea!* A little voice that sounded like a chorus of Hamid and Mariam and, for some reason, his primary seven teacher: *Policeman! Investigating the TRI! Lying to a policeman is a crime! Going out and having a drink and lying throughout would be even worse!*

Then he heard the other little voice that liked very good-looking people buying him drinks and hadn't got laid in far too long. Smaller and quieter, yeah, but when it showed up, he really didn't have a choice, especially not with a man with those dimples and shoulders.

"God, yes."

"What? Really?"

Kit turned back to face him. "Mine's a Bacardi."

Ofori stared at him as if he couldn't quite believe he'd asked and been accepted. He was searching Kit's face, and if he regretted his decision, Kit didn't plan on poking at him to make him back out. A drink was a drink, after all.

In the deserted lobby, they couldn't ignore the tap of approaching footsteps.

"Am I interrupting?"

Ofori dropped Kit's arm and stepped back, turning to face the speaker. "Luke."

Kit spun to face the man, Ofori's son apparently. He looked around the same age as Kit himself, maybe even a little older. A little shorter than his father, his skin was lighter, but now that Kit knew they were related, he could see the similarities in their dark brown eyes and the shape of their features. How bloody unfair that two men could both be so good-looking.

"Evening." Luke held out a hand. "I'm Luke."

"Kit." Kit shook his hand. "Sorry. Didn't mean to steal your dad away." He glanced at Jacob. "Another night, maybe?"

A look passed between father and son. Unless Kit was mistaken, Luke nodded encouragingly.

"Tuesday evening?" Ofori said. "Seven?"

Kit had a feeling he might be grinning like an idiot. His cheeks were aching, so probably. "Sounds good to me." He took out his quill. "Sync me."

They exchanged numbers, and Kit made his excuses and hurried off to find Jenny.

Behind him, he heard Luke speaking to his father.

"Seems nice."

He didn't hear Ofori's reply and was a little relieved. If Jacob Ofori regretted the offer of a drink, Kit didn't want to know about it until he cancelled their date. Until then, at least he could imagine all the ways it could go.

He found Jenny waiting at the souvenir stand, a program tucked under her arm. She smiled knowingly.

"Good-looking man."

Kit made a face at her. "A friend."

"Mm-hmm." She reached up and patted his cheek. "And friends make you blush like a schoolboy, do they?"

"Oh, shut up," he said, grinning.

Chapter Nine

Jacob had his quill out again.

He'd spent Sunday with Luke, trying his best not to think about anything but his son, but the minute Luke dropped him at his door on Sunday night, Jacob descended into a moral crisis with the bloody quill.

All it would take was one message, and he wouldn't be going out for a drink with a man employed by an organization currently part of a major investigation. One message, and he wouldn't be breaching protocol and putting his own bollocks in a vice if everything went wrong.

It was simple. Just a message saying something had come up.

Every time he tried to put the words in, he couldn't.

There were a dozen reasons he should.

And then he remembered Luke's happy face when he thought his father might finally be moving on. If he didn't go and tried to lie about it, Luke would know. He was always too bloody perceptive.

Just one drink.

Didn't need to be more than that, and then he and Rafferty could go on their merry ways and never see each other again except in a professional capacity.

Jacob groaned and tossed the quill to the end of the bed.

What the hell was he doing?

There were other ways to get information out of people. Going out on what could technically be called a date definitely didn't qualify as professional police work. Especially when the target in question was charming in a speaking-before-thinking way.

Jacob crossed his arms over his face and pressed his head back against the mountain of pillows.

Things never went well when a man let his dick lead the way.

That was what was going on here, and he couldn't deny it.

If he were being professional, he would have done things by the book and waited until Anton finished his searches. If he were being professional, he wouldn't have let a younger man with a dazzling smile catch him off guard.

He sat up and reached for the quill again, touching the sensor to activate the screen.

A sensible man would have looked out some porn, stuck his hand down his trousers, and not ended up asking a completely inappropriate person to go for a drink with him.

The alarm on his quill chimed. He never needed it, but especially not today. Every hour, he'd been awake, glared at the quill, and put it down. Every hour, he'd decided to send the message, then changed his mind, and left it another hour.

Maybe there would be new evidence at the office, so he wouldn't have to meet Rafferty.

But then, if he didn't want to meet him, he didn't have to. Therein lay the problem. He wanted to. He hadn't been smiled at like that in a long while. Or flirted with so blatantly. Or eyed like he was worth looking at. Most people who tried to flirt with him were much more subtle, and he could ignore subtle. Kit's guilelessness had hit him like a breath of fresh air.

He swung his legs over the side of the bed, the floor cool beneath his feet.

"Bugger it," he muttered and threw the quill over his shoulder onto the middle of the bed.

When he finally got into the office, Temple took one look at him and went to the coffee machine, filled his mug, and added two sugars for good measure. She followed him to his office and set the mug in front of him.

"Bad weekend?"

Jacob shook his head. He propped his elbow on the arm of the chair and cradled his brow. "Any news?"

"A couple of reported sightings of Sanders to the helpline, but they turned out to be false alarms. Anton said he had some background checks with the Home Office, but otherwise, we're no further on."

With the number of staff employed at the TRI, that could take some time. Jacob recalled seeing and hearing people from different backgrounds. He had no doubt their paperwork would be fine. After all, if the company made such an effort of keeping their books in perfect order, it would be sloppy to screw up the staff details.

He smiled briefly. "Thanks."

She nodded and slipped out of the room.

Jacob switched on his slate, tapping at the screen to bring up the file on the case again. He'd scanned through the images so many times, trying to find something new, something he'd missed. The CSU report had been completed, and it only supported his initial hypothesis: at least two assailants, probably with some kind of getaway vehicle.

He flicked through the images, back to John Smith's possessions.

The design on the coat had been identified at last. Some high-end designer made them for close to a thousand pounds each. From the work on the coat, it wasn't an original, but a very good copy that could be bought at any backstreet market in any city in England. Another lead down the drain.

Jacob skimmed over the descriptions of each item, then paused, frowning.

"Temple!"

She appeared at the door. "Boss?"

"The boots," he said. "John Smith's boots. The reports said they had some grass on them?"

She nodded. "Dried grass."

He pulled up the image of the boots. "If we're going with the hypothesis they came in by a vehicle, why would he have grass on his boots? The pod bay is gravel and directly in front of the house." He looked up at her. "Are we sure he didn't come in across the grounds?"

"CSU couldn't find footprints on the grass, but the wind and rain that day could have destroyed any trace." Her brow furrowed. "Where would he have come from otherwise? There are only fields for miles around the house. I don't think many kidnappers would hike to kidnap someone."

"No," he agreed. "Of course not." He scratched at his jaw pensively. "Suppose he could have been trying to see in the windows. Maybe that's when Sanders saw him and warned his son to hide."

"You'll need to speak to the boy again."

Jacob nodded. He'd been hoping to avoid it. Ben had been traumatised enough. He didn't need a reminder of what had happened. Still, they needed to work out the timeline, and if talking to Ben cleared up some of the facts, it had to be done.

"See if you can't push the analysis on the grass to see if it matches vegetation in the gardens. If not, we might get more ideas of where he came from." He rose. "I'll see if Anton's heard anything from the Home

Office. If I have to go back into the TRI to see Mrs. Ashraf and Ben, I might as well deal with everything while I'm there, if we have any queries."

"You want me to call ahead and let them know you'll be coming?"

Jacob considered the careful way he and Mrs. Ashraf had approached each other. She was sizing him up and vice versa. Better to limit her contact with his team. "I'll call her once I know the details. I think she'd prefer hearing directly from me, since we've talked before."

"Smart one?" Temple guessed.

"And then some," Jacob confirmed. He glanced at the images. "We're going to have to release the scene soon. I think it'll stand as a show of good faith if I tell her that when I see her."

"Here's your friend's house back, tell us what you know?"

Jacob shrugged. "It might work. Unlikely, but possible."

Temple returned to the door. "You want me to go out and do a last sweep?"

He nodded. "Can't hurt. Image everything to be on the safe side."

By the time he emerged from his office, she had already left.

Jacob went to the incident board, trying to put everything in order.

Too much didn't make sense, too many questions needed answering: Where had the kidnappers come from? Where did they go? Why did they target Sanders? Why were the TRI keeping their mouths shut with one of their chief engineers still missing in action? What were they hiding?

Now was not the time to socialise with a member of the TRI.

Jacob thumbed on his quill.

Kit Rafferty's name and number were at the top of his contact list.

It wasn't the time for it, but if they didn't get anywhere with Mariam Ashraf and Ben couldn't tell them anything, then they were going to be working in circles. He clenched his teeth, popping open a new message.

Then he had to take into account how morally questionable it would be to take advantage of Rafferty's good nature, and professionally risky in the middle of an investigation, but they needed answers, and if bending the rules would get them, he would do it.

He typed in a message with a location and sent it before he could change his mind.

Fifteen minutes later, the reply came. Acceptance and a smiling icon.

Jacob stared blankly at the quill.

Jesus, he was a bastard.

Chapter Ten

A speaker system ran through the whole TRI building.

Once in a while, they had a fire drill, and occasionally, rarely, announcements would be made about upcoming visits or events. It was very rare for anyone to be called up individually through the system.

Kit nearly dropped his screwdriver in alarm when his name echoed around the temporal chamber. He'd been doing upgrade work on the temporal gate. To the average observer, it would seem like an oversized metal doorframe, hooked up to wires and cables, but it was far more complicated than anything he'd worked with before. He'd been working on it for hours and had only stepped back to stretch, so the sudden burst of noise made him jump.

"Kit Rafferty, report to Mariam Ashraf's office."

Kit looked frantically at Reg, sitting on the floor, working on rewiring another cable. "What do I do?"

Reg set down the cable and turned to him. "When Mariam calls? You go. It must be important if they're calling through the whole building."

"Well, they couldn't exactly call us down here," Kit said hopefully. "Maybe it's not so serious."

Reg's eyebrows rose. "If you say so."

Kit winced. He spun around and knelt to replace his tools back in his tool tray. Everything had its place there. He took a moment longer than necessary, trying to gather himself. He hadn't seen Mariam since their encounter in the canteen.

A panicked thought surfaced—maybe they knew about his date with the police officer.

He wedged the lid of the toolbox closed and scrambled up. "Don't touch anything," he said with a nod to the gate, then hurried toward the main door of the room. A long corridor linked the gate room to a layover chamber, where agents usually changed and cleaned up after missions. Beyond that, another corridor led to the main halls and the stairs.

The temporal chambers were all located in the second lowest level of the building, far underground, safely kept out of sight. Unfortunately, it also meant they weren't connected to the lift network.

By the time he reached the level where the lifts started running, Kit was puffing and out of breath. He sagged in the corner of the lift, breathing hard and trying his best not to think of the drop below.

They couldn't know about his encounter with DI Ofori. He hadn't mentioned it to anyone, so unless they'd been hacking into his quill, they couldn't know about it. He didn't bring up his love life at work anyway, but mentioning he was having drinks with their investigating officer seemed like the height of stupidity.

The lift whirred to a halt on the tenth floor, and he glanced at his reflection in the mirrored wall. He'd gone white as a sheet, making his freckles stand out in sharp relief. If they didn't suspect he was up to something before, his face practically screamed "I'm guilty of something; ask me what!"

He tried to pat his hair into behaving, straightened his T-shirt, and stepped out of the lift, heading toward Mariam's door.

It was closed, but he tapped lightly before pressing the control to open it.

Mariam was waiting, but she had company.

Janos Nagy rose from the chair beside her desk as Mariam got up.

Kit glanced warily from one to the other. "You called me?"

Mariam nodded. "A few days ago, you asked me what happened three years ago. I'm not the one to tell you." She nodded to Janos. "I'll leave you to it. If you need me back, I'll be in the conference room at the end of the hall."

Janos bowed slightly, an odd little habit he always had around ladies.

Mariam met Kit's eyes. "Hear him out."

Kit didn't know what to say, but he stepped aside and let her leave the room. The door slid closed behind her. He looked at Janos and knocked his knuckles together nervously. "So, you know what happened three years ago?"

Janos motioned with his prosthetic left hand for him to sit. "Please. It is a complicated story to tell you."

Kit sat on the edge of the chair. "Why are you the one telling me? Why not Mariam?"

"Because I am what happened three years ago."

Kit frowned. "I don't think you said that right."

"It is right." Janos laced his hands together. "My name is Janos Attila Nagy. I was born in 1911 in Szerencs region of Hungary." He inclined his head. "I am the reason you have this job."

Kit stared at him. "Bollocks."

Janos met his gaze placidly. "You think I lie?"

"I think there are strict rules to stop it from happening." Kit shook his head. "They wouldn't let it happen."

"They did not let anything happen," Janos said. Kit had never heard him speaking so much. His Hungarian accent was strong, his voice warm and deep. "Sanders told you the gate is left open in time past, yes? They started closing it because of me. I struck one of the agents and came through. They could not kill me, but they had no time to send me back."

Kit stared at him, his fingers wrapped around the arms of the chair.

It went against all the rules they had. Suddenly, fancying a policeman didn't seem like such a major problem.

"Let's say that's true," he said. "So you stayed? Just like that? Travelled in time, and you were okay with it?"

Janos shrugged. He opened his hands, showing the false left one. "There are worse places to be." He met Kit's eyes. "It is small part of big story. Later, one of our people went bad. He tried to change things and broke rules. Dieter went back to stop him."

"Dieter? As in Dieter-the-linguist?"

Janos inclined his head. "He is not official agent. He was not meant to do this, but we had no time to train new person. Dieter did it, but it was bad for him." Janos sighed, scratching the back of his neck. "Now someone has used a gate. We think they have Sanders. It is not us. It is not now, but we do not know who it is or when they come from."

Pieces were fitting into place.

"That's why Dieter looked so bad when Mariam said what happened?" Kit guessed. "He remembered what happened last time?"

Janos nodded. "He cannot stay here now. It brings back bad memories and nightmares. Mariam asked me to tell you this." Green eyes met his. "She say it is important for you to know why we keep secrets. It is my life and my secret, so I must be one to tell."

Kit frowned down at his hands in his lap, then raised his eyes to Janos. "You were really born in 1911?"

"I look good for someone old," Janos said, and a hint of amusement glinted in his eyes, but vanished in an instant. "I was a soldier in Second World War. Now, I am modern man. I live here. I have life and home."

"And boyfriend."

"Yes." Janos leaned forward, propping his forearms on his knees. "You were not told this before because it is a dangerous secret—to know people will try to change things. It happened before, and now, it happens again."

"Someone else has found out about time travel and doesn't care about the rules?"

Janos nodded. "This is how it seems. Maybe it is someone who goes from here, or maybe they come from somewhere else. Mariam says when the police are finished, we will be able to go to Sanders's home and find out more, but we must wait."

"Why not use the gate to go back to that day?"

Janos shook his head. "You know the rules for crossing your own timeline. You cannot be in a world where you already breathe. Anyway, we only open gate to places where we know what has happened. It is a big danger to go somewhere without knowing. People can be hurt."

Kit looked back down at his hands, pressing his knuckles together. "Thank you. For telling me, I mean. I'm sorry I had to push you into it."

Janos smiled, which softened his serious face. "You must know the secrets you are protecting. It is fair." He pushed himself up from the chair, then held out his right hand. "Thank you, for protecting our secrets."

Kit rose and clasped Janos's hand. "If I can help or anything with Dieter, you let me know."

Janos squeezed his hand briefly. "He will be well. Memories are strong, but he is stronger."

"You've been with him all this time?"

Janos was silent for a long moment, but he nodded. "I have lost much, coming to this time, but it is all worth it for what I have here. I am happy."

No wonder they'd kept it a secret, Kit thought as Janos left the room.

The rules of the TRI had been drilled into him. No interference. No changing things. No bringing anything back.

It all seemed like overkill at the time, but if the recent history of the agency involved a refugee from the past breaching their defences and making himself a home, no wonder they were wary about letting everyone know.

Janos was technically over one hundred and thirty years old.

What a mind-blowing concept.

The door opened again and Kit turned around to see Mariam.

She made her way around the desk and sat down. "You see why I had to ask the relevant people."

"Yeah." Kit shook his head. "I...it seems impossible."

"So does our job," she replied with a tired smile. "Now, about Sanders's board. I know you were wary about sharing it, but I need to know."

She opened up the image on her slate and offered it to him. He didn't ask how she'd got it. Probably from the projector's memory in the conference room. Perfectly preserved, clear and sharp.

He knew the key to Sanders's code. With so many of his ideas going straight to Sanders and being bounced back, the key had been passed between them too. He'd logged it so many times, it had become ingrained in his memory.

Kit picked up the stylus for the slate and started decoding as he read.

He didn't know how long he sat there, but his neck ached by the time he raised his head.

Mariam was watching him.

"It's unfinished," he said and slid the slate across the desk to her.

She picked up the slate, and her brow furrowed in disbelief. "This...is this correct?"

Kit rubbed at his eyes. "It's a working theory."

Mariam's eyebrows lifted. "He found a way to jump forward in time?"

"He found a possibility." Kit got up stiffly from the seat. "He already managed to make it possible to teleport to the past. Why not the future too? Maybe that's why no one can find him."

Mariam looked up at him. "You think it could work?"

"I just talked to a man born in 1911 who came through a gate invented by the man who wrote a new theory." Kit's thoughts felt fuzzy around the edges. Even forming words was tricky. "Sanders's science has been right before. It could be again."

Mariam gazed back down at the slate. "Yes, it could."

Between the aching head and the world going a bit spinny, Kit didn't know what else he could add. Decoding was exhausting anyway, and on top of all of the information that had been thrown at him, and working on the gate for four hours already, he wondered if she'd mind if he slid off the chair and went to sleep.

And in a couple of hours, he had an appointment with DI Ofori; he'd be about as stimulating as sponge pudding if he didn't get a break.

"D'you mind if I finish early today?" Kit rubbed at his eyes again. A bit overdramatic, but it caught her attention. "I think I used up the last of my brain on that."

She looked at him with concern. "Are you all right?"

"Too much excitement," he lied. "I'm a bit tired."

She nodded. "I'll let your team know. You go and get some rest."

Kit collected his coat and satchel. Instead of taking the tram, he requested a taxi-pod outside the building. His mind whirled foggily. Time travel and rule breaking, jumping forward and using illicit technology no one else knew about. It was all so much bigger than he'd expected.

He curled against the side of the cab, closing his eyes.

Suddenly, his own little drama seemed insignificant.

So what if he went for drinks with DI Ofori? At least he hadn't let someone from the early twentieth century commit a technically unauthorised time jump to the present and settle down with one of his colleagues. He also hadn't built some new gate and potentially punted himself into the future. Okay, there were things he'd done with homemade gate-bits he probably shouldn't have, but no one knew about it, so it technically didn't count.

If anyone tried to criticise him, he had more than enough ammunition to shut them all up.

Kit smiled wearily at the pod roof.

Now, at least, he could look forward to a night out.

Chapter Eleven

The bar was quiet.

Not that it had ever been an overcrowded social hub, but tonight, there were only a couple of the old regulars nursing their brews at tables in the corners. Jacob had taken a seat, propping up the bar, a drink already held between his hands.

He'd chosen the far side of the bar for some privacy, but he couldn't help thinking the setting was a mistake, too intimate, much more so than a social bistro or a restaurant where people were always coming and going. It wasn't like he hadn't been to the pub before and had any reason to expect heaving crowds. No. He'd picked it because he was a bloody idiot.

"Need a refill?" One of the interchangeable bar staff approached, polishing a glass.

"Not now, thanks."

Jacob took out his quill, checking for both the time and a potential message of cancellation from Rafferty. He could cancel himself, but if he wanted to, he'd have done it the day Luke left.

Seven on the dot and no message.

He flicked the screen off and shoved the quill into his breast pocket, then let his head fall forward with a sigh.

"Aren't you Mr. Enthusiastic?"

Jacob sat up sharply at Rafferty's voice. He hadn't noticed the door opening, and he turned on the stool. Whatever he'd planned to say stuttered to a halt as he ran his eyes over the other man from head to toe.

Rafferty's shaggy mop of hair had been tamed. It shone like copper, pushed back from his freckled face. Dressed in a pale-blue shirt that made his eyes gleam like chips of ice, he didn't look like the rumpled, sleep-deprived engineer Jacob had run into in the lift.

He was too tall, too gangly, not at all Jacob's usual type, but when his face split into the grin that could light up the room, Jacob found he didn't care.

Goddammit.

"You found a comb, then," he said as casually as he could.

Rafferty laughed, dropping onto the stool beside him. "A rare event," he agreed. "I'd say it's a good night to buy a lottery ticket. All kinds of strange miracles are happening." He waved over the bartender and ordered a Bacardi. "So. Here we are."

Jacob looked at his own drink. It was all for the sake of the case. That was what he had to tell himself. "I'm surprised you came."

Rafferty grinned at him. "Likewise. You have to admit my opening line wasn't exactly smooth."

Jacob's lips twitched. "It had a certain subtlety."

"Oh yeah. So subtle." Rafferty shook his head. "The only way it could have been more subtle was if I stripped off and painted a welcome sign on my bum."

Jacob paused, glass halfway to his mouth. "Thank you so much for that image."

Rafferty blushed again, but he smiled. "Trial by fire and mental image. If I don't scare you off in the first ten minutes, I consider this a success."

Jacob looked at him in amusement. "You try to scare men off?"

Rafferty shrugged, turning on his stool to prop himself against the bar. "I like interesting people. People who don't get flustered and awkward when I make a complete arse of myself. Which I do. A lot. Faulty brain-to-mouth connection." His eyes danced. "You may have noticed."

"Once or twice," Jacob agreed.

"And yet, here you are." Rafferty twisted around to take his drink from the bartender and settled against the bar again. "Interesting and interested?" He tilted his glass toward Jacob. "I like that."

Despite himself, Jacob smiled. "I'm not that interesting."

"Oh, come on," Rafferty snorted. "You're a *detective*. That practically screams interesting."

Jacob turned his glass between his fingertips. "You'd be surprised how boring it can be. So much paperwork." He could feel Rafferty's eyes on him and glanced up from his drink. "Being an engineer must be a lot more interesting?"

Rafferty made a face. "It has its moments but with the fun risk of electrocution." He gestured to his hair. "This is the grounded state."

Jacob couldn't help chuckling. "You're an odd one, you know."

Rafferty beamed at him. "You have no idea." He turned on the stool to face Jacob and set his drink down. "What about you?"

"Me?" Jacob had to turn away. "Nothing special." The less personal information given, the better. They needed to be talking about the TRI. Nothing more. Rafferty didn't need to know anything about him. "Just a grumpy old single copper."

"Bullshit."

Jacob almost dropped his glass when a broad, long-fingered hand squeezed his thigh. He looked down, then back at Rafferty, who was smiling in a decidedly interested way.

"It's the truth," Jacob said, only a little hoarsely.

"Partly." Rafferty's hand moved slightly upward, and Jacob clenched his teeth and tried to stop himself from pressing into Rafferty's touch. "Copper, yeah. Single, thank Christ. Old? Call it classic. Vintage." His palm press-rubbed against Jacob's inner thigh, and Jacob's legs opened wider of their own accord. "Grumpy...well, I can work with that."

Jacob reached down and caught Rafferty's wrist. "I'm not sure it's a good idea."

Rafferty leaned closer. "Why not?"

There were a dozen reasons. More even.

"You didn't finish your drink."

Rafferty's face was so close to his he could count every individual freckle. "And?"

Jacob's fingers could completely circle Rafferty's wrist. A twist of his hand and Rafferty wouldn't be touching him. He simply had to move away, and he wouldn't have those cool blue eyes and their copper lashes right in his face. All he had to do was have some bloody restraint.

One side of Rafferty's mouth curled up, and the tip of his very pink tongue brushed his teeth. He raised his eyebrows in challenge, and God damn it all.

Jacob abandoned his glass and sank his other hand into Rafferty's hair, pulling the other man's mouth against his. Rafferty's laugh of delight rippled against his lips, and the younger man fell into him eagerly.

Christ, he was being an idiot, but Rafferty's hot mouth opened to his, and his teeth caught Jacob's lower lip, tugging demandingly. He'd shaken off Jacob's restraining hand and pressed his palm flush against the front of Jacob's trousers, squeezing.

Jacob pulled back, panting. "Wait...wait..."

Rafferty tossed his head, breathing hard. "What?"

"You don't even know me."

Rafferty's eyebrows rose. "So? I'm not asking you to marry me or anything."

Jacob stared at him. "I thought we were just having a drink."

Rafferty slid his hand to a more modest position on Jacob's thigh. "If that's all you want, it can be."

All he'd wanted was a lead to crack the case and to be able to find out what happened to Rafferty's missing employer. All he'd wanted had gone out the window the minute Rafferty had looked at him like he wanted to eat him alive.

Rafferty kept watching him with the same intensity, but concern coloured it now.

"Alternatively," he said and squeezed Jacob's thigh again, "get your coat, honeybuns. You've pulled."

The tension shattered, and Jacob burst out laughing.

Rafferty grinned at him.

"You're an arse," Jacob said.

"It's been said." Rafferty lifted his hand away from Jacob's thigh and retrieved his glass. The heated look had given way to a more genuine smile. "Offer's still on the table, if you're interested."

Jacob gazed down at the front of his trousers, then back up, raising his eyebrows at Rafferty. "I don't think the matter was ever in question."

Rafferty widened his eyes in feigned relief and clutched his heart. "Good. I don't think my fragile ego could take it otherwise." He considered Jacob. "So, if you don't want me for my body, I suppose I'll have to actually engage my brain and make the words?"

"If it's not too much of a trial for you," Jacob agreed.

Rafferty gave a dramatic sigh. "I'll soldier bravely on." He took a drink, then darted his tongue along his lower lip to catch the excess.

Jacob watched the flick of Kit's pink tongue over those now-swollen lips.

He raised a hand to catch the bartender's attention.

He needed another drink.

Chapter Twelve

Kit had a plan.

Part of it involved getting Jacob's trousers off and having a gay old time of it. There were several stages in order to get to the trouserectomy. He'd managed to get a snog already—a good start—and Jacob had definitely shown a lot of interest, which was encouraging.

It was only a matter of taking his time.

So they talked and they drank, and the tension in Jacob's shoulders gradually eased.

For all that Jacob said he was grumpy, he kept on letting those little smiles slip out.

By the time it hit nine o'clock, Kit felt pleasantly buzzed, and Jacob didn't seem like he would tense up again. Kit brushed one hand across the base of Jacob's back. "Want to go?"

Jacob glanced at him, and for a moment, indecision returned.

Stupid indecision.

To help him make up his mind, Kit leaned a little bit closer and kissed him lightly. First on the lips, then the cheek, then the jaw, then the throat, and then up to his ear. He nibbled gently on Jacob's earlobe, and the other man's breath gusted on his skin.

"Not asking for more than a night," he whispered. "C'mon. It'll be fun."

Jacob drew back, staring at him long and hard.

"Why?"

Kit spread his hand on Jacob's back. "Same reason I came for a drink. Same reason I'm having trouble keeping my hands off you." He shrugged. "Not many people catch my eye. You did."

Jacob turned away from him for a moment, pressing his fist to the edge of the bar. "One night? That's all you want out of this?"

Kit grinned. "First is free. After that? Well, that's up to you." He hooked one finger through Jacob's belt. "You're good-looking. I'm moderately all right. I think we could have a good night."

Jacob looked back at him, his eyes gleaming and dark. "Moderately all right?"

Kit slid off his stool. "Modesty is one of my best features."

Jacob tapped his fingers on the bar, then rose too. They were practically the same height, and Jacob caught Kit by the waist, pulling him closer. "One night."

Kit licked his lower lip. "If it's all you want."

"I'm not looking for long-term."

"Good." Kit pulled Jacob's mouth hard onto his. He shivered pleasantly as Jacob's hands tightened against his back. "My place isn't too far."

There were taxi-pods outside, and as soon as they were in and on their way, Kit crowded Jacob back against the seat. It had been a long while since he'd had the urge, but now it had given off great big flashing signs of interest, he didn't plan on wasting it.

Their mouths met, and it was good. Jacob knew what he was doing. His tongue darted against Kit's, and he tangled one hand into Kit's hair. If they'd had longer, Kit would've had his hand down Jacob's trousers right there and then.

They only broke apart when the pod door slid open and the chime indicated they should vacate the vehicle.

Kit didn't hesitate before leading Jacob into the block of flats.

Admittedly, he had a moment where he remembered a policeman now knew where he lived, but since he wanted said policeman to get into the flat, and in or on him—no preference—it kind of became necessary.

As soon as they were in the lift, Kit could not have been happier when Jacob pushed him up against the wall and kissed him senseless.

"You don't like lifts, do you?" Jacob murmured against his lips as Kit clung to him.

Kit shook his head, then hissed between his teeth as Jacob laid a trail of stinging bites down his throat. "Christ!"

If Jacob had any doubts, it didn't show. Especially not in the way he got Kit's belt undone and his hand down the front of his trousers. Kit's head knocked back against the polished mirror, one arm wrapped around Jacob's shoulders, the other clinging to the handrail out of habit.

"There's a camera," he panted out.

Jacob lifted his head, glancing around the lift, and to Kit's bemused delight, he gave the camera a nod and a wink. Kit dissolved into helpless laughter, which earned another of those dimpling smiles from Jacob.

"Was that a hint to get my hand out of your trousers?"

"For two minutes," Kit reluctantly agreed. He pulled Jacob back and kissed him again. "I appreciate the distraction."

"What do you do when there's no one here?"

Kit raised his eyebrows. "Stairs."

"Seriously? We're on the..." Jacob glanced above the door as the lift stopped. "Jesus. Thirteen floors? No wonder you're as skinny as a rake."

Kit made a face. "Pardon me for not enjoying the sensation of being suspended over a terminal drop." He caught Jacob's hand with one hand, and his trousers with the other, and pulled the man out of the lift into the hall.

"You could go for a lower floor."

"I could," Kit agreed as they neared his door. He swiped his key card over the entry panel and pressed his fingertips to the console. The console flashed green, and the door slid aside. "But then, I wouldn't have this..."

The door opened straight into the sprawling living room. The vertical blinds were drawn apart from the balcony door and the floor-to-ceiling windows. Below them, the city scattered like a circuit array, sparking and winking with lights. Jacob walked forward toward the glass, staring.

"Not bad, is it?" Kit closed the door behind them and shed his coat.

"I think I'm in the wrong profession," Jacob said, shaking his head.

Kit came up alongside him, wrapping a hand around his arm. "Where were we?"

Jacob tore his eyes from the view and turned with a flash of a smile. "I think I remember." He pulled Kit closer, one hand getting rid of the belt and shoving Kit's trousers farther down to take a hold of his cock. "There?"

Kit shuddered pleasantly. "God, yes." He groped at Jacob's shirt, twisting buttons undone one by one. "Huh. Fuzzy."

"Oh, shut your face, freckles."

Kit laughed, pushing Jacob back against the glass so he could work his way down the rest of the buttons. As soon as they were undone, Jacob shook both shirt and coat off, letting them land where they fell. His free hand snaked under Kit's shirt, pulling it up, and his broad palm cupped Kit's arse.

"Jesus. I could hold your whole arse in one hand..."

Kit squirmed against his hands. "Not exactly what I had in mind for the night," he said, sliding Jacob's belt loose.

Jacob released Kit's cock to catch his wrist. "I didn't plan on this. I mean..." He raised his eyebrows and nodded down.

Kit grinned so widely his cheeks ached. "Don't move," he said and dashed for the bathroom. He paused at the door. "Or...y'know...undress. Up to you."

In the bathroom, he toed off his shoes and kicked off his trousers. They were only in the way anyway. His shirt followed, pulled off over his head. He rattled through the cabinets, his hands shaking with anticipation, and came up victorious. Never hurt to be prepared for all occasions.

The cool evening air hit him as soon as he came out of the bathroom. The door was open and Jacob stood out on the terrace, overlooking the city below. Better yet, he'd ditched his trousers and was braced, absolutely starkers, against the wall of the balcony.

Kit came to the door, steadying himself against the glass.

Fully dressed, Jacob was good-looking.

Naked, he was a work of art. His shoulders were broad, his waist narrow, and if Kit's arse seemed small enough for him to hold in one hand, his backside was firm and round enough to take both of Kit's hands.

"Enjoying the view?" Kit inquired.

Jacob glanced back, and his lips twitched. "Yeah. You?"

"It's never looked quite as good as it does right now." Kit stepped down onto the terrace, the stone cool beneath his feet. He'd been out there naked before, but never with company, and it made his heart beat a little faster.

Jacob didn't turn. "Find what you need?"

"Armed and ready," Kit replied, coming up behind him. He half expected Jacob to turn, but instead, Jacob pressed back into him, tilting his head to gaze at him. Kit splayed his hand low on Jacob's belly. "What do you fancy?"

When Jacob pushed his hips back against Kit's groin, Kit groaned out loud.

"Surprise me," Jacob murmured against his lips.

Either fate or surprise made him drop the lube.

Kit swore under his breath and went down onto his knees to pick it up. He paused there, admiring a whole other view, and grinned. He left the lube and condoms in a heap and dragged his hands up the back of Jacob's legs, thumbs sinking into the muscle of his inner thighs.

Jacob made no complaint, shifting his feet a little farther apart. He braced his forearms against the edge of the wall, as if he were doing nothing but admiring the skyline.

Kit watched the rise and fall of the other man's ribs as he moved his hands up toward his backside. Maybe Jacob was good at playing it cool, but he couldn't hide his rapid breaths, and when Kit pressed his mouth to the base of Jacob's spine, Jacob shuddered as if an electric current had shot through him.

Kit smothered a grin. Very interested, then. He kneaded at Jacob's backside with both hands, then laved his tongue up the crease of Jacob's buttocks. The muscles in Jacob's thighs jumped, and his head dropped forward as he blew out a breath.

"Been a while?" Kit rubbed his cheek against one buttock.

"Something like that."

Kit nipped at his backside gently. "I'll be kind, then." He slid one hand around in front of Jacob, teasing his hardening cock, while the other pressed at his backside. He nuzzled the base of Jacob's back. "Just say when."

"Mm." Jacob shifted his weight on the balls of his feet and hissed out another breath when Kit's tongue darted against him again. His hips pushed forward against Kit's hand, and Kit grinned at the wordless encouragement, flattening his tongue and licking in broad, greedy strokes.

Jacob's head dropped forward to rest on his arms, and his hips rocked back to meet Kit's mouth and forward to meet his hand. Kit could tell he hadn't had any in a while from how quickly he got hard.

"When," Jacob said hoarsely, only a moment later.

Kit sat back on his heels, groping on the ground for the lube and one of the condoms. He managed to get to his feet without releasing Jacob's cock, though the man groaned as he momentarily tightened his grip.

He draped himself over Jacob's gorgeous bare back, rubbing his cock against the now-neglected buttocks. "How you holding up?" he asked impishly, propping his chin on Jacob's hunched shoulders.

"You're a bugger," Jacob groaned into his arms.

Kit laughed and pressed a kiss to his shoulder. "Hold your breath and count to ten. I'll show you how nice I can be."

Jacob nodded, lifting his head and propping his forearms on the wall. He breathed in, slow and deep. It took three breaths for Kit to get the condom open and on his own aching cock. Another breath to squeeze some lube into his hand, another to warm it up enough not to earn a smack in the mouth.

On the sixth, he pressed his palm to Jacob's hip. On the seventh, slick fingers slowly pushed into Jacob, and he had to bite his own lip to keep from groaning. The eighth breath turned into a shuddering gasp as Kit curled his fingers, and a shiver ran the length of Jacob's body. He started rocking back against Kit's hand, pushing him deeper, until two fingers were buried to the knuckle. Jesus, he was hot.

Kit's mouth felt dry.

"Okay?"

"Hell, yes," Jacob growled. "You now."

Kit withdrew his hand and wrapped his palm around his cock, slicking it.

Jesus.

When he'd flirted with the man at the bar, he never expected the evening to go like this. Not the lack of clothes and shagging thing. A vague hope, yes. But out here, like this? Every inch of them bare to the air, goosebumps all over? With the broad-shouldered, silver fox of a policeman receiving like he was born to? Nope. Never saw it coming.

Jacob pushed back into him as Kit pressed his cock against the older man's arse. Jesus, he was tight. Jacob tilted his head, looking at Kit between his lashes, still breathing hard. As Kit pushed deeper, Jacob slowly straightened, and Jesus, his body clenched. Kit made a small, strangled sound, knocking his forehead against Jacob's shoulder.

Jacob chuckled suddenly, unexpectedly, and the sound vibrated through his whole body.

"How you holding up?" he asked hoarsely.

Kit had to put a hand out to steady himself against the wall. He wrapped his other arm around Jacob's narrow waist, groping blindly for the man's cock. "So...been a while..."

Jacob's hand covered his, their fingers tangling around Jacob's cock. "Fair enough."

Jacob tilted onto his toes, lifting himself up, then as slowly, sank back down. Kit gasped out loud. He could swear he was about to have a bloody aneurysm, his whole body throbbing all the way to his balls.

"Christ..." He pressed his mouth to Jacob's throat, his lips trembling.

He didn't know which of them started moving first. Maybe both of them. Jacob tilted his head enough to find Kit's mouth, and Kit panted against his lips as his hips crashed against Jacob's arse. Their fingers jerked and squeezed together around Jacob's cock, and Jacob's head rocked forward, short, panting breaths escaping him.

Kit's legs were shaking. Jesus. Everything shook. Too little to eat, enough booze, and an eager lover. Everything making his head spin. He buried his face in Jacob's neck.

"Down," he panted out.

"Down," Jacob agreed breathlessly.

Graceless and clumsy, they crashed to their knees.

Easier, Kit thought wildly, as Jacob braced his hands on the wall in front of them and shoved back hard against him. Kit wrapped his hands over Jacob's hips. Pulled him closer. They were both gasping now. He started thrusting harder and saw Jacob reaching for his own cock. Every man for himself, he thought, giggling helplessly.

Jacob went tense suddenly. Tight. Jesus Christ.

It only took a couple more strokes and Kit was done too. He sprawled forward against Jacob's broader back, panting hard. Jacob tipped them both sideways, spilling them onto the rough surface of the balcony. They sprawled there, panting and shining with sweat. Kit dragged himself away enough to let his cock slide free. "Mm."

"Quite." Jacob's voice sounded lower than before.

Kit grinned vaguely at the sky and punched Jacob on the shoulder. "I win."

Jacob turned onto his back, an amused look on his face. "Really?"

Kit squirmed closer. "Yup," he said and kissed Jacob full on the mouth, swallowing the other man's laugh.

Chapter Thirteen

Jacob didn't need an alarm clock to wake him.

A decade of getting up at seven for a run had ingrained itself into his brain. It felt like more of an effort this morning, and as he opened his eyes and found a spread of pale skin on blue sheets in front of him, recollection crashed in on him like a wrecking ball.

He stared blankly at the younger man sprawled out on the bed with him. Kit Rafferty was on his belly, hugging a pillow under his head, his hair sticking in all directions. He was smiling in his sleep.

Shit.

Jacob squinted around the room.

When he'd decided to have a drink or two at the bar, he'd tried to keep a running tally. He was hardly a lightweight. After a certain point, he could still walk and talk and sound completely sober, but the part of him that liked to do bloody stupid stuff came out to play.

Stuff like agree to come home with Rafferty and...

He put a hand over his eyes, a groan of dismay dying in his throat.

The balcony.

Jesus Christ.

As if shagging someone who was part of an ongoing investigation wasn't bad enough! If anyone had seen them, they could be done for public indecency on top of it, and that would be the icing on the cake if his colleagues found out.

On top of everything else, he was dying for a piss.

He rolled over to the side of the bed and stumbled upright. His knees ached; he looked down. They were grazed, and the balcony came to mind again. Brilliant. Just brilliant.

It took him three attempts to find the bathroom. For all that Rafferty dressed like he lived under a bridge, his flat was huge. There were rooms filled with engineering gear. There was what looked like a walk-in wardrobe. And thank God, a bathroom that could have fit Jacob's living room in it.

He did his business, then washed his hands, scooping up a handful of cool water to dash on his face in hopes it might wake him up a bit.

Several problems needed dealing with. How to make a polite but discreet exit was top of the list. Also high up there—resisting the urge to go back to the warm bed and get a couple of hours' more kip. And other things he shouldn't be thinking about doing in the bed as well.

And he hadn't even learned anything useful about the TRI either.

All things considered, maybe he ought to admit it had never really been about the TRI.

It was all about the fact that someone had shown an interest in him for the first time in months, and he'd actually let himself notice. It was his brain getting sick of nearly two years of self-imposed celibacy. It was a grinning redhead with a smile like sunshine.

One night.

That was what they'd both agreed.

One night of shagging and grazed knees.

That was enough of it. No more being bloody stupid because he was gagging for a shag. They'd done enough the night before to stop him being distracted for a while. At least in theory.

He padded out into the flat.

There were clothes scattered here and there. He found his trousers over the back of the sofa and pulled them on. His shirt and jacket were by the door of the balcony, and God only knew where he'd left his shoes. He searched around and spotted one under the coffee table.

By the time he found the second, he heard the shuffle of sleepy feet at the bedroom door.

"Don't you want breakfast?"

Jacob looked over his shoulder, then wished he hadn't. Rafferty didn't seem to have a bashful bone in his body. He stood in the doorway of the bedroom, shoulder against the frame, all pale skin and copper hair and freckles everywhere.

"I need to change before work," Jacob said, sitting down to pull on his shoes.

Rafferty was silent for a moment, then retreated into the bedroom.

When Jacob stood up, shoes on, Rafferty emerged again, this time wearing boxer shorts.

"Some toast, at least," he offered, and his smile was there, still bright. "It'll take what? Ten minutes?"

Jacob frowned at the buttons of his shirt as he did them up. One of them got in the wrong hole and knocked all the others out of alignment. "I shouldn't have come."

"Mm." Rafferty was suddenly in front of him, swatting his hands away from his shirt. His nimble fingers undid the wrong buttons and started to redo them. "I love the smell of regret in the morning." He met Jacob's eyes. "Tell me you didn't have fun."

Jacob closed his hands over Kit's, holding them still. "It's not about that. It's about the fact that you're part of an ongoing investigation, even if it's only in the sidelines. It's about the fact that I shouldn't even be speaking to you in a personal capacity, let alone—"

"Let alone getting buggered by me?" Kit's smile had faded to something softer, more serious. "Don't worry. One-night thing. No one'll know but us. And anyway, it's not like I kidnapped my boss and am holding him for ransom, so you won't need to arrest me or anything."

Relief flooded him to know it wouldn't be held against him.

Jacob squeezed Kit's hands. "And I did have fun."

The grin returned like a flash of fire. "Believe me, I could tell." He leaned closer and dropped a quick, chaste kiss on Jacob's lips. "But now, breakfast. Toast or full English?"

Well, the bridges were already burning...

"Full English."

Kit's face lit up. "A wise choice, sir," he said, doing up the last button. "I find a full English brings out one's cholesterol." He waved a hand toward the rest of the living room. "Have a seat. I'll bring it through when it's ready."

Left to his own devices, Jacob took the chance to examine the room by daylight.

Photographs dotted the wall, most of them of Kit with his mother, though Jacob spotted a couple of group shots. Not many other personal touches though. The flat seemed to be given over to engineering, with boxes of equipment tucked here and there, and sketches and schematics stacked on shelves.

A closer look at the coffee table made Jacob stop short. In the middle of the chaos of wires and tools, an object not unlike the small machines in the Sanders house lay in a tangle of wires.

Jacob sat down on the couch and carefully picked it up, turning it over in his hands. He had no idea what it was for, but it looked practically identical to the devices that had been hanging on the edge of the whiteboard.

"Scrambled or fried?" Kit called through from the kitchen.

"Whatever you like." Jacob took out his quill and scanned and imaged the device. Even though he couldn't really pass the information to the team, later, he could at least compare the machines.

A notification flagged up for a missed call and a message received late the previous night.

He flicked the message open.

Luke, the little shit, had sent: *Congratulations on the sex.*

There were even little fireworks going off around the text.

Jacob smothered a groan. Thankfully, when he did venture on dates, Luke didn't press for too much information. He sent a thumbs-up in reply, waited for a moment, and when no response came, he shut it down again.

His quill was away and the machine back where he'd found it when Kit came through a few minutes later, carrying two generously stacked plates of food.

"Hope you're hungry," he said, offering one of the plates.

"Starved." Jacob glanced around. "Is there a dining table or do we eat here?"

Kit grinned. "If I had my way, I wouldn't even have a sofa," he said, sprawling comfortably against the arm. "Beanbags or pillow piles for preference."

Jacob snorted. "You just want to be a sultan in his harem."

Kit arched his eyebrows. He deliberately skewered a sausage on his fork and gave the end a suggestive lick, but he barely lasted five seconds before bursting out laughing. "Yeah. Maybe a bit."

Jacob cut into his breakfast with the fork. After taking several mouthfuls, he nodded to the coffee table. "What are you working on?" he asked, as casually as he could.

Kit's eyes flicked to the table, then back. Colour spread out from the middle of his chest, upward and downward, an impressively expansive blush. He shoved some egg into his mouth and chewed, and if that wasn't a tactic to give himself time to think of an answer, then Jacob was the king of Spain.

"Just some bits and pieces for work," Kit finally replied, meeting his eyes. "I'm working on a new door function. I'm...probably not meant to have it lying around at home." It sounded like the truth, but there was something in Kit's expression that said it wasn't the whole truth.

Jacob sliced his egg with the side of his fork. It shouldn't have been a surprise that Kit worked on technology similar to Sanders's, but he still wasn't any closer to finding out exactly what Sanders did. It looked like Kit didn't want to answer more questions about it either. He was wolfing down his food, as if to encourage Jacob to eat his own breakfast faster.

Jacob didn't hurry. No need to give himself indigestion.

"Are you working this morning?" he asked.

Kit nodded distractedly, mopping up a smear of egg yolk with his toast. "I left early yesterday. Probably should go in a bit earlier today."

Oh yes. There was something about that object on the table he didn't want to be asked about. He was suddenly too abrupt, making too much of the fact that he was in a hurry and had places to be. He must have forgotten he'd left it out, or never expected it to be noticed.

Out of pity, Jacob set the plate down half-finished though already more than he normally ate for breakfast anyway. "I'll leave you to get ready, then," he said.

Kit was as good at hiding his emotions as he was at hiding his blushes. The relief made his whole body relax, and he scrambled to his feet, smiling. "And you'll have time to get changed too, you dirty stop-out."

Jacob reached for his coat. "And whose fault is that?"

Kit was abruptly right in front of him and caught him by the shirt, pulling him closer to kiss him firmly on the lips. "Well, I didn't make you trip and fall naked on the balcony, did I?" he said, grinning. He rubbed the tip of his nose against Jacob's. "Thanks for a memorable evening, Detective Inspector."

Jacob winced. "Just Jacob here. Not work."

Kit laughed, patting him on the middle of his chest. "I can do that," he agreed and claimed a last kiss. "Off with you, Jacob."

It wasn't until Jacob was standing in the hall, the door closed behind him, that he could breathe easily again. He looked at his coat, held between his hands, then back at the door of Kit's flat.

One night.

That was all he could allow.

That was all he *would* allow.

It had been nice, having company during the night again, even if it technically could get him suspended. They'd laughed a lot, and the sex hadn't been half bad. Kit was cheerful and enthusiastic, not to mention imaginative. It had been a good night.

Jacob stepped into the lift and leaned back against the wall, closing his eyes.

His focus had to be back on the case. Kit's coffee table had helped there. The device he was working on was clearly important enough to get him in trouble for having it outside of the office. It looked advanced, and if that was the standard thing Sanders was working on, who was to say they hadn't been working on other synthetic items? Eyes, for example.

It would explain a lot if the TRI were secretly developing advanced technology. It would definitely explain why Sanders would have been targeted. It would make a hell of a lot more sense than a rogue cyborg beaming in and getting brained with a hammer.

Jacob rubbed at his eyelids with finger and thumb.

Something had to start making sense sooner or later.

Chapter Fourteen

Kit made an effort to keep his head down as soon as he got into the office.

He'd enjoyed the night with Jacob, right up until the moment Jacob noticed the pieces of the temporal gate lying on his coffee table. They didn't look like anything significant, but all it would take was Jacob saying something to Mariam and the TRI would know he'd been playing with a gate at home.

It wasn't as if he'd technically stolen anything from the building. He'd used parts he already had, pieces of other experiments. And they'd never have authorised him to take the blueprints home with him either. So he had a good memory for the details. So what? How did they expect him to develop new features if he didn't tinker in the comfort of his own home?

Still, he went straight to his workstation in the office, got his tools, and headed to the gate room to take up where he'd left off the day before. It felt safer to stay out of the way for a while. Hamid found him there an hour later, screwdriver gripped between his teeth.

"You're in early today."

Kit nodded with a grunt, reconnecting a wire and taking the screwdriver out of his mouth. "Work to do." He glanced back at Hamid. "You're out of your office. Is the world ending or something?"

"Mariam was looking for you. Reg said he saw you come in and head down here. We didn't want to startle you, in case you put a hole in the grid."

Kit stared at him, the bottom dropping out of his stomach. "What's it about?"

Hamid shrugged. "Didn't say. She didn't seem pleased."

Kit's mouth felt dry. There was no way anyone from the office could know anything. Not unless a certain person who had been on a night out had also spilled what he'd seen.

"Oh."

Hamid nodded toward the doorway. "I was trying to be subtle, Kit. Get your arse up there."

"But this needs to be finished—"

"It can be finished after," Hamid replied. "She's already stressed out of her mind. Don't make things worse."

Reluctantly, Kit closed the hatch on the gateway and set down his tools. "Fine. Take me up."

Mariam wasn't in her office when they got there, but Hamid insisted Kit should wait. He left him there, closing the door. Kit sat on the edge of the chair, squeezing his hands together between his knees, hoping to goodness he wasn't in trouble.

Mariam returned less than five minutes later. "Oh good. You're here."

"Um. Yes. Hamid said you wanted me?"

"Yes." She rubbed her forehead as she sat down, her face a lot paler than usual, though it could've been the deep purple hijab she was wearing. "That detective wants you down at the police station."

Kit was turning puce; he could tell. He could remember several things Jacob had wanted, and none of them were anything he wanted his employers to know about. "Oh?" It came out as a squeak.

She didn't seem to notice his expression or his colour. "They have some items they need to confirm as Sanders's work. DI Ofori asked if we can send one of our engineers down to check what they have and see if there's anything there that shouldn't be."

It was as if he was listening through a pillow. "What?"

Mariam spread her hands. "I don't know. Apparently, they have hard evidence, and before they can release the scene, they need to know whether they're holding anything that may have belonged to the attackers."

As excuses went, it was pretty flimsy.

Jesus Christ, he was going to kick Jacob so hard.

"When?" he asked, clamping his hands together. His palms were cold and wet.

"As soon as possible." She sighed. "Since you're our foremost expert on Tom's latest developments, you're the best man for the job. I'll call a taxi-pod. Make yourself presentable, and be careful what you say to the detective inspector. He's a smart one. He might get more out of you than you expect."

Bloody understatement there.

"Yeah." Kit swallowed hard. "Keep things basic, right? Like Hamid said?"

Within ten minutes, he was being escorted down to the lobby. Within twenty, he was in a taxi-pod and halfway to the police station.

Kit watched the city slipping by. Nothing to be nervous about at all. Just a man who was only meant to be a one-night stand bringing him in to be an active part of an investigation.

The police station was a state-of-the-art building. Dozens of floors, glass walls, and the security in the entranceway was enough to make him feel ill, like walking into a top-range cage, even if he was only going in as a consultant.

The officer on reception had his name.

He was taken in a lift to the seventh floor. All the way up, his hands clenched and unclenched. It wasn't the situation or the lift or the fact that he had no idea what he was walking into. Every bit of it combined into a massive Gordian knot of panic.

The officer led him through a series of halls and into a vast room. Images projected up on one wall, including pictures of Sanders, his house, and things Kit didn't want to pay too much attention to. A couple of officers glanced up with interest as he was escorted in, and one even nodded in greeting.

Kit kept his mouth tightly shut and his hands in fists. Easier to say nothing than to try to play it cool.

His destination turned out to be an office at the far end of the room, though the blinds were closed on the windows, concealing the occupant.

Jacob rose from behind a desk. He looked different in his office, sterner, more professional. Even the top button of his shirt was done up, and his tie was fastened. "Mr. Rafferty," he said. "Mrs. Ashraf let me know you'd be coming."

Kit smiled, but not enough to show any teeth. "I was sent. I didn't really have a choice." He took a breath and released it as the door closed behind him. "Is this room soundproof?"

"Not really."

Kit strode across the room, bent over the desk, and hissed when he wished he could shout, "What the hell am I doing here? You know I didn't want any part in this! Why the hell did you ask for me?"

Jacob glanced at Kit's hands, spread on the desk, then up at him. "I asked for the best engineer," he said. "The one who would be most likely to crack Sanders's code and know his technology. I didn't ask for you."

Kit stared at him. "Bullshit! You knew it would be me!"

Jacob leaned across the desk toward him. "And how would I know that?" He sounded so bloody calm. "You're one of a dozen engineers. As far as I know, you're one little cog in a machine. Nothing special in the grand scheme..."

It must've been the nerves or the fact that the bastard was speaking at him like a child. Kit couldn't be sure why, but his hand moved of its own accord, and he slapped Jacob sharply across the face.

Kit recoiled, and they stared at each other across the desk. "Did I just assault a police officer?" he asked weakly.

"Technically." Jacob sighed and rubbed at his cheek as he took his seat. He looked wound up tight again, a deep line between his eyebrows. "I'm sorry about this, but what was I meant to say to her? 'Don't send him. It would be awkward since he had his dick up me last night?'"

Kit subsided into the chair opposite him. "I didn't think about it..."

"Mm." Jacob massaged the middle of his forehead. "Since you're here now, we're going to have to make the best of it. Keep things casual. You going to be able to do that? Without smacking me in the chops again?"

Kit nodded self-consciously. "Sorry. I...it's a bit mental at work now." He shifted his weight on the chair. "You know she could have probably answered your questions, don't you? Identified stuff from the labs?"

Jacob tapped his fingertips on the edge of the table. "We weren't sure," he said evasively. "We wanted people who would know and give us a straight answer."

And they didn't ask for Mariam. Kit frowned. "You think Mariam wouldn't?"

Jacob shrugged. "She plays her cards close to the chest."

Of course she does, Kit wanted to say. *Everyone at the TRI has to. It's one of the clauses you sign.* Mariam was brilliant at keeping secrets. She would have been a better person to sit in front of a policeman with big dark eyes and a weary expression. She wouldn't have felt bad for causing him problems. Anyone else in the TRI would have been better.

Trouble was he liked Jacob, and he'd always found it impossible to lie to a man he liked.

Kit squeezed his hands between his knees until the skin went pale. "I won't be able to explain everything," he said finally. "I'm only an engineer. I don't know what goes on behind the scenes. But if I can tell you something, I will."

The tight lines on Jacob's face softened, and he sighed, relieved. "That's all I'm asking."

Kit sat back on his chair. "Purely professionally."

"Of course."

"No mention of last night."

Jacob nodded. "As far as the world knows, we have only met in your office and here."

Kit nodded slowly. "Okay." He unfolded his hands, spreading them on his thighs. "What do you need me to look at?"

Jacob rose from behind his desk. "Follow me."

They went down a long corridor, passed a dozen doors. Jacob swiped an ID badge at one of the doors and led him into a plain room. White-walled, the room was empty but for a workbench in the middle with a collection of evidence packets. Kit spotted two discreetly placed cameras attached to the ceiling though. A secure room, then.

Jacob offered him a pair of rubber gloves. "As a precaution," he said.

Kit nodded, pulling them on. "Bring it."

Jacob opened one of the packets and withdrew a piece of a temporal gate pretty much identical to the piece on Kit's coffee table that morning. Kit felt the blood drain from his face as he stared at it, then glanced up at Jacob.

There had to be a reason that was the first one.

Jacob had seen it, without knowing what he'd found, and now that he could ask, he wanted to know more.

"Do you know what this is?" The man in front of him was more police officer and less someone he'd spent the night with, sterner, suspicious, kind of dangerous. Kit could only nod mutely. "It's definitely Sanders's work?"

"Yes." Kit swallowed hard.

"You're sure?"

Kit braced his fingertips on the edge of the table. "Yes. He designed it."

To his shock, Jacob nodded and slipped it back into the evidence packet. "Good. We weren't sure. The place was a mess when we got there." He reached for the next packet and opened it up. "What about this?"

It was walking on cracking ice. "You really just want me to identify things?"

Jacob met his eyes. "You know what you're talking about," he said. "We have a whole pile of items found scattered at the scene, and we don't know if they're his or his assailant's. You might be one of the few people who can tell."

Kit's legs were shaking under him. "I can do that." He tried to smile, but he couldn't be sure it worked. "What's next?"

There were a dozen evidence packs. Most of them, Kit could identify at once. Tom had his signature techniques, and once you'd watched him work up close, you couldn't forget them. A couple were trickier, but when he cautiously opened them up, Kit recognised Tom's handiwork on the inside.

With each packet, the panic receded.

Jacob watched him as he opened each sample out and examined it. He stopped paying attention to the other man, putting all his focus on the objects. They were his domain after all, and the ones he hadn't seen before were brand-new designs.

There was something exciting about laying hands on a new piece of tech, enough to make his heart race, and sometimes, when something really special came into his hands, he got a head rush that made him weak at the knees. He'd ended up hiding a hard-on the first time he saw the temporal gate.

The metal, the wires, the fragile and the solid pieces all moulded together. They passed through his hands one by one, some cool to the touch, some warm, most familiar.

"Yup. Another of his," he said, setting another back in the packet. "That one's a transceiver, or it will be when it's finished."

Jacob nodded. He held the last packet in his hand. "This one, we're very puzzled by."

Kit held out his hand demandingly and opened up the packet. There was a small object in it, an orb, off-white with wires emerging from one side, and he tipped it out into his hand. When he turned it around with his fingertip, he yelled in shock. "An eye?"

"Apparently."

Kit gaped at Jacob. The man's expression showed nothing. He had his arms folded, and Kit realised this was why he was really here. The police were suspicious about this thing and wanted him to look at it, but didn't want him to realise how significant it was.

"Where did you find it?"

"At the scene," Jacob replied. "We need to know if Sanders designed it."

"This?" Kit shook his head, carefully turning the eyeball over. He picked up the magnifier, focusing the light on the iris and pupil. The pupil contracted, and he whistled softly under his breath. An automated focusing lens reacting to light like a pupil would. The movement was slow, as if it was running low on power, but still functional.

It was an incredible piece of work. The material of the cover had the same tension and elasticity of an eyeball. The iris contained an intricate array of data receptors. Kit sank onto one of the stools, examining it more closely. Inside, he could make out the processing filters, so tiny and delicate he wanted to cry at the beauty of it.

"Is it one of Sanders's pieces?" Jacob prompted several minutes later.

"No." Kit turned it over to examine the wiring. If it were attached to the optic nerve with delicate enough connections, it would be able to provide better images than a natural eye. "Tom never went for biological stuff. Too messy." He traced the tip of one of the wires. "Have you downloaded the data from the memory yet?"

Jacob's breath hissed between his teeth. "What?"

Kit glanced up. "The data? There's a memory chip inside it. Not any kind I've ever seen before, but they all work in a similar way." He turned the eye beneath the magnifier, peering in at it. "It's smaller as well..."

Jacob was suddenly by his side, so close Kit could smell his aftershave. "Show me."

Kit tilted the magnifier over the pupil, turning the eye away from the light to let the pupil dilate. "There. The gold gleam at the left side. Do you see it?"

Jacob's hand pressed low on Kit's back, broad and warm. "I could kiss you." He was so close Kit felt every breath against his ear. It sent a pleasant twist in his belly.

He should have kept his eyes on the business at hand.

Instead, he made the biggest stupidest mistake he could have and turned to Jacob.

Jacob's face was so close to his, and all it would take was half an inch and their lips would be flush together. They stared at each other, and Jacob exhaled, a short, nearly silent gasp of air.

Kit darted his tongue along his lower lip.

"Camera." Jacob's voice was hoarse and regretful.

Kit leaned back at once, which didn't really help since it pushed him against Jacob's hand. He swallowed hard. "Anywhere without a camera?"

Jacob's breath hitched. "Yes."

Silently, Kit slipped the eye into the packet. He stripped off the gloves as he rose, and Jacob strode out ahead of him. Kit's heart was racing, and Jesus, what a prime idiot he was being, in a police station with a police officer. He felt light-headed, and he hoped to Christ his jeans weren't too obviously straining.

There was a small meeting room, three doors down.

Jacob swiped it open. "In," he growled, and the rumble of his voice made a shudder run all the way to Kit's toes.

Kit almost tripped over his own feet in his haste, and before the door was completely closed, he had Jacob pressed up against the wall beside it, his mouth crushing against the other man's. Jacob's fist was in his hair, and he swallowed a groan, his hips pressing demandingly against Jacob's.

Jacob tasted of coffee and sugar, and Kit couldn't keep from sliding his tongue along every inch of Jacob's mouth. One hand wrapped into Jacob's tie, the other squeezing at his hip, and he bit down on Jacob's lower lip.

Jacob jerked away, panting. "Shit."

Kit knew the feeling. "Seconded."

They stared at each other again, too long, too intent, and Jacob was the one to pull Kit's mouth to his, urgent and hungry, and Jesus...they were in a police station full of people, and he was in little more than a cupboard, making out with the detective in charge of the investigation like they were a pair of teenagers.

They could be caught at any moment.

They *could* be caught at any moment, and the thought of it, the risk, sent a spike of heat right through to Kit's groin.

He twisted his hand into Jacob's tie and pressed his hips forward.

"Need to take care of it," he panted. "People'll notice."

He was amazed the heat in Jacob's eyes didn't singe him on the spot. "Back up," Jacob growled. "Desk."

Kit glanced over his shoulder and nodded with a grin. It took three steps—never relinquishing his grip on Jacob's tie—to hit the edge of the desk with the back of his thighs. He raised his eyebrows in challenge and tugged downward on the tie.

To his shock and delight, Jacob went to his knees. His hands were on Kit's thighs, pushing his legs apart, and then those big, firm hands were undoing his belt. Kit had to brace his other hand on the desk to keep himself from slipping.

This couldn't be happening. Not here. Not in a police station. Not with the scarier official version of Jacob.

The scarier official version who popped the button of his jeans open and slid his fly down. Jacob gazed up at him with his dimpled smile and a flash of his white teeth, and then his mouth wrapped around Kit's cock, and Kit had to bite on his lip to keep from yelling.

There were footfalls in the hall and voices outside the room. Kit whined low in his throat, tugging urgently on Jacob's tie. Shuddering, he cupped the back of Jacob's head, urging him to hurry, to take him deeper, to move...oh God, *that* way. His tongue curled just right, his cheeks hollowing, and Kit panted at the ceiling, his feet scudding against the polished floor.

Laughter in the hall. Someone right outside the door. Detective inspector on his knees in front of him.

Kit jerked his hand up from Jacob's hair to bite down on his knuckles as his hips jerked against Jacob's mouth, and he came so hard his legs shook under him. Jacob gripped his hips and sucked and licked and made sure not a drop fell to show what they had been doing.

When Jacob sank onto his heels, breathing heavily, his lips swollen, he didn't lift his eyes to Kit right away. His hands dropped to his thighs, clenching into fists.

It took Kit a moment to gather his wits and tug on Jacob's tie, his breathing coming too fast to ask anything.

Jacob glanced up at him like a kicked puppy on a leash. He rose so suddenly his tie pulled free from Kit's grip, and he ran a shaking hand over his mouth as if it could hide the evidence of what he'd done. "Shit."

That was never a good reaction. Kit stared at him, heart sinking. He self-consciously tucked himself into his jeans. "Not my usual response."

Jacob didn't look at him. He passed his hand over his eyes, exhaled. "We have work we need to do. This was a mistake."

Kit did up the last button on his jeans. "Just what every man wants to hear." He straightened up from the table, staring pointedly at the door. "Let's get back to work."

"Kit..."

For a moment, Kit could believe Jacob sounded regretful, but he was right. It was a mistake. A bloody good mistake, but a mistake nonetheless. He pulled on his best smile and met Jacob's eyes. "You're right. A mistake. Forget it."

Jacob jerked his head toward the door. "Come on."

Silently, Kit fell into step behind him.

Chapter Fifteen

They were back in the main lab and had been for nearly half an hour.

Jacob could still taste Kit on his tongue.

Kit was acting as if nothing had happened. The best idea in the situation, really. Colour still spread across his cheekbones, but otherwise, no one would be any the wiser.

Outright stupidity and recklessness had got them in that room, the same idiocy that got him on the balcony, stark naked, the night before. The potential break in the case and the light in Kit's eyes—the challenge, pushing Jacob to push back—gave him the buzz of adrenaline and excitement and lust for the first time in five years.

He sipped his coffee, covering the taste, but it didn't change the fact that his throat felt pleasantly abused from an overeager blowjob.

"Well, I'll be..." Temple murmured. "Look at that!"

They'd broken open the eye, and Tisha Glenn, one of the technical team, carefully removed the memory chip from its settings. It was tiny, barely the size of a grain of rice, and so fragile Tisha had resorted to tweezers.

"You know how to connect to it?" Jacob asked as she placed it carefully on the magnifying slide. "Do we have anything that small?"

"There's hardware for these kinds of chips," Tisha murmured, watching the magnifying screen as she turned the chip over. "I've never seen anything quite this intricate before. It may be a special model."

On one of the stools, Kit tilted forward. He had only been permitted to stay due to his part in locating the chip. "It could be a variant of the Arcon data chips."

Tisha glanced at him. "You think? Do they do them this small?"

"Could be they're developing them." He shrugged. "It's a similar shape to some of their more recent models. It would definitely be sturdy enough."

"Arcon?" Jacob inquired.

"They do a lot of work in advanced robotics and engineering," Kit replied without turning or glancing at him, his voice terser than it had been, the back of his neck still red. "They push for smaller memory units, so more space can be used on power and motion."

"You work with them?"

Kit shook his head. "Not as much as I would like. I'm less about robotics."

"I don't think this is one of theirs," Tisha said. "Unless their tech has advanced by at least ten years."

From his vantage point right behind Kit, Jacob saw the colour on his neck vanish as if all the blood had drained away from him.

"What did you say?"

Tisha peered back at him, through the magnifying lenses. "Their tech is too advanced?"

"Oh." Kit leaned forward, staring at the chip, his face reflected on the magnifying screen. "Where did you say this eye came from?"

Jacob hadn't, but Temple helpfully replied, "From Mr. Sanders's assailant."

Kit sat back on the stool, grey in the face. "That's a man's functioning eye?"

"It's been slowing down since we disconnected it from the body, but yes," Temple said. "Why?"

Kit looked awful. Jacob caught him by the shoulder. "You okay?"

"I feel a bit sick," Kit said, staring at the screen. Jacob didn't blame him. He remembered the empty eye socket and the wires all too well. "You didn't tell me where it came from."

"I didn't think it was necessary."

Kit put a hand to his mouth as if he might throw up. "It's amazing how often I've been hearing that lately," he said, a note of bitterness in his voice. "How long until you can download any data?"

"Could be five minutes, could be five days," Tisha replied. "All depends on the software and format."

They all sat in silence, watching Tisha work. A secondary screen illuminated on the wall, and she placed the chip onto the hardware under the magnifier. Jacob wasn't one for working with technology, but he knew enough to recognise the way she lined up the chip with the receiver.

Kit made a small, awed sound.

"Wow..." Tisha pulled the screen closer.

"Wow good? Wow useful?" Jacob prompted. "What do we have?"

"Hell if I know," Tisha breathed. "Look at that coding."

"Tisha," Jacob said impatiently, "for those of us who don't speak computer?"

She glanced up at him. "This is way more advanced than anything I've ever used, boss. I expected it to be simple. Data storage this size normally is." She nodded to the screen. "This isn't basic data storage. It's coded. Could be one of the controllers to the eye."

"It looks like it has audio and video looping," Kit said. He sounded breathless, like he did when someone had their mouth on his dick.

"Audio looping? In an eyeball?" Tisha peered at the screen and scrolled through screeds of coding. "Oh. Oh, yeah. There." She shook her head in disbelief. "If someone is making these, do you have any idea how many people this will help?"

"Not the subject at hand," Jacob said tersely. "Tish, is there anything here we can use to identify Mr. Smith?"

"If there's audio and video, we should be able to get a glimpse of the last things Smith saw and heard." She frowned, squinting at the code. "It's pretty complex though. If we put in an incorrect function, we could wipe everything."

"Let me try?" Kit said. He turned to Jacob. "I work with coding. I can crack this."

Jacob glanced at Tisha. "What do you think of your chances, Tish?"

"Not good," she admitted. "He saw the audio when I didn't. He's probably the better bet."

Jacob hesitated. It was the one piece of evidence they had, and while they could probably call in experts from Arcon, it would take time, with no guarantee they'd even made it. Sanders had been missing for over a week already. Time was of the essence.

"Be as careful as you can," he cautioned. "If you can open anything, do it. We need to see what's there, if anything."

Kit nodded and slid into Tisha's seat, a look of determination on his pale, tense face.

His hands started moving on the illuminated keypad in a blur of motion. Jacob had seen people typing fast, but this was something else. The codes on the screen where changing and shifting rapidly. Kit stared at it, the pale glow from the projection casting his face in shades of green and blue.

Tisha seemed impressed.

"What's he doing?" Jacob murmured to her, not wanting to distract Kit.

She pointed at a row of code that appeared to be unravelling. "There are security protocols to manage the data," she whispered. "He's basically unlocking the safe so we can see what's inside."

"He's good?"

Tisha didn't even look away from the screen as she nodded. "God, yes. I don't know how he's seeing the patterns so fast."

They watched as the screeds of codes moved and changed. Kit had his full attention on it, his lips parted and his breathing coming harder.

Jacob had seen that look on Kit's face before: when he had stared at the projection of Sanders's whiteboard in the office last week. Maybe he hadn't cracked the code then, but he must have been giving it a try.

Seconds turned into minutes, minutes into an hour, and Kit's hands were still moving.

"Maybe he should take a break," Jacob said, frowning. Temple had already headed back into the main office to do some work, but Tisha still sat at Kit's side, watching with fascination.

"Not yet," she said. "He's almost..."

The screeds of letters and codes winked out.

They were replaced with a row of images. Kit touched one of them at random. It expanded into a video of a room, a large one. The walls were metal. Industrial, maybe? Jacob searched the screen, looking for some hint of where it might be. No windows. No defining features. Standard warehouse design, really.

The owner of the eye turned, giving them a glimpse of a face before John Smith looked down at the other person's hand, shook it, and from the movement of his head, nodded. No audio yet.

"So someone sent him," Jacob murmured.

John Smith turned around, and Jacob half expected to see a vehicle or the open doorway of the building, but instead, there was only an empty doorframe, heavy, metal. Before Jacob could look closer, it blazed with light, brilliant enough John Smith held up his hand to shield his eyes.

"What the hell...?" Jacob growled.

"Oh God..." Kit whispered, frantically typing.

John Smith moved forward, toward the light, and as suddenly as it had appeared, the light vanished, and instead of a warehouse or a factory, or anything like an industrial estate, an open field flashed across the screen.

The projection cut out.

Jacob blinked away the afterimage. "What happened?"

"I-I-I tried to get the sound," Kit stammered, flushing. "He must have said something to someone, so there had to be audio, and I—it was complicated code." His hands were shaking over the sensor keys. "I thought I could make it more useful. I'm sorry."

"Do we have a backup of what we saw?"

Tisha nodded. "I set it to copy. Even if we've lost everything else, we'll at least have that."

"Oh good," Kit said, though he sounded more shaken than relieved. He rose on unsteady legs. "I need the loo."

Jacob nodded. "I'll take you down." They walked in silence down the corridor, and he patted the younger man on the shoulder. "You did a good job there. Don't worry about what happened. You got us valuable information."

"Was it useful?"

Jacob squeezed his shoulder. "It could be."

"Good." Kit sounded distracted. He rubbed at his eyes, blinking hard. "You mind if I head back after I'm done here? Or is there anything else you need me for?"

Jacob frowned. "Are you okay? You don't sound too good."

Kit tried to smile, but his lips barely moved. "That level of coding," he said. "It's tiring. Gives me a headache."

Jacob nodded at once. "You did more than we could have hoped for. We've got the footage. We need to try and piece together some details from it."

Another of those frail smiles crossed Kit's lips. "Let me know if you spot anything."

"Of course." Jacob motioned to the door. "You go, do your business. I'll get a taxi called for you."

Kit nodded, heading into the toilets. He really didn't look good.

Jacob rubbed the back of his neck.

It was all getting far too complicated, especially with Kit being involved with the case now, and in a much more complex way than Jacob had anticipated. A wise man would let him be on his way and wouldn't see him again in any way but a professional capacity.

But he looked like shit, and Jacob couldn't leave him like that.

When Kit finally emerged, still pale, Jacob insisted on walking him down to the taxi-pod. "Are you going to be okay?" he asked as they emerged into the daylight.

"I've coded before. I will again."

Jacob sighed. "You're not answering the question."

Kit glanced at him. "It's a headache. I've had worse."

Jacob nodded, watching him. "Call me later." The words came out before he could stop them. "Let me know you're all right, eh?"

Kit said nothing for a moment, then reached out and smoothed down Jacob's tie. It seemed to help him make up his mind. "All right." He stepped back. "Thank you for an interesting morning. Not how I expected it to go for my first visit to a police station."

Jacob cleared his throat. "We should keep that between us."

Kit turned away. "Yeah."

"But you'll call?"

Blue eyes flicked up. Kit nodded. "Fine."

Jacob remained on the steps as Kit headed down to the taxi-pod. He didn't raise his eyes to Jacob until the door closed and the taxi started moving. He looked like death warmed up, and when Jacob raised a hand in half-hearted farewell, Kit didn't respond.

No wonder. Getting dragged into an investigation focussed on your employer and ending up with a horny copper sucking on your knob would scramble things a bit.

Well, Jacob thought as he walked back into the station, it had been a long while since he'd done something completely stupid. This whole affair was a stellar way of making up for lost time.

Chapter Sixteen

The lift slid silently upward.

Kit slumped against the wall, gripping the rail with both hands, and closed his eyes tightly. He needed to get to Mariam and let her know how bad things were as soon as possible. His stomach had twisted in knots, and he was breathing hard by the time the doors opened.

Mariam waited for him on the other side.

"Paulina said you were back," she said. "My office."

"Now," Kit agreed. He ran a hand over his mouth. "Can you get someone to bring me something to eat? I think I'm having a sugar crash."

"Of course." She ushered him along to the office and let him collapse into the seat, while she filled a mug with tea and added a couple of sugars. He wrapped his hands around it and listened as she called down to the canteen. That done, she sat down. "What happened?"

"It's a jumper." He sipped the tea. Probably shock making him shiver. Possibly terror, but he couldn't stop his hands from trembling.

"What do you mean a jumper?"

"I mean a time jumper," he snapped. "Not an agent. Not one of ours. Someone from the future."

Mariam's face drained of colour. "You're sure."

He nodded, tightening his grip on the mug. "Oh, yes. They have the video footage to confirm it."

"Video..." She sagged in her seat, pressing her knuckles to her mouth. She looked as shaken as Kit felt. "How?"

He took another mouthful of tea, scalding his lips and tongue. "Fun fact they didn't tell you: the man they found in Sanders's house had a false eye. Had a real one replaced with something more hi-tech. Direct video feed into the optic nerve, but here's the best part—it has a memory chip."

Mariam's dark eyes fixed on him. "But why would they tell you?"

The hysterical laugh bubbled up in his throat. "Because I'm a twat and didn't realise what I was looking at until I'd told them."

Mariam stared at him. "You did what?"

"What was I supposed to do?" he demanded, his voice breaking. "They had all this gate crap lined up and wanted me to confirm which bits Sanders had built. It was the only thing I didn't think he'd built! How was I meant to know they'd taken it out of some poor bugger's head?"

"And now they have the memory chip and the footage?"

Kit had to set the mug down before he dropped it. "Not much." He clasped his hands together. "I...might have scrambled the coding and destroyed the evidence before they could work out what they were seeing." And bingo: the great big cherry of blatant terror set on the cake of panic. "I—they—" He forced himself to breathe, to speak. "They got a ten-, maybe twenty-second fragment of video. No audio." The laughter had come back, and he wondered how mental he sounded. "I destroyed evidence of a crime in a police station in front of two police officers."

Mariam rose from behind the desk. "Do they know you did it?"

Kit shook his head. Every inch of him felt numb. "D'you think I'd be sitting here if they did?" He shivered. "I decoded the video for them. Got the clip to see if it was important. When I saw what it was, got rid of it. They think I'm very helpful."

"Could the code be unscrambled?"

Kit hesitated. "If they think I did something, they could find someone to undo it. It'd take them a while, but it could be done."

"What are the chances of them thinking that?"

"I don't know!"

A chime from the door made them both turn sharply.

"Food," Mariam said, skirting the desk to go and open it. One of the catering staff held out a tray, which she took at once, then closed the door. She brought the tray to the desk and set it in front of him. "Eat. Calm down. Think."

Kit nodded, snatching the bowl from the tray. It was difficult to eat when his insides were twisting up like overcooked spaghetti, but it would be a hell of a lot worse if he didn't get any food inside him. It was some kind of chicken-and-rice thing. He didn't really care, gulping it down.

The warmth of it spread through him, oddly comforting.

By the time he finished the bowl, his heart had slowed from a thrum, and the tremors had subsided.

Mariam sat on the edge of the desk, watching him carefully. "Better?"

He nodded, wiping at his mouth with the back of his hand. "Yes. Thanks."

"So..." She was probably trying to find some way to interrogate him that wouldn't have him shaking and laughing again.

"I think they trust me," he said before she could ask anything. "I mean, they saw me working on the coding, and their technician told them before I started it might not even work."

Mariam nodded. She pulled up the other seat and sat, facing him. "Tell me about this eye and the footage you saw."

"There's not much to tell."

"Tell me anyway. As much detail as you can."

He described what he could, explaining the tech in the eye and his suspicions of where it might have been developed. When he described the details in the video, Mariam frowned, nodding, a thoughtful look on her face.

"It definitely wouldn't be the TRI, if they sent someone back with a body modification outdating the time period," she said. "Unless someone went rogue and managed to put together their own gate."

"The one they were using did look kind of like Sanders's older designs." Kit picked at his nails, remembering the pieces of the gate he had built in his own home. "I mean, it was basic, but I could see the similarities in the construction."

"Do you have any idea how far they came back?"

He frowned, thinking. "The technology was at least ten, if not more years ahead of us, but the coding could be much more. If technology keeps accelerating at its current pace, I'd say somewhere between twenty and thirty years from now. It wasn't as complex as they believed. Just evolved so much their technician couldn't recognise it."

"But why would someone from the future go after Sanders?" She got up, pacing the floor. "They already have time travel. What could they want with him?"

Kit followed her with his eyes. "All the stuff he didn't tell you."

Mariam glanced at him. "The future-jumping tech?"

"Maybe something else," Kit replied with a shrug. "You didn't know about that. What else has he been working on that no one knows about?"

From the look on Mariam's face, it wasn't a possibility she wanted to consider. "We need to get into his house. DI Ofori said once they identified the pieces that weren't Tom's, they should be able to release the scene."

Kit nodded. "And he's got them all identified now."

Mariam went back to her seat, sinking down. "You'll need to come to the house with me," she said. "You might spot something we'd miss."

"Not today." He didn't know when he'd found the nerve to be so abrupt with her. Probably somewhere between screwing a police officer and destroying evidence. It did tend to put fear of repercussions into perspective. "I'm going home. I've had enough crap to deal with today."

To his surprise, she didn't argue.

"One thing, before you go," she said as he got up.

"Yeah?"

"Do you think you could get a copy of the video footage?"

Kit stared at her in disbelief. "No," he said flatly. "I've already broken the law more than once today, and now you want me to nick stuff from the police?"

"You said they trust you."

"And I'm sure they will continue to do so as long as I don't try to bloody nick stuff." Kit shook his head. "Unless they hand it over to me and tell me to take it, I'm not putting my neck on the line for it."

Mariam looked disappointed but nodded. "Fair enough."

"Fair enough..." Kit echoed, shaking his head. "I'm the one risking everything here." He picked up his satchel from the floor. "If anyone asks, I'm on do not disturb. I...this is...I need a break."

She got up. "Will you be in tomorrow?"

"Probably." He rubbed his forehead. "I don't know. I...I didn't sign up to be lying to the police and hiding evidence."

"I know, Kit." Mariam said quietly. "We're grateful."

He snorted and stumped out of the room.

The nearest stairs were at the far end of the hall, and he started down them. It was always easier going down than up, and he got so lost in thought he didn't realise he'd reached the bottom until the door opened in front of him.

Paulina didn't seem surprised to see him. "You want a taxi?"

Kit shook his head. "I'll make my own way, thanks."

He was at the door when she called after him. "Are you okay?"

He paused. "Do I look it?"

"Not really."

He glanced back. "Well, there you go then." He walked out into the street, breathing in the chilly air. He could have taken a taxi, but his head hadn't stopped thumping from solid coding, and he needed a break where no one could ask anything of him for ten minutes.

An hour later, he trudged in through the front doors of his building.

As luck would have it, Jenny was about to get in the lift and held the door open for him. As soon as he stepped in, she cleared a corner for him and then prattled all the way up to their floor.

"You want me to bring you some dinner over?" she asked as they stepped out into their hallway. "You look like you need that and your bed."

Kit had to smile. "I don't need fed, Jen."

She reached up and fondly swatted his head. "'Course you do." She studied him with concern. "I'll be making up something nice. If you fancy some, you come and knock. I'm in for the night now."

It wasn't until he went into his flat and saw his face in the mirror that he could understand why they'd all tried to check on him. He looked grey, with shadows under his eyes. Normally, after a good bit of sex, he'd be a lot brighter, but Jacob's reaction didn't exactly encourage that. Toss in some intensive coding and law breaking...

He left his bag on the floor, stumbled through to his bedroom, and fell face down on the bed. It still reeked of sex and Jacob, which didn't help. He pulled his pillow up under his head, buried his face in it, and closed his eyes.

Chapter Seventeen

Jacob stood in front of the incident board, gazing at the latest additions.

It had been a long day with a hell of a lot to take in.

Tisha had taken captures from the video footage. The clear ones had been transferred to the board. The ones in need of cleaning up, she'd sent down for the imaging unit to work on.

They had facial recognition software searching for the man who had shaken John Smith's hand, but the imaging technicians warned them a match was unlikely since they only had a distorted, blurred glimpse of him: old, skinny, with a shrunken face like an angry tortoise.

Not much to go on, but more than they'd had only hours earlier.

His focus kept returning to the doorway shown in the fragment. Though not exactly the same, sections of it looked like the technology they had taken from Sanders's study, which gave them a solid, tangible confirmation John Smith had some link with Sanders beyond being killed in his house.

Jacob frowned and touched the board to set the video playing again. He'd lost track of how many times he had watched it, and every time, he hoped he would understand what he was seeing when the man stepped toward the light. Every time, he was left just as baffled.

In the footage, the doorway stood in the middle of a vast room. Stepping through it should not have ended up anywhere except the other side of the room. It definitely should not have deposited him in a field.

They had theories, foremost being they had a teleporter, which would make a lot of sense since John Smith had showed up near Sanders's house without any other means of transportation. From the grass and plant residue on his shoes, the man had walked across some of the nearby fields, but they hadn't been able to locate an origin point.

The only problem was teleportation had never been stabilised. In the first human tests, even fillings in teeth had proved fatal. Jacob had heard an urban legend about a man with dental implants who had used a teleporter. His body had gone through okay, but while his implants had ended up in his skull, it had been in the wrong part. According to the rumours, the pathologist found them nestled between the front lobes of his brain.

Still, that was only one of the rumoured problems. From what he could remember of reports on the later tests, the biggest problem came in the transition stage, where one person's body would be in two places at the same time. There was some scientific mumbo-jumbo he didn't understand, but all the eggheads seemed to nod and agree one-living-body-two-places definitely wouldn't work.

Perhaps the TRI's secrets were something to do with it. Maybe Sanders had found a way to stabilise teleportation. If he had, then they would have access to any historical records they needed to find. Private vaults, locked archives, concealed collections: nothing would be off limits if they could simply hop in and out.

Jacob rubbed the back of his neck and frowned at the board.

That didn't explain why someone would teleport through to jump him. If he'd stabilised the teleportation, then the person using it would have to be one of his colleagues, and none of them were missing or dead.

It also didn't explain John Smith at all.

They were no closer to identifying him, and nothing about him made any sense. His clothes looked like they were based on something from the catwalks of Milan. His eye was so hi-tech the technicians were practically setting up a shrine to it. He had no name, identification, DNA records, dental records.

Jacob had hopes the imaging team would be able to put together some kind of composite of the man who had sent Smith on his way, so they could work backward from there.

He sat on the edge of one of the desks.

Most disappearances he'd dealt with were fairly straightforward. Some were bloody, and others were violent, but none of them came anywhere close to the level of weirdness wrapped around Sanders.

Temple had started work on the image they had from the field. Despite being less than two seconds, the freeze-frame showed the kind of terrain and flora. If she could pinpoint the position in relation to Sanders's house, it would finally give them an origin point to look into.

That was the best they could hope for at present.

They'd gone through Sanders's house with a fine-toothed comb. They'd opened up his computers and gone through his files, backtracking through his business records. Only one file mentioned his theory on teleportation some twelve years earlier, but none of the others suggested he'd pursued it.

With the information Kit had given them about the items they held as evidence, they'd cleared up all the questions about the house itself. They didn't have any excuse not to release the scene.

It bothered Jacob.

They were missing something at the house, something he couldn't put his finger on.

"Boss?"

He turned to Anton. "Anything?"

"Got word from the Home Office." Anton held out his slate. "You might want to take a look."

There was a single file on the screen. Jacob tapped it, opening up the contents. The details related to one of the staff of the TRI, a man by the name of Janos Nagy. At first glance, he couldn't see anything seriously incriminating. Nagy had first registered with the Home Office some three years earlier. He had paperwork and documentation confirming his current residency and domestic situation.

One thing did stand out.

Jacob frowned. "They have no record of his arrival in the country?"

"That's what I noticed." Anton rocked on the balls of his feet. "He's an EU national. Hungarian. They've got right of movement in every EU member state."

"So why didn't he get checked at any of the standard arrival checkpoints?" Jacob finished, frowning. It wasn't impossible for illegal immigrants to get into the UK under the radar, but for an EU national, there was no reason to do it illegally unless you had something to hide. Jacob glanced up at Anton. "Do we have any cause to suspect involvement?"

"The fact that he showed up in the country and immediately started working for the TRI isn't enough?"

Jacob nodded, studying the screen and the image of the man. He didn't look like any kind of criminal, but more often than not, most criminals didn't. Late thirties, computer technician, listed as residing with a partner.

"Get in touch with the Hungarian police and see if you can't dig up his records."

"Already done." Anton flicked to the next file and the correspondence.

Jacob stared at it. "Is this correct?"

Anton nodded. "It can't be a coincidence. First his attacker, now this guy."

Jacob took the slate, rereading the confirmation from the Hungarian authorities. According to all data they held, there were no records of this particular Janos Nagy. They recommended checking if the name and dates were correct. Jacob frowned. Another person who had popped out of nowhere.

"I'll call Ashraf to arrange a meeting with Ben." He straightened up from the desk. "This way, I can see the Sanders boy and deal with questions about Nagy at the same time."

"You think she'll be any more helpful now we've got something on one of her people?"

Jacob shook his head. "She's got a cool head. I think it would take a lot to rattle her." He handed the slate back to Anton. "Good job finding it. Set up a side panel on the incident board with Nagy's details. Not a suspect, but subject to enquiry."

Anton nodded, heading back to his desk.

Jacob returned to his private office and dialled Mrs. Ashraf's number. The call redirected to someone claiming to be in the communication department.

"This is DI Ofori. I'm looking for Mrs. Ashraf."

There was a momentary pause. "I'm sorry, sir," the man on the other end of the line said. "Mrs. Ashraf will be unavailable this afternoon. I believe she is in a business meeting, and her quill is switched off."

Jacob stifled a profanity under his breath. He pinched the bridge of his nose. "Please can you contact her when available and let her know to call me as soon as possible."

"Of course, sir. Would you like to leave a message for her?"

"Just to call me." He gave his number and added, "It's important she calls as soon as possible."

In hindsight, he should have expected it.

One of her staff had found the new evidence and seen the video footage. Kit would have recognised the doorway as something similar to Sanders's constructions. Of course he would have gone straight back to the TRI and informed his superior.

Jacob leaned back in the chair, propping his elbows on the arms, and rested his lips against his folded fingers.

If Ashraf had called a meeting about the video, it meant there had to be something significant in it. Kit hadn't said anything, but if it pertained to his employer, maybe he was under orders to keep it quiet. Wheels within wheels. Someone knew something, but they weren't saying anything.

Kit had to know something.

Jacob grimaced.

He'd brought the other man in, even if it was only by chance. He'd practically gift-wrapped the evidence and presented it to him. Christ. If his superiors learned about that, especially now, he would be well and truly up shit creek without a paddle.

And Kit was the reason they'd lost the rest of the footage.

Jacob's heart sank.

Surely, he wouldn't have messed around with it.

Surely, Tisha would have noticed if he had.

Kit was an honest person. He blushed when he tried to lie. He stammered. He had so many tells it was unfair to put him on the spot. When he left the station, he'd been whey-faced, and his eyes were bloodshot. He looked like crap and blamed the concentration of coding. Jacob had believed it. You couldn't fake looking that bad. But what if it wasn't just the coding?

Jacob stared at the door.

How the hell could he deal with that? If he tried to bring it up with anyone, if he implied he suspected Kit had tampered with evidence, then Kit would be hauled in for questioning. That could lead to a shitstorm of epic proportions. If Kit were accused of any crime, he'd only have to mention he'd slept with the officer in charge, and the case against him would be thrown out.

Jacob could lose his job, his position, his reputation, all because he hadn't got any in months, and a good-natured, amiable young man had paid him attention.

He buried his head in his hands.

It couldn't just be simple.

Chapter Eighteen

Kit was disorientated when he woke up to find the sun setting.

As far as he could tell, only a couple of hours had passed since he'd fallen into the bed, but it had helped, even if his sleep was broken by all kinds of strange dreams.

He sat in the middle of the bed, staring at the rumpled sheets. He could remember Jacob tangled up in them, and no matter how fit Jacob was, it couldn't happen again.

Maybe Jacob had needed him because he worked with Sanders's technology, and maybe they could share information, but it was all getting too intense now. Some crazy person out there had time jumped to abduct people. He had more to worry about than where to put his willy when it got cold.

He ordered the household computer to put the bath on, then sprawled onto his back and gazed up at the ceiling.

Tomorrow looked set to be hellish. The TRI would probably be going into security lockdown. If all went well, the police would release Sanders's house, which would mean a new investigation would start, only this time by people who knew exactly what Sanders was capable of and why he might have been targeted.

That meant tonight would be the last night he could shut the whole world out and pretend everything wasn't shot to buggery.

Nothing said relaxation like lying neck-deep in water so hot it turned him pink, with homemade clockwork submarines puttering around him, while 80s and 90s rock playlists blasted at full volume.

He was still soaking there nearly an hour later, leg dangling over the side of the tub, when his quill buzzed. He frowned, peering through the steam at the display projected on the wall behind the bath.

Jacob's number.

Oh, bloody marvellous.

He stopped winding the mechanism of Mighty Thundersquid 3 and set it back down in the water, then clapped to pick up the call. He paused, frowning, not quite sure what to say to the man who had insisted on a one-night stand, then sucked him off in a back room the next day.

"Kit?"

He stared at the ceiling, wishing he had let the call ring off. Jacob's voice was like all the best sounds combined into one, echoing off the bathroom walls. "Yeah?"

Jacob sighed with relief. "You're okay, then."

Kit sat up in the water, pulling his leg back into the tub. The water sloshed around him, slapping against the sides. "Why wouldn't I be?"

"You didn't look too well this afternoon."

Yeah, but the last thing he needed to encourage was any kind of concern, no matter how good it felt. Not that he was picky when it came to friends or lovers. Being in a job that required secrecy made it so much more difficult to make any casual friends outside of the office, in case of letting something slip by accident.

He propped his arms on his upraised knees. "I got home early. Got some sleep. I'm fine." And once more, his mouth decided the brain's input was unnecessary. "You didn't let me get much rest last night, after all."

As soon as the words were out his mouth, he knocked his forehead on his arms. Shit.

Jacob fell silent for a moment. "Kit," he began.

"I know, I know," Kit mumbled into his arms. "We shouldn't see each other. Investigation blah blah blah." He sighed noisily and lifted his head. "Is that what you were going to say, Mr. I-give-regrettable-blowjobs-in-my-workplace?"

Another silence.

"Actually, no."

Kit looked at the projection of the call details on the wall, frowning. "What?"

"We need to talk."

Kit raised his eyes to the ceiling. Oh, that sentence never led anywhere good. He pushed himself to his feet, water splashing around him. "Talk?" he echoed, stepping out of the bathtub. "What about?"

Jacob sighed. "I'd prefer to discuss it in person."

Kit pulled on his bathrobe with unnecessary force. "So is this a social talk?" He didn't care whether he sounded annoyed. He *was* annoyed. Jacob kept putting out too many mixed messages, and it didn't help with everything that was happening. "Or do you have more evidence you need me to go through before you spring a dismembered body part on me? Or maybe, just maybe, you want to suck my cock again? Is that it?"

"I think you know."

Kit exhaled noisily. "You think I know? Know *what*? Oh, wait, wait. I think I've got this: I abducted Sanders. He's currently hidden in my wardrobe." He stamped over to the mirror and smeared the condensation from the glass. "No more riddles, Jacob. No more surprises. We talk straight or not at all."

Jacob didn't reply right away, his voice guarded. "It's partly to do with the case, and partly to do with us. Like I said, I'd prefer to discuss it in person."

Kit leaned on the edge of the sink. He could say no. It would be simpler. "If I say no?"

"I'd have to get someone else to look into the data chip to see if anything else can be recovered."

Kit stared at his reflection and swallowed hard. It could only mean one thing: Jacob suspected what he had done. "You want me to try again?" Huh. How about that? Voice didn't even wobble.

"I want to talk to you in person," Jacob replied.

Kit drummed his fingers on the counter. On one hand, if Jacob did suspect him, he might be trying to entrap him. On the other, he might be genuinely looking for his help. Or the third option: both.

If Jacob was playing him, then he would choose where. "Fine," he said "Tomorrow night. My place. Eight."

"I was thinking somewhere public—"

"Bugger that," Kit interrupted. "If we're going to talk and it's so important it has to be face-to-face, I want it in my space." He pushed his fingers through his hair, leaving it on end. "If you're worried about us falling back into bad habits, don't worry. I'm not in the mood."

He clapped again and terminated the call.

He wanted to break something.

The only heavy thing to hand was a bottle of hand wash. He eyed it, but all things considered, it didn't seem worth trying to clean soap off the walls and mirror. He grabbed his toothbrush and lobbed it instead. Unsurprisingly, it didn't really help.

He braced his hands on the counter again and looked down at the sink. He'd never been built for politics and deception. A nice, complex code, *that* he liked, but not lying to someone, especially not someone like Jacob. It felt crap. Not only lying to him, but having to maintain it when Jacob wanted his help.

He had to lie though.

People needed him to lie.

He glanced up at his reflection in the mirror. He wasn't good at fooling people, but Janos, the man he needed to protect, was a master at it, his whole life a carefully spun tale. In the three years he'd known the man, Kit had never once suspected anything unusual about him.

Maybe he could give some pointers, especially if it was for his sake.

Kit padded back through to the living room and flicked the screen of his quill on, skimming through to Mariam's name. He tapped in a brief message and sent it on, a simple request, and she would be able to get in touch with Janos about it.

Kit lay back on the couch and stared at the ceiling.

Jumping through hoops for the TRI was one thing, but when those hoops felt like they were on fire and he had to avoid getting burned, he needed help. Who better to help him than one of the men who had lit the hoops up?

His quill chimed, and he tapped the screen, projecting the message onto the ceiling above him: *Janos will be in tomorrow at eight. Come in early. He'll see you as soon as you arrive.*

Not exactly a complete solution, but better than doing nothing.

Kit spent the rest of the night tinkering with the gate fragments he had built, but before he went back to bed, he carefully packed them up in a box and tucked them away in his storage room. While Jacob had already seen them, it was safer not to give him more reasons to ask questions.

It didn't come as a surprise he dreamed of being arrested and locked up. It all seemed so real, the cool metal on his wrists, the cell, the door closing and leaving him in the dark with Jacob looking in through the opening.

When he woke, shivering, he had to check his wrists to be sure it was only a dream.

No matter how he tried, he couldn't get back to sleep.

By six o'clock, he gave up and settled for brooding over a stodgy breakfast instead. The clock had barely struck seven when he left the building and set out in the direction of the heart of the city and the TRI.

For once, he'd remembered his pass and swiped his way into the building. The night warden looked at him in surprise.

"You're early."

"Catching the worm," Kit replied. He shuffled into the lift and closed his eyes, counting under his breath until the doors opened on the tenth level. He didn't know if Mariam would be in yet, but her office seemed like a good place to start.

To his surprise, both Janos and Mariam were in the office when Mariam opened the door.

Kit stared at her. "You look crap."

Her lips thinned to a line. "Thank you." She glanced back at Janos. "You're sure you'll be able to do this?"

Janos rose from the chair. "Yes." He nodded to the door. "You go to collect Ben. He must be priority."

Mariam nodded, then glanced at Kit. "Your friend Ofori is coming in today."

Kit smothered a groan. Something else Jacob had neglected to mention the night before. Of course. If they were lucky, their paths wouldn't cross until tonight, but if they did, at least he wasn't about to be surprised. "I'll stay out of his way."

"Good idea." She motioned toward Janos. "He's all yours."

The door slid shut behind her, and Kit looked at Janos, trying to find the best way to ask his question.

Janos straightened in the chair, completely at ease. "You are staring."

Kit's cheeks burned. "Sorry," he said, approaching and sitting down. "I just..." He frowned down at his knees. "I don't know how to ask this in any polite way: How are you so good at lying?"

Janos raised his eyebrows. "You are right. This is not polite way."

Kit flinched. "I know. I'm sorry. It's..." He pushed his fingers through his rumpled hair, scratching at his head. "Look, I'm an engineer. I never had to keep any secrets because no one outside the TRI ever bothered to ask me stuff, but now, there's a policeman who expects me to be honest with him, and I don't know how to keep from telling him stuff. Stuff that could get you in trouble." He waved a hand at Janos. "And you've been living here, like you've never lived in any other time. You fit in, and no one would suspect anything. How do you do it?"

Janos gazed at him. "Because I have to do it. In my life before this place, I had to be strong man who liked women. For me, this is a lie. I have to do this or I die." He shrugged. "When you have a reason, to lie is not so difficult."

Kit stared at him. That hadn't been mentioned before. "Lie or die?"

Janos held his gaze. "You are lucky. You live in time when people can love where they choose. Other times were not like this." He leaned forward, bracing his right hand on his knee. "I know you have been asked to tell big lies for me, but you do not need to do it this way. You can tell big lies and be afraid of being caught, or you can tell small truths. It is easier for you."

"I don't understand."

Janos drummed his fingers on his knee. "If I am asked, I live here because my family could not accept I love a man. It is true, but it is not all of the truth. If asked what I do here, I work in communication between teams. Again, it is true, but not all of the truth." He offered his rare, solemn smile. "You can do this also with your policeman."

Kit nodded slowly. "Give him enough information to answer some of his questions, without getting all of us in trouble?"

"This is so." Janos sighed. "I am sorry I am problem for you, and for everyone."

Kit shook his head. "It's not just you. I've put my foot in it more than once with the detective. I showed him something I shouldn't have, and I think it's why he's coming back again."

Janos sat back in his chair. "Mariam said you saw video from Sanders's attacker?"

Kit nodded. "I did and Ofori did too." He clasped his hands together between his knees. "I—" He wondered how much he should tell the man. "I think he thinks I know more than I let on, when we saw it."

Janos raised his eyebrows. "You do."

"Yeah, I do, but that's not..." Kit rubbed at his forehead. "How much do I tell him? I mean, without giving away everything? I talk too much. I always do. Especially when there are people I find attractive around."

The other man chuckled. "You find this policeman good to look at?"

Kit felt the blush flood up his face. "He's not bad."

"And this is small truth? Or big lie to hide big truth?" Janos smiled, and Kit felt himself going even redder. Janos patted Kit on the knee. "Don't be afraid. You keep my secret. I will keep yours."

Kit managed a wan smile. "I've been in the basement, working on gates too long," he admitted. "I need to get out more, if I fancy the first non-staff member I see." He sat up a little straighter. "Thanks. I mean, for the pointers."

Janos got up from his seat. "It is selfish too," he said as Kit got up. "I like it here. I do not want to become artefact of history." He wrinkled his nose. "Dieter already makes too many jokes about fucking a museum relic. I do not need to give him more reasons."

Kit couldn't help laughing. "I bet. How is he, anyway? Is he okay?"

Janos's smile warmed. "He is much better now. Still not all good, but much better." He glanced at the door. "Not happy I must be here now, but Mariam asked, and I came for her."

Kit frowned. "Why?"

"For talking," Janos replied. "She has much pressure on her." He patted Kit's shoulder. "You should go. Hide in your basement so you will not see your pretty policeman and go red in front of Mariam."

Kit rolled his eyes. "Shut up." Still, he couldn't help feeling a bit of relief that at least he didn't have to hide absolutely everything from everyone. It was exhausting. "Can you tell Mariam where I went?"

"Hiding in basement." Janos nodded at once. "Yes. Connecting blush to gate for new power source."

"Anyone ever tell you you're a bit of a git?"

"Git?"

"You know? Like an arsehole?"

"Ah. Yes." Janos grinned. "Not many people notice. I am quiet and nice."

"And a git."

"Yes. And a git."

Chapter Nineteen

Mrs. Ashraf met Jacob in the lobby at nine o'clock.

He was there earlier than he'd planned, with insomnia rearing its ugly head. It all came down to whether Kit could be trusted. He hated to think otherwise, especially when Kit was such good company, and he hated being such a suspicious bastard about it.

Mrs. Ashraf looked as worn out, and the shadows under her eyes suggested sleepless nights. No wonder, what with running the TRI and looking after a small, scared child as well. Still, she treated him with every courtesy as he signed into the building.

"How's Ben doing?" he asked, watching the numbers flick upwards as the lift ascended.

"The nightmares are still bad." She stood stiffly upright. "Is this absolutely necessary?"

"We've done as much as we can without speaking to him again," Jacob said with a sigh. "If there was any other way, I'd take it, but he knew his father better than anyone. He might know something that could help."

"He's a child."

"Don't underestimate the things a child will notice." Jacob shook his head. "The number of times my kid caught me out..."

"I suppose." She stepped toward the doors, touched the sensor panel. The doors slid aside. "We'd prefer if you spoke to Mr. Nagy first, if you don't mind. It'll show Ben there's nothing to worry about, and other people will be answering questions too."

"Of course."

Jacob had to admit he was surprised. She hadn't once asked him why he wanted to speak to Nagy. That suggested she had some knowledge of Nagy's history. Whether for good or ill, he wasn't sure yet, but he hadn't expected it.

Instead of taking him to her office, Mrs. Ashraf led him along the corridor to a conference room. Inside, Ben sat on the edge of the long conference table, holding out a toy robot to a man sitting on the chair in front of him. The boy spoke shyly, and the man listened attentively.

Ben was the first one to look toward the doors.

Mrs. Ashraf stepped forward. "Ben, you remember Detective Inspector Ofori?"

Ben nodded. He looked back at the other man. "Can you help me down?"

The man smiled and pushed his chair back, then lifted Ben from the table. Ben caught his hand and tugged him up from the chair to lead him over. Jacob couldn't help noticing Ben had a tight grip on the man's synthetic arm, a prosthetic attached below the elbow.

"DI Ofori," Mrs. Ashraf said, "this is Janos Nagy."

Jacob held out his hand, which Nagy took without hesitation. Nagy looked him up and down, and he did the same. Nagy was a big man, tall and broad-shouldered. He dressed like anyone in an office would, in trousers and a casual short-sleeved shirt that gave the impression it should be loose. On Nagy, it pulled taut around his upper arms and shoulders, only loose at the waist. A physically strong person.

He met Nagy's eyes.

No. Not just physically strong.

Something like iron showed in the man's expression, though he gazed back placidly.

"You have asked to speak to me?" Nagy spoke with a strong accent, which wasn't a surprise, if he had only been in England for three years.

"We have a few questions we'd like to clear up," Jacob said. "I hope it's not too much trouble."

"If it helps, I will answer all things." Nagy turned and crouched to speak to Ben. "You stay with Mariam for now, and then you can answer questions like me, yes?" He smiled at the boy and earned a shy smile back. "Maybe you can show Mr. Policeman your robot too?"

Ben nodded. "Be nice," he said in a whisper. "Jacob is nice."

Nagy ruffled Ben's hair. "I am always nice." He straightened up and nudged the boy toward Mrs. Ashraf.

As woman and child left the room, Nagy returned to his seat at the table. He motioned to the opposite side of the table with his prosthetic hand. He moved naturally, which meant he must have had some time to get used to the mechanism.

"You have questions? It is to help find Sanders?"

Jacob sat down at the table. "Potentially." He folded his hands on the tabletop. "I want to start with your status here."

Janos looked surprised. "This will help to find Sanders?"

"This will answer some questions."

Nagy tilted his head, watching Jacob. "I am suspect now? This is why you have looked at my past?"

"We have looked into all members of staff," Jacob demurred. "Your record was flagged during our checks. That's why we have to ask, and why I hope you'll cooperate, so we can put it aside."

Nagy folded his hands and mirrored Jacob's stance. "Very well. Ask your questions. I will answer what I can." He smiled, a brief tilt of one side of his mouth. "Then you can put a note on case this was all waste of time and go back to find Sanders."

"That's what I'm hoping for." Jacob set his slate down by his right hand. "Your records indicate you came to Britain in 2041."

"Some time like that, yes."

Jacob raised his eyebrows. "You don't know?"

"Not exact date, no." Nagy shrugged. "It was...bad time. I was sick. Hurt." He uncurled his left hand and waved his prosthetic fingers. "Before this."

"How did you cross the border control? We have no record of you entering the country."

Nagy hesitated and looked down at his hands. His flesh hand wrapped around his false one. "The name I leave behind is not the name I come here with." He raised his eyes to Jacob. "Where I came from, they did not agree with me on many things. I left everything behind, including my name."

"You're admitting to carrying false papers?"

Nagy nodded. "I know this is crime, but I had no choice." He met Jacob's eyes. "People I knew then, they hurt me because of who I am." He significantly tapped the back of his false hand. "I run away because I do not want to die. I hide. I come here. Easy country to come to. Good people. Big city for people to hide in."

Jacob shifted in his chair. "You could have come here legally."

"All my papers were with my family." He hesitated, then drew up his shirt, showing a vicious scar down his right side. A knife wound, Jacob guessed. Deep and curving across his ribs. Nagy lowered the shirt, smoothing it down. "It was not possible to fetch papers."

Jacob was thrown. He had expected Nagy to lie about his origins, and his arrival, but instead, Nagy admitted he had committed a crime to enter Britain. He even gave plausible reasons. "Why did they attack you?"

Nagy fell silent for a moment. His prosthetic fingers twisted around a gold band on the ring finger of his right hand. "There is much tolerance in the world," he said finally. "In some places, there is less tolerance. In some places, people condemn for loving the wrong person." His smile didn't reach his eyes. "I loved the wrong person. Some people would have killed me for it."

That was vague enough for Jacob to ask. If the man had some kind of perverted proclivities, they had to know. "The person you loved..."

"A man. Gone now." Nagy looked at the ring on his finger. "Here, I found another. Better." He closed his left hand over his right, then looked at Jacob. "You want to know if I am involved in Sanders's case. I am not. Why would I risk all I have now to hurt my friend?"

Jacob gazed at him, curious. For a man who said he would not risk everything, he had confessed to a crime that could result in his arrest and imprisonment.

Nagy wet his lips with the tip of his tongue. He had another scar there, across his lips and chin. He looked like he had been through the wars. "You will arrest me now, yes?"

On the surface, it seemed like a simple case of identity fraud. Jacob could arrest him, but the man had come here, no doubt expecting to have his past raked over, and had been nothing but honest about his crimes.

If Nagy had been from another country, and he'd fled persecution and claimed asylum, it would have been simpler, but within an EU state, there was never any reason. He could have crossed the borders with his papers, but his scars supported his story and why he had fled without them.

If his story checked out, and his current paperwork was in order, it might be possible to push matters through for him and keep him out of trouble. If it all turned out to be a load of bullshit, then they could cross that bridge when they came to it.

"I'll need your birth name," he said finally, "and copies of your current paperwork."

Nagy nodded. "I will bring it to you." He reached out, then hesitated. "I can type the name for you. It is..." He laughed shortly. "It is very Hungarian."

Jacob opened up a note on the slate and passed it over. Nagy balanced it carefully in his left hand and started typing with his right. He paused, frowned. "You do not mind if I change keyboard settings for a moment? I need accents."

"Whatever you need to get the name down."

A moment later, he slid the slate across the desk to Jacob, who looked at the mess of letters from the arse end of the alphabet. "I definitely wouldn't have been able to spell it." He copied the name over into a message and pinged it to Anton with the instruction to check it. "If you can collect your papers and bring them to the police station as soon as possible, I would appreciate it."

"Of course." Nagy looked relieved. "I am not arrested now?"

"Not for now." Jacob nodded to the door. "If you can let Mrs. Ashraf know we're done, I'd like to speak to Ben."

Nagy rose at once, offering his right hand again. "Thank you, sir."

Jacob shook it. "And for your time." He sat back as Nagy left the room and sent a follow-up note to Anton to look for any violent incidents involving a stabbing, and potentially mutilation of an arm.

A moment later, Mrs. Ashraf returned with Ben.

"Can I show you my robot?" Ben asked, clinging to Mrs. Ashraf's hand.

Jacob smiled. "I'd love to see it." He turned in his seat as Ben came around the end of the table and held it out to him. It was a small two-legged creation with a cartoonish smiley face drawn on the round head. "What does it do?"

Ben carefully set it on the table, and it strolled across to the other side, where Mrs. Ashraf caught it before it could fall. "Kit made it for me," Ben said, looking solemnly at Jacob. "He gave me a present."

The shoebox.

As gifts went, building a toy for your boss's distressed son definitely ranked high.

It provided yet another reason to find it hard not to trust Kit. Kit seemed like a genuinely decent person, something rare in his professional opinion. He hoped like hell his suspicions were wrong, or if they were right, there was a good reason for them.

"You're very lucky," Jacob said. "It's a very good robot."

Ben nodded, running around the table to retrieve it. He returned and stood in front of Jacob, hugging the robot against his chest. "Aunt Mariam says you want to ask me stuff."

"I'm afraid so." Jacob brought himself down to Ben's height, resting his forearms on his knees. "You've been very brave, and now, I need to ask you if you can be a little bit braver for me?"

Ben nodded, hugging the robot tightly.

"When your dad told you to hide, do you know why he didn't hide with you?"

Ben's lower lip trembled. He nodded. "He said he had to put something away downstairs."

Jacob kept the frown at bay. They'd asked Ben the standard questions on day one. Sanders had told Ben to run, and Ben had been so distressed, it had been impossible to get anything else out of him. He definitely hadn't mentioned anything about putting something away.

"Put something away?"

Ben nodded gravely. "He always kept his special things locked away safe."

Jacob glanced over at Ashraf. Her expression gave nothing away, but she had her arms tightly folded and her lips pressed into a thin line. He looked back at Ben. "Do you know what special thing he had to put away?"

Ben shook his head. "I wasn't meant to touch."

Jacob took his slate from the table and opened a picture of the odd mechanism he'd found at the house—the one which had a twin at Kit's flat—and showed the boy. "Is this one of your dad's special things?"

"Dad says it's a spare part." Ben looked up at Jacob. "Do you know where he is?"

"Not yet," Jacob said apologetically, "but I won't stop looking; I promise."

Ben's face fell, and he turned and hurried to Mrs. Ashraf's side. "Can we go home now?"

Mrs. Ashraf glanced at Jacob, raising her eyebrows. He nodded. She put her arm around the boy. "Yes. We can go home." She looked back to Jacob. "Stay here. I'll have someone escort you out."

Jacob rose. "Thank you."

He sank into the seat after the door closed and looked at the image on the screen, then flicked through several of the crime scene photographs. *He always kept his special things locked away*. All the walls were lined with shelves, but nowhere could he see any sign of any cupboards or a safe or anything that could be locked up.

They were missing something.

There had to be something they'd overlooked at the house, something downstairs, somewhere Sanders could lock up his prized possessions. Jacob's mouth opened in shock. Sanders locked up his special things. He had a safe room for his son on the upper level. Who was to say he hadn't done something similar for himself on the lower levels?

When a young woman came to escort him out, he barely paid her any attention, his mind racing. He had to get back to the crime scene. He had to find what Sanders had hidden.

Chapter Twenty

There was something comforting about being left alone to work.

Kit closed himself up in the temporal chamber with the gate. He had been trying for days to replace parts so he could test the lock mechanism, and every day, he'd been interrupted by someone or another.

With tools in his hands and machines opened up before him, he felt more at ease. He could put aside the worries about his appointment in the evening and focus completely on the job at hand. It was so much simpler than trying to think about what he should to say to Jacob.

For the first time since Sanders had disappeared, he had no one bothering him.

People were already twitchy about the thought of a time-traveling kidnapper. With Jacob in the building, people were even more on edge and staying where they were meant to be, which suited Kit fine. He took a break to go up to the canteen, and even then, only for as long as it took him to gulp down a bowl of pasta.

He returned to the engineering bay with the latest readings from the gate. At his workbench, a touch to the console projected the schematics of the gate lock above the tabletop. Kit studied it for a moment, then imported in the new data, moving parts and adjusting the projection to fit it all together.

"How's it coming?"

Kit didn't glance at Hamid. "Technically, the pieces should all fit, but I need to make them work together." He rubbed at one eye with his knuckle. "If all goes to plan, we won't have to redesign the frame."

Hamid clasped his shoulders. "Sanders would be pleased."

Would be.

Well, if that wasn't a morbid outlook...

"He's not dead yet." Kit turned the projection with a gesture, leaning closer to examine some of the connections. "Mariam wouldn't be pleased to hear you say that."

"You know what I mean."

Kit nodded.

The gate needed to be secure. They had been working on it for years before he came along, and Tom would be pleased about it. He still could be, when he got back from wherever he had hidden himself. Or been taken captive. Or both.

Kit put in his earbuds and continued to work on the lock until the rest of the team started packing up and drifting toward the door.

He only set down his tools when his quill chimed, interrupting his music. A new message.

No surprise it came from Jacob.

Running late. Should be there by half past.

Kit glanced at his watch and swore under his breath. Almost eight already.

He bolted out of the office ten minutes later, sprinting for the trams. He barely made it by the skin of his teeth and collapsed, panting, onto one of the seats. At least he hadn't promised any kind of hospitality, but he was bloody starving. He tapped into his list of favourite takeaways, picking one at random and placing his regular order before he even reached his building.

The lobby was deserted, and he swore under his breath, running for the stairs.

At work, he could handle it; he'd fiddled with the cables and wires supporting the lift until he could believe they were stable, but here? He'd asked the building managers here if it were possible to access the lift shaft. He had been refused more than once, despite showing his credentials. As far as he knew, the support lines could be tied together with string. Unlikely, but he still ended up puffing and out of breath when he reached his floor.

He swiped through the security and staggered in, tossed his satchel into the bedroom, and closed the door. No one would be going in there for the rest of the night. He glanced around the living room. Tidy-ish, respectable, with no more incriminating evidence left lying around.

And despite the fact that he was still annoyed with Jacob, he hurried into the bathroom and dragged a comb through his hair. You could be annoyed with the man. It didn't mean you wanted to look like you'd slept with your head in a bucket.

The door chimed less than five minutes later, and he checked the security screen.

Good timing on both parts.

Jacob stood there, along with the delivery boy.

Kit buzzed them through the main doors of the building and tapped in the code to allow them access to the lift. Another quick glance around the room reassured him he looked like a nerd, but not like a criminal nerd.

When he opened the door, he ignored Jacob to tip the delivery boy and took his food, then motioned for the other man to come in.

Jacob remained by the door as it slid closed, watching him, but Kit didn't plan on giving him the satisfaction of knowing how terrified he was. "There's a hook by the door for your coat," he called over his shoulder. "Shoes off too."

By the time he emerged from the kitchen with a pile of rice and curry in a bowl, Jacob had moved to stand by the sofa, one hand resting on the back, as if he was hesitant about sitting down. He seemed knackered as well, like he hadn't slept.

Kit sat cross-legged at one end and looked up at the policeman. He wasn't going to ask what was bothering him, or get invested, or give a damn. He would play it like every cool, collected character he had ever seen in a film, even if he felt anything but.

"You said we needed to talk," he said, gesturing to the other end of the sofa with his fork. "So talk."

Jacob sat down. He tapped his fingertips together and frowned at them. "I know you saw something in the footage that you recognised."

Suddenly, the curry became a brilliant cover. The spices always made his face flush anyway. He tried to remember what Janos had said to him, tried to find a small truth to detract Jacob from the big one.

He remembered the last time they'd sat on this sofa, and Jacob had seen the gate fragment, and he immediately spotted a way he could skirt the topic. "You've got a bit of one of them in the evidence bags at the station," he said, and it came so smoothly and so easily, nothing but the truth.

Jacob looked at him. "And you had a piece of one here."

He had no reason to deny it, even if his cheeks were turning red. "Only a prototype."

"What kind of prototype?" Jacob asked, casual and curious, but the tension in his shoulders said he needed to know if he had the right idea.

Kit chewed on a mouthful of lamb, gazing at him. He remembered the spiel Sanders had given him when he first joined the TRI. "Tom experimented on teleporting years back." Not a lie, but not the whole truth. "If the gate in the video did what it seemed to, maybe someone managed. Maybe they took Sanders's old ideas."

"Maybe," Jacob agreed neutrally. "And why do you have parts of one?"

Kit stirred up some of the rice. "Tom knew I like building stuff." In his early days in Tom's company, he'd been mesmerised by the older man's intelligence and ideas, so excited to meet someone so innovative. "I was curious, and he let me see some of his designs. I wanted to see if I could make one that worked." He didn't have to pretend to look flustered. "You know I'm not meant to do it. If Sanders knew, he'd give me such a bollocking."

Jacob nodded. "Do you know if he ever built one that worked?"

Kit scooped up another forkful of rice and took a moment to chew and swallow. "A teleporter?" His face had to be pink. His eyes were watering too. "Not that I know of. There were too many problems. Physics didn't like it. Can't have two parts of one person on two parts of the world at the same time. And don't even start on what happened to fillings..."

Jacob subsided against the couch. He looked more at ease, but it didn't mean anything. He laced his hands together over his middle and gazed at Kit thoughtfully. "Have you ever been to Sanders's house?"

Kit choked on a mouthful of rice. "Me? Go to his house?" He shook his head. "I wish." He sighed wistfully. "I always thought he'd have all kinds of clever stuff there, but I don't think he let many people from work visit him at home. Keeping his work and home life separate or something."

Jacob tilted his head on the back of the sofa and gazed up at the ceiling. "I'm sorry."

"Come again?" Kit inquired.

"This thing we had." Jacob pushed himself up, folding his hands together again. "I'm sorry. I buggered up. Shouldn't have got involved, not when the case is still ongoing. I shouldn't have dragged you into it."

Kit prodded at his food. "I was pretty much going to be involved anyway." He glanced up over the bowl, and for once, mouth and brain were in full agreement about the next course of action. "You want some curry?"

One side of Jacob's mouth twitched. "You sure you don't want to kick me out, now I've said my piece?"

Kit made a face at him. "I wouldn't offer if I didn't want you to stick around. You might be a grumpy old bastard, but you warned me when we went to the pub." He nodded toward the kitchen. "There's a few boxes of stuff on the counter. I always order too much."

Two minutes later, Jacob dug into a well-filled bowl of korma. He made a sound of appreciation as he ate. "Didn't have time to get something before I came over," he admitted. "It's been a long day."

"Mm." Kit watched him, wondering how much Jacob would be willing to give away now they were actually talking. It helped he'd answered questions, and had been nearly completely honest. The terror of being caught out in a lie hadn't knotted up around his middle this time. "Mariam mentioned you were coming into the office."

A fleeting flicker of wariness crossed his face. "She did?"

Not 100 percent relaxed, then. Still on his guard.

"Mm." Kit used a piece of naan to mop up some of the sauce. "Something about asking a few questions." He met Jacob's eyes. "You get the answers you were looking for?"

"I made a start," He gave Kit an apologetic look. "I really shouldn't discuss the case with you."

"Unless you're interrogating me," Kit pointed out.

Jacob snorted. "If you thought that was an interrogation, you don't want to have a real one."

Kit sprawled back against the arm of the couch. "Would you go all bad-cop on me? Threaten to put me in jail?"

Jacob's expression turned deadly serious. "I would do my job."

"Does that 'job' include the word 'blow'?" Kit asked, widening his eyes.

For a moment, Jacob looked torn between annoyance and amusement. He settled for sighing. "We shouldn't have done that."

"I'm noticing a lot of things we shouldn't have done." Kit set his bowl on the table. He settled back on the couch and stared defiantly at Jacob. "You wanted to do it as much as I did. Tell me you didn't. Tell me you didn't enjoy knowing we were doing it right under their noses. Just like when we did it on the balcony here."

When Jacob looked at him, the heat in his eyes made Kit's heart skip a beat.

"You know I wanted to," he growled, his voice a deep rumble that seemed to come from the middle of his chest. "Don't push me, Kit."

A pleasant shiver curled down Kit's spine. He took a sharp breath, and from the flick of Jacob's eyes, he clearly noticed it.

Jacob stared at him for a moment too long, then set down his bowl and rose. "I'm not doing this again."

Kit draped his arm along the back of the couch. "You enjoy being a celibate monk?"

"Don't," Jacob growled.

That really wasn't the right way to shut Kit up.

"What? It's true. You're so up for it I could hang a flag on your cock, but you're saying you're not. We already set the bridges on fire. What's the point of trying to pretend they're not burning? We started. We might as well keep going."

Jacob snatched his coat from the hook by the door. "No, we shouldn't. We should never have started this. *I* should have controlled myself." He pulled on his coat and shook his head. "I'm a bloody idiot."

Kit vaulted over the couch. "You needed a shag."

Jacob's eyes blazed. "I need to concentrate on my job."

Kit glanced at the front of his trousers. "Well, I see a part of you disagrees."

"I'm a grown man," Jacob snapped. "Not a randy teenager. I have some self-restraint."

Christ, he was gorgeous when he was furious, eyes flashing and teeth bared. Kit felt like a moth drifting closer to a candle flame.

"'Course you do," he said, his heart pounding as he moved closer, close enough to press a hand to Jacob's chest. "Makes sense though. Hormones and things. Some men your age like to ride a big red car." His whole body tingled with anticipation, wondering how far he could push the man. "You just want to ride a redhead."

Jacob grabbed his wrist in a vicelike grip. "You'd do well to shut up."

"Yeah?" Kit leaned closer, grinning. "Make me."

Jacob spun him around and pinned him against the door, Jacob's face close to his. It almost hurt, but Kit didn't care, curling his fingers into Jacob's jacket and jerking him off balance, closer, and crushing their mouths together again.

Jacob groaned into the kiss, but he didn't pull back. He was the one to open his mouth, kissing Kit with a ferocity that stole his breath away.

Kit panted when they broke apart. "There you are."

Jacob stared at him. "You'd take it, wouldn't you? Even if you were nothing more than a midlife crisis fling?"

Kit slid two fingers between the buttons of Jacob's shirt, tracing them against the warm skin beneath, Jacob's heart thumping against them. "I'd take a doing from you any which way I could get it."

Jacob braced his hand against the door behind Kit and raised his eyes to the ceiling. He seemed to be steeling himself. When he returned his gaze to Kit, the anger and the heat had gone, weariness in its place. "I can't do this, Kit. I can't. If it had happened any other time, if we weren't caught up in this bloody case, if it wasn't complicated..." He stepped back. "I thought I could do one night. I can't. And I can't ask more of you now."

Kit stayed where he was, wedged against the door. It couldn't be so easy to walk away. "You want to," he said stubbornly.

Jacob's hands were shivering as he tried to do up his coat. "I do, and it's a fucking mess. We'd be bad for each other."

Kit pushed off from the door and reached for Jacob's coat, did it up. "Not necessarily."

"Then be honest with me for once." Jacob sighed. Quiet. Resigned. "Did you mess with the video?"

Kit's mouth went dry. He had to concentrate on doing up Jacob's coat. "Why would you think that?"

"No more bullshit, Kit."

Kit forced himself to meet Jacob's eyes. He'd lied before. It should be easy to lie again. He just had to say no.

The word stuck in his throat.

Jacob smiled, brief and sad. "Well, no answer is better than a lie, I s'pose." He brushed Kit's hair off his brow. "I know you've got secrets you need to keep for that bloody agency, and I won't ask you to break a confidence, but I'm going to get someone to dig into the video. You can warn them if you like, but I'll have to do it."

Kit dropped his eyes, feeling sick to the stomach. It would have been better if the floor opened up and swallowed him.

Jacob gently pushed him aside and opened the door.

"Jacob." Kit wondered if his voice sounded as reedy and shaken to Jacob as it did to him.

He didn't turn. "Yeah?"

"I had to. I'm sorry, but I had to."

Jacob nodded. "Yeah. I figured as much."

When the door slid closed behind him, Kit sank onto the floor. Jacob knew, had suspected the whole time. If he got the video cleared up, he would know everything, and all because Kit was a bloody tit who couldn't keep his mouth shut. If he'd left Jacob well enough alone, he would never have seen the eye, and they would never have found the video. He pressed his hands to his mouth, trying to fight the rising nausea.

"Shit," he whispered.

Chapter Twenty-One

A folder of paperwork awaited Jacob on his desk when he arrived the next morning.

A glance showed Janos Nagy's formal papers.

They were a secondary concern.

The previous day, when he'd left the TRI offices, Jacob had taken a team back to the Sanders house. They scanned every wall of the crime scene. It had taken close to two hours before they found a door, the security latch hidden on the bloodied shelf.

Sanders did have a safe room.

His laboratory on the ground floor was a front, the real one hidden below the house. The three rooms were filled with the kind of things Jacob had only seen in the TRI engineering bays. Workbenches lined the walls, stacks of tools everywhere, and several computers.

They'd also found another of those damned doorways.

More significantly, there were also the signs of a struggle.

Sanders had reached his safe room, but he hadn't been alone.

From the look of it, Sanders had tried to reach his experimental teleportation gate with blood smeared on the floor and scrabbling handprints, as if he had fallen and been dragged back. The CSU team had found a fainter print, possibly the last one, on the edge of the doorway.

Maybe the doorway had worked, but Jacob wasn't inclined to believe it.

The gateway mechanism connected to a mess of computers, and the machines had been smashed. The questions of the day were to find out whether Sanders had built a functioning teleporter, and whether he'd managed to make his escape through it.

When Jacob left, at close to 7:00 p.m., the CSU team was still going over the room. They'd found three sets of fingerprints in the room. One set were Sanders's, and the child's set had to be Ben's. The last set belonged to the woman he was waiting to see.

He went through to the incident room. "Is Mrs. Ashraf here yet?"

Temple shook her head as she transferred new information from CSU onto the incident panels, with new crime scene images. "It's not nine yet, sir. They'll call up when she arrives."

Jacob nodded. "When she does, have her taken straight to the interview room. We don't let her in here. We don't let her see anything."

If they were curious about his newfound wariness, they didn't ask. He was more curt and sharper than he'd been the day before, and he didn't care if they noticed. He was tired, and the one bright spot he'd had in months had been lying to him.

While he had suspected it, it still hurt when Kit hadn't denied it.

As soon as he'd left Kit's place the night before, he sent a message to Singh on the night shift to get someone in to take a fresh look at the memory chip. After, he'd gone home and drunk himself into a stupor. The headache pressing behind his eyes reminded him what a bad idea that had been.

He returned to his office to read through Nagy's file.

It gave him something to do to keep himself from being angry with Kit, frustrated, even disappointed. Maybe he had reasons for deceiving him. Maybe they were good reasons, but it still hurt like hell. The intensity continued to surprise him.

He sighed, picking up the file and opening it out.

It came as no surprise Nagy had included everything. While Kit was hiding something, Nagy was being as transparent as possible. He'd even included a thorough medical report from a Dr. Bellevue, which detailed his injuries when he had arrived in the country.

Jacob glanced up from his reading when Temple tapped on his door.

"Sir, Mrs. Ashraf arrived. We put her in interview room two."

Jacob set down the papers. "How did she seem?"

"Calm," Temple replied. "She thinks she's here for some follow-up questions."

"Well, she's not wrong." Jacob got up, picking up his slate. "You good to sit in?"

Temple nodded. "I'm up-to-date on everything. Anton can cover the desks."

Jacob motioned for her to lead the way.

They had called Mrs. Ashraf shortly after the discovery of the room, to arrange for her to come down to the station in the morning. She didn't know they'd found it, and until they had more details, they weren't willing to divulge any additional information.

She looked up when Jacob and Temple entered the room. "DI Ofori."

"Mrs. Ashraf." He took a seat on the opposite side of the table. "Good morning. We have a few questions we need to clear up. I hope you don't mind if we record this interview? Standard protocol and all that."

"Of course not. Any assistance I can offer."

Jacob smiled, but it felt like more of a grimace. He tapped the code into the side of the table and set the system to record, stating time and date and those present. He laid his slate against the sensor.

"You are aware we have had footage from Sanders's attacker come into our hands."

She barely even blinked. "Kit did mention something had been found."

Of course he had.

Jacob's fingers darted across the screen of his slate. Captures from the video illuminated on the table in front of her, starting with the blurred shots of the man. "Do you know this man?"

Ashraf leaned forward, studying him, then shook her head. "I've never seen him before."

That seemed honest at least.

Jacob nodded and shifted onto the next image: a crystal-clear shot of the gate. "Can you tell me what this is?"

Ashraf stared at the image. He saw the way she wet her lips, the way the tips of her fingers whitened on the edge of the table. "It looks like some kind of gate."

"We found pieces of a device like this at the crime scene." Jacob opened up the images of the mechanisms Kit had identified. "Mr. Rafferty confirmed Sanders had worked with these machines."

She nodded. "They look like his attempts to build a teleportation device."

"Do you know if he succeeded?"

Ashraf shook her head. "It never got beyond the initial development stages."

Jacob flicked through some more images on the slate. "Have you ever worked with Mr. Sanders on these projects? Or is it something he told you about?"

"I'm not really a technician." She shrugged. "I wouldn't be any use to him."

There, Jacob thought grimly.

"Perhaps, then," he said, "you'd be able to explain why only your fingerprints and his were found on this machine?"

He brought up the image of the gate from Sanders's basement. It looked identical to the gate from the video.

She managed to hide her shock well, but her lips trembled as she stared at the picture. When she spoke, she seemed to be picking her words carefully. "He thought I could help with some kind of coding for it. He thought it could make a difference."

Jacob set his slate in his lap and folded his hands on the table. "Here's where I'm confused, Mrs. Ashraf." He kept his tone pleasant. "You said you didn't know Sanders until after he lost his wife, but all the information we have on him shows he stopped working on teleportation over ten years ago. Before his wife vanished."

The hesitation lasted just long enough, and he could practically see her mind whirling. "He stopped working on it publicly, because of all the attention it drew. He didn't want to get people's hopes up, only for it to fail again."

"I see." Jacob inclined his head. "Remind me again how he lost his wife."

Ashraf blanched. "You're not suggesting he used his wife as a subject in his experiment?"

"You tell me. She went traveling, isn't that what you said? And vanished, with no trace?"

"If you're implying what I think you are, you better stop now." She rose sharply, pushing the chair back. "I didn't come down here to listen to you slandering one of my dearest friends."

Jacob met her eyes. "Sit *down*, Mrs. Ashraf. You are here to answer questions, and believe me when I say I have a lot of them. Most specifically, I want you to tell me about this gate, and this time, please try not to lie to me."

She remained standing. "Am I being charged with anything?"

"Not yet." He gestured to the chair. "Please sit down."

She complied, tucking her hands in her lap. "Very well."

He brought up all available images of the doorways on the tabletop. "Tell me everything you know about these, and why Rafferty is still familiar with them if Sanders stopped working in teleportation." Ashraf fell silent for so long he prompted, "Mrs. Ashraf? Now, if you don't mind."

She raised her eyes from the pictures to look across the table at him. "Sanders never stopped working on his teleportation technology," she said, her voice flat. "He had ambitions that one day it would work, but up until now, he's hit all the same problems as previous tests."

"Up until now?"

She lifted her shoulders in a tight shrug. "He was still tinkering with it. Maybe he finally got it right, and that's why you can't find him." She pursed her lips. "Or maybe it still went wrong, and you should be looking for pieces."

Jacob leaned back in his seat, watching her. It was like Kit all over again: telling him a lot of useful information, but he couldn't help feeling they were missing something important, something that would make the whole case make sense.

He set his slate back against the sensor and flicked up the image of the destroyed machines at Sanders's house.

This time, she didn't bother trying to hide her dismay. "What happened to them?"

"Best guess, someone took a wrench to the casing and tore out whatever was inside them." Jacob scaled up the image. "You've seen the machines before. Do you know what he had on those units?"

She looked back up at him. "Oh, yes," she said quietly. "Those machines contained the details and schematics of his original designs." She touched the edge of one of the images. "If they couldn't get Sanders and his brain, they got the next best thing."

"How much information would he have stored there?" Jacob asked.

Mrs. Ashraf smiled, brief and tight and painful. "All of it."

Chapter Twenty-Two

Mariam wasn't at the office when Kit got in.

He wasn't in any state to focus on work, his mind all over the place. He'd tried to find the way to tell her what had happened on the quill, and it hadn't worked. He'd even got to the point of writing down what he had to say on paper, but in the end, he'd binned it.

Face-to-face and honesty was the best option.

He asked to be contacted when she came into the office, but when an hour passed and then another, he had to tell someone, and if anyone ought to know about how badly he'd screwed up, it had to be the man who it would affect the most.

Janos had apparently joined Dieter on compassionate leave, but Kit sweet-talked their address out of Paul in HR. The man had looked at him doubtfully when he'd asked, but relented when Kit insisted it was important, and it related to three years ago.

He made his excuses to Hamid, then headed out of the office and held out his quill to catch a taxi-pod. Janos and Dieter lived on the outskirts of the city, and given the choice of changing from tram to train and the potential for delays, a pod made things simpler and quicker.

In the back of the cab, Kit stared blankly out at the city as it flashed by. He'd bitten his nails down to the quick but couldn't help chewing on them again until they stung and bled.

If Jacob was as smart as Kit suspected, he would join the impossible dots and turn Janos's life upside down.

Kit shivered. How the hell could he tell a man *oh, sorry, thinking with my dick just ruined your life*?

He had an hour to find a solution, but even as the pod pulled up outside the small house, he was drawing a blank. He stood at the front gate as the pod sped off and tried to find the balls to go in.

It wasn't anything like he'd expected: a cottage from the early 1900s, tucked off the main road, and with enough land attached to keep the housing estates on either side at a distance. Old-fashioned and probably what Janos had grown up with. It even had a garden and a hedge.

Kit opened the gate and walked into the garden, heading for the quirky little bridge crossing the winding stream which bisected the lawn. A ceramic gnome stood on the bank of the stream and might have seemed out of place if he hadn't been holding something that definitely wasn't a fishing rod.

Ahead of Kit, the door of the house opened.

He forced himself to keep walking.

Janos wiped his hands on a dishcloth, and he seemed puzzled. "Kit?"

"Hey. Um. You got a minute?"

Janos's frown deepened. "Something is wrong?"

Kit sagged miserably, and he didn't know what to say. The air left him all in a rush, and he pressed the heels of his hands to his eyes. "I'm sorry," he blurted out, his voice shaking. "I fucked up so badly, and it's going to ruin everything."

He didn't hear Janos come closer and jumped when Janos's broad arm wrapped around his shoulders.

"Come inside," he said. "This is not a conversation to have in garden."

Kit let Janos guide him into the house and obediently complied when he asked him to remove his shoes. The inside of the house stood in stark contrast to the outside, a beautiful modern sprawling living room with thick dark beams serving as a staircase up to the next level.

Dieter reclined on one of the sofas, reading something on a slate, his glasses perched on the end of his nose. He pushed himself upright, frowning when he saw Kit, and looked askance at Janos.

"Kit is upset," Janos murmured, guiding Kit around the end of the couch.

"Yeah, so I see." Dieter swung his legs down, sat up properly, and set his slate on the heavy wooden coffee table nestled between the oversized couch and the fireplace. "I also can't help noticing he's...here?"

Kit sat down. His legs wouldn't hold him any longer. "The police are going to find out the truth about the TRI." He swallowed hard. His words were tripping over one another in their haste to be out. "I cocked up, and I accidentally helped them find the footage, and now, the detective knows I tried to hide something, he's going to go back and look, and if he does, if they're speaking on the video, he's going to find out and when he does and when he comes back to the TRI and he knows about the time travel..." He took a shaking breath. "I had to tell you first. It's your life."

Janos and Dieter were both silent.

Kit looked down at his hand. His thumbnail was bleeding.

"You gave him the footage?" Dieter's voice sounded flat.

"I didn't mean to," Kit said in a whisper. "I tried to scramble it, but he figured me out, guessed I'd try to hide something."

"Fuck." Dieter pulled off his glasses and covered his eyes with one hand. "Jesus fucking Christ on a cake."

"It's okay."

Kit looked at Janos in astonishment, but Dieter spoke first.

"What do you mean it's okay? Didn't you hear him?" He stood up suddenly, throwing his glasses down on the table. "This stupid fucking arsehole has practically handed your identity to a fucking copper on a silver platter!" He swung around and stormed over to the window, slamming both hands down on the sill. "Christ! Why do we work with fucking morons who can't leave things well enough alone?"

Kit started to rise, but Janos pressed his shoulder in silent command. He subsided and watched as Janos walked across the room and stopped behind Dieter.

He laid his hands on Dieter's shoulders and murmured something in Hungarian, calm and placating, but it wasn't enough to stop Dieter from whirling around, his eyes blazing.

It could have been an argument for all Kit could understand: Dieter shouted, his voice high and breaking, and Janos caught his hands, took his arms, spoke more calmly, quietly. Finally, Janos drew Dieter into an embrace. Dieter struggled and punched weakly at his chest, but Janos curled his hands in Dieter's hair and against his back, and all the anger seemed to sap out of Dieter's body.

Janos continued to murmur, rubbing his right hand slowly up and down the back of Dieter's neck, and Kit had to look away when he realised Dieter's shoulders were shaking with silent, quaking sobs.

He self-consciously stared down at his hands when Janos returned to the couch with Dieter and sat down beside him. Dieter leaned mutely into him, clinging tightly onto Janos.

"I'm sorry," Kit said again, quietly. "I really am."

"We know." Janos sighed. "We have been waiting for this day. Every day I live in this time, I wait for someone to notice, someone to see." He looked at Dieter, then back at Kit. "The TRI is hiding a big secret. Big secrets cannot hide forever."

"And the day that secret comes out," Dieter said unsteadily, "is the day they lock Janos up in a fucking freak show."

"We do not know that," Janos murmured.

Dieter's hand tightened on Janos's, and he wrapped his other hand around their linked ones. "I know what this world is like. If those fuckers try and take you, then they're taking me too."

Janos pressed a kiss to Dieter's brow. "So sentimental."

"Fucking right I am." Dieter took an unsteady breath and blew it out. He looked at Kit, and his eyes were bloodshot. "You said this detective's going through the footage again? Mariam said you thought he trusted you."

"Turns out not so much." Kit shifted on the edge of the couch. "Last night, he pretty much said he knew I'd played with the footage."

"Last night?" Janos frowned. "He only comes to the office during the day."

Kit groped in his pocket for a tissue, coming up with a crumpled knot of one, but at least it wasn't snotty. He pressed it against the side of his bleeding thumbnail. "I..." He frowned at his hand. "Um. I might have shagged the policeman."

Dieter burst out in explosive, sharp laughter. "Well bugger me with a fish fork and call me Sebastian," he said. "Isn't that useful?"

Janos looked at Kit. "More than good-looking?"

Kit's face burned. "I wasn't meant to get involved in any of this, and the bastard dragged me in."

Dieter's eyes were on Janos. He said something in Hungarian and made Janos's expression tense.

"No."

"Why not?" Dieter said. "He's screwing someone in the TRI. It could get him off the case."

"And make him pissed so he will tell his other policemen what to look for, and make it easy for them." Janos shook his head. "We do not say anything to him about this. If he asks, I will talk to him, but this..." He sounded adamant. "We do not stoop low."

"Jan," Dieter began.

"No." Janos looked at Kit. "He does not trust you now? Tell us what happened."

The floodgates opened: he told them everything right up to the point where Jacob had showed all his cards and left Kit sitting in a heap on the floor.

"What a bastard," Dieter murmured.

Kit released a shaky breath. "No. We both buggered up. I shouldn't've gone near him, and he shouldn't've gone near me, and we still both did it, because we were stupid and horny."

"You like him?" Janos asked.

Kit glanced up at the other man. "'Course. He's good-looking and—"

"No," Janos interrupted. "I did not ask if you want him. I ask if you like him."

Kit's stomach flipped. "Like him?"

"He says if things were not as they are now, if he had no case, he would be with you." Janos lifted his shoulders in a shrug. "If things were different and there was no case, would you like him enough to be with him?"

Kit gaped at him.

He hadn't thought about it.

They'd both agreed to one night, and then it became a night and a day. All at once, there were emotions there that shouldn't have been, and the anger and the frustration had become too intense for something that was meant to be a one-night stand.

"I-I don't know."

Janos raised his eyebrows. "Really?"

Kit took the tissue away from his thumb and stared at it, willing it to bleed again to give him something else to focus on. Did he want to be involved with Jacob? Shagging was one thing, but spending time with him?

Two hours of chatting in a pub and some great sex weren't anything to base a relationship on, but a man who had similar tastes, who could tell when he freaked out in lifts and tried to help, and who checked on him when he seemed poorly? That was another story.

"Shit." His voice sounded tiny.

Janos murmured something to Dieter, who rose and circled around the couch, heading for the door to another room. When he disappeared through the doorway, Janos moved a little closer and patted Kit comfortingly on the shoulder. "You should not feel bad."

Kit looked up at him. "Why not? I've made a mess of everything for everyone. For you. For Dieter. For the TRI. For him."

Janos laughed, a warm sound. "You are very silly man," he said, the smile on his face comforting. "You did not come from the future. You did not attack Sanders in his home. You did not bring the police into this." He squeezed Kit's shoulder. "Even if you did not tell this detective all the things you have, he is a smart man. He would see things do not make sense. He would come back to the TRI to find the answer."

Kit blinked. "I forgot you met him."

"Yes. I met him. He is not bad to look at." Janos's eyes twinkled. "He is also good man. He listens well and does not jump to conclusion. I think this is why he asked you for truth, instead of arresting you. He knows you are good man, and so you must have good reasons."

"You can tell all that from one meeting with him?" Kit snorted.

Janos nodded. "I can tell because he did not arrest me when I told him I came here under false name. He listened to my reasons and did not act like I was a criminal. He could have arrested me, but he did not. He is willing to give people a chance to prove themselves."

Kit squeezed his hands between his knees. "I screwed it all up, didn't I?"

Janos held out a hand, swayed it from side to side. "There is some screwing up, but it is not all your doing. He screwed up also. The man who attacked Sanders also screwed up. There is lots of screwing up. You are only small part of it."

Dieter rattled back through the door, looking calmer and carrying a tray laden with mugs and a teapot. A tower of biscuits on a plate tilted ominously over the middle of the tray. "Is he being philosophical at you?" he asked as he set the tray on the coffee table. "If he is, kick him."

"A little," Kit admitted.

Dieter poured each of them a mug of tea, then settled beside Janos, laying his hand lightly on his lover's thigh. Janos looked at him and smiled affectionately, then covered Dieter's hand with his own.

Kit wrapped his hands around the mug. "What's going to happen?" he finally asked. "I mean, with everything?"

"Fuck knows," Dieter sighed, leaning against Janos's side.

"But we deal with it when it comes," Janos said. "Like we deal with crazy Hungarian soldier who comes through gate."

Dieter pressed his cheek to Janos's shoulder. "Maybe not exactly like that."

Janos chuckled. "Maybe."

Chapter Twenty-Three

Temple was bringing Ashraf to the crime scene.

Jacob went ahead of them to do a last look over the site before they arrived. CSU were long gone already, leaving it empty. He'd already descended into the hidden laboratory when Temple radioed to notify him of their arrival.

It must have been a pristine environment to work in before the intruder got in, brightly lit and polished. The remains of the computers were installed along one wall. Small neon evidence markers had been placed at random points around the room, with bright blue tabs indicating where the scanners had registered and imaged fingerprints.

Another opening led into the room containing Sanders's mysterious doorway.

It looked harmless, ridiculous even—an empty doorway standing in the middle of a room, rooted into a metal bed and connected up with so many wires and cables, it looked like it had a nervous system.

Jacob approached it.

This place had to be the reason for everything that had happened to Sanders, important enough to be concealed and secret. He felt it in his gut. Potentially, Sanders had created a successful teleportation gateway like the one in the video. Or something else entirely but equally controversial. Jacob wasn't a scientist or an engineer, but he could tell without question it had to be something significant.

He was still standing there when Temple escorted Mrs. Ashraf down. She looked pale, drawn, and he could imagine why. It couldn't be easy coming to the place where a friend had been attacked.

Jacob went over to her. "If you want to leave or need some air, let us know, okay?"

She nodded, taking a deep breath. "Where do you want me to start?"

"You tell me," Jacob replied, gesturing around. "CSU have finished, so if you need to move anything or touch anything to check what's missing, do what you need to."

She nodded and went straight through to the computer consoles. Some of the casing remained intact, and one of them even booted up when she switched it on, but it whirred, then shut down at once.

She crouched on the floor, checking over each machine. "All the hard drives," she said, rocking back on her heels. "They've all been ripped out."

"Surely, he'd have backups of his work?" Temple said, frowning.

Mariam nodded. "You'd think so, but this was his private project. I don't know how much information he stored on those, and how much he stored elsewhere. If he had backups, he put them somewhere he considered safe."

"Do you know where?" Jacob asked.

The frustration on her face suggested she was telling the truth when she shook her head. She got up, brushing dust off her hands. "I won't say Tom was paranoid, but he didn't like people working with his new developments until he could be sure they worked, in case anything went wrong."

Jacob rubbed at the hollow of his cheek with his thumb. "You said he brought you in to do coding? Doesn't it count?"

"Not when he didn't let me see the details of his latest developments." She hesitated. "The board upstairs was his latest project. I'm not sure of the specifics, but he included some of the coding I'd offered for his older designs."

Jacob lowered his hand, watching her thoughtfully. "The whiteboard? The coded whiteboard you said no one in your office could decode?" He inclined his head. "And how long have you known what it said?"

She grimaced. "We set someone working on it, with what we had left of Sanders's codes and keys. It's not a full translation, but it does support the idea he'd developed some kind of teleporting system."

Jacob glanced at Temple and nodded toward the stairs. She took his meaning and disappeared up them.

Jacob sat on one of the stools, gazing at Ashraf. "Mrs. Ashraf, until now, I have been patient with you, but my patience is rapidly wearing thin. I'm more than aware you are keeping things from me, but if there is anything I need to know, now is the time to tell me."

Mrs. Ashraf rubbed her palms together. "I've told you what you need to know now."

He smiled without parting his lips. "And we both know it's definitely not enough." He braced one hand on his thigh and leaned forward. "I'm giving you a last chance to come clean here. Tell me everything. Give me all the information I need, not these scraps you've been tossing me until now. Otherwise, I'm not going to hold back anymore, and if I have to take your institution apart brick by brick, I *will* do it."

A muscle in Ashraf's cheek twitched. "I don't know what you're expecting me to tell you."

"Did Sanders successfully manage to teleport someone? Is the gate functional? Is there any way to check whether he used it?" He spread his hands. "I could go on all day. Just give me the answers I need to help me find a motive for someone attacking your friend, and hopefully, we'll be able to find him."

She stared at him, then rushed through to the doorway to the other room and the empty gate. She was circling it when he caught up with her, looking it up and down, as if she could see...what? He didn't know.

"Well?"

"I think there are ways to check if it has been powered up."

"And if it worked?"

She glanced at him. "As far as I knew, this was only in development. It shouldn't have been at this stage. If he managed to power it up successfully, then it's more than he ever told me."

Jacob watched her. "And how do you tell if it has been powered up?"

"I'd need to get one of the engineers down here," she replied, and Jacob—his heart sinking—knew at once who she'd ask for. "Kit Rafferty has worked on a lot of Sanders's technology. He would be able to confirm it."

He couldn't protest either, not without raising questions.

After all, she had sent Kit to him before. If she thought he was the one they needed to look at the gate, then he'd be the one they called in.

Still, there were innocuous questions he could ask without incriminating Kit and his household experiments. "Would Rafferty have any experience with teleportation devices, in his role in your agency?"

Ashraf's weary expression gave way to something like amusement. "That boy has no doubt tried a bit of everything in his time. If he saw a button for the apocalypse, he would take it apart to see how it worked." She touched the quill button on her bracelet. "I can get him out here right away."

Well, it was going to be awkward, but if it had to be done, it had to be done.

"As soon as possible," he agreed.

In the hour and a half it took for Kit to be shuttled out from the city, Ashraf went through the basement, picking through the items knocked off the shelves and left scattered on the floor. She paled when she saw the handprints on the floor, but she swallowed hard and continued to sift through the debris.

As far as she could tell, only the hard drives were missing.

As far as he could tell, she wasn't lying this time.

They both looked up as footfalls clattered down the staircase.

Kit stopped short on the third step from the bottom. "Mariam?"

Jacob stepped aside and let Ashraf take charge, explaining in brief, clipped tones what they needed him to do. Kit didn't glance Jacob's way, but from the flush riding up the back of his neck, he was definitely aware of his presence.

Ashraf took him through to the mysterious doorway, and Jacob heard Kit swear under his breath, apparently as surprised as the rest of them had been.

"Do you know how it works?" Jacob asked, remaining at the entrance of the room.

"I've seen the concept in development." Kit's voice sounded flatter than usual as he walked straight to the doorway. He hesitated. "Is it okay to touch?"

Jacob bit back the urge to ask if he'd ever asked that question before. It wasn't the right place, and it sure as hell wasn't the right time. They weren't friends. They weren't lovers. They weren't anything to each other, and if Kit chose to blank him, he could be equally blank and professional in return. "Be my guest."

He stayed by the door, watching, to ensure no foul play. Not that he could be sure of recognizing it. He hadn't seen it the last time when it had happened right in front of him. But it felt better to keep both eyes on the pair and make sure they didn't take anything away with them he hadn't seen first.

Kit made it a hundred times more difficult with the way his bony hands moved on the framework. He moved his long and elegant fingers like a pianist touching a keyboard, tracing power lines and rivets, opening panels, and plucking lightly across the wires within. Jacob remembered all too well what those hands were capable of.

Kit murmured under his breath, too, as he had when he'd worked on the video, as if reciting what he'd found, cataloguing it, and putting it aside for later assessment. He checked the inside of the frame and the exterior. He opened cavities Jacob hadn't spotted, occasionally brushing his hair back from his brow.

Jacob found it fascinating to watch him work.

Ashraf fetched one of the stools from the main room before Kit turned to ask for it, his focus entirely on the gate. When he reached out for the stool and found it there, he didn't seem surprised. He didn't break his pace, climbing up on it and working along the top of the gate.

"Does he even know we're here now?" Jacob asked quietly.

Mrs. Ashraf shook her head. "You give him a challenge, and it's like he flips a switch somewhere under that mop."

They remained there, watching him work for what felt like hours. Mrs. Ashraf had sunk onto a spare stool, and Jacob continued to lean against the wall, hoping and praying his scrutiny of Kit looked like nothing more than casual interest.

Kit dropped down from the stool suddenly and turned. He looked like hell, all the colour gone from his face, and he held out his hand as he came over to Ashraf. In the middle of his palm, there was a blackened lump.

"What's that?" Jacob demanded.

"It was the stabiliser," Kit said, his voice unsteady. "It should have controlled the flow of power. It means the gate has been powered up." He met Mrs. Ashraf's eyes. "When they smashed the consoles, the power surge would have short-circuited the whole thing, but it would have to be using power when they did it."

Ashraf's eyes widened. "He tried to use it?"

Kit nodded stiffly. "Looks like."

Jacob looked between them. "You're saying he created a functioning teleporter?"

Kit looked at him for the first time since he'd arrived. "No, I'm saying he switched on this thing, which might not have worked, and they shorted it out when he tried to escape through it."

Jacob felt out of his depth, groping in the dark. "What could that mean?"

Mrs. Ashraf's face had drained of colour. "It means, Detective Inspector, that your suspected abduction may have just become a murder investigation."

Chapter Twenty-Four

It felt wrong to be sitting in Sanders's living room without Sanders there. It felt wrong to be drinking the man's scotch. It felt wrong to be surrounded by photographs of Sanders and his wife and child.

It all felt wrong.

Kit's hands were still shaking around his glass.

He'd always assumed it would turn out fine in the end. It would all be nice and neat. Sanders would show up as if nothing had happened. The people who had tried to abduct him would be apprehended. Everything would go back to normal.

Christ, what a naïve tit he had been to assume that.

He never imagined he'd be the one to find proof that Sanders could be...was...might be...

He took a shaking breath and lifted the glass to his lips. The liquid burned all the way down his throat, and he shuddered.

Jacob had got them out of the basement as soon as they told him. He'd hustled Mariam off outside as well, and through the window, Kit had watched numbly as Mariam covered her face. Crying, he realised. He stayed long enough to see Jacob put a comforting hand on her shoulder.

Inside the house, Kit had turned in circles, trying to find something to do, something to make things fit and be right again, but there was nothing he could do.

He'd wandered numbly back into the room with the whiteboards. A plastic sheet covered a dark stain on the floor. For a moment, he didn't understand, and then he did. He backed out of the room, and the policewoman found him standing in the hall, still staring at it. She took him through to the living room and suggested he sit for a moment, that it might help.

It hadn't.

He'd lasted less than a minute after she left him there, and then he was up and walking around the room. He'd found the drinks cabinet, opened a bottle, and poured himself half a glass, his hand trembling so much he sloshed it across the tabletop.

Now, only a trickle remained in the glass, and he couldn't find the energy to rise and refill it. He felt sick to his stomach, couldn't stop himself from rocking back and forward. Stupid response. Pointless. Useless. It didn't have any benefit, but he couldn't stop himself. His throat felt tight and raw, too, and it was all wrong.

He looked up when someone stepped into the room.

Jacob.

Oh Christ, just what he needed.

The man who had shown concern about him before being there when he needed someone to hug him.

"Mariam?" Kit's voice broke, and he looked back down at the glass.

"She wanted a few minutes to herself." Jacob's shoes tapped across the floor. Toward him. Christ, no. Stay at arm's length. It would be easier. "I'm sorry. We couldn't be sure of what had happened down there."

It was like watching in slow motion as the glass slipped between Kit's fingers and fell. It clattered onto the wooden floor, bouncing and spinning. A fine spray of scotch patterned the wood. The glass cracked, with a chip out the rim. He started to reach down for it, but Jacob got there first. He crouched in front of the couch, in front of Kit, and looked up at him.

"It's okay," he said, his voice low and gentle, and that made things so much worse.

"Don't," Kit whispered. "Don't be kind."

His eyes stung, and they felt hot and wet. He lifted his hand to hide them, to hide his face, to hide from Jacob, because he didn't need to be stupid and pathetic and emotional in front of Jacob. He didn't want Jacob to look or care, because it was all wrong and messed up, and if he looked and he cared and he acted on it, then it would get even more twisted up and knotted, and Kit didn't know how to undo it and didn't even know if he'd want to.

He heard the glass being set down on the coffee table, and then a warm hand touched his knee. He flinched.

"Kit, look at me." Jacob was so close, and he sounded worried.

Kit shook his head. "Please," he whispered.

He didn't know what he wanted, if it was invitation or dismissal. He didn't know anymore, and his hand was wet, and his throat closed up with the tears he couldn't hold back.

"He was meant to come back," he choked out. "He was meant to come back, and this was meant to be a whole load of bollocks."

"I know," Jacob murmured. "We hoped that would be the case."

"But it's not!" Kit crammed his other hand over his eyes, pressing the heels to his eyelids to try to stop the bloody tears. It was stupid, and it wasn't helping anyone, and they wouldn't stop, no matter how hard he pressed his hands against them. "It's not, and he's dead!"

The word hung on the air in the echoing silence.

Jacob's hands were suddenly on his shoulders, broad and warm and solid, someone safe and here, and Kit couldn't stop himself from leaning forward. He dropped his head forward, his brow coming to rest on Jacob's shoulder. The tears kept falling like they wouldn't stop, and he felt lost.

More than a quarter of a century of life, and he'd never had someone he knew and liked die on him.

It was wrong.

Ben needed his dad. It wasn't right or fair to take his dad away from him. It wasn't.

Kit didn't know when his hands moved to grasp the front of Jacob's coat. He didn't notice when Jacob's hand had curled across the nape of his neck, his other hand rubbing in circles on Kit's back. He only noticed both things when the tears finally stopped, leaving him hollowed out and raw.

He stared at the wet stains on Jacob's jacket. He wanted to lift his head, but his body seemed weighed down with exhaustion, nothing left in him.

"I never lost someone," he confided. "Not someone I knew."

Jacob nodded, and his beard brushed Kit's ear. "It's hard," he murmured. "Losing someone is never going to be easy, no matter what your relationship is." His fingers curled under Kit's hair against the back of Kit's neck, moving gently up and down. "It's not wrong to grieve for them."

Kit nodded as much as he could without lifting his head.

They only pulled away from each other when the front door opened and footsteps came toward the door of the living room. Jacob straightened up, one hand still on Kit's shoulder, as Mariam came into the room.

She looked crap, but he probably matched her. Her eyes were on Jacob. "Do you mind if we go for now?" She still sounded impressively steady and calm. "I don't think we can be much more use to you today."

"Of course," Jacob murmured. "I'll arrange for Temple to take you back."

She removed her glasses and rubbed at her eyes. "Do you want to come to the office, Kit? Or go home?"

"Office."

The idea of going back to his empty flat with nothing but the thought of Sanders stepping through the gate rolling around in his brain made him recoil. It was true they wouldn't be able to do anything more in the office, but they could point him at machines, give him something else to think about, and he could try to hold himself together.

Temple travelled with them. She and Mariam occasionally said something to each other, but Kit didn't want to listen. He stared out of the window as they shuttled toward the city, wondering how much he would need to drink to forget what a gate malfunction could do.

He'd created a dozen hypothetical scenarios when he first started with the TRI: What would happen to someone in transit if the gate shut down, or if they were midway through the trip back and lost the connection. He had a whole array, and the worst by far was the short-circuit option.

He posited that a short-circuit in the grid would not only destroy the connection, but completely obliterate anything or anyone in transit at the time. Sanders had agreed with it. Kit shuddered. He wished he'd never come up with the theory, no matter how accurate it might be.

Temple dropped them outside the TRI building.

"What are we going to tell them?" Kit asked as they walked up the steps.

Mariam gazed up at the tower. "What we know."

He nodded, following her in. Paulina nodded in greeting. Kit thought he returned the gesture, but he couldn't be sure. He propped himself in the corner of the lift, closed his eyes, and held on to the handrails as tightly as he could.

The doors closed, and the lift started moving.

"Is there something you want to tell me?"

He opened his eyes. "About the gate? I don't know what I can tell you. It worked, but I don't know where he was trying to go, or when."

"No." She wasn't looking at him. "Not about the gate." She wet her lips and turned to face him. "I'm talking about you and Detective Inspector Ofori."

Maybe the lift jolted, or maybe his stomach dropped to his toes. He didn't blush for once. Instead he felt cold, his reflection in the mirrored wall of the lift ashen. "What do you mean?"

She looked wearily back at him. "Don't lie to me, Kit. I was outside the house. I saw you through the window."

"I-I was upset." The words tangled on his tongue, and the rails were cold and hard against his palms. "He was trying to calm me down."

"You didn't see the way he looked at you." Her face was lined with fatigue. "What have you done?"

He pressed into the corner of the lift, breathing hard. "Mariam..."

"For pity's sake, Kit." She sounded like she was on the verge of tears. "You knew we were going into lockdown. What were you thinking?"

He shook his head. "I think it's pretty clear I wasn't, isn't it?" His lips trembled, and he pressed them together, trying to keep them still.

"He's investigating us," Mariam said quietly. "Don't you understand that? He wasn't getting information out of us, and then he's what? Flirting with you? And suddenly, he knows Tom had built a teleportation device, he has video footage that could compromise us, and he knows where Tom's lab is?"

Kit flinched as if she'd slapped him. "He—it wasn't like that!"

He didn't know what was worse—the condescension or the pity in her eyes.

"I know you want to believe that," she said, "but he didn't have anything on us before."

"And you think I told him everything, because I shagged him?" Kit's heart fluttered against his ribs. "Is that how much you trust me?"

Mariam winced, but she didn't have a chance to say anything as the lift chimed, notifying them they were on the tenth floor. She stepped toward him, touched his wrist. "Kit, it's not about not trusting you."

He shook her hand off, pressed his palm to the door sensor, and stepped out into the mercifully empty hall. "Bullshit." His voice sounded like a stranger's, raw and angry. "You accused me of deliberately telling him everything! I didn't tell him anything about Sanders's house! I hadn't even been there before today!"

"Kit—" She reached out again, but he recoiled.

"Don't!" he snapped. "You don't get to play nice, Mariam. The only thing I told him about was that bloody eye, and the only reason I did *that* was because you sent me down there. You know what I'm like when I find some new, exciting tech, and you sent me there!"

"I know," she agreed, "and I did. I'm sorry about that."

"About that. But not about calling me a traitor." He shook his head. "I've changed my mind. I want to go home." He pushed past her to get back in the lift, slapping his hand against the console to shut the door. He grasped the handrail again, pressing his brow to the cool metal of the wall.

She was wrong.

She had to be wrong.

He hadn't told Jacob anything, apart from the details relating to the eye. He couldn't remember saying anything incriminating. He hadn't. Had he? Okay, maybe Jacob had seen some of the tech, but that didn't tell him anything. Not really. Did it?

Jesus, he didn't know.

He stumbled out of the lift on the ground floor and didn't stop to speak to Paulina. Four blocks away, he realised he'd left his bag and jacket in the engineering bay. All he had with him were his pass and his quill.

He stopped, turning on the spot.

He could go back, get his stuff, but he didn't want to set foot in there, not now, not when he was fizzing over with anger and distress, and they were people who didn't trust him or give a shit about him. The only people in the TRI who had ever shown him any real concern were the man who had died and the man he'd lied about to protect.

He withdrew his quill and opened out the screen. Yeah, he could get home without his stuff, and Jenny had a spare security pass for his door, but he didn't want to be at home, sitting there, looking at gate pieces and trying to find a way to make it impossible for it to short-circuit. He would work himself to exhaustion, and it wouldn't make a damned bit of difference, not now.

Home or the TRI. Isolation or a place full of people who probably believed he'd spilled his guts to the investigating officer.

He sank onto the step of a nearby building, his legs shivering.

A message registered on the quill, and he opened it.

Jacob's name and number.

A message offering the number of a bereavement support group. A kindness he hadn't asked for from a man who—if Mariam could be believed—only got close to him to pick him dry of information.

Yes, Jacob did ask a lot of questions. Hell, Kit had joked about it only the other day, but he couldn't believe it, not about Jacob. Jacob had chosen to step back. He'd said it wasn't good for them to be together, not when they had the case as a wedge between them.

Kit stared blindly at the message.

His thumb moved.

The bar. An hour. Please.

It took him more than half that to get to the bar where they'd met only three days earlier. It felt like much longer than that, when he'd still been stupid and giddy with the thought of meeting a handsome man for a drink.

This time, he took a table in the corner and another glass of scotch. He didn't normally like it, but with one glass of the stuff already sitting heavily in his stomach, mixing in something else seemed like a bad idea.

He didn't know if Jacob would come. If they'd been in each other's shoes...

Hell, he didn't even know then.

His eyes stung again, and he rubbed at them with his fist.

Wouldn't help anyone.

The chair opposite him scraped the floor as someone pulled it back. He lowered his hand from his eyes to find Jacob sitting there, and silently, he reached across the table and offered Kit his hand. Kit threaded his fingers between Jacob's, and Jacob curled his to hold Kit's hand.

"You okay?" he asked gently.

Kit shook his head.

"Can I help?"

Kit looked at their linked hands. His throat felt tight, and hot tears streaked down his cheeks. "Tell me the truth," he said, trying to keep his voice even. "Did you only come near me to get information about the case?"

"Kit—"

"Please. Please. Just tell me. I won't be angry; I promise. I just...I need to know."

Jacob stayed silent for too long, and it was like a punch in the stomach.

Kit started laughing sadly. "No answer is better than a lie, eh? Just my luck. Couldn't be that you were interested in me."

"Kit, I didn't—"

"No, no," Kit said, trying to smile. "Daft of me. 'Course you only wanted information. Stupid Kit. Showed an interest. Made it easier for you."

"Kit!" Jacob said sharply. "Will you let me finish?" Kit mutely looked at their hands. Jacob sighed, but his grip tightened. "Maybe at first, I thought it might be useful. But what kind of wanker do you take me for? Do you really think I could shag someone if I didn't like them?"

Kit shrugged. "Dunno."

Jacob released his hand, and Kit stared dully at his empty pale fingers lying on the table. He didn't want to see Jacob walking away, but that meant he didn't see Jacob circle around the table, until Jacob sat down right beside him.

Jacob's fingertips touched his cheek, tilting his head up.

Jacob was there, beside him, looking at him with frustration and affection. "Getting information gave me an excuse," he said, his hand cradling Kit's cheek, his palm warm. Kit tilted his face into it, shivering. "Give me one good reason why I wouldn't be interested in you."

Kit blinked hard, and his cheeks were wet again. "Because I'm a bloody great tit with no brain-to-mouth connection."

When Jacob smiled, the lines in his face deepened beautifully and his eyes were bright. "All a part of your charm, you daft tosser." He stroked the tears from Kit's cheeks with his thumbs. "Try again."

Kit stared at him. "It wasn't only about the case?"

"Why d'you think I left?" Jacob sighed. "I didn't want to compromise you."

Kit choked on something between laughing and crying. He couldn't find any words, so he leaned forward and buried his face in Jacob's neck, wrapping his arms around him, and when Jacob embraced him, it felt all right.

Chapter Twenty-Five

There were pork chops sizzling in the pan.

Jacob prodded at them with a fork.

He'd done something very stupid, and hiding in the kitchen seemed like the wisest course of action, at least until he could scrape together his wits and try to figure out how to undo the mess he'd made.

Kit was in his flat.

It hadn't been intentional.

He'd gone to the bar to check on him and make sure he was holding it together. He wasn't. He was far from okay. Jacob couldn't leave him sitting there, alone and falling apart, so he'd done the first thing that came into his head: invited Kit back to his place.

He jabbed a chop, frowning at it.

He should be angry with himself, but he had more to be worried about. It said a lot about Kit's situation that he'd chosen to contact someone who could have been using him, rather than a friend to comfort him. That could only mean he didn't have a close circle of friends.

Jacob flipped the chop over. There were potatoes cooking as well, but it was a poor man's feast. He hadn't been to the shops in days, and he'd had to hack eyes off the potatoes before he tossed them in the pan.

He didn't want to think about the state of the flat.

Not that he had bad habits. He just never got around to doing anything in the house when he had a case. Laundry would pile up, dishes would form citadels in the washer, the bed would go unmade, and yeah, he would look like a lazy bastard to anyone who came to visit.

"You want a drink?" he called through the door to the living room, before wondering if he'd left more than one bottle of beer in the fridge.

"I'm okay."

Jacob left the chops sizzling and stepped into the living room, wiping his hands on a cloth. Compared to Kit's flat, his whole place would fit in Kit's bathroom. He had the bedroom on one side of the living room, kitchen on the other, and a small bathroom at the back. Technically, he could've got something bigger, but after two and a half decades, being frugal had turned into second nature.

Kit had curled up on the couch.

Jacob stopped short, eyebrows rising. "What are you doing?"

Kit had the basket of fresh laundry between his feet. He looked up guiltily, a half-folded pair of socks clutched between his hands. "I needed to be doing something, and it was this or try and fix that piece of crap you call a TV."

Jacob glanced at his sturdy, outdated media unit. "It's a classic."

Kit snorted, ducking his head over the laundry basket. "Fossil," he muttered.

Jacob tossed the towel at his head. "I thought you appreciated vintage things."

When Kit looked back up at him, a tentative smile played on his lips. "So you remember what I said?"

Jacob braced his shoulder against the kitchen doorframe. "I pay attention. It's my job." Kit looked back at the laundry basket and hesitated before picking up a pair of boxers to fold. Jacob couldn't help smiling wryly. "Shy about touching my smalls?"

"Didn't know if you'd mind."

"I think once you've handled the goods, handling the wrapper is allowed."

Another of those small, cautious smiles passed over Kit's face, showing a glimpse of a new side to him Jacob hadn't seen before, a much more fragile side.

Jacob withdrew into the kitchen to check on the chops, a little of the weight lifting from him. He had to admit he'd been worried it would be strange to have Kit here. Unexpected, true, but it didn't feel all that strange.

Five minutes later, he scraped the chops onto a pair of plates and added a pile of potatoes for each of them. He couldn't offer much, but it was better than nothing, and he had a feeling Kit probably hadn't eaten anything since they were at Sanders's house.

"Grub up," he declared, carrying both plates through.

Kit set down the shirt in his hands and pushed the laundry basket back with his foot. "You didn't need to feed me."

"And you didn't need to fold my laundry." Jacob handed him the plate. "Let's call it even."

Kit cleared his plate in a matter of minutes. For a skinny rake of a man, he didn't seem to have any trouble with his appetite. He set the plate on the floor and resumed his work on the laundry basket.

Jacob watched him as he continued eating.

Kit folded the clothes as methodically as he'd gone over the gate, each thing checked, then folded into a neat rectangle, which fitted in a nice, neat stack of rectangles, which were arranged in the bottom of the laundry basket.

"Why did you invite me here?"

The question came after minutes of silence, and Jacob blinked. "What?"

Kit smoothed out a T-shirt over on his lap, turning it into another tidy rectangle with four quick folds. "You could've seen me home. You know where I live. Why'd you decide to bring me back here?"

Jacob picked up Kit's plate. "If I hadn't, you'd have been going home alone, wouldn't you?"

"Yes."

"You shouldn't be alone tonight."

Blue eyes looked up at him. "You said it yourself, that this is too complicated."

Jacob nodded. "But tonight, it's simple. You shouldn't be alone." He offered a tired smile. "No funny business. Just company."

Kit gazed at him for a long time, then nodded. "Company." He glanced over at the media unit. "If that thing works, we could watch something."

"If it works?" Jacob said indignantly.

For a moment, Kit's eyes glinted with a little of their usual mischief. "Just checking."

Jacob sighed, shaking his head. "Arsehole."

Kit bowed his head over the basket, but Jacob saw the brief smile. He left him to finish the laundry and returned to the kitchen with the plates. It took all of five minutes to fill up the dishwasher and tidy up the surfaces.

By the time he returned, Kit had finished folding the laundry and stood beside the bookshelf, examining the display of photographs as the frames flicked from image to image.

"He's a good-looking man, your son." He didn't turn.

Jacob approached him. The array of images showed Luke at various ages and, in pride of place, his graduation photograph, his face split in a beaming grin. "He turned out well."

"A doctor?"

Jacob smiled, nodded. "He likes taking care of people."

Kit darted a glance at him. "Wonder who he gets that from. He doesn't live near here, does he?"

Jacob shook his head. "London. Where I came from before here. He visits every couple of months."

Kit curled his fingers on the edge of the shelf. "My family's all down Brighton way." He frowned at his fingers, pressing them until the tips went white. "They worry, y'know, me being all the way up here on my own. No one nearby to check on me. Bet your family worries too."

And that was a topic Jacob didn't want to think about.

Luke might worry, but the rest of the family were...negotiable. He remembered the last time he'd seen them, and the reason he hadn't seen them since then.

"Well," he said, "we're not on our own tonight." He laid his hand lightly on Kit's shoulder. "How about we find something to watch?"

In the end, they chose something they both enjoyed. Monty Python might well have been older than either of them, but they could appreciate it without having to engage their brains.

Jacob wasn't surprised when Kit curled against him on the couch.

Less than halfway through the film, Kit's head drooped against his shoulder, listing sideways against him. Jacob stopped the film, then gently pressed his hand to Kit's shoulder.

"You need to sleep."

Kit squinted at him. "I'll take the couch."

Jacob shook his head. "It's not big enough. You'll put your back out." He slipped his hand under Kit's elbow. "Come on. My bed's big enough for both of us, and I promise I won't bite."

"Shame."

Jacob smothered the smile. Even when miserable and exhausted, Kit could still be a blatant flirt. Jacob slipped his arm around Kit's waist, supporting him all the way to the bedroom.

Compared to Kit's expansive bedroom, Jacob's room looked bare. A chair stood in one corner, stacked with clothes, in the space left by a wardrobe, a chest of drawers, and the bed, which was flanked by mismatched bedside cabinets. Still, it was warm and comfortable, and all a man really needed.

Kit paused in the doorway and looked at him. "You really don't want anything to happen tonight?" His pupils were wide and dark.

"Not tonight. You need to rest."

Kit nodded and stepped forward into the room, pulling his T-shirt over his head and dropping it at the foot of the bed. He hooked his thumbs over the waistband of his trousers, then paused. "Starkers, or do you need my boxers to protect your virtue?"

Jacob lingered in the doorway. "Whatever you want. As long as you're comfortable."

Trousers and boxers promptly landed in a heap on the floor.

Kit glanced back at him. "No funny business," he said quietly, looking vulnerable and very young, "but can I lie with you?"

Jacob walked into the room, letting the door slide shut behind him. "Of course."

Kit reached for the buttons of Jacob's shirt, fumbling to undo them. As soon as the shirt gaped wide enough, he wrapped his arms around Jacob's waist and dropped his head to rest on Jacob's shoulder, pressing their chests together, bare skin on skin.

Kit's breath gusted against Jacob's shoulder, and Jacob lifted a hand to stroke through his hair. "Come on," he murmured. "Get to bed. I'm here."

Kit nodded. "Sorry."

He started to pull away, but Jacob caught his wrist. "Don't apologise." Kit looked at him in tired confusion. "You've got nothing to feel sorry for. You've lost someone. You're allowed to be upset." He cupped Kit's cheek with his other hand. "You're going to be all right."

"Yeah?"

Jacob nodded and leaned closer, kissing him, gentle and chaste, but Kit shivered all the same. "Yes."

Chapter Twenty-Six

Kit jolted awake with a gasp.

The nightmare had left his heart racing, his whole body shaking. He called out for light, but the lamps didn't come on, and it took him a moment to remember why. He wasn't in his own home or his own bed and that wasn't his hand on his side.

He sank back onto the bed. "Shit," he whispered.

"Bad dream?" Jacob murmured sleepily.

Kit nodded into the darkness.

Jacob's fingertips pressed lightly to his side. "C'mere."

"It's okay," Kit whispered. "Don't need to."

Jacob pulled a little more insistently. "C'mere," he said again, voice thickened with a yawn.

Kit turned over to face him, sliding across the space between them. The sheets were cool where neither of them had been lying, but Jacob was warm and mostly naked. Jacob buried his hand in Kit's hair, fingers stroking along his scalp.

"Better?"

Kit sprawled beside him, and the chill that had washed through him eased a little. "Mm." He settled there, his arm curving on Jacob's broad chest, fingers toying with the dark mat of curls.

Jacob continued to stroke through his hair, then downward, kneading lazily at Kit's neck and shoulders until the tension eased away. Kit laid his head on Jacob's chest, focussing on the beat of his heart and rise and fall of Jacob's ribs beneath his ear.

"Wanna tell me?"

Kit shivered. "I saw what happened to Tom, when the gate…" The words stuck in his throat, the image seared onto his retina. "Like I saw the whole thing. Saw him get disintegrated."

Jacob's hand went still. "That's what would happen?" He sounded more awake now, and horrified. "If the gate were damaged?"

Kit nodded, releasing a shivering breath. "Best guess." He splayed his hand suddenly on Jacob's chest. "Poof."

"Jesus." Jacob tightened his arm around Kit's shoulders. "I'm sorry."

Kit and clasped Jacob's hand on his arm. "Wasn't you."

Jacob squeezed his arm. "I put you in a situation where you had to look into that as a possible result. That's not the way you should have found out about it."

"You didn't know," Kit murmured, tracing a circle in the middle of Jacob's chest with the tip of his index finger. The curls were soft to the touch, and he smoothed them out and felt them spring back beneath his finger. He tilted his head and pressed a brief kiss to Jacob's collarbone. "Thanks."

"For what?"

"Not leaving me on my own." Kit craned up to try to search out Jacob's face in the darkness, but he couldn't see a thing. He frowned in the dark. "You've got bloody good curtains."

Jacob chuckled. He called for light and the bedside lamp illuminated softly. "Night duty," he said by way of explanation. He looked up at Kit, propped up over him. "Any reason you need it?"

Kit tried to smile, but it faltered. "Wanted to see you too. Remind myself I'm not alone."

Jacob mussed his hair. "How about that?"

Kit squirmed away from his touch and had to fight down a tired smile. "Piss off."

Jacob struggled not to smile, too, his dimples showing in sharp relief. "We need to make sure," he said, then flicked at Kit's earlobe. Kit tried to duck, bringing himself down lower over the other man. He lost his balance and ended up sprawled on Jacob's chest, and Jacob laughed out a gusting breath. "Convinced yet?"

Their faces were so close, and Kit felt every breath, from the ribs rising and falling against his to the soft puffs of air against his lips. He stared at Jacob, well aware he should back right the hell off because, Christ, they'd both agreed no funny business, no carrying on, only company.

Jacob's hand sank in his hair again, a warm weight against the back of his neck. Kit swayed downward, stifling a quiet moan when their mouths met again.

It wasn't the height of romance, not when they both had morning breath and dry lips, but none of that mattered. Jacob arched his head up from the pillow, and Kit opened his mouth greedily, demanding his kiss. Breathless and urgent, they pressed closer together. Kit gasped out loud when Jacob rolled them suddenly, pinning Kit beneath him. Jacob's eyes gleamed, and he caught his lips again, kissing him as if he never wanted to stop.

Kit clutched at him, fingers scrabbling up and down Jacob's back. He pressed his feet to the bed beneath him, pushed his hips up demandingly, and felt the answering rock of Jacob's body against his. He still had his bloody boxers on.

Kit tried to concentrate on that problem, but Jacob stealing every little breath he took should've come with a warning: addictive and distracting. In the end, Kit did the only thing he could think of and pinched Jacob sharply on the arse.

Jacob pulled away, looking both amused and offended. "What?"

Kit pressed his hand low on Jacob's back. "Too many clothes."

Jacob glanced down his body, then at Kit. "We're shit at this whole restraint thing, aren't we?"

Kit tugged at the waistband of Jacob's boxers again. "Speak for yourself. I never said anything about being restrained." He looked up at Jacob. "If you don't want to, you don't have to."

Jacob kissed him. "Want isn't the issue here."

Kit slid his fingertips beneath the waistband of the boxers. "Yeah?"

In response, Jacob pushed up onto his knees and shoved the offending shorts down and out of the way. Kit looked him over, and God, he liked the view. But more than that, he wanted and desperately needed to push the nightmares away.

"Y'could put someone's eye out with that thing, if you're not careful," he said, propping himself up on his elbows.

Jacob braced himself over Kit. "And whose fault is that?" He caught Kit's hair with one hand and claimed his mouth again in another heated kiss. Kit slid his hands between them and wrapped one around Jacob's hardening cock, giving it a squeeze. Jacob groaned into his mouth and pushed against his hand.

Kit broke off from the kiss, breathing hard. "You got johnnies?"

Jacob stared at him. "Crap."

Kit couldn't help grinning. "My jeans. Back pocket."

"You're kidding."

Kit shrugged expressively. "You never know your luck." He held up three fingers in the Scout salute. "Always be prepared."

Jacob shook his head with a rueful smile. "You're making me feel like a disorganised old man," he said as he crawled across the bed and reached down to the floor to retrieve Kit's jeans.

Kit stretched out his leg, poking Jacob's backside with his toe. "Vintage." He couldn't help smiling as Jacob shot a mock glare over his shoulder. "Mature." He gave another more emphatic poke. "Like cheese."

Jacob whipped around, quick as a snake, and caught his ankle in an iron grip. "Ah, ah." His voice sank to a low, rich purr, and the look in his eyes—so heated Kit would swear his blood had turned to molten steel. "My bed. My rules."

"Yeah?" Kit pushed up onto one elbow. "What do you want to do?"

Jacob's grip on his ankle tightened. "I have a few ideas."

Before Kit could think or say anything, Jacob jerked his ankle hard enough to throw him off balance and flipped him onto his stomach. He fell face down among the pillows and exclaimed in surprise, but when he braced his hands against the mattress and pushed himself up, Jacob neatly pinned him to the bed.

Jacob was over him, knees straddling his thighs, and he brought his lips close to Kit's ear, his voice little more than a breath. "What do you fancy?" His hands settled on Kit's shoulders, kneading slowly.

Kit dropped his head forward. He had no idea. He only wanted something that wasn't a nightmare, something to push away the afterimages. He curled his fingers into the bedding. "Distract me."

He shuddered pleasantly when those broad, strong hands slid down his spine, massaging every knotted inch, leeching the tension from him. It would have been innocent, except for the way Jacob's fingers kept brushing his arse before moving back up.

Kit was squirming in moments, trying to demand more than those fleeting touches. "Bloody tease," he complained cheerfully. He managed to wriggle enough to get himself onto his knees, pushing his arse up demandingly.

"Sometimes," Jacob agreed, sitting on his heels, his fingers tracing the curve of Kit's buttock. "Could do with some KY."

Kit tilted his head to slant a glance through his hair, grinning. "Oh, so no johnnies, but not entirely useless?"

"I'm single, not celibate." Jacob snorted and swatted him sharply on the arse. It was a light smack, but the sting of it sent a rush of heat straight to Kit's head, and he yelped. Jacob went still, then gently brushed his fingers against the tingling skin. "Sorry."

Kit swallowed hard, a little more...interested than he'd have expected. Hadn't really been in with an adventurous crowd back in the day. Hadn't thought about it really either. But now, with his arse warm and pink under Jacob's hand, the thought had surged up along with other things.

"Kit?" Jacob sounded concerned.

Jesus. Well, there was something to find out for the first time...

"Do that again," he whispered into his arms, burying his face in them, the blush spreading across his shoulders. If it kept going, every inch of him would be scarlet, and his knob would be as limp as an overcooked noodle, but Christ, it felt good once, and maybe...

Jacob only hesitated for a second, then smacked him again. Not only the fingers this time. The palm—and the sound, the sharpness, the stinging heat sending a shudder through Kit from head to toe. And then Jacob made it worse by tracing his fingers across the tingling flesh.

"Like that?"

"Mm." Kit caught his breath when Jacob used his nails instead. "Jesus..."

Jacob leaned over him again, bracing his hands on either side of Kit's arms, and nuzzled at his shoulder. "Didn't know you were into that."

Kit tilted his head enough to see Jacob through the tangled strands of his hair. "Well, when you know what comes after a spanking..."

Jacob paused, puzzled, then actually laughed aloud. "Mm. And I know you like that."

Kit's cheeks hurt from grinning, and he buried his head back in his arms. He shuddered again when Jacob smacked him firmly, and a little harder. The heat rushed through him, and he groaned, rolling his hips.

Jacob shifted behind him, and both his hands caught Kit by the hips, pulling him up onto his knees. Big hands, so broad his thumbs met over Kit's tailbone. He drew his thumbs up Kit's back, then dragged his hands down.

Each time he slid his hands up, they moved just enough, until Jacob's fingers raked over Kit's chest, teasing across his nipples, over his ribs, curving down Kit's belly to graze by his cock. He adjusted the pressure, changed from light to firm, and by the last stroke of his hands, he barely skimmed Kit's skin, leaving it thrumming in anticipation.

Kit couldn't help arching like a cat, sharp demanding sounds escaping him. His whole body tingled with sensations, and Jesus, his head was spinning with overstimulation.

As if reading his mind, Jacob smacked him suddenly on the other buttock, hard after light and teasing touches, and the delicious surprise of it made Kit yelp again, only made worse when Jacob cupped his arse with both hands and squeezed.

"Don't go anywhere."

Kit wanted to say that wasn't an option, but Christ, he couldn't even put the words together anymore. He pressed his mouth to his forearm, breath coming fast, and squeezed his eyes shut, dizzy and basking in it.

Somewhere by the bed, he heard the familiar sound of a wrapper opening.

Kit swallowed, his heart racing with anticipation.

The mattress shifted behind him when Jacob knelt on the bed. Another light smack followed, enough to warm, not enough to hurt, and then he nearly bolted forward in surprise when Jacob's tongue laved the offended skin.

"Christ!"

Jacob chuckled and blew a soft breath over the damp, tingling flesh. Kit bit his arm to stifle a whine, his hips jerking. Jesus, he wasn't going to beg, definitely and absolutely not. He shifted and pushed one hand beneath him, reaching for his cock.

"Ah, ah." Jacob caught his arm.

Kit kicked the sheets. "You bastard!" he moaned.

Jacob knelt up behind him, close enough for Kit to feel the warmth of his body, but not enough to bloody touch him. Fingertips ghosted the length of Kit's back, making him jerk and clutch at the bedding under him.

Suddenly, Jacob caught his hair, giving it a tug. Kit arched his neck and pushed his hips back demandingly. Only then did Jacob—bloody great bastard that he was—push forward and stroke his slick cock against Kit's arse.

Kit knocked his head on his clenched fists, hissing between his teeth as Jacob pushed into him, his thighs twitching with the effort of staying still. He had knots of the sheets bunched between his fingers and rucked up under his knees and toes as he panted and shivered.

"I know," Jacob said, his voice thicker. "It's not oral, but you going to complain?"

Kit rocked his head from side to side. No. Jesus no. "I'll cope," he gasped out.

It felt like a reward for giving the right answer when Jacob pulled out, then thrust hard enough to make his legs buckle. He pawed at the sheets and pushed his hips up in wordless encouragement. Jacob, thank God, took the hint.

No more light touches. No more teasing. Just one hand at his hip, another under his body, grasping his cock, and then Jacob started to move in earnest. Not fast. Not rough, but slow and, Christ, deep. Every stroke of his hand matched a stroke of his cock, and every bloody time Kit tried to up the pace, the hand on his hip held him still.

"My bed," Jacob reminded him hoarsely, and as he withdrew again, a sharp, reproving smack to Kit's arse made stars flare behind Kit's eyes. Kit dropped his head forward again. Christ.

He babbled helplessly, panting, and so bloody close when Jacob released his cock and stopped moving. Kit almost yowled in protest, but before he could, Jacob caught his hips and lifted him, angling him, and then thrust into him, and Jesus Christ! Right there! Kit gasped out a cry smothered in the pillows, and he came, his whole body shuddering with the force of it.

Jacob kept moving, his grip on Kit's hips so strong Kit would probably have bruises come morning. Kit felt only a little guilty about not moving more, but not his fault he'd gone all limp and boneless and good. Not like Jacob needed the help anyway. His pace quickened, each stroke sending fresh flickers of pleasure through Kit, and he hardly made a sound when he came, only a long, slow sigh, and then he went still.

As Jacob slipped himself free, he released Kit's hips. Kit heard the condom hit the bottom of the bin, and then Jacob brushed his fingers lightly down Kit's sides before smoothing Kit's sweat-damp hair off his face. "Okay?"

His cheek pressed to the sheets, Kit uncurled one fist to give a thumbs-up. "Mm."

Jacob stooped over him, hands depressing the mattress on either side of Kit's shoulders. "Mm?"

Kit peered up at him, warm and sated. "Thank you, sir, I'll take another to go."

Shaking with silent laughter, Jacob broke into that beautiful smile of his. "You're such a little tit."

With effort, Kit managed to roll over and lift one arm—Jesus, it felt like it weighed a bloody ton—to wrap it around Jacob's shoulders. "C'mere." He tugged Jacob over him and kissed him clumsily. "That," he declared, "was a good effort."

Jacob settled his body over Kit's, a warm weight, and he braced himself on his forearms, an amused look on his face. "A good effort? Is that all?"

Kit ran his fingers down the curve of Jacob's cheek and traced them along his full lower lip, admiring the pinkness of Jacob's tongue as it darted out to lick his fingertips. "Well, you know what they say about practice."

The furrow had reappeared between Jacob's brows as he tilted his head into Kit's palm. "You know this is probably a bad idea, don't you?" he murmured, his breath warm on Kit's wrist.

Kit shrugged as much as he could. "I can walk out that door tomorrow, and we avoid each other, if you like."

Jacob turned his head enough to kiss Kit's palm. "That's not going to happen."

Kit drew Jacob's face to his. "Good."

Dark eyes met his. "Is that so?"

Kit answered by pulling him in to kiss him again.

Chapter Twenty-Seven

The office was already buzzing when Jacob walked in the next morning, an hour late and armed with the feeble excuse that he'd slept in.

Temple raised her eyebrows and glanced at Anton, who gave Jacob the filthiest leer this side of a sexual harassment case. Knowing they weren't exactly wrong made it worse.

After they'd shagged, Kit had curled up against him, the skinny little spoon to Jacob's big spoon, and they'd both slept. Not a big surprise, given the exertion of the night, but quite a surprise in the morning when Jacob woke to his quill trilling.

The fact that he hadn't made it into the office at his usual time had worried everyone enough to call him to make sure he hadn't—as Anton put it—"fallen and broken your hip or something."

They hadn't had time for breakfast or even more than a handful of words. He'd scrubbed up quickly in the bathroom while Kit pulled on his clothes in the bedroom. Better that way. Less chance of Kit doing or saying something to catch his attention.

When Jacob came out, showered and changed, Kit popped out of the kitchen, toast in hand. He rushed over, grabbed Jacob by the tie, and pulled him into a breath-taking kiss that tasted of marmalade.

"Tonight?" His eyes were shining.

Despite himself, Jacob caught him by the hips and pulled him closer. "If you behave, and work isn't..."

"Arresting me?" Kit's lips pressed to his again. "Maybe, then?"

"Maybe," Jacob agreed and released his hips. "Now, piss off."

"That's all I'm getting?" Kit looked offended. He tilted his head, half closing his eyes and parting his lips. "Go on. You know you want to."

Jacob did, but once in a while, he had restraint. At least some. Instead of kissing Kit, he smacked his arse hard through his trousers. Kit's eyes flew wide open, and his freckled face flushed.

"Like I said." Jacob bit down on a grin. "If you behave."

He nodded toward the door and couldn't help noticing Kit's walk had turned a little stiffer as he headed for it. Jacob licked the marmalade off his lips and shook his head, knowing he was a royal tit but, for a moment, not giving a shit about it.

Having an indulgence didn't hurt anyone, and no one needed to know. Hell, outside of his flat, he couldn't even afford to let himself think about Kit, if he could help it.

Thankfully, the case had provided him plenty to do. The initial assessment of Sanders's lab by the CSU had come in, and there were signs of minor clean-up in the basement. Technicians were also working on the computers. Even if the additional hard drives were gone, there could be some kind of information left behind, but the encryptions on the machines were buggering everything up. Tisha insisted she could unlock them eventually, but it would take time.

He skimmed through the CSU images, frowning.

Every door they opened seemed to raise more questions than it answered.

An abduction made sense, with Sanders being an infamous technical genius. The fact that they'd stolen much of his material suggested he had something they wanted. Jacob wondered if they'd shorted the teleportation gate to try to stop him escaping, and killed him by accident.

Then they had to take into account the frail possibility that Sanders might be alive, either if his assailant had stopped him or if the teleporter worked. But from the look on Ashraf's face, she didn't believe it had. Kit's knowledge of the mechanics gave credence to his theory as well.

He rubbed his eyes.

The investigation had to take on board all the possibilities, but when the possibilities were piling up by the day, it was exhausting.

A coffee mug clinked down on the desk.

Jacob lowered his hand, relieved to see Temple. "Morning." He reached for the mug of thick, black coffee and clung to it as if it were a sugar-laced elixir of life.

"Just about." She tilted her head, looking at him. "Long night?"

He winced. "So you've been sent for details, eh?"

She lifted her shoulders. "The tech team are taking forever. Anton's bored. We need something to keep us occupied."

"Well, you can tell him my love life is off the table."

"So there *is* a love life, then?"

He glared at her half-heartedly. "I had a bloody long day yesterday, Temple. Last night wasn't much better. I can sleep in once in a blue moon."

Temple smiled. "You know we like to see you happy, sir."

"Laid and laid-back, you mean."

"Six of one," she shot back, grinning. "And given how grumpy you are this morning—"

"You don't want to finish that sentence." He took a mouthful of coffee. "Any updates I've missed?"

"Nothing yet. The man from the video is still proving as elusive as John Smith. The DNA searches are being reset again, to try a different combination. We've got nothing." She nodded to the desk. "Did you get the Nagy paperwork?"

He glanced at the envelope. He'd had a flick through the papers, and as far as he could see, it confirmed everything Nagy had said, even including an address for the family in Hungary. Everything written up all nice and neat, which—naturally—made him suspicious. Nothing about the TRI or Sanders was straightforward, but Nagy's story seemed too good to be true.

"Do you know anything about Hungary?"

Temple shook her head with a frown. "I went on a Danube cruise once. Nice goulash. Peppers everywhere. Why?"

"I'm wondering how prevalent hate crimes are there."

She shrugged. "Probably no worse or better than anywhere Catholic or Communist. That whole right-wing surge a couple of decades ago has left some nasty scars. I think they even fought with the Nazis or something back in the day? Part of the axle?"

"Axis." Jacob shook his head. "Never mind. I'm looking for trouble where there isn't any. This bloody case is messing with my head." He sighed. "Take Nagy off the board. He has no motive and has been the most helpful person we've spoken to."

"Apart from Rafferty." She sounded too thoughtful.

Jacob glanced at her. "What's going on in that brain?"

She tapped on the chair in front of her. "Rafferty. Any chance we could get more information out of him?"

"No."

"Boss, he got us the footage—"

"No." His tone was too sharp, and she would notice, being far too good at her job not to. Her eyebrows rose, and if he didn't give a reason, she would go looking for one. "He was the one who confirmed that Sanders is most likely dead. You saw him yesterday. Right now, I don't think he'd be any use to man nor beast."

"He knew how that gate in the basement worked."

"If it worked at all."

Temple shook her head. "It's important. You know it. I know it. Hell, even Anton's getting something out of it, and you know what he's like."

"I heard that!" Anton's voice drifted through from the other room.

"That doesn't mean we should interrogate him."

Temple stared at him. "That's exactly what it means! That gate could be the explanation for everything. That poor bugger in the fridge used one, and if Sanders has created a functioning teleportation device, what the hell is he doing working for a historical research club?"

"Rafferty and Ashraf both think it's a prototype teleportation device."

"That Rafferty happens to know how to dismantle? Which happens to be identical to the one Sanders's alleged attacker used?" Her lips thinned to a line. "He has to know more about what the gate does. You need to bring him in."

She was right, which made it all worse.

He tapped his fingers on the edge of the desk. "I'll head down to the TRI. See if I can get them in or at least try and get something out of them." He pushed himself up from the chair. "It's not the kind of thing you want to say in a call."

Temple watched him. "Want me to tag along?"

"I need you to keep on the technicians." Jacob demurred. "One of them is bound to find something, and I need you to let me know as soon as they do."

She straightened up. "Yes, sir."

Something in her tone made him glance at her as he pulled on his jacket. "You have something to say, Temple?"

"I'm wondering why we haven't got a warrant yet." She met his eyes. "They've admitted concealing data and evidence from us. Surely, that would be enough to get a warrant approved?"

He looked down at his buttons as he fastened them. "Get us the warrant, but give it twenty-four hours. I think they may be more cooperative now that they know what happened to their colleague." He hesitated, then looked back at her. "They were warned. This is their last chance to give us what we've asked for. If they don't, we go in with the warrant tomorrow."

"You think they will?"

Jacob shook his head. "I have no idea. I hope so, but..." He shook his head again. "I hope they'll see sense."

And I hope Kit understands why it has to be done.

Chapter Twenty-Eight

The mood at the TRI was unsurprisingly grim.

When Kit entered, Paulina rose from behind her desk and hugged him. News of Sanders's passing had probably been issued while he had been...well, technically in a mood, but justifiably so.

At least he hadn't been left alone with it.

There had been no more nightmares through the rest of the night. Boneless exhaustion helped, but he'd always found something comforting about having another person wrapped around him, keeping him warm and making him feel safe.

It wasn't until he'd left Jacob's flat that he remembered why he'd ended up there in the first place. His smile had faded by the time the taxi-pod dropped him at the TRI's front steps.

"Is Mariam in yet?" he asked.

Paulina shook her head. "She said she might not be. Ben."

Kit felt ill. Of course. Ben. Ben would have to be told. "Yeah."

"Janos is in though. He said you might want to see him."

Kit stared at her. He couldn't guess why Janos would think that when they weren't even that close. Hell, Kit happened to be one of the many people who had had a hand in bollocksing up Janos's life again. "Did he say where he'd be?"

"Conference room on ten."

Kit clung to the rail of the empty lift and stared at the ceiling as it whirred upward.

He'd need to apologise to Mariam for yelling at her. Technically, yes, he did have some justification, but it was a bloody childish way to react. She had every reason to think he might have blabbed. God only knew he couldn't keep his trap shut, but this was TRI business. She *had* to trust in his professionalism at least.

Said the man currently shagging their investigating officer.

He closed his eyes.

No.

He wasn't shagging the police officer. He was sleeping with the good-looking, kind man with the big knob and fantastic shoulders.

The lift chimed, and he reached out for the sensor. Stepping out into the hall, he saw a few familiar faces hurrying here and there, every one of them drawn and unhappy. No big surprise there. Sanders might have been a hard taskmaster, but he was *their* hard taskmaster.

He continued down the hall to the conference room and swiped his pass.

The door remained closed, the sensor showing red.

Kit frowned.

He hadn't thought the conference room even *had* a lock.

A moment later, the door opened from the inside. Janos looked out at him, then stepped aside, motioning for him to enter.

"What's going—" Kit's question died on his lips as he looked around the walls. Projections lit every one of them, and he recognised some of the images. He turned to stare at Janos, who looked back at him. "What did you do?"

"We need to find out what happened," Janos replied innocently. "The police would not tell us, so we had to find out."

Kit gawped at him. "Find out? Janos, these look like the police records!"

"Yes." Janos headed back to the table, the surface illuminated with floor plans and the layouts of Sanders's house.

"Yes, they look like...?" Kit trailed after him.

"Yes, they *are* the police records." Janos scattered a series of evidence shots and the photos of the whiteboard up onto the wall. "We need to know all of the parts of this."

"Okay, yeah, that, of course. Just steal the police files. Naturally..." Kit turned on the spot, staring around, then exploded, "Jesus Christ, Janos! What the hell? How the hell did you get a hold of the police files?" He pressed his hand to his forehead. "No. No, never mind. I don't... Do I want to know?"

Janos shrugged as if he hadn't broken a dozen laws. "When he interviewed me, he let me put my name into his computer."

"And that's how you did it? You hacked it?"

Janos raised his eyebrows. "Your brain has switched off, yes? No. I did not hack. I only have a few seconds to do this. I cloned the computer." He held up his false hand. "I put small machine inside my hand. People try not to stare at false hands. It took me time to get through firewalls, but they were not too difficult."

Kit sank into the nearest chair. "We're all going to jail; I hope you know that. I mean, lying to the police is bad enough, but stealing their information?" He pointed a shaking finger at Janos. "You don't get to lecture me about banging Jacob now."

Janos flashed a wry grin at him. "I would not lecture. I am in relationship with a man born one hundred years after me. How can I judge you?" He sat down at one of the other chairs. "I found the video file. Can you fix it now? Undo what you did?"

Kit hesitated. "I don't know. I can try."

Janos nodded in approval. "This is your job today. We do not have many people to do this. We do not want too many people getting worried." He glanced around the room, then scaled up one of the images, distorted but recognizable as a man's gaunt face. He had pale eyes, a crooked nose, a high round forehead, and receding hairline. A thin beard and moustache circled his mouth. "You recognise this man?"

Kit nodded. "He's the one in the video."

"I thought so," Janos said. "He is older than this John Smith. I would say sixties. Maybe seventies. With medical advance, it is difficult to tell now." He gazed at the image. "If you can work on video, find out what he says. This is most important now. If he is the one who sent this Smith, then we must know who he is."

Kit nodded. It made sense. Based on the estimated time of the technology in Smith's eye, his benefactor could be alive and accessible in the present. "Do we have any access to facial recognition software?" he asked, shedding his coat and picking up a slate.

"Your policeman is ahead of us there. They have run searches for him and for Smith. Neither of them have any trace."

"He must look very different," Kit mused, staring up at the face. "And Smith. Don't they have his DNA?"

"Now, yes, but not on any present records." Janos pulled up an image of the dead man, and Kit had to turn away, feeling nauseous. "They keep searching with different specifications."

"You know what they're doing now? I thought you said you'd cloned what he had?"

Janos waved a hand dismissively. "I check time frames for searches. They have been changing the parameters all the time. I think they will still be doing this."

"Do we have any ideas about him?"

"We know more than they do," Janos replied. "We know a parameter they will not search."

Kit looked up at the body. "We know he might not even be alive yet."

Janos nodded. "If they follow time-travel rules, a man should not go back into his own timeline."

"For people who came to the past to abduct someone? You really think they'll follow the rules?"

The other man sifted through some of the images. "This is the problem, yes." He got up from the table. "You must work in here today. The less people who know of this is better."

Kit, already opening the video files, glanced up. "How many people, exactly, know what you've done?"

Janos's expression turned opaque. "Two."

"Two apart from you?"

Janos shook his head. "Two."

Kit laid the slate on the table. "You didn't tell Dieter? Jesus."

"I tell no one else, because if no one else knows, then no one else can be in trouble."

"Apart from me." Kit sagged back in the seat. "This is what I get for lying to the police for you?"

"This is what you get when you know more than everyone else about everything," Janos countered. "Much of this, you already know, so if you are asked, you can say you saw it all in police station. If truth is revealed, I will be in trouble anyway. This way, at least someone in the TRI will know what has happened, but will not be compromised."

Kit stared at him. "You'd be locked up."

"If I am identified as man from the past," Janos said quietly, "Dieter is afraid I will be closed up like a specimen in a lab. I think he is not wrong." A brief, sad smile crossed his lips. "If it happens, then I want to make sure we find the ones who harmed Sanders. He saved my life with Dieter and Dr. Bellevue. I owe him for three years of good life I should not have had."

Kit's throat felt tight. "You don't need to risk your freedom on an off-chance."

"They cannot solve this," Janos said simply. "We may be able to."

"But still—"

Janos pushed his chair back and rose. "It is done now anyway." He nodded toward the slate. "You work here. I will lock the door now and change your security access, but now, I must go and speak to my team."

Before Kit could make any further protest, Janos strode toward the door and swiped his pass over it.

Kit stared at the door, then looked back at the slate Janos had left for him. He didn't know if he could undo what he had done, but Jacob's team would be working on it already, and if anyone had a chance of beating them to the punch, it could only be him.

He toed off his shoes, making himself comfortable. Decoding was a bastard at the best of times, but since he had scrambled the code, he'd only made it worse.

At some point, Janos returned with food, but Kit barely noticed. He might have eaten some of it as he worked. He was finally getting somewhere when one of the screens projected on the wall illuminated, and a data transfer window opened.

Kit blinked at it in incomprehension.

He touched his ear, triggering the earpiece, then routed the call to Janos's team, requesting his presence.

Janos showed up two minutes later. "You have done—" He burst out with a furious litany of Hungarian, bending over the desk, shutting down the screens and projections, until the room was darkened by their absence.

"What is it?" Kit asked, blinking away the afterimage of the blueprints.

Janos looked at him. "I left an automatic trigger for your policeman's slate."

His brain still sloshing with code, Kit blinked at him. "Eh?"

"It means that any time the original computer is in range of my hardware, it will update the copy." Janos seemed to realise his words weren't getting through. "It means your policeman is within a hundred meters of the building."

The conference room phone hub illuminated.

"No," Kit corrected, feeling light-headed. "He's in the building."

Chapter Twenty-Nine

Mrs. Ashraf was not available or even in the building, which shouldn't have been a surprise given the circumstances. Jacob sighed when the woman on the front desk apologised for the inconvenience, which meant he only had one other choice. Kit was going to kill him.

The woman put a call through and relayed Jacob's message, then informed him someone would come down to escort him, if he could have a seat in the waiting room.

Jacob sat in the same seat he'd occupied on his first visit, barely even two weeks earlier.

It felt like so much longer, but also like no time at all.

He sighed, resting the back of his head against the wall.

Whatever had started in this room when Kit stuck his head around the doorframe, it had turned into something a lot more complicated than he'd ever intended. He really didn't want to give a damn about a man several years younger than his son. He hadn't been looking for a relationship. Even a one-night stand was stupid. True, he'd had them before, but they really weren't his thing. And this? Now? This was something different.

It wasn't a relationship, really. Not yet. But it definitely had the potential to be something more than he'd first expected.

Down the hall, the lift doors opened and footsteps approached. They were too heavy to be Kit, who moved as light as a skinny cat. Jacob had already started to rise when Janos Nagy appeared in the doorway.

"Detective Ofori." He held out his hand.

Jacob shook it once. "Mr. Nagy. You're here to escort me?"

Nagy nodded, motioning for Jacob to follow him. "Since I know some of what is happening, it is better for me to do this. Especially after news from yesterday."

Jacob fell into step alongside him. "I'm sorry for your loss. Did you know Sanders well?"

"He gave me this job and opportunity," Nagy replied as they stepped into the lift. "He was a good man. This is not the end he deserved." He folded his arms casually, sitting against the rail, mirroring Jacob's stance. "Mariam is staying with Ben today. He needs her more than we do."

"Understandable," Jacob murmured, thinking of the poor, scared little kid. Ben had trusted him to find his father. He should have been there to tell him. He'd promised he would try to find him, and he had failed. He cleared his throat. "How's Rafferty? He was the one who confirmed what happened."

Nagy's expression showed nothing, but he inclined his head. "As good as can be expected." He stepped forward as the lift came to a stop and pressed his palm to the console. The door opened. "This way."

Jacob recognised the room before they entered: the conference room where Jacob had first met Nagy, but this time, Kit sat at the table, eating a sandwich. He hastily snatched up a napkin to wipe his mouth and nodded in greeting, but he looked like hell, nothing like the mischievous man who had run out of Jacob's flat that morning. His face was pale and his eyes bloodshot, a symptom Jacob recognised at once.

"Coding?" he guessed.

Kit nodded, swallowing the mouthful of food. "They didn't let me know to expect you." The accusation hung on every word.

With Nagy still standing there, Jacob couldn't say anything overt. "Unfortunately, we have questions we need answers to. Given everything that's happened, we were hoping Mrs. Ashraf or yourself might be willing to help us."

Kit methodically folded the napkin and laid it on the edge of his plate. "So it's to be an interrogation?" The sharpness to his voice said he was on edge already, and no wonder. No one liked to be surprised by a policeman, even if they were sleeping with him.

"It's a request for information," Jacob said quietly. "We need to know what we're dealing with, and why someone would be willing to kill Sanders."

Nagy went to stand by Kit's chair. "I think we must tell him," he murmured, and Kit looked up at him, clearly startled. Nagy pressed his hand to Kit's shoulder. "Tell him what Sanders was working on. Maybe this will help."

"You know Sanders wouldn't—"

Nagy lowered his voice. "Sanders is gone. His ideas can't hurt anyone anymore."

Pieces fitted into place.

"You're the one who decoded the whiteboard?" Jacob wondered why he hadn't realised before.

A muscle in Kit's cheek twitched. He turned from Nagy to him. "Mariam told you?"

"She mentioned it had been decoded, but she didn't say who'd done it." Jacob approached the table, sat down. "Look, I didn't want to be here. I didn't want to be asking these questions, but two men are dead, and we need to know why."

Kit stared blankly at him, then pushed his plate away. "Okay."

"Okay?" Jacob eyed them warily. He hadn't expected such immediate acquiescence.

Kit propped his forearms on the table, leaning forward. "Okay," he repeated. He looked like death warmed up. "I'll tell you about those whiteboards. You know he'd experimented in teleportation."

Jacob nodded. "We were told the tests were abandoned, because of the usual problems."

"They weren't as abandoned as he suggested." Kit turned his hands over, picking at his thumbnail. "He wanted to develop teleportation that moved people forward."

"Forward? Forward how?"

Blue eyes met his. "In time."

Jacob stared at him. "Time travel?"

Kit shrugged and looked back down at his hands. "Call it what you like. The problem with teleportation is the existence of matter being in two places at the same time, as well as the messy stuff. According to his theory, if you went through a gate and it took you forward a couple of seconds, there would be no overlap."

Jacob felt like he'd stumbled into the middle of a science fiction film. "Seriously? Time travel?"

"I'm telling you what was on the board. You wanted to know. I'm telling you."

"Would it..." Jacob shook his head. He could scarcely believe it, not when teleportation itself had proved impossible. "Could that even be possible?"

Kit laid his hands flat on the table, his jaw clenched, and pressed his fingertips against the tabletop, watching them whiten.

Jacob leaned forward. "Could it?"

Nagy pressed his hand to Kit's shoulder.

Kit curled his fingers into fists. "Based on the equations on the board, I don't think so." He took a slow breath and released it. "It's impossible to go forward, because until that moment happens, there is only the potentiality of the future."

Jacob frowned. "So what did the gate *do*?"

Kit shook his head. "He built it himself. It could do anything or nothing. We didn't know. Maybe he thought it worked. He was definitely desperate enough to try." He looked across the table at Jacob. "If we had the settings, I can bet you anything he wanted to get to Ben."

"So could it plausibly have worked to teleport him?"

Kit hesitated. "Maybe. Without all the schematics, I don't know."

"It is a big risk," Nagy said, "but he must have believed it was worth a try."

"To save his son?" Jacob nodded. "I can understand that."

"And he died because of it." Kit propped his elbows on the table and pressed his face into his hands, rubbing at his eyes. "I don't know what else you want me to tell you."

Nagy patted his shoulder. "I will fetch us tea. We need it."

Kit nodded into his hands, but as soon as the door closed, he looked up. "What the hell, Jacob?"

Jacob rose from his chair, circling around the table to sit closer to him. "I'm sorry, but I had to come. People were wondering why I wasn't asking questions."

Kit looked away from him. "I get it. I do. But you could have warned me."

Jacob touched his knee. "I didn't plan on bothering you. I hoped to speak to Mrs. Ashraf."

Kit's gaze drifted to Jacob's hand. "And yet, here you are, bothering me. Is this turnabout? I come to your work and now..." He covered Jacob's hand on his thigh, dragging it upward.

"Kit..." Jacob protested half-heartedly.

Kit reached out his other hand and caught Jacob's tie, hauling him closer. "I have had a shit morning," he said, his voice lower than usual. He searched Jacob's face, his breath warm on Jacob's lips. "I'm going to kiss you now."

"Does it help?"

Kit shrugged. "Can't make it worse," he said, and kissed him.

Jacob drew back. "Is this a distraction?"

Kit rose from his chair and pressed Jacob deeper into his. "Does it matter?" He straddled Jacob's thighs and yanked him in by his tie, claiming his mouth again.

Jacob let himself indulge for a moment, sliding his hands up Kit's thighs and squeezing his arse through his trousers. Kit made a low, appreciative sound, shifting closer on his lap, his hand still clenched in Jacob's tie, his tongue darting against Jacob's.

When Kit reached down between them, Jacob broke away from the kiss, but Kit's grip on his tie held him in place. Jacob swatted him sharply on the backside, shook his head, and Kit retreated at once.

"Not right now?" he guessed.

"Not when Nagy will be back any moment," Jacob replied.

Kit reluctantly braced his hand on Jacob's shoulders and pushed himself to his feet. Jacob's tie trailed between his fingers as he stepped away. "You might want to get back to your seat." He nodded downward. "You'll be able to hide that under the table."

Jacob's cheeks warmed. "You're an arsehole."

It was worth the risk to see the small, pleased smile light up Kit's face. "Sometimes," he agreed.

Chapter Thirty

All things considered, Jacob's unexpected visit didn't go as badly as they'd feared.

He went away with the answers he needed to the questions he'd asked and, quite possibly, a cock still coming down from half-mast. Janos saw him out, and as soon as he left, Kit collapsed in one of the chairs, hoping the tremors in his hands had gone unnoticed.

He was still slumped there when Janos returned.

"You did well."

Kit rolled his head to the side, wincing. He felt wrung out. "I told him time travel was possible. Mariam's going to kill me."

Janos waited until the door slid closed, then typed in a code to lock it. "You implied it might be," he corrected. "This is very different. He does not think it could happen, and there is no reason he would suspect the TRI is using it." One side of his mouth turned up. "Small truth, hiding the big truth."

Kit pushed himself back up in the seat and ran his hands over his face. "You said he was like a dog with a bone. It might be enough to make him wonder."

"Wonder what?" Janos returned to the table and sat down. He started opening up the new files, including the CSU report from Sanders's basement. "Everyone knows time travel is impossible. What could make him think this is the reason for the attack on Sanders?"

Kit pulled his slate toward him, to return to the task at hand. "I don't know."

"You let me worry about such things." Janos offered him a brief smile. "I am used to it." He nodded to Kit's slate. "You have had any luck?"

Kit rubbed at the middle of his forehead with his thumb. "I think I'm getting somewhere, but it's taking a while." He shook his head. "I need to try and remember where I'd reached before he got here."

Janos fell silent for several moments. "He had a blush when I came back, I think."

Kit peeped tentatively over the edge of his slate. Janos raised his eyebrows.

Kit ducked his head, his cheeks warming again.

To his mortification, Janos chuckled. "Ah. Not so parted as you thought?"

Kit glanced up warily. "Did Mariam tell you what happened when we got back yesterday?"

"Mm." Janos didn't look at him. "You were both upset. It does not go well."

"I was upset," Kit agreed quietly. "I asked Jacob if he'd done what she'd said."

"And you did not mind his answer?"

"He said it might have started out that way, but he..." Kit set his slate down, frowning at it. "He looked after me last night. I was in a mess, and he didn't leave me on my own with it. I wanted to be angry with him, but he...shit." He pressed the heels of his hands to his eyes. "He was kind. He didn't have to be. Why is he kind?"

"Because he is a good man," Janos murmured, all the teasing gone from his voice.

"Yeah." Kit couldn't deny it. "He is."

"And he is the man who knows if you have freckles on your ass."

Kit's hands dropped from his eyes. "You what?"

Janos sorted serenely through the files. "Oh, it is no matter. Only I have a wager with Dieter."

"Over my bum?"

Janos shrugged. "We all have questions that need answers."

Kit stared at him in disbelief until Janos slanted a look at him, and one side of his mouth tilted up.

Kit couldn't help releasing an explosive laugh. "Oh, you bastard! You're messing with me, aren't you?"

"Maybe a little," Janos admitted. "You look like you could use laughter."

Kit smiled. "I never realised you were such a sarcastic git."

Janos laughed, then put his finger to his lips. "Is secret."

Somehow, it broke the tension that had been weighing on Kit since he'd arrived. He picked up his slate again and took a deep breath in, then released it. "I won't tell anyone if you won't." He ran his fingers over the screen of the slate. "You mind if I get back to this?"

"Pretend I am not here," Janos replied. "We both have much to do."

Kit turned his focus back to the code. Remembering where he'd left off was the tricky part, but once he found his place and resumed the rhythm of the unscrambling, it became much easier, although not what anyone would consider "easy" by any stretch of the imagination.

His eyes and mouth were both dry when an unfamiliar voice echoed out from the slate.

"You did it?"

Kit stared at the screen. "I think so."

Janos came around the table to watch over his shoulder. "Play it."

It started at the same place as it had before: the owner of the eye walking into the makeshift temporal chamber. Something seemed off about that, but Kit couldn't put his finger on what.

"—hopefully within five miles. You know what you're looking for?"

Their John Smith spoke. "Yes, sir." He turned, glanced down at a hand held out to him.

"Good luck," the owner of the hand said.

John Smith nodded, turned, and the gate blazed to life.

"I stopped it here," Kit murmured as John Smith emerged from the gate. "Everything from here is new."

Smith turned, scanning the surroundings. They were in a field at the edge of a forest, lit by the early morning sun. The camera that served as his eye tracked the area, identifying structures, and a mapped outline appeared, showing the lay of the land. The man turned on the spot as the map pinpointed landmarks, then paused, zooming in on a faint glimpse of red showing between the trees.

"There. Less than three miles," he said and turned to his unknown companion, the missing attacker. And there she was.

"Freeze it," Janos said at once.

Kit nodded, capturing the image, and flicked it onto the wall projection. Brunette, Caucasian, around the same age as Smith, so that could make her anywhere from midtwenties to midthirties. The kind of person who would be an ideal TRI agent: someone who could blend in by virtue of being average.

"Okay."

Kit set the recording to play.

"If we're lucky, it should be too early for anyone to be around. The house should be empty anyway." John Smith turned around, and where there would normally be the trace outline of a gate, open fields spread as far as the eye could see. "We're on our own for now."

"You might want to..." He looked at his partner, who tapped beneath her eye. "It's glowing. It freaks me out when it does that."

John Smith laughed. He sounded so young. "Fine. We don't need the maps now anyway." He blinked, and the feed went blank.

Kit stared at the blank screen. "They thought the house would be empty. Do you think they meant to steal the data? Maybe Tom caught them in the act?"

Janos frowned at the image of the woman.

"Janos?"

"Maps."

"What?"

Janos reached down, dragged the video back several seconds, and hit Play again.

"We don't need the maps now anyway."

Kit shook his head in confusion. "I don't understand."

"The gate they came through closed behind them." Janos looked back up at the image of the woman on the wall. "They travel as a team. He carried the data for their mission in his head." He nodded at the picture of the woman. "She took the hard drives, but where did she go? He had the maps."

Kit's heart skipped a beat. "You mean she's still on the loose somewhere?"

"If she does not know where to go, then maybe, yes." He sank into a seat. "Your policeman, he could put her face into his computer and search for her in all the cameras in the city."

"But if we do that, we have to admit what you've done."

Janos nodded. "We can send anonymous tip for them. Say we saw this woman fleeing the scene."

"You think they'd believe that?"

Janos sighed. "You think we should take the honest choice?"

Kit looked back at the image of the woman. "If we can get an angle that looks like an image from someone's pod camera, it might work."

"I can create an e-mail account for this." Janos reached for one of the other slates. "Send it directly, with no name, through different IPs in different places. Too many for them to trace back to a source."

Kit glanced at him. "Think it'll work?"

"It is anonymous tip. They have to follow up." He rubbed his chin thoughtfully. "Kit, you will see DI Ofori again soon?"

Kit tried to ignore the way his heart did an embarrassing hop and skip at the thought. "I don't know. We had talked about it, but I don't know. Maybe it would be better if I don't for now." He frowned at the slate. "I don't like lying to him."

"But maybe he will suspect something is going on if you change your mind." Janos reached over and touched his wrist. "He is a good man, and we are helping him. Don't forget. We are helping as much as we can without compromising the TRI."

"Doesn't mean we're not lying to him."

"Keeping the whole truth from him," Janos corrected.

Kit rubbed at his forehead. "Same difference." He turned his attention back to the slate and flicked several more screen captures onto the wall. "Okay. What now?"

Janos dragged one of them down onto his screen. "You leave this to me."

"And what do I do now?"

Janos didn't look up from his screen. "Go. Find your policeman. Take what pleasure you can. Life is too short not to."

Kit hesitated. "I don't—"

"Kit," Janos interrupted quietly. "You like the man. He likes you. It may not last long. Enjoy it while you can." He looked up from his screen. "Trust me, you will regret it if you do not."

"What about you? Shouldn't you be with Dieter?"

Janos smiled. "Once I am done here, I am going back to him, and we will do things I will not discuss with you." He set down his slate and offered Kit his hand. "Good luck."

Kit stared at him as he shook his hand. "You're going to be fine."

Janos didn't meet his eyes. "I know. Now, go."

Chapter Thirty-One

Jacob was bloody tired.

His day had gone from all right first thing to downright ridiculous, and he couldn't help but feel like he was being slowly and steadily wound up.

It only got worse when he returned to the station.

As soon as he entered, Temple got to her feet. "Sir."

"We have something?"

"A few things, actually," she said, following him to his office. She held out a slate to him as he hung up his jacket. "The technicians were able to salvage some data from the computers in Sanders's basement..."

He looked around, startled, then snatched the slate. An unbroken stream of numbers covered the screen, but there didn't seem to be any pattern to them. He sank onto the edge of the desk, scrolling through them. "Do we have any idea what this is? Is it coded?"

"It could be, but I have a theory." She leaned alongside him and tapped the screen. Red lines broke some of the mess of numbers up into eight-digit clusters. The breaks were erratic, and he could see no pattern otherwise.

"Dates?" He frowned. Some of the numbers would have been centuries earlier. "Maybe he used it to research projects for his work?"

"It's only a vague theory now," she replied, "but we're looking into the code option as well. It could be a case that all the text was scrambled when the computers were smashed, but it's better than nothing."

"We'll see." Jacob rubbed his eyes tiredly.

"The TRI was that bad?"

Jacob grimaced. "If what they told me is to be believed, Sanders sounds like either a genius or a lunatic. I can't decide which." He rested his hands on the edge of the desk. "You said you had something else."

"Potentially." She hesitated. "We're double-checking it because it doesn't make any sense."

"How so?"

"We have a match on John Smith's DNA."

Jacob stared at her. "And you didn't think you should have let me know this as soon as you had an ID?"

Temple looked uncomfortable. "That's the problem, sir. The ID. It's impossible."

Jacob sighed impatiently. "The DNA matches?"

"It matches exactly."

"So what's the problem?"

"He's a fortnight old."

Jacob blinked slowly. It had been a long day already. "What?"

"We got a flag on the DNA after a call went out for blood donors for the baby. He has a rare blood type, and no familial donors."

"And you're sure it's a match? Not a system glitch? Or maybe a mismatched sample?" Temple gave him a look, and he held up a hand. "No, I know. You checked already. You sent someone to get a new sample for a comparison?"

She nodded. "I thought it would be better if we had it from the source in case of contamination when they registered it on the system. It'll be sent to the lab as soon as Singh gets back with it."

"Let me know as soon as it's in." He sat down and rubbed at his temples. The warning twinges of a headache of epic proportion were already there. "Did you manage to dig up those files on Sanders's thesis on teleportation?"

"On the incident board." She studied him. "Did they tell you what the gateway did, sir?"

"Apparently," he said, wondering how ridiculous he sounded, "Sanders thought the problem of teleporting could be resolved by sending people forward a couple of seconds in time."

Temple's mouth opened, then closed, her expression a picture. "He was trying to build a time machine?"

"So they say. But according to Rafferty, it wouldn't have worked."

Temple shook her head. "Well, no, because the future doesn't technically exist until it's the present, so you can't really go there until it's...well, there."

Jacob had to smile at that. "That's what Rafferty said."

She looked pleased. "Oh?"

"Mm." He closed his eyes, kneading at his temples. "Nice in theory, not possible in practice."

"It's a shame," she sighed as she headed back toward the door. "It would have explained a hell of a lot about this case, wouldn't it?"

Jacob's eyes flew open.

It would.

Maybe the machine wouldn't work for going forward, but maybe sometime in the future, it would work to go back to a time that had already happened.

He sat up in his chair, reached for his slate, and flicked through the most recent data. In addition to the DNA, Temple had also managed to get a hold of a copy of the baby's medical record. The parents must have been too exhausted and distracted to mind that the police were looking into their newborn.

The file already had a lot in it, despite the baby only being a fortnight old. Jacob scanned through the information, most of it about blood tests and transfusions.

His mother had gone into premature labour the same day Sanders disappeared. The baby had arrived seven weeks early and been in a critical condition since birth, requiring a full transfusion now. The notes showed that his parents and siblings had been checked for a match, but were unsuitable.

A couple of words leapt out at him, and Jacob looked them up, heart pounding. If he was right and not completely losing his marbles, he had proof of a scientific leap that no one believed possible.

Baby Robertson presented with a severe coloboma in his right eye and showed early symptoms of microphthalmia. Both conditions could potentially cause blindness, one due to damage to the retina and optic nerve, and the other due to an underdeveloped, undersized eyeball. Sometimes, the eyeball would even be removed and replaced with a synthetic.

He sat back in his seat, staring at the slate.

It had to be a coincidence.

It couldn't be the straw he was tentatively grasping.

He pulled up the images of the gate parts again: the fragments from Kit's flat, the image from the video, CSU photographs from Sanders's basement. John Smith—Baby Robertson, if his blood could be believed—had come through one of those gates.

He tapped open the file of Sanders's teleportation research to dig out any sign Sanders had moved into a far more advanced mode of transportation.

Halfway through the file, a thought crept up on him. The TRI verified historical events. They found information and evidence somehow overlooked by historians and scholars.

A quick search of the database brought up details of the Potiorek conspiracy.

The official report had been issued by a university somewhere down south, but it didn't mention anything about the TRI. There were hundreds of websites about it in dozens of languages, some supporting the theory, some denouncing it. A good number of them were querying the source of the new information.

Jacob frowned, staring at the screen, then pulled the TRI files up again. They had an extensive client list, but few mentions online. They weren't cited as sources or given credit for information. In a story as big as the Potiorek conspiracy, it could have had their name in lights and made them a fortune, but instead, they had stayed on the sidelines and out of sight.

That was...odd.

Unless...

Unless you were using time travel to find your evidence, and rather than letting people look too closely at what you were doing and how, you sat on your hands and kept your company quietly on the peripheries.

Jacob laid down his slate and dabbed at his eyelids with his fingertips.

It was insane.

Even if Sanders *had* been able to stabilise teleportation to the point of transporting people, how on earth did that transition into time travel?

The office door chimed a moment before sliding open.

Jacob looked up. "Yes, Anton?"

"Got something." Anton approached the desk. "This came into the digital helpline."

Jacob sighed, reaching out, and took Anton's slate. "You could have sent it to me."

Anton beamed at him. "Not this, boss. Good news needs a courier."

Jacob turned the slate around to see a photograph of a woman glancing over her shoulder, half turned away from the camera, and a message with a place, time, and date. No name. No details. "What am I looking at here?"

"The coordinates are from the road leading to Sanders's house."

Jacob raised his eyes to the man. "A witness?"

"Anonymous tip," Anton replied. "I've set one of the techs to find where it came from, but so far, they've tracked it through a public ISP, which means it'll be tricky to narrow down."

Jacob looked at the photograph. It might not be much use, given the angle of her face, but they had a glimpse of her clothing—high-collared shirt under a dark jacket—and her colouring, which was something.

"Interesting," Jacob murmured, studying her.

"Could be she was waiting for a lift," Anton said.

Jacob shook his head. "Look at her coat."

Anton took the slate back. "Looks fancy." His eyebrows rose. "Kind of like John Smith's."

Jacob rose, circling around the desk. "We may well have been given the face of our second assailant." He strode through to the incident room. All eyes turned to him at once. "Everyone, we have a lead." He nodded to Anton, who flicked the image onto the incident board, scaling it up. "We received an anonymous tip about this woman who was seen at the road leading to Sanders's house on the morning of the attack."

Foley peered up at the woman. "Is this a suspect?"

Jacob nodded. "Priority one is now locating this woman. Temple, I need you to put together a statement for the news. We need to find her and as soon as possible."

"How much information?"

He scratched at his beard. "Keep it simple. Looking for a witness. Basic description. We don't want to scare her off." He glanced at Anton. "You're good for putting her in the search filters to see if she's been picked up on CCTV?"

"On it." Anton headed for his desk. "You want the picture to be issued with the statement?"

Jacob hesitated. On one hand, getting her face out there could be as useful as the facial recognition software. On the other, if she knew the police were looking for her, she might well bolt.

"Yes," he decided. "We need to find her. If she panics and tries to run, that's when she's likely to make mistakes."

The office sprang to life around him.

A fresh lead could do that when it seemed like a case had gone cold.

He looked up at the image of the woman.

They had to find her, not least so he could know he wasn't going nuts and seeing science fiction where there should only be hard fact.

Chapter Thirty-Two

Despite Janos's advice, Kit hadn't contacted Jacob, as much as he wanted to.

It felt awful, lying to him when he came to the TRI. No, not lying. Janos was specific about that. But omitting the truth still counted. Kit hated keeping secrets from people he cared about. He'd avoided getting too attached to people ever since he started his job for that reason. It was bad enough not telling his mum.

He retreated to his flat and took refuge in the oversized kitchen. Sometimes building machines helped. Other times, nothing distracted him like trying to construct a meal from whatever he had left in his fridges and cupboards.

He'd calmed down a lot by the time he took the bubbling stew off the hob and shoved it into the oven, even though he had a sneaking suspicion it would taste like crap with the mix of stuff he'd thrown in. His culinary experiments tended to be potluck, sometimes awful, sometimes fantastic, but if all else failed, he had more takeaways at his fingertips than he really needed.

He'd started scrubbing down the surfaces when someone rang the door buzzer.

Kit frowned, picking up a cloth to dry his hands, and went to the security monitor.

His heart did a little flip.

Jacob stood there.

"Hey."

Jacob looked up at the camera. "Can I come up?"

A sensible man would have found some excuse. Kit prided himself on being smart, but he couldn't honestly admit to being sensible. He pressed the entry button and watched Jacob step through the door.

He had two minutes before the lift reached his floor. He'd timed it before.

He raced back across the living room, looking out for anything incriminating, then skidded across the floor into the bathroom, where he pulled a comb through the stress-tangled mess of his hair. Bloodshot eyes couldn't be neatened up so easily. A splash of cold water would have to be enough.

Jacob was waiting when he opened the door.

He looked as bad as Kit felt, one side of his mouth twisting up in a strained smile. "I'm sorry. I should have called ahead."

"It's okay." Kit reached out and caught his wrist, tugged him in. "You okay?"

Jacob laughed wearily. "I look that bad?" Kit frowned in confusion, and Jacob clarified, "You don't normally ask. I must look like shit."

"Yeah." Kit stepped closer and wrapped the other man in a hug. Jacob tensed in surprise, then lowered his head to bury his face against Kit's neck. Splaying his hands on Jacob's back, Kit rubbed them in comforting circles. "I think you need this."

"You have no idea," Jacob murmured.

After several minutes swaying together in silence, Jacob touched Kit's hip and drew back.

"Thank you."

Kit leaned closer and pressed a chaste kiss to his lips. "You helped me. It's only fair I help you when you need it."

Jacob searched his face. "I should go."

Kit should've let him, but if Jacob felt half as bad as he had the night before, no way could he let him walk out the door. "Not tonight," he said, catching Jacob's belt and swiping his other hand to lock the door behind him.

It seemed as if the cord holding Jacob tense snapped.

"No funny business," Kit offered, an echo of the man's words from the previous night.

Jacob tried to smile, the attempt much frailer than usual. He rubbed at his forehead. "I don't know about you, but it's been one hell of a day." He studied Kit, then frowned. "More coding after I left?"

"Yeah." Kit nodded toward the kitchen. "I have an experiment cooking. It'll take about an hour." He pulled Jacob a little closer, and even if there was no funny business, there were ways of being warm and comforted without it. He started working his way down Jacob's buttons. "But now, you're going to have a bath and relax."

Jacob's hands hung by his sides, and he watched Kit, unresisting. "You sure that's a good idea?"

Kit glanced up from the shirt with a tentative smile. "Have you seen my bath? Of course it's a good idea." He spread the shirt open and touched Jacob's chest. "I can even give you a back rub, like you did last night."

Their eyes met, and abruptly, Kit remembered what had followed.

"Still blushing?" Jacob lifted his hand to run his thumb along Kit's cheek. "Almost makes me think you're an innocent little thing."

Kit snorted. "Sod that." He leaned forward to kiss Jacob. "Bath. You look like you need to relax."

Jacob followed him through to the bathroom. He whistled in awe.

He'd seen it before, but Kit supposed Jacob hadn't really paid all that much attention to the tub in his haste to get dressed. Kit'd had it custom-made a foot longer than the average tub, and twice as wide, because whoever wanted to limit its function to bathing was sadly unimaginative.

"Is it big enough?"

Kit bent down to touch the taps, choosing the foam one as well as the hot water. "You know what they say about a man with a big bath tub."

"That his toes are as wrinkled as his balls?"

Kit shot a grin over his shoulder. "Something like that." He straightened up. "Have a soak. I'll go and see how badly I've destroyed three days' worth of food. Yell if you need anything."

He didn't hang around to see whether Jacob took his advice, but neither did he close the bathroom door.

The stew, on the whole, didn't look like it would kill anyone. A lick of the spoon even made him wonder if it might taste all right. He turned the heat down and left it simmering, then set to work on a salad of some kind, trying not to think about the naked and wet man currently in his bathroom.

He lasted another ten minutes.

Restraint could only go so far, and hell, it was his bathroom.

He padded back toward the doorway.

"Jacob?"

"Mm?"

"You need anything?"

The door muffled Jacob's voice. "I'm okay."

He sounded so tired, and Kit couldn't help poking his head through the doorway to make sure he had at least got as far as the tub. Jacob had, sitting upright in the steaming, foamy water, arms propped on his upraised knees, his head bowed forward and resting on them.

Kit hesitated, then approached the tub and knelt beside it. He saw Jacob tilt his head enough to glance at him from the corner of one eye, but pretended not to. Instead, he leaned over the edge of the tub and scooped up a handful of water to pour over Jacob's tense shoulders. Another followed, then another.

"You want me to rub your shoulders now?" What could have been flirtatious came out too quiet, too serious, and when Jacob nodded, Kit couldn't help feeling they were crossing another one of those invisible markers in their relationship.

He considered his options.

Stretching over the side of the tub was possible, but tricky.

Stripping off his own clothing and climbing into the tub to kneel behind Jacob made more sense. The water swirled around them, the foam deep enough to preserve what modesty they had left. Kit reached for a bar of soap and worked up a lather before pressing his hands to Jacob's shoulders.

Jacob didn't make a sound, not even when Kit kneaded the meat of his shoulders and worked down his back. He barely moved, his head resting on his forearms, his ribs rising and falling under Kit's hands.

"Did something happen?" Kit finally asked when his hands were beneath the water, working the last knots from Jacob's back. "I mean, I saw the picture on the news. The woman. Did you find her?"

Jacob shook his head without lifting it. "You know I can't talk about it."

Kit rested his hands at Jacob's waist and leaned closer, propping his chin on Jacob's shoulder. "You're thinking too much. Anything I can do to help?"

Jacob stayed silent for so long Kit wondered if he'd maybe drifted off, but then he tilted his head. "This case is driving me mad," he confided. "I have so many facts, but none of them make any sense."

Kit slid his hands back up to press against Jacob's back. "Don't all cases do that?"

He didn't expect Jacob to pull away, to turn and face him. "If I ask you something, no matter how insane it sounds, would you answer me?"

Kit's mouth went dry. "It depends on the question."

Jacob searched his face. "Did Sanders build a time gate?"

Christ, Kit wished he hadn't got into the tub. It would've been much easier to leg it if he weren't waist-deep in hot water, literally and metaphorically. Bugger, bugger, bugger.

"I told you earlier," he began, trying desperately to remember what he'd said back at the TRI. "I don't think it would be possible going—"

"No," Jacob interrupted. "Not going forward. Did he make a gateway that can go back?"

Kit's world contracted to a very tight circle, fixed around Jacob's face. The rest faded to black, and he groped for the edge of the bath. "Everyone knows time travel isn't possible." He managed to get the words out.

"Kit, I know what everyone knows. That's not what I asked. Did Sanders make a time gateway?" Jacob didn't sound angry or impatient. He sounded exhausted, and that made it so much worse. "Please, tell me if I'm barking up the wrong tree here, because if I am, if I'm thinking like this, if I'm cracking up..."

Despite the heat of the water, Kit felt icy cold. "I can't tell you," he whispered. "I can't."

Jacob closed his eyes, and Kit knew at once that he should have lied, should have said no. But he was such a crap liar, and if he had tried, if he had bluffed, Jacob would have seen right through him, and he would have felt even worse about lying to him again.

He groped for the edge of the bath. "I should go and check the food."

Jacob reached out and caught his wrist. "Kit."

Kit couldn't bring himself to look at him. "Yes?"

"Thank you."

Kit curled his fingers into a fist. His wrist tensed in the loop of Jacob's hand. "For what?" he asked, his voice unsteady.

"For not lying to me."

Kit turned his head, looked at the other man. He tried to smile, but it faltered. "I hate this," he confessed. "I hate all of this. I hate not being able to help you. I hate not knowing what's going on. I hate—I hate that we met this way."

Jacob's hand didn't loosen. Instead, he pulled Kit toward him gently. "But not that we met?"

Kit's eyes roved over him. "God, no. Never."

He didn't know which of them moved forward to close the gap between them. They met in the middle, water and foam swirling about their waists, and their lips met in a hungry, almost-violent kiss.

Chapter Thirty-Three

The blinds were open.

The elevation of Kit's flat meant the light from the city below didn't bother them, but the crescent of the moon shone bright in a cloudless sky. It cast a pale, silvery glow into the bedroom, and Jacob watched it slowly move across the sky.

He was exhausted, but also at the stage of being too tired to sleep.

Kit had all but confirmed that time travel was possible, leaving Jacob's mind reeling. No wonder Kit hadn't been able to say anything. If it came out that the TRI used time travel, that time travel even existed, the world would have to change.

Kit had a confidence to keep, and Jacob had been chipping away at it for days.

Beside him, Kit stirred, curled on his side, his head resting on Jacob's outstretched arm, his back against Jacob's side. He hadn't been asleep for some time. He reached out and touched Jacob's palm with his fingertip, tracing a circle on it.

They hadn't done anything.

Despite nearly flooding the bathroom when they'd embraced, it hadn't gone much beyond that. Jacob's brain had filled to overflowing, and even with a nimble hand touching him, he couldn't think about anything else, too distracted, too tired, too...too everything to be roused.

Kit hadn't been offended. In fact, he'd backed up first, teasing that age was clearly coming into play, and they could try again later. He'd hopped out the bath, dripping and pink, to fetch them both towels from the heated rack by the wall.

Jacob had watched him from the tub, wondering how on earth he could quantify their relationship. A good 60 percent had to be lust and horniness, maybe 15 of developing affection and concern, 10 for the thrill of taboo liaisons, another 10 for mutual loneliness, and the last 5—and decreasing by the encounter—of residual guilt.

He'd never been any good at one-night stands. He'd tried them, and it always came down to the other person to ensure it only stayed as a one-night thing. He liked being involved with people too much. He missed it.

And now, the wires of work and relationships had crossed again.

Just over two years ago, he'd got home to the house he shared with Rory, late. He hadn't realised how late. Much later, it dawned on him he'd spent their anniversary in the bloody morgue.

Rory never got angry, which made it so much worse. He just quietly made it clear he had been struggling for the last eighteen months of what Jacob still called a relationship. He was tired of coming second to the job, and tired of Jacob dismissing his concerns. Jacob had asked what he wanted. Rory, fighting back tears, had told him to pack his things.

Jacob hadn't argued, not when everything Rory had said was nothing but the painful truth.

He'd wanted to say that he worked for Luke, to put him through medical school, to make sure he didn't end up in debt for the rest of his life, but it was bullshit. The job had been his priority, right up until that moment, and he hadn't realised. More than seven years of being with Rory, and he hadn't noticed how much he'd neglected him.

So he didn't argue. He packed his things without protest. He stood helplessly, trying to work out if he could even kiss Rory goodbye. In the end, he hadn't. They hadn't seen each other again.

Work and love life. Love life and work.

He'd made the wrong choice then. He'd promised himself that next time, next time, he wouldn't let his work affect his relationship.

What a colossal arse-up he'd made of that.

Kit brought him back to the present, touching each of his fingertips in turn, then tracing down to his palm.

"Can't sleep?"

Jacob dragged his eyes from the moon, and instead watched the way the light played on Kit's hair, the wild dandelion-fluff of it sticking in all directions. "You either."

"Mm." Kit rubbed his cheek against Jacob's arm. The first hints of stubble scratched against Jacob's skin. "Trying to work out how much trouble we're in."

Jacob curled his fingers to catch Kit's. "I'll go out on a limb and say a lot."

Kit pressed a kiss to his arm. "Yup. That's what I thought." He sighed, and his ribs rose and fell. "You'll need to come into the TRI tomorrow. Mariam'll need to know that you know."

Jacob turned onto his side until his chest pressed against Kit's back, and he wrapped his other arm over Kit's waist. "You think she's likely to tell me anything now?" he asked doubtfully.

Kit fell silent for a moment. "If she doesn't, you could push anyway, couldn't you? Formal searches and all that crap." He drew up his hand and covered Jacob's wrist at his waist. "You need to come in. There are people you'll need to speak to. To explain things."

Jacob nodded, though he seriously doubted Ashraf would say anything. Even if she knew he suspected their true purpose, she seemed the type to let him think he was imagining it, rather than risk the privacy of her organization. How many years had they been hiding the true nature? Had it ever been a proper research foundation? Or had they already made their scientific leap all those years before, with the TRI's foundation?

"Tomorrow afternoon," he murmured. "I have a meeting in the morning. The DCIs want an update, since we didn't have a lead until today."

He could feel the way Kit tensed in his embrace. "What are you going to tell them?"

"What we know for certain." He laid his lips against Kit's freckled shoulder. "They don't need to know about my speculation. Yet."

Yet.

It had to be *yet*.

With a case this convoluted, he wouldn't be able to keep the secret indefinitely.

If the DNA checks confirmed that Baby Robertson was their John Smith again, if they found and questioned their missing woman, if Sanders's computer records were decoded, if any number of events happened, the TRI would have to be opened up to public scrutiny, and when that happened, there could be no hiding any of their secrets anymore.

Kit nestled against him. "That's all I need to know for now." He squeezed Jacob's wrist lightly. "You think you could sleep if I shut the curtain?"

"Could you?"

Kit shrugged. "I'm tired. We can live in hope."

Jacob stroked Kit's belly. "We can try, then." He kissed Kit's cheek lightly. "Curtain us."

Kit's smile stretched across his cheek, and a sweeping gesture from his hand sent the curtain skimming across in front of the broad windows. For a moment, it seemed like the room had been plunged into complete darkness, but little by little, Jacob's eyes adjusted.

"Better?"

Jacob nodded, laying his head down on the pillow. "Better."

He might have slept. Kit certainly did, limp with fatigue in Jacob's embrace, out like a light when Jacob drifted, and still that way when Jacob drifted to full awareness, his mind muzzy.

He squinted at the clock on the bedside cabinet. Seven. As bloody usual.

He eased off the bed as carefully as he could, trying not to disturb Kit. The younger man had looked worn out the night before, and if his eyes were any indication, he'd been coding extensively. Jacob remembered he'd said it led to headaches.

Better to let him rest while he got ready to head to work.

Ten minutes later, Jacob heard the shuffle of bare feet coming toward the door of the kitchen where he'd rustled up some eggs for a scramble.

Kit appeared in the doorway, rubbing one eye with a fist, dressed in an oversized, patched dressing gown, and his hair—always unruly—even wilder than ever. "You stayed for breakfast?" He sounded pleased.

"I think we're both going to need it," Jacob admitted, stirring the eggs. "You're okay with scrambled eggs with cheese?"

Kit padded over and slipped an arm around his waist. "I'm okay with anything." He propped his chin on Jacob's shoulder, nuzzling against his neck drowsily. "I like it when you make food. Means I don't have to."

"Lazy bugger." Jacob couldn't help smiling. "Can you get the toast? Or is that too much like hard work?"

Kit grumbled amiably and padded over to the toaster. As he stacked the pieces of toast carefully onto a plate, Jacob watched him from the corner of his eye. He couldn't put his finger on what had changed between them, but something had. A tension that had been there every time their paths crossed had vanished.

It probably came down to the fact that Kit's secret had been revealed, and they didn't have to circle around each other, avoiding it and trying to hide it. Kit always seemed like an open, honest kind of person. It must have been tearing him up, concealing anything.

Kit hardly said anything beyond sleepy mumbles until he'd scarfed down half of his food and drained a mug of coffee. "D'you get anymore sleep?"

"Not as much as I'd like," Jacob admitted as he skewered a piece of toast and stacked some more eggs on top of it. "You?"

"Enough." Kit shifted closer on the couch until his knee knocked against Jacob's. "Is it daft that I'm glad you stayed?"

Jacob glanced at him. "Yeah?"

Kit nodded. "I mean, I know when people find out what we've been doing, we're going to be up shit creek without a paddle, but I…it's better. I mean, now that you know stuff." He smiled tentatively. "Y'know what I mean?"

Jacob set his plate on his lap and gave Kit's knee a squeeze. "I do."

Kit returned his attention to his plate. "So what do we do?"

"We get on with things and hope my bosses don't find out about us." Jacob cast an apologetic look at Kit. "It's a massive breach of protocol. I don't know how far they could take it. If I'm lucky, they'll let me keep my badge."

He didn't want to imagine it going all the way or think about being stripped of his rank, and maybe even of his job and badge. It still weighed down on him, the ticking time bomb, and yet, for a smile like sunshine and a man who could make him laugh, he'd put it aside.

Maybe because he'd lost that chance before, out of his own stupidity.

Maybe because he was lonely.

Kit gazed at him. "You could be in real trouble? And you kept coming back? No offence, but are you stupid? I'm not worth that."

Jacob looked down at his plate. "I think I'd have to disagree with you there."

Kit fell silent, and then his plate clattered as he set it aside. He leaned closer and pressed a kiss to Jacob's cheek. "You," he said, his voice thick with emotion, "are a very silly old man." He laid his cheek on Jacob's shoulder. "Thank you."

Jacob prodded the last of his eggs around his plate. "You want these?"

Kit's smile was palpable through the sleeve of his shirt. "All right." He nuzzled Jacob's shoulder. "Daft old fart."

Chapter Thirty-Four

Dull grey fog wreathed the city.

Kit watched the world shuttling by from the window of the tram.

The last fortnight had been very odd already, but this morning was something special. When it all started, he hadn't expected more than one night of eager, hasty shagging. When it turned into something else, he was pleasantly surprised.

Somehow, he'd never really considered how seriously it could affect Jacob's position. Part of him had assumed Jacob would be sensible enough not to take anything too far, or do anything that would get himself in trouble. After all, he was a copper and a good one. Kit had assumed Jacob always told him not to bring up the police thing to keep work and sex separate.

Turned out he'd been very wrong about that.

Kit tore his attention from the window and looked at the quill in his hand.

He'd tried hunting down the disciplinary procedures for the police force, but there weren't any specific details about punishments. It varied on a case-by-case basis, depending on how close the police officer got to misconduct.

Shagging someone involved in the case, however, was marked down as very problematic.

Kit slid his quill into his jacket pocket and pushed himself upright as the tram came into his stop. He hadn't gone in expecting anything out of a fling with a bloody gorgeous older man, but he'd got it all the same, and he didn't know what to do with it.

The thing was…

Well, he'd avoided having anything more than casual flings because of the TRI, because it could be bloody difficult to try to keep a secret when you were in a relationship, especially when you spent five days a week surrounded by said secret.

He'd never considered what would happen if he ended up banging someone who knew the TRI's biggest secret. Admittedly because the rest of the TRI staff were generally too hetero, too taken, too female, too boring, or about as attractive as the back end of a bus. He'd never considered the possibility of an outsider knowing.

That meant his biggest concern wasn't relevant anymore.

Three years of brief flings and one-night stands, and now this?

He frowned as he made his way up the steps toward the building. He shouldn't be worrying about it when there were bigger things going on. The TRI wouldn't be able to keep their secret much longer. He should be worrying about that, but his brain kept on veering back to the potential relationship, which felt so much more significant.

A couple of the agents were waiting for the lift when he entered, so he ran to join them, settling in his usual corner. He would be expected in engineering, but Mariam needed to be warned.

To his surprise, when he stepped out of the lift, she was standing there waiting for him.

"Kit."

He gave her a cautious nod. "Mariam."

She waited until the lift doors closed and they were alone. "I wanted to apologise," she said quietly. "What I said the other day was out of line, and I'm sorry. I didn't really think you told DI Ofori anything. You've been much more discreet than some of our agents."

Kit looked self-consciously down at his satchel. "Yeah. About that." He hesitated, gazing back up at her. "He knows."

Mariam's face went waxy and unreadable. "Knows what, exactly?"

Kit licked his lips nervously. "Is Janos about? He'll help me explain."

She nodded, leading him to her office.

When they entered, Janos started to rise from the chair by the desk. "I told you I am in hurry. Why you are..." He stopped short at the sight of Kit. "Ah. Something tells me this is not a good time to be in here."

Mariam locked the door behind them. "Explain."

Kit didn't look at her. He looked at the man who had more to lose. "DI Ofori knows."

Janos stared at him and slowly sank back down into his seat.

"Knows what?" Mariam demanded again.

"What we do here," Janos said, his face bleaching of colour. "He came here with demands yesterday. We have to tell him something. So we tell him what Tom was doing—trying to go forward." He shook his head. "He is very clever man. He listens too well."

"He worked it out himself," Kit added quietly. "I don't know how."

Mariam reached out to steady herself on the desk. "He knows about the time travel?"

Kit nodded, swallowing around the lump in his throat. "He said he won't tell right away, but this isn't a secret he can keep. He's going to come here this afternoon. He wants to talk to you." He looked at Janos. "I think you should talk to him. I think you need to."

"We need to convince him that he got it wrong," Mariam began.

"No."

"Kit, you know why Sanders never went public with time travel," she protested. "It needs to be regulated. It needs to be controlled. The fewer people who know about it and use it, the better."

He looked at her in disbelief. "Tell that to the people who attacked Tom. He knew this day was coming. Don't tell me you haven't been thinking about it." He nodded to Janos. "I know he has, and Dieter." He snorted. "You just don't want it to be on your watch."

Mariam sat down stiffly. "I've been working with Tom on this project since he lost Olivia," she said, her voice low. "He only started the TRI to get him enough funds so he could try and find her. He never wanted it to go public."

"Olivia?" Kit looked between them.

"His wife," Mariam replied.

The world seemed to tilt under his feet. "You're telling us losing his wife was..." He felt sick. "Jesus Christ. He used his wife as a guinea pig?"

"She was never a guinea pig," Mariam said sharply. "They worked together. She chose to take the risk."

"Oh, that makes it so much better." Kit shook with anger. He'd worked with Sanders, one-to-one, for days, weeks, months, and he'd had no bloody clue about what had happened to the late Mrs. Sanders. Jesus Christ. So much for mutual respect and trust. "Loses his wife with his invention and then uses hundreds of people to get him money so he can find her and apologise."

"How else could he afford to keep looking?" Her voice rose in anger. "He failed at teleportation. This was the only thing he had. Do you think he should have left her? Or sold the rights to anyone? Do you think he should—"

Janos's false hand slammed down on the table like a pistol crack, making them both jump.

He was breathing hard, and his eyes were fixed on the ring on his right hand. He curled his fingers into a fist. "We are not going to fight," he snarled. "Maybe Sanders did not want public access, but he is *dead*. We are the ones left with this mess. We must make as much damage control as we can." He looked from one to the other. "You are understanding me?"

Kit nodded. He assumed Mariam did the same.

"So…" Mariam tapped her fingertips on the desk. "Janos, this is your life. What do you want to do with it?"

Janos slowly turned the ring on his finger with his thumb. He looked up at Kit. "He is giving us time to be honest. This is more than he should do."

"I think we need to tell him everything, except where you came from." Kit sat in the empty chair by the desk. "We can cover that, but he's figured out so much without any help from us. If we hold back, he'll come in all guns blazing. They need answers, and if he has to, he'll come in and take them." He glanced at Mariam. "He knows we've been screwing him around enough. We try and hide anything big now, and that's it—the straw that breaks the camel's back. We don't want him as an enemy. He will tear this place down, if we lie to him again."

"He is giving us an opportunity," Janos agreed. He lifted his right hand, pressing his lips to his knuckles, silent for a moment. He then lowered his hand. "We do not lie to him. Not at all. I will call Dieter. We will tell this policeman the truth."

"But, Jan—" Mariam began.

"No," he interrupted. "No. This policeman, he will not be fooled again. If we try to hide anything, he will know. He already sees that my papers were wrong. If he knows about TRI secrets, he will start to wonder if maybe papers are wrong for a reason. We need to tell him. Better to be on the good side, than on the bad side."

"He's not a bad person, Mariam," Kit said quietly. "He knows this is something big. He knows it's going to change everything. He's giving us a chance to do it on our terms, instead of dragging us into the spotlight, kicking and screaming."

Mariam removed her glasses and rubbed at her eyes. "Kit, you may be biased."

"Janos met him too," Kit replied, pushing down the annoyance at her words. Did she really believe him incapable of thinking when his knob was involved? Okay, maybe a little, but she didn't have to keep bringing it up.

"He is decent man," Janos confirmed. "He has been generous until now. We have done nothing to deserve generosity. You know he was good with Ben. That is not something you can pretend."

Mariam nodded reluctantly. "I just..." She sighed. "Tom set this place up. It's...I can't wrap my head around breaking the biggest rule we had." She ran a hand over her face. "We really don't have any choice anymore, do we?"

"Not if he's on the case," Kit murmured. "Janos has it right about him. He's like a dog with a bone. If he spots something is off, he'll keep on coming back to it until he figures it out. That's how he must have found out about Tom's basement. That's probably why he kept it a closed scene as long as he did. He pays a hell of a lot of attention, even if you don't think there's anything to see."

Mariam leaned back in her seat. "I suppose it's all down to how we do this, then." She glanced at Janos. "You're sure you want to tell him everything?"

Janos nodded, suddenly looking much older, and so pale. "I will call Dieter. We have spoken of this before. He will not be surprised." He rose from the chair. "I will go up to roof now. I would like some air."

Kit rose too. "D'you..." He hesitated. "Is there anything I can do? Do you want company?"

Janos straightened his shoulders and, without a word, walked toward the door, rigid as a soldier. A soldier about to go into battle knowing he might lose his life.

"What will they do with him?" Kit asked when the door closed.

"Who knows?" Mariam reached for her slate, her hand trembling. "At least it can't be as bad as the life he left behind. If he's very lucky, he might only be locked up."

That, Kit thought bleakly, wasn't much of a comfort.

Chapter Thirty-Five

Jacob's head buzzed.

The meeting with DCI Crawford had gone as well as expected. Or as badly.

Thankfully, Jacob had come in to a lead on the potential witness—or suspect—and that kept Crawford from tearing him a new one for the lack of progress. Like Temple, Crawford wanted to push harder at the TRI, and Jacob was only grateful he'd already made plans to go over there.

He returned to his office and slumped into his seat for five minutes' respite.

A mug of coffee sat on his desk, waiting.

No doubt the team had suspected how well it might go.

He pulled the mug toward him and retrieved his slate. He'd barely had a chance to skim over the details of the newest lead before he'd been called into Crawford's office.

Their missing woman had been sighted in the city, which meant she would start showing up on CCTV. Anton was already working on that angle. Foley and Singh had been dispatched to take statements from eyewitnesses.

Temple had taken charge of the other calls, the ones that were the most significant. She'd already scheduled a meeting with a Patrick Harper, the most promising of the callers, a businessman in the city. He claimed the woman had been in his offices.

That was the real reason for the coffee. He had the meeting in half an hour, and he needed to be sharp to catch any little detail Harper might give them. Jacob picked up the mug, gulped down the coffee, and read through the information they had on Harper.

As far as the records showed, he was a shipping magnate who'd made his fortune transporting goods internationally. He'd started young and now, in his early forties, was considered one of the key players in the shipping industry. Not exactly the kind of man who'd be interested in historical research or time travel.

Still, the woman must have gone to him for a reason.

Temple accompanied him to the man's office, a second pair of ears. They were greeted by his secretary, who took them up to Harper's office on the top level of the building, a grandiose and over-the-top affair, with expensive furnishings and artistically placed photographs.

Patrick Harper sat behind a wooden desk, which somehow dwarfed his bulk. He'd clearly enjoyed the spoils of his success, judging by his tailored suit and his girth. Everything about the man seemed large: his waistline, his broad hands, his wide shoulders. Only his features looked too small for him, close together beneath a high, round forehead, as if they'd been designed for a much slighter man.

He rose, walking with that careful gait Jacob had seen in many large people, and held out a pink hand to Jacob. "Detectives."

"Mr. Harper," Jacob said. "We've come to ask you some questions about the woman from the news bulletin."

Harper returned to his seat, subsiding into the chair. "Ah. Yes." He motioned for them to sit and nodded. "I barely spoke to her myself." He poured himself a glass of water.

Taking a moment to decide how to proceed, Jacob thought.

"My people said she insisted on delivering a package to me personally. Security were...wary, but agreed to let her in." He shrugged those wide shoulders. "She came in. Saw me. Said she had made a mistake."

"A mistake?" Temple frowned. "What kind of mistake?"

Harper spread his hands. "That, I can't tell you. She left as soon as she realised. One of my receptionists recognised her on the news and thought we ought to call in."

"Did she tell you what she had to deliver?" Jacob asked.

Harper shook his head. "She told reception it came from someone called Sanders, but I don't know anyone by that name." He tilted his head, watching them thoughtfully. "Isn't that the man who disappeared a few weeks ago?"

"Yes," Jacob replied.

"And this woman was involved?"

"That's what we're presently trying to ascertain." Jacob leaned forward in the seat. "Mr. Harper, I expect you have top-of-the-line security equipment in this building? Cameras? Even a few microphones in public areas?"

The man's pale eyes glinted. Something about them caught Jacob's attention, something familiar that he couldn't place. "If you're after my footage, Detective," Harper said, bringing him back to reality, "we've already got it downloaded for your attention."

"And your other members of staff who encountered the woman," Temple put in. "We would need to speak to them as well, in case she provided any other information."

"Of course, of course." Harper motioned for the secretary to come in. "Marco will take you to one of the meeting rooms and arrange for the relevant people to be brought along." He frowned. "It won't take all day, will it? I have a business to run after all."

"We'll keep it as short as possible," Jacob promised.

It would have been quicker and easier if they'd left with the security footage. They learned next to nothing from the staff. Sometimes, it irritated Jacob how little attention people paid to their surroundings. They didn't notice much, though they were fairly sure she couldn't be someone local. Her accent sounded more southern, definitely the home counties. Not much to go on, especially when she hadn't given a name, but better than nothing.

"Maybe the footage will have something more," Temple said as they made their way to the pod outside.

"I doubt it," Jacob murmured, glancing back at the building.

Temple darted a look at him but kept quiet until they were back in the pod and the doors were closed. "You think he was lying?"

"I think there's something he didn't bother telling us, even if most of it was probably true. I get the feeling there's more to her seeing him."

Temple pinched the bridge of her nose. "Just once, I would really, really like it if we could deal with people who weren't unfamiliar with the concept of complete disclosure."

Jacob smiled. "If everyone was honest, we would be out of a job pretty quickly." He opened up the files on his slate, dispatching them ahead to Anton back at the station. "I'll leave you guys to go through them. Maybe have Anton skim through Harper's records. He has a good eye for anomalies." He shut down his slate. "I have an appointment at the TRI. Again."

"You really think they'll say anything new, sir?"

Jacob considered his conversation with Kit the night before. "This time? They have to."

Temple sighed. "I hope you're right."

He dropped her at the station before inputting the TRI address into the pod nav. He sent a message to Kit to warn him of his arrival, then leaned back in the seat.

The case was a mess of loose ends. If he'd guessed right—and the TRI wasn't bullshitting him—Sanders's attackers came from the future. If so, the missing woman was either from the future as well, or an innocent witness. But innocent witnesses didn't tend to carry packages from missing men who were presumed dead.

He closed his eyes, wishing he could stave off the impending headache.

The ride to the TRI didn't take long, but offered a brief respite for him to push down the fatigue and look as professional as he could when he walked into the building. His shirt and suit were rumpled from too many hours in the office, as tired and creased as he felt himself.

Kit met him in the lobby. A brief, tight flick of a smile crossed his face.

"Hey."

"Mr. Rafferty."

Kit held out an ID pass to him. "Mariam is waiting for us upstairs."

Jacob let his fingertips brush against Kit's. Whatever they were going to tell him, it was the line in the sand. Either they were honest and they moved forward, or they would lie again, and he'd have no choice but to bring in warrants and tear the place open by force.

He and Kit didn't speak as the lift ascended. Jacob didn't know what he could say, and Kit spent the whole ride staring up at the tiles on the ceiling, as if it would stop him thinking about the drop below them.

"Kit."

Kit pulled his eyes down. "Mm?"

Jacob straightened up from the wall. "Whatever happens, this isn't personal."

Kit almost managed a convincing smile, then skimmed his hand over the scanner. He led Jacob along the hall, but instead of going to Ashraf's office, they headed to the conference room once more.

"Why here?"

"They'll explain," Kit said and opened the doors.

Ashraf was sitting at the table and rose as they entered. She wasn't alone. Nagy sat there, too, and another man Jacob didn't know, slender with bleached hair, bloodshot eyes, and a guarded look on his face. He had to be around the same age as Nagy.

Behind Jacob, the door slid closed.

"DI Ofori." Ashraf motioned to the table and the vacant seat opposite the two men. "Please, take a seat. You know Janos Nagy. This is Dieter Schmidt." The blond nodded. "They both need to be here for this."

Kit remained by the door, arms folded and staring at his shoes.

Jacob sat down. "You have something you need to tell me."

Ashraf looked at Nagy, who nodded and glanced at the man on his right, who took a shaking breath. Schmidt's lips were trembling.

"Just fucking tell him already," he whispered.

Nagy's right hand moved under the table, and from the way Schmidt's arm matched the motion, they had reached for each other's hands. "Kit says you know what the TRI does."

"I believe Sanders successfully created a way of moving backwards in time," Jacob said, getting it out before he could change his mind. "I believe this is how you do your research. I believe the people who attacked him used a similar system to come back from a point further in the future. And I believe you have suspected this all along, and have kept it from us to protect your agency from public scrutiny."

Ashraf closed her eyes, a muscle in her cheek twitching.

Nagy's expression remained placid and unreadable. "You are correct."

Jacob breathed out as steadily as he could. Christ. It was true. He'd half wondered if he'd lost the plot, but no. They confirmed it. They were serious. It was all true, and time travel was real.

Nagy tapped his false fingertips on the tabletop. "Only employees of the TRI know about the technology. How did you come to this conclusion?"

"I ask the questions." Jacob propped his elbows on the arms of the chair. "How long has this been going on?"

"Around seven years," Ashraf replied. She didn't look at him. "Sanders worked on teleportation for years before that, and it led to temporal experiments. He never explained how he made the leap. He...kept a lot to himself."

"So, you've been time traveling for seven years?" It felt strange to say it. "This incredible leap in technology, and Sanders kept it restricted to your select group to make a quick profit?"

"He had his reasons," Ashraf said evasively.

"His wife." Kit spoke quietly from behind him. "He lost his wife. He needed the money so he could afford to keep developing his tech to try to find her."

An unpleasant chill ran down Jacob's spine, and he looked over at Ashraf. "Lost while traveling. That's what you said."

She met his eyes. "I didn't specify what kind of traveling."

Shit.

He looked at Nagy. "And what's your part in all this? Are you some kind of computer genius? Is that why he brought you in without papers or genuine documents?"

Nagy met his eyes. "You solved the TRI mystery, Detective Inspector. You know what I told you. My mystery is much simpler. Think for a moment."

Jacob frowned. Yeah, Nagy had come to the country on false papers, and had never come through border control at any of the sites around the country. He hadn't even had paperwork until three years ago, when he just...

The thought hit him like a hammer.

He stared at Nagy, open-mouthed. "When?" he asked hoarsely. "When are you from?"

Schmidt made a small, shrill sound of distress. Nagy turned to him and murmured something in what had to be Hungarian. He slipped his hand free of Schmidt's and put his arm around Schmidt's shoulder.

When he returned his attention to Jacob, he looked older, tired. He touched the sensors on the tabletop with his false hand, and the walls around them illuminated with images, security feeds and footage: a filthy man—bleeding and armed—stumbling through a doorway of light into a room that resembled an industrial tank.

Jacob watched in silence as a man—Schmidt—entered and managed, despite the gun to his head, to calm the furious Nagy. Another frame: a woman joined them in another chamber, uncovering Nagy's wounds, the mutilated limb, the ragged knife wound in his side.

Beside Nagy, Schmidt had his eyes closed, his face white as a sheet.

Bad memories, Jacob guessed.

"I was a soldier in the Second World War," Nagy said quietly. "All of my story is true. The only part I did not tell you was when I came from. It was an accident. I saw the gateway, when the TRI were on a mission. I was dying." He swallowed hard. "They hunted me, my comrades. They would have killed me. I came here. I was saved."

"Why kill you?" Jacob asked, though he could already guess the answer.

Nagy looked at Schmidt, who had silent tears rolling down his face. "Because I looked at men." He looked back at Jacob. "Because I loved a man." He took a steadying breath. "I tell you this now so you understand why Mariam and Kit have lied. They did not lie to stop you. They lied to protect me."

Jacob nodded slowly.

If they put the TRI under public scrutiny, and the world found out that some soldier from World War II existed in the modern world, he would become a living museum artefact. He would be dragged into the spotlight and displayed, forced to relive horrific events from his past. For a man condemned for his sexuality, he would become a symbol for people, a token icon. He would be an exhibit, and that would be his life.

No wonder Ashraf and Kit had tried to keep it—and him—under wraps.

"You know your operations can't remain secret anymore," Jacob said finally. "If there are people using time travel to commit crimes from the future, we need to bring this to public knowledge now. It needs to be controlled, regulated, managed."

Nagy nodded stiffly. "Mariam is preparing a statement. We know this must happen now."

Schmidt leaned into Nagy, trembling and breathing hard, his face wet. "We can go somewhere else," he whispered. "Fuck it all. Let's go and find an island somewhere, get out of the way, go where no one will ever know who we are. Let them deal with this."

Nagy pressed his cheek to the man's hair. "You know we cannot. I cause these problems for everyone. I cannot leave people with my mess."

Schmidt said something in Hungarian, short and shaking, and Nagy gathered him in his arms, murmuring comfortingly to him.

Jacob ran a hand over his mouth, watching them. There could be no mistaking the genuine emotion between the two men, and he remembered all Nagy had told him, about his better life, about what he had left behind. No man deserved to have years of abuse and violence dragged back up.

He glanced back at Kit. He looked unhappy, his lips pressed together in a tight line. He didn't meet Jacob's eyes. No wonder. This was what he'd really been hiding. Schmidt and Nagy had ended up together, despite war and violence and being born a century apart. It would be brutal to knowingly separate them.

"Ashraf." Jacob turned to the woman. "You control all the files here?"

She nodded tersely. "We have a lot of paper and digital records."

"What about his records? Reports into his arrival?"

Ashraf thought for a moment. "Most of the details of his arrival were restricted to a couple of machines. There were a few paper files, but the rest of it, you've seen—his documents, his medical records, all that stuff."

Jacob nodded, his heart pounding, and Jesus, if anyone from the force found out what he'd done, it wouldn't just be career suicide. He'd most likely end up behind bars. He didn't dare glance at Kit. They'd only started out. If he ended up locked up, they hadn't really had time to get attached yet. Nagy and Schmidt, on the other hand...

"Destroy it," he said. "All the digital data. Anything that shows his arrival. Anything that might make people question his origins and compromise his current identity. Get all digital copies and wipe them, then smash the hard drives."

"What?" Nagy's voice hitched.

"Everything on the records you provided checks out. As far as anyone knows, you're an upstanding modern citizen. I don't see why you should be punished for something out of your control, not knowing what would happen."

Nagy's eyes were wide, and he pressed his hand, shaking, to his lips.

"You're serious?" Schmidt's voice broke. "You're not fucking with us?"

Jacob nodded. "Full disclosure on everything else. That's the condition. You give us everything else. No lies. No cover-ups. As far as anyone will know, Janos Nagy came here three years ago from Hungary. No one needs to know anything more about him."

Schmidt started laughing, wrapping his arms around Nagy.

Nagy didn't move, tears spilling down his cheeks, his false fingers crushed to his lips, bleaching them white. Shock, Jacob guessed. Relief too. Having his life handed back to him.

"Thank you," Schmidt said, running his fingers through Nagy's hair and hugging him tightly. He was crying too. *Thank you.*

Chapter Thirty-Six

Jacob and Mariam had left the conference room to go to Mariam's office.

Mariam suggested it to give Janos and Dieter a little time, and Kit dithered in the doorway, unsure where to go. He wouldn't be any use to Mariam or Jacob. But then, he didn't know what he could do for Janos and Dieter, and if he went anywhere else in the building, people would grill him about what had happened.

He glanced at Jacob, who didn't meet his eyes.

Not Mariam's office, then.

That left lurking around in the conference room and trying not to be a creepy, overemotional bastard.

His eyes were still wet, and he didn't have any right to that. It wasn't his life that had been on the line. Of all the people in the room, he had the least claim to relief, but he couldn't help feeling it.

He'd wanted to run to Jacob and hug him in gratitude. He wanted to kiss the man senseless for such a kindness. He wanted to do a hundred and one things that would probably get him fired if he did them at work.

And then he remembered that Jacob had ordered them to destroy evidence.

A lead weight seemed to settle in his belly.

No wonder Jacob hadn't looked at him when he left the room.

Janos had barely moved since Jacob had given Mariam the order, and Dieter had wrapped around him, holding him tightly.

Their whole morning had been spent together in the belief it was the last chance they'd have. Kit had been the one to fetch them down from the roof, and he'd found them sitting in the garden there, not even speaking, holding each other's hands.

Silently, Kit went across the room to the drinks machine and filled two cups with tea, adding milk and sugar to both of them. First aid training, many moons ago, told him warmth and sugar helped people in shock, and from the look on Janos's face, he needed it.

He carried the tea over to the table, setting it in front of them.

Dieter's smile lit up his face. For the first time, he'd come in without makeup, and despite the lack, and the sleep-shadowed bloodshot eyes, his happiness made him radiant. "Thanks."

Kit shrugged with a small smile. "Seems like he could use it."

Dieter nodded, leaning closer to nuzzle Janos's cheek. He murmured something in Hungarian, then kissed Janos's cheekbone. Janos only blinked, sending fresh tears rolling down his cheeks.

"Is he going to be okay?" Kit asked.

Dieter nodded, picked up one of the cups, and pressed it into Janos's trembling hand. "We are."

"Why did he do that?" Janos burst out. His voice sounded different, thickened with emotion. "He had no reason."

Dieter shook his head. "I don't know." He looked to Kit. "Why?"

Kit wrapped his arms around his middle. He could say simple compassion from a good man, but it was so much more than that, and he didn't—couldn't—understand why Jacob would make such a sacrifice for people he barely knew.

His cheeks felt wet again, and he could only shake his head.

Janos, who'd been staring blindly at the spot where Jacob had sat, turned to Kit. "He is a good man. Don't let him go."

Kit's lips trembled.

If Jacob were found out, he wouldn't get a choice about that, even if...

No. No *if*.

He wanted Jacob. He liked him. He liked him a lot, too much. Christ, if Jacob were taken away now, when they were making a start of it, what the hell was he meant to do?

Janos murmured to Dieter, who immediately scrambled up and came around to Kit. To his utter astonishment, he yanked Kit into a hug. Kit recoiled in shock. Dieter didn't strike him as the kind of person to hug anyone, but here he was, and Kit's arms moved of their own volition. He clung to Dieter.

"He's a cunning fucker, that policeman," Dieter murmured, rubbing between his shoulders. "Don't you worry. He'll be fine."

Kit stepped back, scrubbing at his cheeks with a fist. "Sorry. I'm sorry. I'm pooping on your party."

Janos rose from his seat, reached out, and pulled Kit toward him. He hugged him warmly. "You have reasons," he murmured against Kit's hair.

He stepped back, clapping his hand to Kit's shoulder. "We should go downstairs. Dieter has not eaten all day."

"You either," Dieter snorted. He studied Kit. "You're coming with us."

"Jacob..."

"Will be arguing semantics with Mariam for hours," Dieter said.

"People'll ask us what happened," Kit protested weakly.

Janos shook his head. "Not if you are with us. They know better. Come. You should not be alone now. Trust me with this."

He couldn't really protest, and to his surprise, they were right. People who saw them in the corridors stared curiously, but no one said a word. Even when they got to the canteen, he could tell people wanted to ask them questions, but no one did.

"You are hungry?" Janos asked. He had his hand back on Kit's shoulder, a solid support.

Kit shrugged. "Don't know."

"We will get food. If you are hungry, you can eat it."

Kit glanced at Dieter, who smiled his perfect white smile. "Is he like this a lot?"

"You have no idea," Dieter admitted. "I swear to God if I ate everything he put in front of me when he thought I was upset or worried, I'd be the size of a fucking house."

"He exaggerates," Janos said, propping a tray against one hip and arranging three plates on it, which he started filling from the buffet selection. "Anyway, you like food. We have seen you eat your own weight in bacon."

That made Kit smile briefly. "I do like bacon."

Janos nodded at once, searching the counters. "Do you want bacon? They must have some for the breakfasts. I will go..." He set the tray on the counter and looked around for one of the kitchen staff, a determined look in his eye.

Kit yelped, reaching out and grabbing his arm. "You don't have to! This stuff is all fine!"

"If you are sure?"

Kit nodded emphatically. "Really. I'm sure."

In the end, he managed to persuade Janos that one plate of food would be more than enough for him, while Dieter stood by, looking on with indulgent amusement. It must be rare, Kit supposed, that Janos's attentions were on someone else.

He ate in silence while Janos and Dieter spoke to each other, switching between English and Hungarian. Kit wasn't really listening, but from the rapid, excitable tone of their voices, he could tell they were happy, and that was good.

He wished he could be as happy and relieved as they were.

"You are done?"

Kit looked up from the plate. He'd eaten half of the food mountain and pushed the rest around with his fork. No appetite, which wasn't normal. But then, his almost-boyfriend committing a crime to save two of his not-quite-friends didn't class as a part of his everyday routine.

"I s'pose." He glanced toward the door, frowning.

"You can go up if you want," Dieter said, "but you know how much they're going to need to let out to the world. It's better not to get in the way."

Kit nodded. "What are we meant to do now?"

Janos shrugged helplessly. "I did not think I would be free from today. I had no plans."

"Fucking." Dieter took a spoon out of his mouth to speak. "Fucking everywhere."

Janos's face lit up in a grin. "Yes. That is a plan."

Dieter's eyebrows lifted a little. "Fucking here?" he inquired optimistically.

A thoughtful look crossed Janos's face. "Like old times..."

Kit held up his hands. "Too much information, guys." He shoved his chair back. "I'm going to go and wait upstairs. You go and do...whatever you want to go and do."

Janos rose so quickly his chair fell over, and Dieter scrambled up right behind him.

"If anyone asks," Dieter called over his shoulder, "we're working. Hard."

Janos's laughter rang back.

Kit watched them go, then plodded out to the corridor.

He couldn't make any sense of Jacob's actions.

No one could be that good or generous without a reason.

He headed up the stairs toward the conference room. His stomach churned, and he was bloody tired. It had been a long day of trying to get things organised, watching Janos getting increasingly pale and drawn, and wondering if he'd end up hating Jacob for doing what he had to do.

How wrong he had been.

The room seemed much bigger now that it was empty and silent.

Kit sat down, folding his arms on the table and propping his chin on them. He wanted to do something, but his mind felt so scattered anything he tried to do would end up wrong.

Soon, the TRI would be unveiled to the world, and people would be asking questions and poking at the agency, and if Mariam couldn't find some way to keep it controlled, it might even get shut down. Unlikely, but possible.

Hell, even if it didn't get shut down, everyone in the TRI would know he was one of the people who'd given it away, and that would go down like a lead balloon. He might get driven out by the people he'd considered colleagues.

He buried his face in his arms.

It would be a bloody great joke if he ended up losing a lover and a job all because he was too bloody honest.

Chapter Thirty-Seven

Jacob prayed he didn't look as wrung out as he felt.

For three hours, he and Ashraf had gone over the options. They had to go public and show the links to the case, but without confirming they suspected the involvement of a time traveller.

She had unsurprising concerns about how the TRI operatives would be perceived when the news broke. People would be furious that such an advance in technology had been hoarded by such a small group.

Unfortunately, they both agreed the easiest solution would be laying accountability at Sanders's door. He had created the technology and restricted its use, but Ashraf said it felt unfair to blame the man when he couldn't defend himself.

"If you make it clear it was for his wife," Jacob suggested.

She shook her head. "They'll think he used her as his guinea pig."

Privately, Jacob wondered if that wasn't exactly what Sanders had done. Just because the woman had agreed to try out his technology didn't mean it wasn't using her.

They turned over options, trying to find a way that wouldn't bring the whole world crashing down on them. Ashraf even suggested shutting down the system, destroying all the parts.

"It's too late for that," Jacob said. "You've been using this stuff. If you think they'll be angry about you not letting them know about it, imagine how much worse they'll be if they find out you've destroyed it."

Ashraf nodded unhappily. "It needs to be controlled."

"Then make sure it's put into the right hands?"

She gave him a blank look. "Who could we possibly trust with this? The government? The United Nations? The reason he limited the access meant less chances of someone betraying us." She sighed. "Even then, it wasn't enough."

Jacob frowned. "What?"

"One of our agents went rogue," she replied, passing her hand over her eyes. "He tried to change something significant. It went wrong. He's being cared for in our medical facilities."

Jacob sat back in his seat. "Significant how?"

"Stopping a world war."

The killing Hitler theory. Change a historical event to stop wars and disasters.

Jacob shivered. "What happened to him?"

Ashraf met his eyes. "Because he intervened and it went wrong, history remembers him—his false identity in that period—as being complicit, and he ended up being blamed for it all in the history books. He couldn't cope with it, and now, he's the living example of why you can't change things."

"Jesus," Jacob breathed. He shook his head. "Christ, you people…"

Ashraf's cheek twitched as she clenched her teeth. "It may seem ruthless, but it made our point clear to our agents. It made a point of why we have to be neutral."

"So you keep him closed up here? A specimen to remind people what not to do?"

Ashraf took a deep breath, clearly trying to keep her temper. "He's still one of our agents, DI Ofori," she said, her voice sharp as a blade. "He had no family. If we gave him over to the local authorities, he would be another patient on a ventilator, checked by nurses and left to fade away to nothing. Here, he is cared for by people who knew him, and know what he did and why. Here, he is looked after for as long as he will live." Her eyes were bright, and her voice turned brittle. "We protect our own, DI Ofori. We always will."

He had the good grace to avert his gaze. "He's still your cautionary tale."

"He is," she agreed quietly. "We might not like it, but he made himself the perfect example of why the rules exist." She returned to her desk and sat down. "They'll ask, when we go public. They'll ask why we don't interfere. Why we don't stop conflicts before they start."

Jacob understood. He didn't like it, but he understood. "And you'll tell his tale."

She set down her glass. "The world already knows about the Potiorek conspiracy. This will be the full stop at the end of that story."

By the time he left, they had come to an agreement.

A press conference would be arranged for the next morning. That would give them twelve hours to gather and purge all the data relating to Janos Nagy, and him time to put together a report with his theory of what had happened.

If all went well, he could time his meeting for just before the press conference, and ensure that his team learned about the whole thing before they made the official announcement. That way, they wouldn't have time to think he'd cracked, and none of them would be able to let it slip by mistake. It wasn't that he didn't trust them, but it only took one person saying the wrong thing to the wrong people, and everyone would know.

The door of the conference room opened as he passed, and it came as no surprise when Kit poked his head out. Christ, Jacob wanted to turn and reassure him that everything would be okay, but he couldn't lie. For all he knew, anything could happen.

He paused, though, at the aborted half gesture Kit made.

"I need to get back to the station," Jacob said.

"Oh. Right." Kit's hand fell back by his side.

It felt shit, leaving it like that, but better for both of them, until they knew how things would turn out. He couldn't let Kit get attached to him, not now. He wanted to sink his hand into Kit's hair, ruffle it, tell him they'd be fine, but he couldn't, so he turned and walked away.

He stood by the lift with Ashraf, and from the doorway, he heard Kit call, "By the way, Detective Inspector Ofori, Janos says thank you."

Jacob pressed his lips together. He remembered the shock and relief on Nagy's face, and the joy on his lover's. It was only fair to give him that chance, in a place where prejudice wouldn't hurt him. After what he'd been through, the poor bugger deserved it.

He nodded silently but couldn't turn to Kit.

When the taxi-pod pulled away and no one else would see it, he let himself sink into the seat and bury his head in his hands. Christ, he'd never been so tired. It was all so bloody complicated.

Anton glanced up from his desk when Jacob got back to the station, and his smile vanished at the look on Jacob's face. "You okay, boss?"

"The TRI gave me the information we requested," he said.

"Seriously? About bloody time!" Anton rose. "Do you have anything for me to update on the incident board?"

"It's nothing that'll make a difference tonight," Jacob demurred. "But I need all hands in for a meeting at nine forty-five tomorrow morning. Compulsory attendance. I need everyone there and I need them to be punctual."

Anton frowned. "If it's that important..."

Jacob kneaded at the back of his neck. He felt twenty years older. "It's sensitive information, so I'd rather give it to the whole team in one go, instead of people wandering in and seeing it on the board."

"Fair enough. You okay, boss? You look...well...shit."

Jacob laughed tiredly. "I got chewed out by the DCIs this morning, then had a useless meeting with Harper, then spent the rest of the day trying to get information out of the TRI."

"Eugh." Anton winced. "Yeah. If I'd had that day, I'd look pretty shit too." He jerked his head toward the door. "You done for the night?"

"Just need to catch up on any developments."

The other man snorted. "Yeah. So many." Off Jacob's look, he held up his hands. "One or two more sightings of our missing woman, but nothing conclusive about her current location. The DNA sample is being run again in two separate labs, in case of cross-contamination. Oh, and Temple says you're a bastard for leaving her with those videos."

"She get anything?"

Anton shook his head. "Nothing more than we already had." He nodded toward the incident board. "All video footage of her is up there."

Jacob glanced at it. He was shattered, but if he went home, he would sit and worry about what might come. "I'll have a look over it and see if there's anything Abby missed."

"She'll love that," Anton said dryly.

"She can deal with it," Jacob replied and headed into his office. His slate lit up when he touched it, but he didn't open the files at once.

Instead, he checked his quill. There were messages from Kit, received throughout the day. The most recent one must have been sent after he left the TRI: *Come by if you want. Or if you want company, let me know. K*

He closed the message up and shakily laughed at the irony that he'd discovered restraint at the worst possible time. What a crap time to be alone, especially when you were a people person. All those nights with Kit had reminded him how much he liked having other people around. He didn't want to be alone.

There was one person he had to see, regardless of what might happen.

He opened up a new message.

I need to see you. Please can you come up as soon as possible.

He pressed Send, then set the quill aside to open the video files on his slate.

Jacob cupped his chin in his hand and watched them in order, one by one. There were four altogether: the external shot of her entering, waiting in reception, coming back through the reception on her way out, and an external shot of her leaving.

On first glance, he had to agree with Temple. The woman waited in the reception, spoke little, and said nothing about her purpose, only that she had a parcel to be personally delivered.

He played them through again, watching her carefully.

She had a package, about the size of a shoebox, which had to contain the hard drives. She seemed nervous too. While she waited, she avoided the camera, so subtly it seemed natural. That explained a lot about why they had little to no surveillance footage of her if she knew how to avoid cameras, and perhaps had even trained in the art of covert operations.

Could be military, could be private. Hell, if she came from a future where people used time travel, she could even be a government agent. He frowned. If she came from the future, then why look up someone born years earlier? Unless she'd met him somewhere in the future.

Jacob stared into nothing.

Harper. He'd said he didn't know the woman, and that the woman had said she didn't know him either. Maybe she didn't know him in this day and age. Maybe she knew him as someone older. And if that was true, and Harper had sent her...

No.

The present-day Harper couldn't possibly know about time travel, and if he did, why had he sent the woman on her way, still carrying her box?

Jacob ran the footage again, watching intently. The timestamps suggested she'd only spent a few minutes in the building, but something in the footage seemed wrong.

It took three more runs before he realised what, and when he did, he smiled grimly.

"Gotcha, you lying bastard." He rose and went to the door. "Anton!"

Anton turned from his work, rearranging the recent data on the incident board. "Boss?"

"Any of the techs still around?"

"You got something?"

Jacob nodded. "I think I do."

Chapter Thirty-Eight

Kit's day had gone from bad to worse.

Mariam issued an order for all available members of staff to attend a meeting in the canteen. She stood on a table and laid out the situation ahead of them.

Kit kept to the side of the room, out of the way, and listened to the voices rising in disbelief and shock. People looked his way, as he expected, muttering and whispering. Sooner or later, the finger-pointing would start, and the thought of it made him sick to his stomach.

"I know none of you signed up to be in the public eye," Mariam said, "but we have no choice anymore. DI Ofori has made it clear that if we don't step forward ourselves, we will be dragged by the full weight of the law." She fell silent for a moment, as if trying to come to a decision, then said, "If any of you want to leave us before this happens, you are free to do so. You will not be penalised. I will put in place support for you, and references will be provided if you choose to go."

"So we have to go public or quit?" The voice rose from the crowd. "How is that fair?"

"You don't have to quit," Mariam replied. "That's your decision. Unfortunately, we don't have any say in the rest of it now. A press conference is scheduled for tomorrow, and after ten o'clock in the morning, we will be public. There are no two ways about it. Take some time. Think about it. If you want to leave, let me know."

She stepped down from the table and disappeared into the crowd. Kit took the opportunity to slip out of the room to head down to the deserted engineering bay. He'd left his latest experiment spread out on his workbench, and he sat down, staring at it.

He could take Mariam's offer and run. It wasn't as if he couldn't find a job in any other engineering company in the world, but therein lay the problem: the TRI needed people who knew what they were doing.

They'd lost their best technician with Sanders's death, and if Kit abandoned ship, Hamid and his team would be left with the weight of the tech. They were bloody good at what they did, but they didn't have Sanders's eye for the tech, or Kit's intuition. They could keep things running, but if they failed and the TRI went under, everyone else would lose their jobs.

Anyway, what kind of engineer abandoned one of the greatest technological innovations of his lifetime and let it fall apart because a few people—okay, probably a lot of people—thought he was the idiot who'd forced the TRI to go public?

Footsteps approached him.

He looked up, laying down the gears.

Hamid stood a few steps away. "You knew about this?"

Kit nodded unhappily. "Thrown in at the deep end," he confessed. "He figured it out, DI Ofori. If Sanders hadn't...if this hadn't..." He shook his head, feeling like a child in front of the principal. "I didn't mean for the TRI to get found out."

"I know, but we can't cry over spilt milk now." Hamid sighed, then reached out and patted him in the shoulder. "It was good working with you, Kit."

Kit blinked. "You...you're not leaving?"

Hamid nodded. "I think it would be better. I have a family. They're going to come after anyone involved here. They'll want gossip. Stories. Secrets from the TRI. Anything about what we do. Especially from us techs. They'll want us to go private, build gates, all the things Tom tried to prevent. I can't let my family be harassed by them." He smiled, brief and sad. "I spoke to my wife. We're heading to stay with her parents for a while, until it starts to blow over."

"You could stay!" Kit protested.

"For all the reasons I told you, I don't think I can," Hamid replied.

Kit stared at him, then threw himself forward and hugged the man hard. Hamid staggered, surprised, then hugged him back.

"I'm sorry," Kit whispered.

Hamid patted his back comfortingly. "You didn't do this, Kit. The ones who attacked Sanders did this. That policeman and his team did this. You just got caught in the middle of it." He stepped back. "I need to gather my things."

"You'll need to tell Mariam..."

"Already done." Hamid looked around the room. "I'm going to miss this place."

Kit could only watch as the man who had been his manager since his first day went into his office and started to pack up his few possessions. It felt like Kit was sitting a thousand miles away, watching something he couldn't stop.

Others followed.

Three of the other engineers packed up their belongings, and Kit wanted to apologise to every one of them, but not one of them would meet his eyes. He turned back to his desk and, with shaking hands, tried to work on the gears. It was that or going out to see how many others were departing. A tight knot twisted in the pit of his stomach as he wondered how many staff they would have left.

Even if he wanted to leave, he couldn't. Not when so many were jumping ship.

By the time he finally dared to leave the engineering bay, most of the building had gone dark, but he ran into Mariam in the lobby, grey-faced and drawn. She saw him approaching and nodded in greeting.

"I'll see you tomorrow?" It sounded like more of a plea than a question.

He nodded at once. "Someone has to fix the lock on the gate." His voice sounded like a stranger's.

The relief that lit her face was like a blow. "Good. That's good." She offered a hand, and he clasped it. It wasn't a handshake but a lifeline, and they were both holding on. "I'll see you tomorrow, then."

He tried to smile.

Outside, the wind wailed along the street. He hailed a taxi-pod and clambered into it as quickly as he could. A check of his messages showed that Jacob still hadn't responded, and sending yet another message felt futile.

It was typical though.

The one time Kit really wanted and needed company, when his whole world had slipped sideways, he couldn't ask for it because it might make things worse.

He made his way home, keeping his quill gripped tightly in his hand in case anyone—Jacob—tried to contact him. No one did. Not even when he got home and sank onto the couch, holding the quill in front of him.

That only really left one other person he could call.

He set the quill down and projected the screen above it as it connected.

His mother's face appeared when she answered. A few more lines curved around her eyes and mouth, but her hair remained the same warm red. "Christopher?" Her eyes lit up. "Hello, love!"

He raised a hand, trying to smile. "All right, Mum?"

"Can't complain," she said warmly. "How are things up in the north? Not too cold?"

The way she talked, people would think he'd moved to Norway. "It's not bad now." He leaned forward, shifting the quill for a clearer angle. "You busy?"

"I'm out to Dora's this evening, but I've got some time, if you don't mind me putting on my face while you talk."

His mouth curled up. "Like old times."

She carried her receiver through to her room and sat at her dresser, where she started sorting through her makeup. "So what's wrong, love? You don't usually call unless it's the end of the world."

Kit's words stuck in his throat, and he could feel the moment his mother's silence went from waiting for an answer to concern.

"Christopher?"

"Things at work," he said haltingly. "Mum, stuff's happening, and it's all gone tits up."

She looked into the screen, frowning. "Are they letting you go?"

He shook his head. "No. No, nothing like that." He looked down at his hands. "Y'know how I couldn't tell you about it? Confidentiality clause and all that stuff?"

"Yes. All very hush-hush, you said."

He clenched his hands into fists, staring blindly at them. "There's going to be a press conference on the news tomorrow. I think you should watch it. It's...people might come and ask you stuff about it all, Mum. I don't...I never wanted you to get caught up in it."

His mother's face paled. "You're not involved in something illegal, are you?"

"No!" Kit said quickly. "Honest, Mum. It's just...bad things have happened to Sanders. My boss." His voice shook. "Mum, he died. Someone killed him."

"Oh my God. Kitten, why didn't you call me sooner? I would have come up!"

Why indeed?

If he had, what could he have told her? The TRI would have gagged him, and she was his mum. He couldn't keep secrets from her, not without moving halfway up the bloody country and only calling every couple of weeks.

"Watch the press conference," he whispered. "It'll all make sense."

"Do you want me to come up?" She watched him, worried. "I could get a shuttle up tomorrow. Or there might be an overnighter. I could be there, if you want me."

He did. God, he did. If he hadn't had Jacob there to hold him through his nightmares, his mum would have been his first choice. But with the TRI going public and the world inevitably swarming them, he didn't want to have the media crashing in on her.

"I'll be all right," he lied. "I wanted you to know what's happening."

She nodded, lifting her hand and touching the projection. He mimicked her, his fingertips touching her transparent ones. "You know your room's here if you need it," she said. "We'd only need to chase the cats out of it."

He nodded in return, his lips trembling. "Thanks, Mum." His cheeks felt cold and wet, and he hastily wiped them with the back of his hand. "You go and get your face on."

"You're going to be all right, love."

He couldn't say anything more. He pressed his fingertips to his lips and blew a kiss, which she pretended to catch, then disconnected the call. It would be so easy to get on a train and run off to Brighton, away from all of the coming fallout.

He sprawled on the couch, hands over his face.

Trouble was, he could never back away from a challenge, and this one promised to be the biggest one of his life. He just needed to hold himself together until the aftershocks passed, and it would be all right.

Jacob had enough to deal with already, bogged down in the case and preparing for the press conference, so he'd have to do it on his own. He needed to think about something else, and only one thing ever helped with that.

Kit pushed himself off the couch and all but ran to the room where he'd stashed all his engineering supplies. He still hadn't finished the hard copy of the gate's mechanism. Sanders's last instruction had been to ensure the security of the gate, and he was damned well going to do it.

The mechanism lay in his hands, cold and heavy, and he gazed at it.

Definitely time for a coffee and bass night.

Chapter Thirty-Nine

Jacob had barely slept and ended up in the office earlier than he'd intended.

He'd tried to contact Harper the previous night, but to no avail. Anton had dug up his address first thing, but no one answered at the house or office. Jacob couldn't help thinking it was deliberate. Harper had lied to them. There had to be a reason.

He disconnected the call and massaged his eyelids with his fingertips.

Temple rapped on the edge of his office door, walked in, and held out a gently steaming and grease-speckled paper bag.

"What's this in aid of?" he asked, accepting it.

"Anton said you looked crap last night." She shrugged. "I figure a hot roll to start the day won't hurt."

He smiled gratefully. As usual, when things were going royally tits up, breakfast didn't rank high in his priorities. "You know me too well." He opened the bag up, peering in. "Egg *and* bacon? Do I look that bad?"

Temple swayed her hand from side to side. "Safe to say you need all the help you can get. You want a coffee?"

"Better make it a tea." He'd already had a coffee at home, and one on the way in, and he remembered the last time he'd done a meeting with a caffeine-induced headache. It hadn't gone well.

She winced. "So it's that important?"

"Mm?" He glanced up from the roll.

"The meeting. Anton mentioned it."

He didn't need to ask how she knew. All of them had their tells when they were worried or stressed or upset. He didn't know what his were, but Temple could spot them every time.

"It'll explain everything," he said, opening up the roll to poke the errant bacon back into it. He raised his eyes to her. "Don't ask me for more now, Abby. It's not something I'm going to explain twice. Not this."

She nodded. "Understood."

By the time the rest of the team rolled in, he'd abandoned half the roll, and the tea had gone cold as he prepared everything in the conference room. There were ten officers below him and two DCIs attending, each of them looking as bemused as the next.

Jacob waited until they all filed into the room and the door slid closed behind them.

"Well?" DCI Crawford sat down at the head of the table. She looked irritable, but given the early hour, that was no surprise. "You believe you've broken the case, DI Ofori?"

Jacob nodded. "The TRI has provided information which explains the trouble we've been having." He tapped the console in the table, illuminating one of the walls with the video-link to the press conference. "Mrs. Ashraf is going to make a statement for the press regarding the TRI, and since it connects directly to the case, I want everyone to hear it"

"Surely, it would have been more appropriate to have her make a statement here?" DCI Lender said.

Jacob shook his head. Ashraf sat at a table, her hands folded in front of her. "Not for something this big." He turned up the volume and fixed his gaze on the desk. He didn't need to see her face as she broke the cardinal rule of her operation.

His colleagues shifted impatiently, waiting for the conference to start. When it did, he raised his eyes and watched their faces.

Ashraf spoke clearly and succinctly. He couldn't help admiring how cool she sounded. Her whole life and her business suddenly thrust under the spotlight, all while dealing with an orphaned child and the loss of one of her closest friends, and she sounded completely calm.

He didn't need to listen to what she said, more than familiar with it all already. Around the table, looks exchanged in disbelief, shock, confusion. Temple glanced across at him for verification. Jacob could only nod.

He looked back down at the table, cupping one hand over his forehead. Even without the caffeine, a headache throbbed behind his eyes. Everything would have to change now; the only saving grace was that it wouldn't be his burden alone anymore.

When Ashraf stopped talking and the feed cut out, Jacob shut down the projection.

"She's...joking, right?" Anton sounded dazed. "I mean, she can't be serious. Can she?"

"She is." Jacob turned to Crawford and Lender at the head of the table. "You can see why I felt this would be better to reveal to the group as a unit, rather than finding out from the incident board. The TRI are willing to cooperate in any way they can. Until Sanders was confirmed dead, they were bound by his orders not to divulge anything about the true nature of their business."

Crawford nodded slowly. "The DNA sample," she said. "We have a confirmed match between the infant and the man we have in the morgue?"

Jacob hesitated. "We are having it checked again to be certain, but yes. John Smith appears to be the Robertson baby."

Crawford looked shaken. "My God."

Temple cleared her throat. "So do we tell his family? I mean, that he's dead? It..." She shook her head, frowning. "How do we do this, sir? We have their dead son, but they have him, and he's still alive. Do we tell them how he's going to die?"

Jacob wanted to laugh aloud, or lay his head on the table and cover his ears. The same thought had been running through his head since he'd found out the truth. "I don't know." He shook his head. "I don't know."

There were so many variables. If they told the family, they were giving a newborn child a death sentence before he even left the hospital. Wouldn't they try to change things to stop their son from going on the journey that resulted in his death? It could change everything, if he never came back, if Sanders had never been killed.

But if they didn't tell them, sometime in the future, their son would leave and never return.

Lender rubbed his jaw. "We're going to have to call in the Ashraf woman and pass it up the line. This is beyond anything we've ever dealt with before. We'll need to proceed with care. Upstairs will have to deal with this one."

"I have her direct line," Jacob said at once. "She may appreciate the chance to avoid the media."

"Do we have any more leads on the missing woman?" Crawford asked.

"I suspect Mr. Harper knows more than he let on," Jacob replied. "He should be coming down to the station as soon as he's available. I have a few questions I need to ask. Anton will keep eyes on the CCTV, and tabs on any reported sightings."

Crawford tapped her fingertips on the desk. "Do we have any indication what this...why this man came from the future?"

"It could have been for something specific that Sanders developed, or for something general," Jacob admitted. "We can't be sure. We only know that the hard drives and backup data from Sanders's private computers were all taken by John Smith's accomplice."

"And the TRI don't know either?" Temple frowned. "That seems unlikely."

"Turns out Sanders was very secretive about new developments," Jacob said. "It's possible someone from the future heard about the developments and decided to come back and take them ahead of their time."

"But they already have time travel." Anton shook his head. "Why would they need it?"

"Was he still working on his teleportation development?" Lender asked.

"We don't know," Jacob said. "His colleagues don't either."

"Are you sure about that?" Crawford said.

"Yes." Jacob met Crawford's eyes. "They have guaranteed full access to all available information. I don't believe they have anything left to hide." He nodded across the table to Temple. "I'm going to send Temple and several of the technicians down there to work with the TRI operatives to see if they can shed some light on the situation."

"What about the memory chip from the eye?"

Jacob glanced over at one of the technicians. "Leo?"

One of the youngest members of the team in the meeting, Leo blinked in alarm at being put on the spot. "Still working on it," he said. "The coding is a mess, but I'm working through it."

"How long do you think that's going to take?" Lender asked.

"How long's a piece of string?" Leo fidgeted. "I'm doing the best I can, but it's more advanced than anything I've seen before."

"Take your time," Jacob said. "We need to save what we can. Don't risk losing data by rushing it." He glanced around the table. "Our main priority has to be finding our missing woman. If she's Smith's partner, she's the only one who can explain everything. We have to focus on that. Everything else pertaining to time travel gets passed up the line."

Crawford and Lender didn't look thrilled about it, but frankly, Jacob was dealing with shit so far above his pay grade that he deserved a raise.

Lender rose. "We want discretion from here on in," he said. "No one speaks to the media. If we have any information showing up in the press that is part of this investigation, believe me when I say the department will come down on you like a ton of bricks."

Silence lingered as he and Crawford left the room.

As soon as they were gone, the tension shattered, and a babble of voices washed over Jacob, wanting to know how long he'd known, how he'd worked it out, when he'd planned on telling them if the TRI hadn't released the information.

He pushed his chair back. "It was only confirmed to me yesterday," he said. "Temple gave me the answer."

"Thanks, sir," Temple said with a wry smile. "Not sure how, but thanks."

He tried to smile in return. "You gave me the idea. I just had to dig further to prove it." He rose from the chair and glanced around at them. "Temple, you pick two people to go with you to the TRI. I'll call ahead to let Ashraf know you're coming. Leo, you keep working on the decryption. Anton, you're still on CCTV and incoming. Use as many people as you need for it. This woman must be found." He glanced at his watch. "And I have to go and chase down Harper again, to find out what he knows."

He walked out of the door, only to collide with a nervous-looking sergeant.

"Sorry, sir!" She held up her hands.

He could only imagine how the DCIs had reacted if they'd walked out and crashed straight into her, when they were already on edge. "How can I help you, Sergeant?"

"There's a Mr. Harper downstairs, sir. He said you'd left messages for him?"

Jacob stared at her. "What? He's here?"

"Yes, sir. He arrived about fifteen minutes ago."

Jacob frowned. It felt off. What had changed? What had happened in the last hour that got Harper...

The press conference. He must have seen the press conference.

"Have him brought up to interview room three," Jacob said.

The sergeant nodded and hurried away. Jacob watched her go, flexing his hands by his side. The familiar tension ran through him, the sense that he was on the edge of something. Harper had only come in because of the TRI going public.

Jacob hurried to the toilets, relieved himself, and freshened up. He did up the top button of his shirt and straightened his tie. You could look like crap in front of colleagues, but in a case like this, you didn't expose your throat to someone like Harper.

By the time Harper reached the interview room, Jacob had settled at the desk. He rose with a polite smile and held out his hand. Harper's palm was cool and damp against his.

"Mr. Harper. I'm glad you could make it."

Harper subsided into one of the seats, breathing heavily, his face flushed with exertion. "Always happy to be of assistance to you people."

Curious that you didn't think so last night.

"You don't mind if we record this meeting?" Jacob smiled without showing his teeth as he sat back down. "Protocol and what have you."

Harper waved a hand, motioning for him to continue.

Jacob set the monitor to record, providing name, date, and time. He folded his hands on his desk. "I suspect you know why you are here, Mr. Harper."

"My secretary said you had some questions for me." Harper mirrored Jacob's pose, one hand folding around the other.

Jacob tapped the desk, bringing up the two videos from Harper's reception. He kept his attention on Harper, catching the way his eyes moved from one video to the other. "We have examined the footage you gave us. It was very helpful."

"I'm glad to hear you say so."

Jacob gazed at him. "Even though someone had tampered with it."

Harper's already-rosy cheeks blotched with red. "What?" he sputtered.

Jacob didn't reply at once. Instead, he played each of the videos, watching as Harper stared down at them.

"You're saying they have been tampered with?" Harper jabbed a finger at him. "You insult me, DI Ofori. I see nothing there that suggests tampering."

"Nor did I, at first," Jacob replied mildly. "But it's there." He brought up captures from both videos. They looked identical, except for the shaft of sunlight cutting across the floor. "I passed the footage on to one of my scientists to confirm it. We're very curious about how the clock shows five minutes passing, but the movement of the sun indicates at least half an hour has elapsed."

Colour drained from Harper's face. "There must be some mistake."

Jacob wanted to smile. Harper had come for his own reasons. He didn't imagine he'd been compromised. "I think now is the time to stop acting innocent, Mr. Harper. Our missing woman stayed in your building for over half an hour." He inclined his head. "Explain."

"She was in my office for less than five minutes!"

"Yes, I expect so," Jacob retorted. "But that begs the question where she went for the other twenty-five minutes. She doesn't strike me as the type to go and powder her nose." He leaned forward. "Believe me, Mr. Harper, I am not having a good day, and if you lie to me, I am not likely to be lenient."

Harper stared back at him, those odd, pale eyes narrowed, the expression of a man trying to work out how deep in the shit he really was.

Finally, he sat back and unfolded his hands, spreading them flat on the desk. "I humoured her. She said I wasn't who she expected. She got...upset. I tried to calm her down." His lips twitched in something masquerading as a smile. "Do you find that hard to believe, DI Ofori?"

"That's not for me to say," Jacob replied, though he privately doubted it very much. "Did she give you her name? Your receptionist said that the girl brought a delivery from Mr. Sanders. She couldn't recall the company the woman claimed to work for."

Harper shrugged his massive shoulders. "Marla? Carla? Something like that anyway." His lips tugged again. "As I said, she'd worked herself into a right state when we spoke. Hardly making any sense, barely coherent. I felt it was...kinder to calm her down, rather than press her for information."

Jacob tapped his fingers on the edge of the table. "Did she say why she was upset?"

"Oh, she spouted a lot of nonsense." Harper took his time, clearly putting thought into each sentence. "I didn't understand much of it. Something about information she had retrieved. She was quite hysterical. I let her sit in the staff room, gave her a cup of tea, tried to make some sense of it."

"And she mentioned Sanders."

"Yes. The man from the news."

"And this morning's press conference."

Harper was good, but he couldn't conceal the flicker in his expression. "Press conference?"

Jacob smiled placidly. "I believe you are aware of it. The Temporal Research Institution's press conference this morning."

"Ah. Yes." Harper's cheek twitched. "I saw something about it on the news. Some agency has managed to travel in time or some such nonsense?"

"Nonsense that could be very useful to a savvy businessman," Jacob observed. "Especially a businessman who happened to be visited by a young woman who is known to have stolen a great deal of information relating to it."

Harper's mouth widened unpleasantly. "So this is your game, Detective? Make grand assumptions that I've been plotting to steal this...time travel information? Before I even knew it was a reality?"

Jacob tilted his head to one side. "Were you? After all, it could make you a fortune."

Harper leaned forward, his eyes glittering slits. "Let's say we follow this little story of yours, Detective. Let's say she talked about time travel. What kind of savvy businessman would even believe a fairy tale like that?"

Jacob's slate chimed. He tilted it up, glancing at the screen. DNA confirmation had come in. John Smith was definitely Baby Robertson. He directed it up to the DCIs. Not his responsibility anymore.

"A fairy tale," he said. "Yes." He laid the slate down. "Now, Mr. Harper, I need you to tell me what our mystery woman said to you. No matter how nonsensical."

Harper gave them nothing they didn't already know: she had hard drives with data on them, which he—Harper—knew nothing about; she wanted to find someone familiar to help her deal with them; she laboured under the misapprehension that she knew Harper himself.

Jacob folded his hands, listening to the man. Most of what he said had to be true, but it felt like he'd done some strategic editing. "She came to you, sir. That suggests she knew who you were. The fact that you didn't immediately dismiss her suggests she said something that might have convinced you to listen, no matter how ridiculous her words were."

Harper chuckled. "Do you enjoy grasping at straws, Detective? I have told you what I know, and that I comforted a poor, distressed young woman, then sent her on her way. As you can see in the footage, she left still carrying her precious box of stolen merchandise."

"And you didn't ask to see any of the drives she had before she left?"

"Why would I?" Harper said. "I had no idea what she had on them, or that she had killed a man to get them."

Jacob tilted his head slightly. The news reports had been deliberately vague regarding what had been taken from Sanders's home. "I never said she killed a man to get them."

Harper's mouth opened and shut a couple of times. "Well, I assumed that's why she's being hunted in connection with Sanders," he sputtered. "I thought that's what must have happened to him."

"You knew."

"Of course I didn't!"

Jacob smiled thinly at him. "Let me put forward what I think happened. This woman comes to you. Why, I don't know, but she seems to think you will assist her, and something she says convinces you to listen. She's distressed, as you said, and she tells you she may have killed a man to get the information she is now carrying. You hear something useful in what she says, so instead of reporting her, you let her go on her way and cover up after her until your receptionist recognises her on the news."

Harper's face turned thunderous. "You are bordering on slander, DI Ofori."

"And you, Mr. Harper, have perverted the course of justice," Jacob retorted, voice as sharp as a pistol crack.

Harper rose. "You can't prove anything, DI Ofori. I stand by what I said. I spoke to a confused and upset young woman. When she calmed down, I sent her on her way. All you have is a glitching video. That's hardly evidence."

Jacob looked up at him. "Give me time."

Harper's eyes blazed. "You'll hear from my lawyer first."

Jacob rose from the chair and smiled. He had perfected a slight crook of his lips that always pissed off anyone he was interrogating. "Until then, you're free to go."

He followed Harper into the hall and watched the sergeant escort the man away. Harper was the last piece of the puzzle. They had to find the girl to make sense of it all.

"Sir?"

Jacob turned. Anton leaned out of the incident room. "Yes?"

"You have a call."

Jacob nodded. He'd been expecting it since the previous night. "I'll be there in a second." He glanced back along the hall as the lift doors closed on Harper. God, he wanted to bring the bugger down. He turned and headed back to the incident room. "Keep on it," he said to Anton as he passed. "We need to find her."

Chapter Forty

Reporters had flooded the street outside the TRI building.

Kit stared down from the canteen window, watching them milling around. There were a few police officers around as well to make sure things didn't get out of hand.

He'd seen Mariam leave earlier in the day, and it made him think of cheesy old horror films, when piranhas scented blood in the water. The police had to flank her on all sides to get her to the squad pod, but it hadn't been enough to stop her getting buffeted around.

They'd left a few officers and technicians inside as well.

Kit had spent two hours with one of them, explaining the technical side of things. It wasn't as if he could have passed her off onto anyone else either. They'd lost around twenty percent of their staff across the board. People were on edge, especially since they were under siege by the media, and Kit knew there'd be more departures before the week was out.

When the policewoman had moved on to a different department, he had fled to take refuge in the one room the police weren't actively interested in. After all, food couldn't answer questions.

Someone approached him from behind.

"They will still be there," Janos said. "For days, they will be there. We are a new thing. It is exciting for them."

Kit pressed his forehead against the window, looking down. "How long will that last?"

Janos's reflection shifted in the glass. "Until they find another new thing. It is always the same with them. They are like small children with a new toy. For now, we must wait. They will go eventually."

Kit turned to the other man. "It's now I'm worried about."

Janos patted his shoulder. "They will not hurt you. Push, yes. Shout, yes. But they cannot hurt you."

"I guess you've had a lot worse than cameras in your face, huh?"

"Mm." Janos's hand rested on his shoulder. "This is small fish. Frightening if you have not had small fish before, but not so frightening when you have been bitten by a shark." He smiled briefly. "If you want, when we leave in an hour, you can leave with us. Dieter wants to shout at them. You can run while he shouts."

Kit was surprised. "He wants to shout at them?"

Janos grinned suddenly. "You only see the cheerful man with words and history. He is not happy all the time. He is angry a lot when people are stupid and judge on first sight. He does not like news people. He does not like the way they spoke of Sanders before. He is still angry with Sanders and for what happened. Until now, he had no one to shout at."

It wasn't unusual to see Dieter yelling, but usually, he accompanied it with a grin and a lot of swearing, even when he was in a good mood. Especially when he was in a good mood. It made Kit wonder how bad it could get if someone really pissed him off.

"Are you sure it's a good idea, letting him out there?"

Janos shrugged. "Maybe not, but it will give them something to distract them from Mariam, and it will give him someone to let steam out on."

Kit looked back out of the window. "Yeah," he said. "I'll leave with you."

Janos patted his shoulder again. "Where we can find you, in an hour?"

Kit considered it. "The engineering bay. I'm working on the gate lock again."

"Any luck?"

"I've finished the prototype based on the schematics, and it should work." Kit shrugged helplessly. "Until I can test it, I have no idea, and I have no idea if we'll still..."

"Still do our job?" One side of Janos's mouth tilted up. "We will. Everyone will want to know about time travel."

"Yay," Kit said morosely. He pushed his fingers through his hair. "I should get back down. Standing around here and watching the vultures circling isn't good."

"You will be well," Janos said as he walked away. "We all will."

Kit wished he could believe it.

He felt like he was walking across broken glass, treading carefully to keep from causing more damage. He didn't have the excuse that his life had been bollocksed and thrown out the window.

With so few people left, the quiet in the engineering bay seemed more morose than usual, and he slouched at his workstation in silence. He'd brought in the lock he was working on from home as a security precaution, to keep it all internal, especially since the police were everywhere now.

Coffee, insomnia, and anxiety weren't a good combination.

By the time Janos came in to fetch him, he was still sitting, staring blindly at the lock. Janos didn't speak at once. He lifted the lock from Kit's hand and put it on the workbench, then took Kit gently by the elbow and pulled him to his feet. "You need to get rest," he said.

Kit nodded, letting the older man lead him through the halls.

Dieter waited by the lift, his makeup a lot starker than usual, the eyeliner so sharp it looked like he could cut someone with it. He smiled, showing a glimpse of teeth, his lips a dark, bloody red. "I hear I'm your human shield tonight."

Kit looked at Janos. "I never said—"

"Neither did he," Dieter interrupted as they stepped into the lift. "Those fuckers outside want something to write down, and I'm going to give it to them."

"Is that why…" Kit gestured to his face with one hand, the other on the rail.

"Game face on," Dieter confirmed, his grin feral. "Mariam's got enough bullshit going on. This, I can do."

"Will they actually be able to print any of it?"

Janos snorted. "They want to know what we do. We will not tell them that."

"I'm going to tell them about Sanders," Dieter said, his smile grim. "The man they ignored in their news bulletins. The man they've forgotten about. They want words. They're going to get a fucking earful."

"It is best for you to run," Janos said as the lift doors opened. "Do not stop. Go as fast as you can."

Kit looked between them. "Thank you."

Despite their best intentions, at least four media blocks were still shoved in Kit's face, red lights blinking, lenses clicking. He raised his arm to shield his face, trying to push through the swarm, and then Dieter's voice rang out. "Leave the fucking electrician alone, you bastards!"

Janos's hands were on Kit's shoulders, steering him firmly through the crowd.

"You want to hear what someone from the TRI has today? Is that what you're waiting for? Fine! Let me tell you—"

"Go," Janos hissed in Kit's ear and shoved him hard, breaking him through the scrum of reporters. Kit staggered, but kept his footing, and bolted off as fast as he could. A couple of the reporters yelled after him, but he had long legs and a head start.

Half a dozen streets away, he flagged down a taxi-pod and fell into it, panting.

The pod shuttled away from the curb, and he groped in his pocket for his quill, digging it out. With exhaustion weighing him down, no way in hell could he risk cooking anything, and if he got an order in now, it'd be waiting for him when he got home.

Kit frowned.

A message blinked on the screen, and his heart skipped a beat.

It wasn't from Jacob.

His frown deepened. Jenny? She only ever sent a message if there was a problem with the flat.

He pressed to dial, calling her. "Jen?"

"Oh good!" she whispered urgently. "You got my message!"

"Yeah. What's going on?"

"Some reporters were hanging around like a bad smell outside the building," she said. "I checked now, and they're still there." Kit's stomach clenched. "I saw your work on the news. I thought they might be looking for you."

"Yeah..." He stared at the windscreen of the pod. "Yeah, they probably are. How many are there?"

"At least four, maybe six." She sounded worried. "Maybe you should stay somewhere else tonight? Go and stay with a friend or something?"

A friend.

If only it were that easy.

"I'll see what I can do." He tried to smile. "Thanks, Jen."

"You keep safe. You can buy me dinner for letting you know."

He almost laughed. "Anyone ever tell you you're a grabby old bird?"

"I'll have steak," she replied and hung up.

Kit lowered the quill, gazing at it. She was right. Staying somewhere else would be better, but he didn't have many people he could call friends, and he could only think of one person he might go to, and that was a bad idea. Jacob had to be kept at arm's length until the case was cleared up. They'd both agreed.

He couldn't work out how he'd gone from staring at his quill in the pod to standing at Jacob's front door. The backside of his brain seemed to be taking charge an awful lot, taking over from all the run-ragged higher functions.

Bad idea or not, he needed to at least see a friendly face, and maybe even get a hug before buggering off and finding a hotel.

He rapped the door once, and as soon as it opened, he stepped forward and hugged the man on the other side. He tried to drop his head to Jacob's shoulder and noticed, confused, the shoulder seemed to be two inches lower than usual.

Kit blinked.

The man he was hugging stood very still, tense with surprise.

Kit blinked again. "You're not Jacob."

"No," the man agreed.

"And I'm still hugging you, aren't I?"

"Little bit."

Kit stumbled back a step, mortified. Jacob's son looked at him, both amused and concerned.

"You okay?"

Kit pulled at the sleeve of his jacket. He knew he should go, but he was tired and scared, and he didn't want to be on his own. His lips were trembling, even though he tried to stop them, and he could only shake his head.

Luke stepped out of the doorway and put an arm around his shoulder. "Come on," he said, pulling Kit forward, then called out, "Dad!"

Jacob emerged from the kitchen and stopped short, wiping his hands on a towel. He looked as drained as Kit felt, and Kit wished the ground would swallow him. Of course he would be stressed about the case. How bloody selfish was Kit to imagine he could show up and expect Jacob to be fine too?

"Kit?"

"I'm sorry," Kit said unsteadily. "They're at my house. I didn't know where else to go."

Jacob glanced past him at his son. "Luke..."

"I don't mind," Luke said. "He looks like he needs the company."

"Can you...?"

Luke headed into the kitchen, and Jacob steered Kit over to the couch, gently pressing him to sit down.

"The papers?" he asked.

Kit nodded. "They were all over the office when I left." He looked down at his hands. He'd picked his nails raw again during the day, and one of them stung and bled at the edge. "I was going home, but Jen—she's my neighbour—she let me know they were there too." He trembled. "I don't know how they found my house. I couldn't go there."

"No, I bet." Jacob rubbed his back in soothing circles. "You can stay put here. Not much room, but for tonight, if you need to—"

"I can get a hotel," Kit protested. "I just...I needed to see someone I feel safe with. Just for a little while."

Jacob sighed. "You poor, daft bugger." He leaned closer and wrapped Kit up in his arms, hugging him. Kit clung onto him, squeezing his eyes shut. Jacob was so solid and warm and real, and it pushed back the misery and the gut-knotting fear a little. "You're staying here tonight, Kit. You need it."

"I'm okay."

"Your eyeballs are pink, and you're shaking."

Kit made a sound halfway between laughing and crying. "Yeah. Not good days."

"Know that feeling." Jacob sat back enough to meet his eyes. "How bad is it on your side?"

"Lost around forty staff, give or take." Kit looked down when Jacob took one of his hands and used the corner of the towel to stem the bleeding. "I know I can't leave, but I really don't know if I can stay either." He shivered. "It's all falling apart, and I want to hold it together. It's so important, and I don't know if I can do it."

Jacob gently cupped Kit's cheek. "You've not slept either, have you? Christ, what a pair we are." He ran his thumb along Kit's cheekbone. "I'm under doctor's orders already. Dinner and an early night with something to help me sleep."

"Doctor's?" Kit paled. "You're not—"

"He means me," Luke called from the kitchen. He poked his head around the doorframe. "You okay with sausage and mash?"

"Yes. Good. I mean, thank you." Kit tried to smile. "I'm sorry. For getting in the way."

Luke waved a hand dismissively. "Hardly in the way. I planned on feeding him and getting him to bed. Now I can do the feeding part, and you..." He winked. "Well, let's say you might be more comfortable there."

Kit blushed to the roots of his hair. "Um."

Luke laughed and withdrew into the kitchen.

"So, about my son being an annoying little tosser..." Jacob said loudly.

"I heard that!" Luke's voice drifted back through.

"He...knows? And he doesn't mind?"

Jacob smiled. He looked tired. "Right now, he just wants me happy." He rested his brow against Kit's. "At least we're both buggered by this together."

Kit sank into his embrace, nodding. It made it easier, knowing he wasn't in it alone.

Chapter Forty-One

Rain drummed against the window.

Jacob wished he could blame it for keeping him awake, but it would be a lie. He lay on his back, staring into the dark, Kit curled beside him. He'd pillowed his head on Jacob's chest, and one fingertip tapped in time with Jacob's heartbeat.

All things considered, given the circumstances, it hadn't been a bad evening.

There'd been comforting food, some beer, and mostly casual chat. It wasn't how he'd pictured Luke and Kit meeting properly. The fact that he'd pictured it at all told him how deep he had fallen. Still, it had happened, and on the surface, they seemed to get along, even if Luke did try to ineffectually give the "if you hurt my dad" speech.

Jacob moved his hand from Kit's shoulder to bury his fingers into Kit's hair, much more tangled than usual. He combed through it, loosening the knots.

Kit sighed against his chest.

"You okay?" Jacob murmured.

Kit spread his fingertips on Jacob's chest. "Does he know?" he asked quietly.

"Know what?"

"What you did."

Jacob drew a fingertip along the curve of Kit's ear and felt his lover shiver. "He knows I did something that could end badly. I think he thinks it's just my involvement with you." Kit tensed against his side. "I mean as a part of the case."

"Oh." He didn't relax much. "Yeah. That."

Jacob exhaled slowly. "I don't think it would be prudent to spread around what happened with Nagy's files. The fewer people who know, the better. That way, it's less likely to leak, and if we're lucky..." He trailed off.

That was what it came down to: luck.

Kit rubbed his cheek against Jacob's chest. His hand curled into a fist. "Why did you do it?"

Jacob kneaded at the back of Kit's neck with his fingertips. "You know what would have happened to him if the world found out."

Kit nodded. "But why?" he whispered. "Why risk yourself, your whole bloody life, for him? You don't even know him."

Jacob closed his eyes. "He deserved it."

Kit leaned up, and Jacob could picture his incredulous expression. "So you wanted to give them a happily ever after?" He sat up, pulling the sheets with him. "Jesus, Jacob. Just because they pull on your heartstrings doesn't mean you need to risk jail. You don't have to be a bloody hero!"

Jacob brought the lights up. Kit sat there, arms wrapped around his legs. "You heard what he lived through, what he survived, Kit."

Kit nodded, propping his chin on his knees.

"And you know how he ended up here. What he went through."

"Yes." Kit's voice sank to a tiny, frail whisper.

Jacob pushed himself up the bed and slipped his arm around Kit's waist. He kissed his freckled shoulder. "The poor bastard has suffered enough," he murmured, Kit's skin warm against his lips. "He lost everything. His friends and family turned on him. He nearly got killed. And now, for the first time in his life, he's somewhere safe, where he won't be hurt. Could you let him get locked up? Put on display like a sideshow? Stared at and pointed at and picked apart all over again?"

Kit shivered, shaking his head. "I don't want you to be locked up either."

Jacob wrapped the younger man up in his arms, framing Kit's hips with his legs. "I know."

Kit leaned back into him. He was still shivering. "If you do...if that happens, Luke'll kill me."

Kit's heart thundered against Jacob's ribs. "If it's because of Nagy," he murmured, "Luke'll understand."

"He will?"

"Mm." Jacob drew his hand slowly up and down Kit's chest.

Kit twisted in his embrace, searching Jacob's face. "What aren't you telling me?"

Jacob gazed back at him. If he told him, it would be letting some of the facade fall away and letting Kit see things weren't as simple as he seemed to think. It would be letting him even closer, letting him see something Jacob kept closed up because it hurt like hell to think about.

"Jacob?" Kit touched Jacob's cheek. "Tell me? Please?"

What the hell, he thought. Why keep fighting when you were in this deep already? No harm in pushing the boat a little farther out into shit creek.

"D'you know why they targeted Nagy, back in the day?"

Kit frowned in confusion. "Because the Nazis were homophobic bastards?"

A muscle twitched in Jacob's cheek. Christ, it shouldn't have been so hard. "You have no idea how lucky you are, people of this generation."

"You're not that much older than me," Kit began.

"Kit." Jacob's ribs heaved, tight as a vice, his voice more strained than he wanted it to be. "Please. Listen."

Kit stared at him, then nodded, leaning into his embrace.

Jacob swallowed hard, both of their hearts thrumming now. "I was born in Ghana. We moved to London when I was six. Different world." He looked down at his hand, resting on Kit's arm. "My parents were—are—traditional."

He heard the sharp intake of breath, but thankfully, Kit didn't say anything.

"I knew by the time I turned thirteen." It was a struggle to continue. "We used to go back to Kumasi every year to see relatives." He smiled sadly. "I should have been an actor. Fooled every one of them." He threaded his fingers between Kit's. "You see, there were laws there. Most of the family agreed with them."

"Jesus," Kit whispered. "Did they find out?"

Jacob watched their fingers overlapping; Kit's were long and thin, his nails bitten down. "Eventually. I had a choice, they said. Be a good, respectable, decent man or get out." He sighed. "It's a long time ago now. Luke keeps me up-to-date, but..." He shook his head. "Let's say I've been where Janos is. Not as badly, but I know how bad it can get."

Kit twisted around fully and reached up to pull Jacob's lips down to his, a cautious kiss, and every second of it drained a little of the tension from Jacob's body.

When Kit drew back, he looked at Jacob, searching his face. "That's why you did it, isn't it?"

Jacob met his eyes. "He had it so much worse than I ever did. He deserves to have some of the happiness I've had. He's got someone who loves him. He deserves a chance to live it."

"And you don't?"

"Deserve a chance to live?"

"Have someone who loves you." It was barely above a whisper, but so vehement.

Jacob stared at him. Surely, he couldn't be saying...that. Christ, they didn't—they couldn't—not when everything was falling apart around them. He was tired. That had to be it. "Kit," he began, then faltered.

Kit fell silent, as if he'd realised what he had implied. "We should sleep."

Jacob nodded. He lay back down, but when Kit lay down, too, he turned away, curling on his side. Maybe he thought he'd said the wrong thing. Maybe the fact that Jacob hadn't given the reply he wanted upset him.

"Here," Jacob said, pulling the covers up and curving himself against Kit's back. "You'll get cold."

Kit's fingers caught his wrist, pulling Jacob's arm tight around him. "You're a good man, Jacob."

Jacob pressed a kiss to his shoulder. "I'm all right."

Kit shook his head, his hair rustling on the pillow. "No. You're good. You're far too good, no matter what your parents told you. To me. To Janos. To everyone but yourself."

Jacob laid his head down behind Kit's. "Just a man, Kit. No worse or better than anyone." He snapped his fingers, and the lights winked out.

Kit pressed into him, and Jacob felt his heart beating. "You're wrong."

Chapter Forty-Two

Kit woke in the dark, his cheek resting on Jacob's chest.

"Morning," Jacob murmured.

Kit squinted around. "Is it?"

Jacob's hand rubbed at the back of his neck, fingers curled into his hair. "Mm. About seven." He still sounded tired. "Sleep okay?"

Kit shrugged, smothering a yawn.

There'd been sleep of some kind, but it had been fragmented by strange dreams. A memory surfaced from the night before, of saying something he hadn't intended to say out loud. He pushed himself up on one elbow, groping for the edge of the sheets. "I should go."

Jacob brought the lights up. He looked half-asleep. "C'mere," he murmured, motioning Kit closer.

Kit hauled himself up the bed, and Jacob curled his fingers deeper into Kit's hair and drew Kit down to him.

"What are you doing?"

Jacob's fingertips dragged across his scalp. "Kissing you."

"My mouth tastes awful," Kit warned.

"Had worse," Jacob replied and kissed him.

Kit sank his hands into the pillow on either side of Jacob's head, half sprawled on top of Jacob. He should leave. It would be sensible, and Jesus, Jacob nibbled on his lower lip, and he changed his mind about going anywhere.

It wasn't as rushed or urgent as their previous encounters, but when Jacob pushed his hips up against Kit, and his free hand caught Kit's arse, Kit felt the same shiver of pleasure.

"We probably shouldn't," Kit whispered against his lips.

"Mm." Jacob squeezed his backside, then dragged his nails up.

Kit laughed breathlessly. He trailed his mouth off Jacob's, down to his ear. "Luke's right next door," he whispered. "He might hear."

"Then you'll have to be quiet," Jacob murmured into his hair. He slid his other hand down, both palms hooking under Kit's arse, and pulled him up over him, their cocks rubbing together.

Kit smothered a groan in his throat. "Like that'll happen."

"Mm." Jacob guided him into rocking slowly.

Beneath Kit, Jacob shifted his legs, bracing his feet against the mattress to push up against him. His hands were wandering, too, up Kit's back, then teasing lightly back down, over his buttocks.

It was sleepy and sensuous, and Kit hissed through his teeth, kneading at the pillows when Jacob's teeth scraped against his throat. His hips stuttered, his cock hardening, and he pressed his lips to Jacob's ear.

"Good?" Jacob murmured, the fingers of one hand tracing the crease of Kit's buttocks, and the other hand slowly kneading at Kit's backside and hip.

"Yeah..." Kit's voice petered out as Jacob pushed his hips up, rubbing against him. Christ, his cock was hot. He started stroking more demandingly, that heat rubbing against his own. "Jesus..."

Jacob's chest shook with a low chuckle. "Keen," he murmured, slipping one hand down between them. He wrapped his fingers around both of them, and Kit yelped when he squeezed. "Sh." Jacob's voice thickened with sleep and sex, and one hand stroked them both, while two fingers teased around Kit's arsehole.

Kit tugged at the pillows, rocking his hips. Back or forward? Which was better? Jesus bloody Christ, he hadn't even had coffee yet.

He clumsily found Jacob's mouth with his own, kissing him, their teeth clicking together as he started thrusting harder, more demandingly. Jacob's laughter rumbled against Kit's ribs, deep in Jacob's chest, soft on his lips, shaking him, shaking them both.

Jacob kept teasing, nudging against him, but then not, nearly squeezing tight enough, but then not, and Kit huffed, whimpering and squirming with frustration.

"You bastard!" he panted out. "You absolute bloody bastard!"

Jacob caught Kit's lower lip between his teeth and tugged on it. His hand went still and tight around both of them, unmoving. "Ask nicely."

"Christ!" Kit yelped "Please!"

Three things happened at once: Jacob's hand moved on their cocks, slick with sweat and precum, while the fingers of his other hand pressed into Kit, curling and hitting just right, making his back arch and hips jerk, and his mouth caught Kit's guttural groan.

Kit's mind went white. The press of fingers, the heat around him, the warm, teasing lap of Jacob's tongue made his head spin. He sagged on his forearms, his hips jerking helplessly, and just took Jacob stroking two fingers a little harder. He gasped explosively into Jacob's mouth as his cum spattered Jacob's belly.

Jacob's hand kept moving, though, and he wasn't spent.

"Wait," Kit panted out. "Wait, wait, wait..." He pulled himself free of Jacob's hands and flopped onto his side. Could go for hands, but just once, he wanted to taste him. Likely as not it was the last time they'd get the chance, and he wanted to.

He shoved himself down the bed, still breathing hard, and pushed the sheet down, down over Jacob's hips. Jacob's fingers were still around his cock, but Kit batted them away and sprawled over Jacob's belly to lick at the head of his cock.

Jacob's chest heaved under him as he swirled his tongue around the head, tasting his own cum and Jacob's. He leaned closer and took as much of Jacob in his mouth as he could, licking, then swallowing, then dragging back, and Jacob groaned like he was dying.

"Good." Jacob's voice sounded even hoarser. His cum-spattered hand tangled into Kit's hair, and he pushed his hips up.

Kit shifted over him, alternating licking and sucking. He dipped one hand between Jacob's thighs and squeezed his balls, kneading them with the same rhythm as his mouth.

Jacob was close already anyway, and when Kit moved his hand onto Jacob's shaft, it only took a few rapid strokes and licks. He never made any real noise when he came, only clenched his fist in Kit's hair and groaned long and low.

Kit squirmed around, cum on his lips, and wiped his mouth with the back of his hand. "One for the road?" he guessed, propping himself on Jacob's chest again.

Jacob stroked his fingers through Kit's hair, gazing at him. "One for the road," he agreed, then pulled Kit's mouth to his for a brief kiss, their lips barely grazing and his thumb brushing Kit's cheek.

"What I said last night..." Kit began, then trailed off.

"Don't worry about it." Jacob withdrew his hand from Kit's hair, smoothing it fondly. "You need to get a shower."

Kit winced. "Yeah. Some tit rubbed cum in my hair."

Jacob's soft, sleepy smile made Kit's heart skip a beat. "Daft bugger," Jacob murmured drowsily. He nodded toward the door. "Go on. I'll go and check we haven't traumatised Luke."

Colour surged up Kit's face. Well, as a grace note to their relationship, embarrassing Jacob's kid was a fine way to do it. He rolled over to the side of the bed and stooped over to find his boxers. He wiped himself off, then hopped into them and looked back over his shoulder. "Thank you."

Jacob smiled, tired but sated.

By the time Kit emerged from the shower, Jacob and his son were in the kitchen, both in T-shirts and boxers.

Kit hesitated in the doorway, buttoning up his shirt. "Um. Morning."

Father and son turned to him, and Luke's eyebrow rose, one side of his mouth crooking in a smile as dirty as his father's, activating Kit's blush like flicking a switch. Kit scowled down at his rosy chest as he fumbled with the buttons and wondered if the floor would obligingly open up and swallow him.

"Um. So. Um. I'll be going now."

"You're not staying for breakfast?" Luke asked. "I'd say you need your energy."

Kit felt more than heard the squeak that escaped him.

Jacob swatted his son across the back of the head, earning a snicker from Luke, as he walked around him to get to Kit. "Ignore him," he said. "You can go if you want to."

Kit nodded. "Should get to the office. Might be less reporters about."

Jacob looked at him with concern. "Yeah. Probably best." He watched as Kit pulled his shoes and jacket on, then walked with him to the door. "You take care of yourself, you hear me?"

Kit tried to smile. "Yeah." He shoved his hands into his pockets, rocking on the balls of his feet. Anything to stop him from grabbing Jacob and kissing him again. "We had some fun, didn't we?"

Jacob's dimples appeared. "I'll say," he agreed as he unlocked the door and opened it. "And you have my number. If you need to talk to someone. Or whatever."

Kit stepped out into the hall. He'd fisted his hands in his pockets, and he really didn't want to walk away. "Jacob," he started, raising his eyes to the other man's.

The words stuck in his throat, and he could only lean closer and press one last kiss to Jacob's lips.

Jacob touched his shoulder. "Take care."

Kit managed a weak flick of a smile, then turned and hurried away before he changed his mind. He didn't see the other man standing in the hallway until he crashed squarely into him, sending him stumbling, knocking against the wall.

"Shit! Sorry!" Kit exclaimed. "Are you okay?"

"Don't move!" The man held up a hand. "My contact lens!"

Kit almost asked why he didn't get his eyes fixed, but it wasn't the time or place. Instead, he crouched with the man, searching the floor. A shimmer caught his eye, and he picked up the tiny disc between his fingers.

"Huh." He tilted it into the light. "Is this it? It looks like a digi-lens?"

The man snatched it and pulled a small case out of his pocket. With a practised hand, he rinsed the lens off. "Yes, that's it," he snapped as he pulled back his eyelid and put the lens back in. Kit rose, watching him.

Digi-lenses weren't all that common. For people who didn't want a retinal implant or didn't like the effort of carrying around a quill or a slate, wearing the monitor on one eyeball was an option, but they were so rigid they could pop out easily.

A glow centred over the man's pupil, the tiny screen illuminating for him.

"Is it okay?" Kit asked hopefully, praying he didn't have to add repair bills to his current worries.

"No thanks to you." The man glared at Kit, and the colours on his eye danced and shifted. He frowned. "You don't live around here."

"No." Kit jerked his thumb toward the stairs. "I was just leaving."

The man glanced along the hall. "You're a friend of Jake's?"

Kit shrugged. "I know him and his son." He stepped around the man. "Excuse me."

By the time he got on the tram, he'd started wondering why a man with such a hi-tech lens had been skulking around in the halls of Jacob's building. Jacob didn't live in a high-end part of the city. Even people who were well off didn't really bother with those kinds of lenses anyway. And come to think of it, he couldn't remember anyone calling Jacob "Jake." He didn't seem the type who would like it.

Kit took out his quill to let Jacob know about the encounter, especially that those lenses were often used for keeping a discreet eye on people. If they'd followed him, fair enough, although most of the reporters chasing the TRI story weren't exactly being subtle about it. But the man had mentioned Jacob.

Perhaps days of paranoia were catching up with him, but with everything that was going on, it felt better to be safe than sorry.

His quill buzzed in his hand.

He called me Jake?

Kit typed in an affirmative, then waited.

Okay. Jacob's messages came in rapidly, one after another. *Don't worry about this. I think I know what it might be about. FYI, Luke is laughing himself sick at the thought of anyone calling me Jake.*

Kit had to smile at that. He typed a brief message: *Let me know what happens.*

A tiny image of a thumbs-up appeared on the screen.

"You are such a dad," Kit murmured, shaking his head with a tired smile. He slipped the quill away and folded his arms over his chest, trying not to think about what the man in the hall might be after.

He didn't have long to worry about it.

As soon as the tram pulled up to the stop nearest the TRI with the huddle of reporters still hanging around outside, he had much more pressing problems to focus on. He stepped out onto the platform and took a deep breath.

Time to face the press, and hopefully get out alive.

Chapter Forty-Three

Jacob left Luke at his flat. They'd talked over breakfast, and while there'd been some teasing about him being a dirty old man with a toy boy, Jacob got to say all the things he wanted and needed to say.

It felt better to be prepared for the worst, even if it didn't happen.

The whole ride down to the station, he stared unseeing out of the window.

Cutting Kit loose was the end of it. It would be better for Kit, in the long run to find someone who didn't get himself in trouble so often, because Jacob was a moron who couldn't think. Kit had been right about that.

In hindsight, Jacob had dived headlong into situations without thinking about the repercussions so many times it was embarrassing: shagging his then-girlfriend in a desperate attempt to prove to his heterosexuality to his parents, dropping out of college to join the police force to make money to help raise his son rather than get an education, taking his first boyfriend to meet the parents on the bloody stupid assumption it would open their minds, and then getting so determined to pay Luke's way through university that he went and buggered Rory's life up instead.

Better for Kit, for both of them, to end on a good note.

One for the road.

No matter what Kit had said the night before. No matter if he meant it. No matter if Jacob was starting to wonder if maybe, possibly, he might be able to feel the same. One for the road. A final line under the hot mess that had been their relationship.

He pressed his hand over his eyes.

"Bloody idiot," he whispered.

He didn't know which of them he was talking about.

A few reporters were loitering outside the station by the time he got there, trying to see in through the frosted glass of the reception doors. He brushed by them and went into the building and paused at the front desk, registering his arrival on the ID sensor.

"Detective Inspector Ofori?"

Jacob paused, glancing into the reception area. "Mrs. Ashraf?" He headed toward her. Like him, she had been screwed over by the case, and now, at least, he could sympathise in earnest. "How are things going?"

She rose and shook his hand. He hadn't seen her since their last meeting, though he knew she'd been called in by people much further up the food chain. She looked drained. "I think you can imagine."

He didn't have to, but he nodded all the same. "And Ben? Is he all right?"

"As well as he can be, really. My husband is looking after him and our boys at the moment. We're keeping him out of the limelight."

"Good."

"Mrs. Ashraf?" Both she and Jacob turned. DCI Crawford stood in the doorway and nodded to Jacob. "If you'll come with me, Mrs. Ashraf, we're ready for you upstairs."

Mrs. Ashraf picked up her coat and bag. "Perhaps I'll see you later, Detective Inspector."

He stepped aside to let her pass, then went to the second lift to head up to his own department. The office already bustling, he glanced at the incident board. The TRI had been relegated to a single folder at the bottom of the screen. Now, the focus had turned to the mystery man—presently Baby Robertson—the missing woman, and Harper.

"Anything new?" he asked Temple as she transferred data across from her slate.

"One possible lead," she said, tapping a finger to the slate and scaling up an image on the incident board. "We finally managed to get the video clip cleaned up enough to be visible."

Jacob went closer and studied it—footage from outside Harper's building, distorted, but clear enough to see the woman they were looking for. She ran down the steps, and a moment later, a pod drew up in front of her. She glanced back, climbed in, and off she went.

"This is good," Jacob said. "It looks like a taxi-pod, doesn't it? That means the company will have it tracked. We can find out where she went from there."

"You'd think so," Temple replied, scratching the hollow of her cheek with her thumb.

"Oh?"

"We contacted the taxi firms first thing to find the one that did this pick-up, but haven't had any luck so far." She shrugged. "It may look like a taxi. Could be she had a friend who sent it for her."

Jacob stifled a groan. He rubbed at his eyelids with his forefinger and thumb. "Okay. Have you got someone trying to track it on other cameras?" She nodded. "If we can get a clear shot, and the registration panel isn't visible, set someone to follow it on the cameras..."

"My thoughts exactly." She reduced the image back down. "Also, there are a few messages for you. Mr. Harper called. He wants to arrange a meeting with you. He asked for you to call and schedule it as soon as possible."

Jacob hesitated. "When did he call?"

"Less than half an hour ago. Why? Is it important?"

Jacob rubbed his jaw, recalling Kit's unexpected message. Someone had eyes on him, and if it wasn't a reporter, he had a feeling he knew who it might be. "I think it could be. You okay doing what you're doing?"

Temple nodded, frowning. "You all right?"

Jacob smiled, tight and forced. "Yeah. We're getting somewhere. Keep people looking for the pod. I'll be in my office."

His messages were illuminated on the small board beside his desk, and he dragged Harper's number into the call box, touching his earpiece as it dialled. He wasn't surprised that Harper had been in touch. He'd been expecting it.

Harper's secretary answered, but she couldn't tell him anything specific, only that Mr. Harper wanted to see him privately, at his earliest convenience.

Jacob gazed at the calendar projected on his message board. He had nothing scheduled, but if his assumptions were correct, he didn't want to go rushing in half-cocked. Plus, he highly doubted Harper had grown a conscience overnight and decided to hand over a sheaf of useful information. Not given the note their last meeting had ended on.

Now, he needed the man to be at ease, and how better than to let him think he was holding all the cards?

"Shall we say one o'clock?" he said with false brightness. "His office?"

The secretary agreed, and Jacob ended the call, then removed his earpiece. A glance at the clock showed nine thirty. Enough time to make a few calls, speak to the right people. He ran his hand over his mouth. No time like the present.

He rose from his desk and went to the door. "Temple, do you know if Ashraf is in with anyone but the DCIs?"

Temple shook her head. "They didn't say."

He nodded, tapping his fingertips on the doorframe. "Right." He glanced back at his desk, then walked back out into the incident room. "If anyone is looking for me, I'm going to be upstairs for a bit."

"Something come up, sir?"

Jacob hesitated at the door, looking back at her. "I need you to keep on top of this case for me for now, Abby."

She frowned. "Of course." She studied him and came closer. "Sir, is something wrong?"

He tugged at the cuff of his sleeve, then jerked his head for her to come with him. He led her into one of the meeting rooms. "Mr. Harper wants a meeting, and upstairs need to know that he was being vocal about causing trouble for us. I might have pushed his buttons."

Temple groaned. "Not again."

"He's concealing evidence," Jacob said. "Maybe more. I...we need..." He sighed. "Look, I'll focus on him for now, and make sure he's only gunning for me, not the department. I need someone running point on everything else. It might only be temporary or it might be until that wanker stops playing silly buggers with us, and God only knows how long that could take."

She knocked his arm with her fist. "One day, you're going to learn to use that mess of stuff between your ears and stop riling people."

Jacob's lips twitched. "One day, maybe. You'll be okay with this?"

She laughed. "I know how you work, old man. Told you I'd take your job eventually, even temporarily."

He rolled his eyes and swiped his hand to open the door. "Get back to it then, Temple."

She threw a mock salute his way as she left. He blew out a breath. One person down. Only several ranks to go.

By the time he'd finished with DCI Crawford and gone two levels higher, it was coming up to noon, and he felt wrung out like an old cloth. In some ways, it had gone as expected, but then Harper had changed the rules, and Christ, he hated lawyers.

He returned to the incident room and watched Temple giving instructions to Foley. She always managed to keep up with him, no matter how bad a case got, a rare gift in a DS.

"Temple." She turned, looking over. "You got a minute?"

"I'll be with you in a second," she confirmed. "Get yourself a coffee. You look like crap."

By the time she joined him in his office, Jacob had finished his coffee and had his head in his hands. He'd tried massaging at his temples, but nothing seemed to work with the headache pounding behind his eyes.

Temple closed the door behind her. "You want to tell me what's actually happening, sir?"

He looked up at her. "Harper's lawyers have been pulling strings. I've been...advised that my attitude toward him the other day could be deemed as unnecessarily aggressive."

"Unnecessary my arse." Temple sat down opposite him. "You said it yourself—that bloated wanker has been keeping information from us. We have the tapes that prove it."

"Inadmissible," Jacob said. "They intend to use 'technical glitch' as an argument."

Temple propped her arms on the edge of his desk. "So what happens now?"

Jacob sighed, leaning back in his seat. Upstairs had made their instructions clear: no more pushing of buttons, no more encouraging a wealthy businessman to sic his very expensive lawyers on the department, no more aggressive pursuit without due cause.

Still, he planned on hauling her in with him, so she had to know what was going on.

"I think he may have been keeping eyes on our team."

Temple sat back, shock written on her face. "How? I mean, our records aren't meant to be publicly accessible."

"Don't know." Jacob glanced over to make sure she had closed the door entirely, then tapped the digital lock on his desk to ensure they wouldn't be interrupted. "There was a man in my block, acting as if he knew me. According to my source, he had high-end digi-lenses and...well, you know where I live."

"That rotten bastard," Temple growled. "I'll rip his nuts off."

Jacob had to smile. "Not yet. We don't know if anything shady is going on, but he's the one who called for the meeting. I suspect that means he thinks he has something on us. Or on me, at least. I want to see what he's going to do with it, and I want you to be there as my backup if it all goes tits up."

"You think he'll show his hand?"

Jacob lifted one shoulder. "If he does, I want to be ready for it."

Temple nodded at once. "You need a wire."

"Already one step ahead of you there." He tapped a pack on the desk. "Don't let the others know about this, not until we have confirmation of what's going on."

Temple eyed him curiously. "You sure that's all, sir? You've been off all morning."

Trust Abby to notice something. Still, until they knew how things were going to play out, there was no need to worry her.

"Isn't this enough?" He pushed his chair back. "I don't want this spilling over and affecting the rest of the team."

"As always," she murmured. "Anything else I need to know?"

"I need you to be my eyes and ears, and play along with whatever I say."

She nodded, rising. "And keep you out of a harassment suit, if worse comes to worst?"

"I'm hoping it won't. For now, get the others organised and grab a bite to eat. I'll call you when we're going."

She headed for the door but glanced back. "This case is a bundle of fun, isn't it?"

He opened up the case and took out the wire to fit it on his jacket. "You have no idea."

They left for Harper's office half an hour later. Jacob elected to take one of the blue-and-white squad pods, instead of the unmarked ones. They were going in as police officers, and he intended to make that as clear as possible.

Harper's secretary had been notified and waited for them at the door.

Jacob was pleased to see the flicker of concern in the woman's expression when she noticed Temple.

"Mr. Harper didn't expect anyone else," she said as she led them into the building. "I'm afraid the meeting room is only prepared for him and yourself, Detective Inspector."

Jacob smiled benignly. "I expected as much. Don't worry about it. One of the DCIs insisted that we come together, but I'm sure Temple would be more than happy to have a seat somewhere with no one asking her questions."

"It's been a busy day, sir," Temple agreed, stone-faced. "Does Mr. Harper's meeting room have a waiting area? Or somewhere out of the way?"

The secretary hesitated. "I think there should be a conference room available, if that's all right."

Temple smiled. "Somewhere quiet to catch up on my notes would be fine."

The secretary looked relieved and picked up her pace. Jacob glanced at Abby with a quick nod of approval. When she was ushered into a room, she reached up and pointedly tucked her hair behind her ear. She was listening already.

"This way, Detective Inspector," the secretary said, leading him onward.

Mr. Harper waited in a room several doors away, as unlike his office as possible, sterile and plain with a digital desk in the middle of the floor. Two bland landscapes hung on the wall, each just off-centre, and the monotonous ticking of the clock was uncomfortably loud. It had to be some kind of interview room, definitely designed to make people feel uncomfortable.

"Detective Inspector." Harper rose from the seat behind the desk. "I'm glad you could come."

And so, Jacob clasped the man's hand briefly, *the game begins.*

"I was told your lawyers have been in touch," he said as he sat opposite Harper. "I hope they've advised you to provide all and any information you might have pertaining to our missing woman."

Harper smiled, but it didn't reach his eyes. He sat and folded his hands together. "I feel we got off on the wrong foot, Detective Inspector. We could help each other."

Jacob inclined his head. "If you provide the information I asked for, then yes, I do believe you could."

Harper's eyes were cold. "I was thinking of a different type of information. It would be a shame if there were some questions raised over the people involved in this case."

Easy does it. Jacob leaned slowly back in the seat. The man had to hang himself, but he had to take a hold of the noose first. "I'm not sure I follow, Mr. Harper. What are you implying?"

"Discretion is beneficial."

Jacob pushed back the chair in a show of impatience. "I didn't come down here for you to speak in riddles and waste my time," he said, rising. "Unless you have something useful for me, I have a lot of work to be doing."

Harper looked up at him. "I would sit down if I were you, DI Ofori."

"Give me one good reason why."

When an image of Kit's face appeared on the desk, he couldn't help feeling both disappointment and relief in equal measure. Sometimes, it was frustrating to be right about people.

Kit appeared mussed and sleepy, as he had been when he left Jacob's flat that morning. It had to be a still frame from a live feed. Not his best look, and Jacob stared at it a little too long, and a little too hard, schooling his face into an expression of guarded shock.

"What the hell is this?" he demanded.

"Sit down, Mr. Ofori."

No more DI. Jacob forced down a tight smile. Instead, he obliged and, in doing so, handed Harper a little more rope. "Where did you get that picture?" he asked quietly.

"That doesn't matter." Harper tapped his finger on the desk. "What matters is that I have it. You know why I have it, and I know why you wouldn't want anyone to know about it."

Jacob looked down as he clenched his hands into fists in his lap and bunched his shoulders. Tense and tight. Exactly what Harper would be expecting. "So it's to be blackmail, is it?"

Harper chuckled. "That's a very nasty word, Mr. Ofori. As I said before, I think we can help each other." He flicked the image to show a frame of the last kiss, then Kit leaving, and Jacob standing in the doorway, watching him go. "Cooperation."

Jacob folded his hands together and looked slowly back up at Harper. "I only want to find the girl. Why are you protecting her? What the hell is she to you?"

The man laughed again. "Her? Nothing."

The pieces slipped into place. She had Sanders's technology on hard drives. Maybe Harper hadn't believed her entirely, but he had suspected the value of the data. Now, with the TRI going public and the revelation of what Sanders had created, Harper could have access to a potential goldmine.

"And if I pursue you?" Jacob put just enough tightness in his voice. "I know you have her hidden away. What's to stop me coming after you?"

Kit's face flitted back onto the desktop. Harper tapped the surface, smiling benignly at him. "Are you really willing to risk your career, your reputation, on the off-chance I might know where she is?"

"You think this is relevant?" Jacob nodded toward Kit's image.

"I think," Harper murmured silkily, "you were investigating the TRI, and have ended up shagging one of your suspects, Mr. Ofori. Regardless of whether I have the girl or not, I don't think your superiors would be too happy to know about that, do you?"

Somewhere in the building, Temple would be having kittens, but right now, Jacob couldn't care less. He had baited and set the trap, and Harper had blundered straight into it, with Abby as the witness on the other end of the wire.

"They weren't," he said, smiling.

Harper frowned. "What?"

"My superiors," Jacob replied. "They weren't happy when I told them, but given the circumstances, I had no choice."

Harper's face went paler. "What the hell are you on about?"

Jacob rose from the chair. Maybe he'd just flushed his career down the toilet, and he'd likely get dragged through the dirt by the press. That didn't matter. What mattered was that he'd nailed the bastard and nailed him hard.

"Your little spy wasn't very discreet, Mr. Harper." He braced both hands on the desk. "I knew you had these images before you did."

"Bullshit!"

"Temple," Jacob said. "If you don't mind joining us?"

Harper's face blotched with red. "What?"

Jacob turned the collar of his jacket, revealing the wire. "You tried to blackmail a police officer, Mr. Harper. You have also practically admitted to hiding our missing girl, which means you are also guilty of perverting the course of justice."

Harper surged up from the chair, scrabbling at the desk to conceal the images. "If that's the case, why don't you arrest me?" He looked furious. "All this showboating! It's a bluff!"

Jacob stepped to one side as the door opened. He didn't dare look at Temple. "I'm afraid I have no capacity to arrest you, Mr. Harper. Rather than risk this case and the wrath of your expensive little lawyers, I have tendered my resignation." Despite Abby's sharp indrawn breath, he kept his eyes on Harper. Now he'd said it out loud, he felt light-headed, his stomach knotting. "Temple, this is your case and your arrest, if you don't mind."

"Yes, sir," Temple said, voice tight with emotion.

It should have been a victory, he thought, as he watched Temple cuff Harper and read him his rights. It should have been, and yet the exhilaration and triumph were being swallowed up, and it took all his effort to keep standing, his legs shaking beneath him.

"Are you coming back to the station with us, sir?" Temple asked once they had loaded Harper into the back of the squad pod.

Jacob forced himself to look at her. "I don't think that's a good idea. Better for me to stay out of the way for now."

"Sir..."

He shook his head. "The DCIs will make an announcement. Give it a few days for the dust to settle." He held out a hand. "You'll do well, Abby."

She looked at his hand, then took it in hers. "Thank you, sir."

He tried to smile. "Jacob. It's just Jacob now."

Chapter Forty-Four

The mood in the TRI had been grim all day.

Running the gauntlet of reporters, all pushing and shouting questions, had been terrifying but it got worse when he got inside. From the subdued discussions around the building, Kit realised a few more people had left the previous day, and Mariam had been called to the police station again. He didn't know what else she could possibly be telling, and he was glad he wasn't in her shoes.

All things considered, he had an easy job.

He went to the gate room to finally install the lock for testing within one of their three gates. The mechanism seemed to be finished, and it only needed to be adjusted and fitted within the body of the gate itself. Not the most difficult thing he'd ever done, but time-consuming.

Still, better to be there, out of the way of anyone who might make a snide comment. He'd even planned ahead and snagged a couple of sandwiches from the canteen, so he didn't have to go upstairs to eat or face anyone.

He turned up the volume on his quill until the beat bounced off the metal walls, safe in the knowledge no one would care, and got on with his task. He was so engrossed in it, hours later, that he didn't notice the door open behind him.

The music cut off suddenly, leaving him singing tunelessly along with silence.

"What..." He turned, then blinked. "Mariam?"

She held up his quill. "Do you have a minute?"

Kit hesitated, glancing back at the gate. His hand currently held a bundle of four wires inside the body of the machine. "Give me a second..."

She nodded, and he turned back to the wires. It took him nearly five minutes to get them all reconnected and attached to his satisfaction.

That done, he climbed down from the ladder. "What's going on?" From the look on her face, the news wasn't good, and it felt like his heart had dropped through his stomach. "Are we being shut down? Are they taking the gates?"

She held out the quill to him. "There's going to be a review. A big one. The government has demanded it. They feel we have had too much power, using this technology without international approval." She sighed, removing her glasses to rub at her eyes. "The rest of the world is breathing down their neck about it."

"Shit."

"Mm." She looked up at him. "We might still lose it. I don't know. But for now, everything is on hold."

He glanced at the gate again. "Including the lock?"

She fell silent for a moment. "How close is it to finished?"

"Two days. It would need to be tested, but it would be finished by then."

Mariam approached the gate, looking it over. She reached out and ran her fingertips lightly down the frame, then turned back to him. "Finish it. If you can get two more made for the backups, I know Tom would have wanted the locks in place, no matter what."

"It might not work," he warned. "It could block travel in either direction. No coming or going."

"If the gates are taken from us, then that might be a good thing."

He turned his quill around in his hands. "People might ask me what I'm doing."

"Just say you're keeping them up to Sanders's specifications." She exhaled a shaking breath. "We need the locks in place. If they take them, if they use them, we need to make sure they don't make the same mistakes we did."

"I'll see to it," he promised.

Mariam stepped back from the gate. "Have you heard from Detective Inspector Ofori?" She said it casually, but something in her tone made the hairs on the back of Kit's neck rise.

"Not lately."

Her shoulders rose and fell with the release of a breath. "Oh." She turned back to face him. "He quit."

Kit stared at her. "What?"

"Detective Inspector Ofori. He quit."

"Quit?" Kit echoed. "Quit what? The case?"

She shook her head. "The police force."

Kit tightened his grip on his quill. "What?"

"DS Temple is taking over the case," Mariam replied quietly. "She said DI Ofori has stepped down."

Kit swayed on his feet. Shit. Had he got Jacob in so much trouble he had to quit? "Did she say why?"

"She only said his resignation is pending."

A swoop of nausea made his throat tighten. His hands were trembling so much he had to curl them into fists to hide it. Jesus. He'd done a lot of things in his life, but he'd never buggered up anyone else's so badly before.

"I didn't know."

Mariam awkwardly patted him on the arm. "This situation hasn't been good for anyone."

He nodded, staring past her. It didn't count, not like everything else that had happened. He'd pursued Jacob, and even after Jacob had warned him it could lead to trouble, he'd kept going to him. Jacob had been screwed over and lost his job because of Kit. Not anyone else. It wasn't the case or the TRI or anything else. It was just him.

"You okay?"

Kit brushed by her. "I think I need to make a call. 'Scuse me." He bolted for the door, through the layover room and out into the hall, taking the stairs two at a time.

Three flights up, he had to stop. His ribs ached, like someone squeezing them with a giant hand, and he stumbled against the wall, gasping. He sank to sit at the foot of the wall, trying to catch his breath, and his hands shook as he opened up Jacob's number.

He stared numbly at the dial key.

What the hell was he meant to say?

What the hell was he meant to do?

The quill clattered when it hit the floor, and he pressed the heels of his hands against his eyes. Christ, what kind of selfish bastard did it make him if he started going after Jacob all over again? The man had already lost his job because of him.

Kit was still sitting there, arms wrapped around his legs, when Mariam caught up with him. She didn't speak at once. Instead, she knelt and picked up his quill, and widened the screen with a touch. She held it out to him.

"You should call him."

Kit wanted to argue, but it came out as a breaking laugh.

She sighed and took one of his hands in hers, turning it over. "He thought you were worth the risk, Kit."

She laid the quill in his hand, and he closed his fingers around it as she stepped around him and made her way up the stairs.

He called, eventually, but—no shocks there—Jacob didn't reply.

Kit slipped his quill away. Later, he decided. He would try again later. He rubbed his eyes. He was so bloody tired, and he should've left hours ago.

Half an hour later, he managed to sneak out of the building and out of sight of the lurking reporters, and flagged one of the taxi-pods. While he waited, he tried Jacob's number again. It didn't even go to the inbox. No wonder. If he'd dropped his job as quickly as Mariam said, then everyone would be trying to reach him. Who could blame him for avoiding everyone?

Kit clambered into the taxi-pod and tapped his quill against the destination sensor. He slouched back in the seat and closed his eyes, trying to think what he would say to Jacob when he finally got through to him.

The journey home didn't take as long as expected, and when the pod chimed, he sat up with a frown.

He was outside Jacob's tower block.

Kit stared at the building, then at his quill. Of course. The bloody thing picked up on the last location he'd used in the taxi network. Either that or the universe enjoyed having a good laugh at his expense.

Still, he had to apologise for ballsing up Jacob's life, and maybe it was better to do it face to face.

It felt like a lifetime since he'd walked down the hall, even if only a dozen hours had passed. It all felt different.

His hand shook as he pressed the door chime.

He didn't know what he should say. He didn't know what he could say, but he had to say *something*.

The door opened.

Luke stood on the other side. "Kit."

Kit looked down at his shoes self-consciously. "Your dad—"

"He's not here," Luke interrupted. "He didn't come home."

Chapter Forty-Five

People were arguing in the hall.

Jacob took another mouthful of beer from his bottle and tried not to listen. The trouble with going for a downscale hotel somewhere out of the way meant thinner walls and doors, and a less considerate clientele.

He'd taken a basic room with a bed, small couch, table, and chairs. A small bathroom with a grotty shower took up one corner of the room. It felt more like a holding cell than somewhere to rest and relax.

Jacob stood by the window, looking down into the street.

The worst of rush hour was over, but still pods still shuttled here and there, back toward the city centre. He had idly toyed with the idea of wandering out, finding somewhere to eat, but put it aside at once. He always hated eating out alone. Without someone to talk to, it didn't feel right.

Instead, he'd called down for room service. Holing up in the room and staying there with his quill turned off felt like the simplest course of action. His colleagues would want answers, and he wasn't ready to give them yet.

He turned from the window, letting the curtain fall back in place. If he called, Luke would come running. His son had insisted on staying in town after Jacob called him to let him know what had happened at Harper's offices. He wanted to be there, he said. What kind of son would he be if he wasn't there when his father's world fell apart?

And yet, Jacob had run off to hide out in a hotel and told his son to let him be.

He didn't even know why.

Force of habit, he supposed. Pride. Retreating into a corner to lick his wounds and try to work out what to do next.

He didn't know.

He sat on the edge of the bed and drained the rest of the bottle.

Thirty years on the force. What the hell was he meant to do with himself? He had no real formal education. Police work, especially detective work, had been his life for more than twenty years. Those weren't the most transferable skills.

And then there was Kit.

They'd gone their separate ways. It had been a clean break. The trouble was that the job—the case—was the reason they couldn't see each other, but that obstacle had been removed. Another factor to think about, another decision that needed to be made, and right now, Jacob's head wouldn't stop buzzing.

He picked up another bottle of beer from the pack at his feet.

In the hall, the argument had trailed off. A door slammed somewhere beyond his walls.

He opened the bottle and took a drink, enjoying the brief silence.

The door chimed to notify him someone was waiting, and he glanced at his watch. For such a basic place, the room service was bloody fast.

He set the bottle on the nightstand and went over to open the door.

His heart leapt to his mouth.

Kit stood there, worn out and dishevelled. "Hello." He looked down at his feet, then back up. "We need to talk."

He was right, of course. There were decisions to be made. Conversations they needed to have. All the things a sensible adult would do.

Jacob couldn't give a shit about any of them. He grabbed Kit by the front of his jacket and pulled him into the room, and before Kit could say a word, Jacob had him pressed up against the back of the door, kissing him as if his life depended on it.

Kit froze, startled, but it lasted less than a heartbeat. His taut lips softened, parting, and his tongue darted against Jacob's. Jacob laughed with relief, sinking his fingers into Kit's tangled hair.

Kit's hands were wandering, too, and Jacob shuddered pleasantly as one of them undid the buttons of his shirt and slipped between the folds to press to his skin. Kit curled his fingers, and his nails scratched down, drawing a groan of want from Jacob's throat.

He pulled back from the kiss reluctantly, nipping Kit's lower lip in reproof, and searched the younger man's face.

Kit's pale cheeks had flushed, and his lips were already swollen. He met Jacob's eyes as he undid the rest of the buttons of Jacob's shirt, pushed it open, and slid his hands up to the back of Jacob's neck to tug him back for another kiss.

Jacob didn't know which of them moved first, but all at once, they were stumbling toward the bed. Clothes fell in their wake. He shook his shirt off his arms, Kit peeled his T-shirt over his head and threw it aside, and both of them were kicking their trousers off as they crashed onto the bed.

Kit landed on top of him, chest to chest, and pinned him in place with his body, his hands sunk into the covers on either side of Jacob's head. Kit's heart thundered as rapidly as Jacob's own.

"Hey," Kit said, eyes shining.

Jacob splayed his hands on Kit's back, sliding them down to squeeze his arse. "Hey."

Kit's mouth met his suddenly, hotly. His tongue teased along Jacob's lips and thrust lazily between them, over and over, as he rocked his hips playfully against Jacob's and squirmed encouragingly when Jacob swatted his backside.

Jacob dragged his hand up to tug on Kit's hair, drawing his head up enough to meet his eyes. "Fancy going out with me some time?"

Kit stared at him, then dropped his head forward to burrow his face in Jacob's neck. "I'm naked and wriggling on top of you." He nibbled his way up Jacob's throat, earning pleasant shivers. Jacob jolted as teeth closed on his earlobe and tugged. Kit's breath warmed his ear. "What do you think?"

Jacob curled his fingers, raking his nails across Kit's scalp. "I'm not sure. Maybe you should paint me a sign."

Kit lifted his head and they stared at each other. Kit broke first, dissolving into giggles. Jacob couldn't help smiling as Kit sprawled on top of him, his knees pressing into the mattress on either side of Jacob's body.

"I like you," Kit informed him and kissed the tip of his nose.

Jacob trailed his fingertips lightly up Kit's back. "Same."

It was the first time he'd really said anything of the kind, the first time he'd felt free to, and he saw the moment when Kit recalled why. His smile winked out, and he hastily knelt over Jacob, straddling his thighs. He braced his hands on Jacob's midriff, frowning at them.

"Sorry about your job."

Jacob propped himself up on one elbow and reached up to catch the back of Kit's head. "I made the call." He ran his thumb along Kit's cheek. "You helped me, you know. If it wasn't for you, I'd have been fired and never got the bastard."

Kit's expression brightened. "You caught him?"

Jacob grinned. "Oh yes." For all that losing his livelihood felt like the rug being pulled out from under him, he still had the satisfaction of knowing he'd outsmarted Harper. "He tried to blackmail me. Thanks to you, I knew to expect it, so I played my hand first. The son of a bitch didn't know what hit him."

"Good." Kit's smile returned, though not as brilliant as it had been. "That's good."

Jacob sat up and slid his hand to knead at the back of Kit's neck. "Don't give me that look."

"What look?"

Jacob raised his eyebrows. "That kicked-puppy look." He drew Kit closer and kissed him again. "You haven't noticed the bright side, have you? I can take you out in public now and get us arrested for indecent exposure the next time we shag on the balcony."

Kit's face lit up like a beacon, his grin returning, and he smacked Jacob's shoulder. "You're a twat."

"Mm." Jacob brushed his lips lightly along Kit's, teasing him into another kiss.

"Jacob..." Kit began, drawing back.

"Not tonight," Jacob murmured. "I just...let's not think for a bit, eh? Just tell me you're all right with this. With us."

Kit ran his hand along Jacob's shoulders. "Have you looked at you lately?" The echo of that first date, that first night, rang in the words. It felt like such a long time ago.

Jacob wrapped his arm around Kit's waist, pulling him flush against his own body. "That doesn't answer the question."

Kit cupped Jacob's face between his hands and met his eyes, his expression solemn. "I say again, I'm naked and wriggling on top of you. What do you think?"

Jacob rubbed his cheek into Kit's hand. "Not enough wriggling."

Their mouths met again, and Kit rose on his knees over him, cradling Jacob's head as he drew every breath from Jacob's lips, hungry and demanding, and Jacob stroked at Kit's back and down, curving over his arse and squeezing.

The door chimed, and Jacob pulled away. "Shit."

"Ignore it," Kit suggested, nibbling on Jacob's ear.

"Ignore my first meal since breakfast?"

Kit sat on Jacob's lap, indignant. "Bugger," he declared, swinging one leg over and getting to his feet. "Yeah. You need to eat something." He scanned the floor, then snatched up his trousers and pulled them on. "I'll get it."

By the time he returned, carrying the tray, Jacob had rearranged himself in his boxers. Thankfully, he wasn't nearly as up as he could have been, though he couldn't help notice the reproachful look Kit gave his groin.

"Nothing personal."

Kit wrinkled his nose. "We'll say it's low blood sugar."

Jacob smiled. "I'm not sure that's how it works."

Kit slouched into one of the chairs by the table and pushed the other one out with his foot. "Let me stroke my poor, feeble ego." He loosened the waistband of his trousers and shoved his hand down, wincing. "I need something with a more comfy seam."

"That's your feeble ego?" Jacob picked up the fork.

Kit made a face and raised his eyebrows. "Funny." He settled back in the chair, watching Jacob eat. "How bad was it? Today?"

"I'm not ready to talk about it yet," Jacob replied without meeting his eyes. He used the side of his fork to cut up a sausage, then skewered one of the pieces. "I'm guessing Luke told you where to find me?"

Kit nodded. He combed his fingers through his hair, leaving it more rumpled than before. "I came to apologise. I think he felt sorry for me, and since he's worried about you, two birds with one stone."

"He's a conniving little shit," Jacob said with his mouth full. "I told him I didn't want him to come over. He didn't want me to be on my own." He pointed the fork at Kit. "You solved that for him."

"He's worried." Kit stretched out his leg and brushed his toes along Jacob's bare calf. "But he didn't tell me to get you on the bed and naked."

Jacob laughed quietly. "Yeah. I bet." He pushed the plate toward Kit. "Hungry?"

Kit stole a chip, swirling it in the ketchup. "Do you want to come back to mine?"

Jacob looked at him in surprise. "What?"

"You don't need to stay in this dump," Kit said. "I mean, if you want."

Jacob wiped his mouth on the napkin. "Any reporters still lurking about?"

Kit grimaced. "Yeah. Balls. I forgot about them."

"It was a kind offer." Jacob glanced over at the bed. "There's room for two here though. If you don't mind sharing a dump with me."

Kit stole another chip. "I think I can manage," he said and smiled.

Chapter Forty-Six

Something was ringing.

Kit grumbled in protest, but the computer didn't switch it off. Only when his warm pillow pushed him off did he remember where he was.

The lights went on, and he gave a pitiful moan, rolling over and burying his face in the pillow. Jacob patted him apologetically on the back as he picked up the hotel telephone receiver. At least, Kit thought muzzily, the ringing had stopped.

The night hadn't gone at all as he'd anticipated.

He'd shown up determined to apologise and sure that Jacob would show him the door. He hadn't expected to be kissed. And even after they were interrupted, he hadn't expected the invitation to stay.

They hadn't even gone back to shagging either. Jacob was shattered, and Kit had to admit he knew the feeling. They'd rolled into bed by nine o'clock, and though he'd teased Jacob with the offer of a hand job, they ended up watching some daft film on the telly, and Kit had dozed off before it finished, his head on Jacob's chest.

Jacob was talking in a low voice, and Kit reluctantly rolled over to where he sat on the edge of the bed. Soft light played across his back and shoulders, highlighting how tense he was.

It took him a moment to understand why.

Jacob's quill had been turned off, which meant the only person who could be phoning through the hotel for him had to be Luke. Whatever it was about, it clearly had to be important for Jacob to switch his quill back on.

Kit dragged himself closer and curled around Jacob as much as he could. Comforting, he decided. Could do that. The quill chimed as it disconnected, then another series of beeps.

He knocked his brow against Jacob's side. A wordless reminder he wasn't alone, and things were all right.

A broad hand stroked through his hair, Jacob's voice a low murmur. Someone else, a more serious voice this time. Kit tried to force his bleary eyes open, to listen, but sleep had its claws back in him.

A moment later, Jacob shook him awake.

"Kit." Jacob's voice was still soft, but more urgent now. "Kit, wake up."

He squinted up. "Mm?"

"Kit, I need you to wake up." Jacob patted his cheek. "We need to go."

Kit's heart clenched, and he struggled upright. "What's wrong?" He blinked, puzzled at the sight of Jacob fully dressed. Oh, that wasn't good, not in the middle of the night. "Is it Luke? Is he okay?"

Jacob rose from the bed and went to fetch Kit's clothes. "He's fine." He handed Kit his trousers and shirt. "Temple called me about the girl from Sanders's place."

Kit pulled on his trousers, staggering. "You found her?" His brain, slow with sleepiness, caught up. "You have his tech?"

Jacob had his own quill out and scanned through the messages. "Get dressed. You'll understand when we get there."

Kit nodded, yanking his shirt over his head. He groped around under the bed for his socks, and by the time he had them and his shoes on, Jacob had their jackets and had opened the door of the room.

Mercifully, there was a twenty-four-hour coffee window two buildings down from the hotel. Kit tottered along to get them both a generous dose of caffeine, while Jacob waited for the taxi-pod. There were a limited number of taxi-pods available at night, and if a passenger wasn't waiting as soon as it showed up, some other bugger could ping and summon it.

By the time they reached their destination, Kit was more or less awake, a couple of his fingers twitching. Too much caffeine on an empty stomach.

Kit climbed out of the taxi and stopped short, staring. They were at the central infirmary, the biggest hospital in the city, all gleaming glass and chrome.

"What happened?" he asked in a hushed voice as Jacob hustled him into the building.

"They found our girl," Jacob murmured, keeping his voice low. "She's on life support now. It looks like she fell in front of a train."

A shudder ran down Kit's back. "Looks like?"

Jacob pressed his hand low to Kit's back, steering him along the identical hallways. "That's what I've been told."

"Bullshit." Kit felt Jacob's eyes on him. "Bullshit," he said again. "She's kept out of sight and off your radar for this long, and we're meant to believe she accidentally fell in front of a train?"

"Does seem a little suspicious, doesn't it?"

Kit frowned. "Why are we here, though? You..." He hesitated, not sure how to approach the subject. Directly, he thought. Easier. Like taking a plaster off. "I mean, it isn't your job anymore."

Jacob stopped walking. "They weren't calling for me. They need you."

Kit stared at him. "What? Me? Why?" He'd barely finished speaking when he understood. "Tom's stuff. She had Tom's stuff."

Jacob nodded. "You didn't seem awake enough to understand before coffee," he said apologetically. "Abby needs you to check over what they've got if you can. She's in charge of the case now, and if we can help her, then all the better."

"But why here? Why not down at the station? And why in the middle of the night?"

"Because the minute it's down at the station, it'll go up the ladder," Jacob replied. "This is TRI business. All of that is going straight to the top of the tree. Abby needs to know what we...what they have or haven't got. If they can finish all of this..."

He trailed off, but Kit understood.

Closure. Helping him finish the last case of his career.

He rubbed his eyes. It was too early for all of it, but if Jacob needed him to, he would bloody well do it. "Right. I'll do what I can."

Jacob caught his hand and gave it a grateful squeeze. Wordlessly, he led Kit into the hospital. Kit didn't want to ask how Jacob knew his way around without checking the signs. It spoke of many visits, and that didn't bear thinking about.

Jacob finally stopped at a nurses station in the cross-section of four corridors. The nurse sitting in the circular booth glanced up as he approached. She could only be a little older than Kit, and rose from the desk when she saw Jacob. "DI Ofori."

"Louise. Temple said she would meet me here."

The nurse—Louise—nodded. "Room nine."

She glanced askance at Kit.

"One of our consultants," Jacob said smoothly. "He's been working with us on this case."

She seemed to accept that, pointing down one of the spurs. "Fifth door on the left."

Kit glanced at him as they walked. "You forget to tell her something?"

"Necessary," Jacob replied tersely.

Temple rose from her seat inside the door when Jacob opened it, nodded at him, and then studied Kit. Something in her expression gave Kit the impression he was being assessed and taken apart.

He forced himself to look beyond her at the bed where the time jumper lay, covered in a mess of tubes, wires, and bandages. The machines were beeping, and the air hissed as it was pushed into her lungs and released. He could barely see her face at all, and a glance the bed showed one leg sheared off at the knee.

He turned away, feeling sick.

"Do we know what happened?" Jacob asked. "Suicide attempt, accident, or something else?"

The policewoman shook her head. "No witnesses, and the CCTV at the station was out of order. The train was one of those high-speed freight trains. Skeleton staff. The driver didn't even see her until the proximity brakes shut the whole thing down."

"Well, that's convenient," Kit muttered. It earned him another sharp look from the woman and a hand on the shoulder from Jacob. "What am I here to see?"

Temple went over to on the girl's belongings on the table beside the wall. They were all bagged up and labelled. Some had clothes in them, some of them speckled with bloodstains. He took a deep breath. Temple pushed through them and pulled out a single small bag. "This."

Kit approached, accepting a pair of rubber gloves from her. "This is it?"

"She had this in her pocket. Everything else she had on her was smashed to pieces by the same train that hit her. CSU are recovering what they can from the scene, and we've got someone coming in to get what evidence they can from her body."

"So the only person who could tell us what happened and had valuable information is practically dead in an accident that no one witnessed and all of the data is destroyed or missing?" Jacob shook his head. "It's all too neat."

Kit tilted the lamp to examine the small object inside the bag. Rectangular, metallic, the size of a box of matches, and it looked dented, with one small socket which seemed to be blocked up. Kit smiled. Typical Tom. "Only the old data."

Temple caught her breath. "Explain."

Kit looked up at her. "Tom likes to..." His voice caught as he remembered. "Liked. Tom liked to keep new data to hand, where only he could reach it until it was ready. Somewhere no one would notice." He turned over the bag and pressed the barely visible sensors in Tom's usual pattern. The seamless sides slid open, and Temple swore under her breath. The inside of the drive was flawless and undamaged. Kit looked over at the patient. "She knew what she was looking for. She kept this on her. I don't think that's a coincidence."

Jacob and Temple exchanged looks.

Temple said, "She didn't trust whoever—"

"We don't need to mess about, Abby," Jacob interrupted. "She didn't trust Harper."

"We don't know that."

"Who else could it be?" Jacob countered. "You heard him yesterday. He practically admitted hiding her away, and now that we finally have her, she's in no state to answer any questions about his involvement? If that's not ringing alarm bells, I didn't train you well enough."

She nodded. "Unfortunately, it's only conjecture now. We need evidence."

"Where was she hiding anyway?" Kit inquired. "Somewhere nearby?"

"We still haven't found that," Temple said. "But the station was one of the rural ones. Nowhere she could have stayed nearby."

"And where there's less upkeep and fewer people," Jacob murmured. "Handy place to stage an accident when you need to get rid of a pesky living piece of evidence. Get them to check under her nails. Could be she fought someone off."

"Harper's been locked up from the moment I arrested him," Temple said, then caught her breath. "Shit."

Jacob glanced at her, and Kit suspected they had some kind of psychic police communication going on. "When did he call the lawyers in?"

"As soon as I had him in the cell. It took them an hour to get in, and they stayed for forty-five minutes. He was making a call as he left the building."

Jacob nodded. "Do we know when she was hit?"

"Around four hours ago." Temple rubbed the back of her neck, frowning. "So we have a five-hour window."

Kit had been looking from one to the other, trying to understand what that meant. "What happened in the five hours? How does that help?"

Jacob looked at him, his expression grim. "It means we might be able to work out where they collected our mystery lady from before they brought her to the train station and pushed her in front of a train."

Chapter Forty-Seven

"What the hell were you playing at?"

Jacob stepped forward. "Ma'am—"

DCI Crawford turned a blazing look on him, her dark eyes flashing. "The question was not addressed to you, *Mr*. Ofori."

Jacob flinched, retreating a step. He'd made the mistake of agreeing to accompany Temple to the station, and, by bad luck and bad timing, DCI Crawford was still in the building. A stern woman at the best of times, the matter of the TRI was weighing hard on her. They'd been summoned to her office at once, and now, she tapped a fingertip on the desk in front of her.

"I would appreciate an answer, DI Temple."

Temple's hands were in fists by her side, and Jacob couldn't see her face, but he could imagine her taut expression. "Jacob was in touch with Mr. Rafferty. We had tech we needed identified. I thought it would be advisable to do it as soon as possible."

Crawford's lips thinned. She leaned forward, the lamp on the desk carving sharp shadows across her face. "And neither of you considered the fact that this case now hinges on Mr. Harper? The very man Mr. Ofori sacrificed his career to apprehend? How do you think his lawyers are going to take it if they find out Mr. Ofori has been impersonating a police officer to gain access to a hospital ward? And that his...companion from the TRI has been involved too?"

"Ma'am, I didn't—"

"You are in quite enough trouble, Jacob," Crawford snapped. "Don't make this worse. Perhaps you didn't mention to the nurse that you were no longer in our employ, but you know as well as I that a lie of omission is still a lie."

Jacob nodded reluctantly. It had been the height of stupidity, agreeing to go to the hospital, but if they hadn't, who knew what would have happened to the tech? Kit wouldn't have been allowed anywhere near it, being as compromised in the case as Jacob himself.

"Ma'am." Temple did a good job of keeping her voice level. "Ashraf has previously said that Mr. Rafferty has the best knowledge of Sanders's technology. If we hadn't asked him to examine it, it may have been overlooked by his other colleagues."

Crawford raised an eyebrow. "And this couldn't wait to be done in the station, following the correct protocol?" She shook her head. "You were aware of the circumstances, Temple. You knew about Rafferty's involvement, and that Harper was aware of him."

"Ma'am, the information was vital—"

"That's as may be." Crawford rose from her chair. "But the point remains that Rafferty was not meant to be involved in this anymore." She pressed her hands to the desk, her fingertips whitening against the surface. "We have no idea if Harper still has eyes on Ofori. We have no idea if he's had people tailing Rafferty. For all we know, his people may be aware that an ex-police officer and a member of the public who works for the TRI have had access to evidence they had no business with."

Temple's shoulders slumped. Jacob wished he could say something to make things right, but he and Temple had both made a bad call. For the right reasons, yes, but Crawford was right. They had screwed up.

"What happens now?" Jacob asked. After all, he had technically broken the law by impersonating a police office and allowing a civilian to handle evidence.

Crawford gazed down at her desk. She looked tired. He wondered how long it had been since she'd seen her house. "Rafferty's involvement can't be avoided," she said finally. "The evidence has been altered since you bagged it up. I don't imagine we can gloss over that." She raised her eyes to him. "If anyone asks why you were there, you were dropping him off. That's all. You didn't see or touch or discuss anything. Am I understood?"

"Ma'am."

"As for you, Temple..." Crawford sighed. "I already lost one of my best DIs because of this damned case. I don't have the manpower or the capacity to suspend you until this blows over. We need evidence, and we need it now. Everything you do from this moment must be by the book. Clear?"

Temple nodded sharply. "Yes, ma'am."

Crawford looked at Jacob. "Where's Rafferty now?"

"My office," Jacob replied at once. "He wanted to wait for me."

He'd tried to persuade Kit to return to the hotel, but Kit was having none of it. He wanted to help and even offered to work on the scrambled video footage from the eye. Even as sleep-deprived as he was, Jacob knew it would only be asking for trouble to follow that avenue.

The DCI nodded. "You're free to go for now, Jacob, but please explain to your friend that he will be helping us with this investigation. Go and get some sleep. Make sure he comes down here first thing."

Jacob shot a look at Temple, but she had fixed her eyes ahead. "Yes, ma'am," he replied and retreated from the room, knowing Temple was about to receive the bollocking of a lifetime, but he couldn't help her now.

He made his way to his old office. Kit had found the recline function on his old chair and had curled up and fallen asleep on it.

Jacob circled around the desk and crouched to gently shake Kit's knee. "Hey."

Kit squinted at him blearily. "Hm?"

"Time to go." He caught Kit under the elbows and drew him to his feet. "We need to get some sleep."

Kit, barely awake, tilted into him, putting an arm around his waist. "Mm. Sleep's good."

The few officers who were in stared at them as they headed for the door. Jacob ignored them as best he could. No doubt they'd all heard about his indiscretion and wanted to have a good look at the man Jacob had sacrificed his career for.

By the time Jacob helped him into the waiting taxi-pod, Kit was more aware of his surroundings. "Sorry."

Jacob slid in beside him. "For what?" he asked as the pod moved off.

"Being clingy." Kit picked at his fingernail, a nervous tic Jacob had noticed more than once. "They were staring. The other police people."

Jacob slipped his arm around Kit's shoulder, pulling his lover back to his side. "Let them. The cat's out of the bag now anyway." He pressed a kiss to Kit's temple. "I need to tell you something."

Kit tensed. "You've not been arrested, have you?"

Jacob chuckled wearily. "I'm in a pod with you, not a cell."

"Oh. Right." Kit gave him a sheepish look. "Tired. What's up?"

"You're to help them on the case."

Kit's eyes widened. "Me?"

Jacob nodded. "Since we were seen going to the hospital, and you've opened up the tech for Abby, DCI Crawford thinks it's necessary, in case questions are asked about why we were there. It won't be anything complicated. Only dealing with Sanders's tech. You don't need to cover anything up anymore."

Kit fell silent for several seconds, then in a very small voice said, "Shit."

"Shit?" Jacob echoed. "What's shit?"

Kit fidgeted. "There's something I should have told you."

Jacob's heart sank. "Don't tell me you covered up other stuff."

"Not...exactly." Kit knotted his fingers together. "The picture of that girl. The anonymous one..."

A suspicion crept up on Jacob. "How did you know it was anonymous? We never mentioned that in the press reports."

Kit stared at his knuckles. "Something they didn't tell you about Janos—he's a bloody genius with computers. He...might have cloned your slate so I could decode the video."

Jacob thought he heard wrong. "What?"

"Your slate. Janos copied the files." He took a shaky breath, and the words came out in a torrent. "We just...we kind of knew what was going on, and we couldn't tell you, but we couldn't not tell you either, so we...the video... I undid what I did to it, and Janos sent you the picture, so you'd know who you were looking for."

Well, he definitely hadn't expected that.

"You hacked a police computer and stole the files?"

"We wanted to help." Kit looked imploringly at him. "There was so much we couldn't tell you. So much we had to keep under wraps. It was the only way we could think of to get the information to you without everyone finding out about the TRI."

"Shit." Jacob sank against the seat. He withdrew his arm from Kit's shoulders and rubbed at his face with both hands. Just when things couldn't get any more complicated.

Kit touched his knee, then drew his hand back at once. "I'm sorry. I had to tell you. Now everything's in the open, you had to know."

Jacob lowered his hands and looked at him. "Is there anything else in the footage that might be useful?" He kept his voice calm with effort. "They have someone working on it, but if there's anything we could use, you need to tell me now."

Kit shook his head at once. "Just her and the man saying they're going to Tom's house and that they don't think anyone'll be around."

"Good." Jacob blew out a sigh of relief. "That's something." He studied Kit, and how pale and nervous he looked. "It wasn't your idea, was it? Any of it? Nagy did it all."

Kit chewed on his lower lip. "He thought we might be able to solve the case where the police couldn't. Tom helped to save him when he came here. He wanted to find whoever…" His distress was audible in his voice. "He wanted to help."

Jacob sighed and slipped his arm back around Kit's shoulder, pulling Kit against his side again. "And that went well." He rested his temple against Kit's hair. "Your lot didn't find the culprit. My lot were chasing an impossible killer. The only person who could have told us anything is probably going to snuff it so we'll never find out." He gazed at the roof of the pod. "And it's four in the sodding morning and I'm unemployed."

Kit squeezed his thigh. "Could be worse. Could have crabs."

Jacob tilted his head to peer at him. "Anyone ever tell you you're an odd one?"

Kit dropped a kiss on Jacob's lips. "Once in a while." He shifted on the chair to snuggle against Jacob's side, his head on Jacob's shoulder. "How long do I have before I have to get back to the station?"

"As long as we need to sleep," Jacob replied. "Bugger them all. We've earned the break."

Kit shivered and let out a soft sigh of relief. "Good," he whispered.

Back at the hotel, they tumbled into the unmade bed. Kit managed to fall asleep at once, but Jacob couldn't. Even with the warmth of Kit's arms around him and the whisper of breath against his bare chest, his mind kept drifting back to the case. All the evidence they had wasn't enough, and if they weren't able to find some connection between Harper and the woman, Harper would walk with nothing more than a slap on the wrist.

Jacob had no part to play anymore, and he knew it was going to drive him crazy, like an itch in the middle of his back, just out of reach. And Christ, he wanted to be able to walk back in there and pick apart the evidence until he found what he needed to condemn Harper once and for all.

He stared at the ceiling.

Maybe he didn't have access to the station. That didn't mean he didn't have access to the files.

In the darkness, he smiled.

Chapter Forty-Eight

Kit wanted to find somewhere to hide.

Going to the police station with Jacob was bad enough. Going into the station on his own and facing Jacob's colleagues, when they probably all knew the part he'd played in Jacob's resignation, was so much worse.

DI Temple met him at the front desk and escorted him up to their department, explaining that a desk had been assigned to him, and she would brief him shortly on his tasks. Kit could only nod gratefully when she led him to a desk in the corner of the room.

Other officers glanced at him occasionally. It gave him the impression of being put in the naughty chair.

One of them, a big blond man, came over ten minutes after Temple left him. "So you're Rafferty? Work for the TRI?"

Kit flicked the screen of his quill away and nodded. "Kit."

The man tilted his head, examining him. "I heard you're one of the people who slowed down this investigation to cover for your boss."

Kit felt a cold knot in his gut, but he looked back at the man, setting his jaw. "Unless I'm mistaken, I gave you the break in the case with the data from the eye." He lifted his chin defiantly, meeting the man's eyes. "The only thing I didn't tell anyone about was the time travel."

The man continued to gaze at him, his arms folded over his chest.

Kit fidgeted.

"Anton." Temple's voice made him look away from the man. She gave the blond man a warning glare. "Don't you have work to do?"

Anton touched his fingertip to his forehead. "On it, boss." He shot Kit a frown, then walked away.

"Ignore him," Temple said. "First off, I need you to give me a description of the man you saw skulking outside Jacob's place; then we'll need you to get into Sanders's drive. The upper levels and your boss need to know what he was working on."

Kit nodded. "I want to help however I can."

Temple's stern expression softened slightly. "I know. Jacob spoke well of you."

"It feels strange being here, knowing I'm the reason he had to leave."

Temple patted him on the shoulder. "We all know Jacob made the call. He always did what he had to, to break a case. You help us tidy up this one and let him go out with a cherry on top, yeah? I think he'd appreciate it."

"I might not be able to get into it," he warned.

"As long as you do what you can."

She left an officer with him to get the description, then brought him a slate and the evidence bag with the drive in it. They had decent equipment, even faster than some of the TRI tech, but even so, he knew Tom and Tom's keys. It was going to be a long day.

He didn't know how long he'd been trying to break through the encryptions, but a gentle buzz in his pocket distracted him. He frowned, pulled out his quill, and drew out the screen to find a message from Jacob.

What do they have you working on?

He glanced around, then replied. *Sanders's drives. They want to know what he was doing.*

Tell Temple you need to work on the eye.

Kit's frown deepened. *The eye? Why?*

Tell her you think there might be more data on it. Trust me.

DS Temple was talking to the blond man, over at his desk. Kit hesitated, then got up and went over to her. She held up a hand, motioning for him to wait, and finished her conversation before turning.

"Rafferty?"

"Could I have another look at that eye, when you have a minute?" he asked, hoping Jacob had the right idea. "I think there might be more data apart from the video."

Temple's dark eyebrows arched. "Like what?"

Kit shrugged. "It could be information about where the eye came from. Or about the man and where he came from. I don't know exactly," he said, and then suddenly, he did. He remembered the video. Maps. They had maps. He stared at her, his heart racing. "It might even have information about where they were meant to take the stuff they stole."

Temple spun to face the man beside her. "Anton, get to the evidence bay. Get me that eye. We need to get all the data from it, if we possibly can. It could give us our link to Harper."

The man's craggy face broke into a smile, and he shoved his chair back. "Yes, boss."

Temple looked back at Kit. "You think it's possible?"

"Even if there isn't anything new, we have to try," he replied. "What do you want me to do with the memory drive?"

"Keep on it now," she said. "Anton'll bring the eye as soon as he can."

Kit nodded and retreated back to the desk. He opened out his quill. *How did you know there was more stuff on the eye?*

You can take the man out of the CID, but you can't take the CID out of the man. Janos sends his regards.

Kit stared at the message.

"Rafferty?"

He snapped the screen shut and turned, startled. "Yes!"

Temple was standing right behind him, a knowing smile playing around her lips. "I wondered how long it would take for him to try and stick his nose in."

"I—" Kit wrapped his hand around his quill. "It's not—"

"Don't worry about it," Temple said, her voice low and conspiratorial. "This was Jacob's case. I knew it would bother him. If he wants to drop us hints, we'll keep it between us. He told you to look into the eye, didn't he?"

Kit nodded with a sheepish smile. "Is he always like this?"

"Stubborn to the bitter end?" Temple laughed. "Yeah. He never knows when to stop." She gestured to Sanders's drives. "Any luck there?"

He shook his head. "I've run it through the TRI decryption program, but he's used his key as well. It'll take me a while."

Temple ran her finger along her lip thoughtfully. "Right now, I think the eye has to be the priority. How much time will you need?"

Kit winced. "As much as you can give me. It's not exactly easy work."

"You do what I tell you to. Leave the rest of it to me."

"I don't want to get you in trouble as well."

Temple smiled. "Believe me, if I get in trouble on this case, it's not going to be your fault." She indicated to the drive again. "Keep working on that until we get the eye. We'll set you up somewhere quieter, make sure you're not disturbed. That way no one'll see what you're focusing on."

Kit tried to laugh. "No pressure, then."

Temple patted him on the shoulder. "You'll do fine."

Chapter Forty-Nine

Jacob jolted awake when the taxi-pod chimed.

He rubbed at his eyes and tried to get his bearings. It took him a moment to recognise his shithole of a hotel, but then consciousness and recollection came crashing in on him. He slid out of the taxi-pod and headed for the door, withdrawing his key card from his pocket.

It had been a long day.

As soon as Kit had headed for the station, he'd done some digging, spoken to people at the TRI, and shuttled himself out in the direction of the Schmidt-Nagy house.

While Nagy had been wary about admitting his crime, as soon as he realised Jacob wanted to conspire with him to find the man responsible, he'd had his slate out and had flung up projections all over the smooth white walls of the living room.

A lot of it, Jacob already knew, but the additional video footage was what he'd wanted to see. He'd watched it in silence four times, his smile growing wider by the moment. Less than ten minutes later, he knew his colleagues would be on the right track.

It hadn't stopped him going over every single file with Nagy, looking for anything he might have missed. They had every file from his slate, as well as the extra information Nagy and Kit had unearthed.

It had been a long, focused day, only broken by a brief call from Luke to check on him, and a heated argument in Hungarian between Nagy and his lover. Judging by the raised voices and angry gesticulating, Schmidt hadn't been aware of Nagy's hacking, but the fond impatience in his expression suggested he wasn't really angry, only concerned.

Jacob hadn't bothered calling Kit. Even if he had, he probably wouldn't have got any reply. When Kit slipped into coding mode, he didn't seem to notice there was anything else going on. If a fire alarm had gone off, he probably would have sat through it until the flames were licking his feet.

It came as a surprise, then, when he opened the door and the lights were already on.

"Kit?"

"Mm?"

Jacob shucked off his jacket, hung it in the wardrobe behind the door, and went farther into the room.

Kit was sprawled on his belly on the bed, stark naked, his chin resting on his folded wrists. He must have showered recently, his hair still in damp disarray. He had his quill in front of him, the small screen projecting a foot from the end of his nose. From the look of him, he wasn't watching whatever was displayed on it, his eyes half-closed.

Jacob crouched at the end of the bed and tapped the quill to switch off the screen. It winked out, and Kit opened his eyes a little wider, peering up at him. A drowsy smile crossed his lips.

"Y'r back?"

"Looks that way." Jacob propped his arms on the end of the bed. "Busy day?"

Kit rubbed his cheek against his forearm and yawned. "Eye. Drives. Stuff. Lots of stuff." He managed to unfold his arms enough to reach out and run a finger along Jacob's sleeve. "Smart boyfriend. Big brain."

Jacob's heart skipped a beat. "You found something?"

Kit nodded, smoothing Jacob's sleeve. "Maps." He shook his head, as if it would wake him up, and forced his eyes open. "Eye had maps. The meeting point." He smothered another yawn, blinking hard. "They came to the wrong place."

"The wrong place?" Jacob echoed. "They weren't meant to go to Harper?"

Kit rubbed at his forehead with the heel of his hand. "Wrong," he said, shaking his head. "Time. Wrong time. Maps weren't right. Maps were from ten years ago."

Jacob stared at him. "Ten years ago, when Sanders first developed the technology? They were trying to steal it before Sanders even started using it?"

"Their gate doesn't work right," Kit explained. "They missed the time they wanted to hit." He stretched out like a cat, kneading at the blanket beneath him. "Wrong times. S'pose they wanted Tom's plans before the TRI happened. 'Magine being first people to get it. Could make a fortune."

Jacob covered Kit's hands with his. "Do we know who they were taking it to? Or where they were taking it to?" If they knew that, then they might be able to make sense of it all, and maybe even figure out who had sent them.

Kit's face split in a sleepy grin. "Yep."

"Well?"

Kit curled his fingers over the end of the bed and wriggled closer until they were nose to nose. "A shipping company," he confided. "Just getting successful ten years back." His eyes were shining. "They moved, four years ago, to bigger offices. Fancier offices. Some daft DI quit so they could arrest the boss."

Jacob stared at him, holding his breath. "We have the link to Harper?"

Kit beamed at him. "Mm-hm."

Jacob sank his hand into Kit's hair and kissed him hard. "You," he said, between kisses, "are a bloody marvel."

Kit smiled into the kisses. "Yep."

He caught the front of Jacob's shirt and pulled at him, and Jacob was happy to take the hint, crawling up onto the bed with him. He kicked off his shoes, and both of them made quick—if clumsy—work of his shirt buttons.

"You're not too tired for this?" Jacob asked, burying one hand back in Kit's hair.

Kit reached down and squeezed him through his trousers. "You can do the work." He laughed. "Gets you off, doesn't it? Fighting crime?"

Jacob grinned crookedly. "Only a little." Kit squeezed him again, pointedly. "Okay, a lot." He caught Kit round the middle, hauling him closer. "You got johnnies?"

Kit caught the front of Jacob's shirt, rising up onto his knees. "Who d'you think you're talking to?" He jerked his head toward the bedside cabinet. "Good Boy Scout, me."

Jacob wrapped one arm around his lover's waist, then reached over and groped in the bedside cabinet. He came up with a handful and gave Kit a look. "An optimistic Boy Scout."

Kit shrugged with a pleased, lazy smile, slowly tugging at the front of Jacob's shirt. It gaped open to the waist, but he didn't make any moves to take it off.

"I'm feeling overdressed," Jacob observed.

Kit's smile turned wicked. "I like it. Feels naughty. All naked and you all dressed."

He couldn't help laughing. "Yeah?"

"Mm." Kit leaned down and nuzzled at his throat. "Should have kept the handcuffs."

Jacob's eyes went a little wider at that image, and his trousers were feeling uncomfortably tight. He reached down between them, undid his belt. Kit's hand joined his, fumbling with the button and fly, and all at once, a warm, skinny hand wrapped around his prick.

"Lemme," Kit said, snatching one of the condoms.

Jacob ran his hand down the length of Kit's back, watching those pale clever hands stroking him, then smoothing the condom neatly on. "You're more awake, then?"

Kit raised those drowsy eyes to him. "Nah. Can do it in m'sleep if I have to." He straddled Jacob's thighs, his own thighs pressing to Jacob's ribs. Their bodies were flush against each other, and he wriggled, rubbing their cocks together. "C'mon. Lube me."

Jacob snorted, squirting some lube into his hand. "Such sexy talk," he said, then hissed through his teeth when Kit's tongue teased his ear. His teeth caught Jacob's lobe and slowly tugged.

"Could talk dirty," he murmured as Jacob squeezed his arse, stroking his fingers against Kit's opening. "Could tell you how much I liked your arse. Noises you made first time. Could have done that for hours." He moaned against Jacob's throat when a finger pushed into him, hips shifting, cock rubbing against Jacob's bare belly. Jacob had to close his eyes, breathing hard. The air rushed from him in a gasp when Kit bit his throat. "M'ready already," Kit breathed, hot and wet on his skin. "Fuck me, yeah?"

Jacob nodded, swallowing hard. Christ, with the break in the case getting him started, and Kit being a filthy little bastard, he wasn't going to last any time at all. He slid his hands under Kit's thighs, hauling him up. Kit clung to the back of his neck, panting against his throat, and they both groaned together as he lowered Kit down onto his cock.

Kit's thighs tensed against Jacob's arms, and his body clenched tight around Jacob's cock, for a moment, all too much in one go. And then he had to go and make it worse, rolling his hips. He uncurled one hand from the back of Jacob's neck to slide under Jacob's shirt and rake his nails up Jacob's shoulder.

"Christ!" Jacob panted at the ceiling.

The laughter rippled against his neck; then Kit lifted his head, that pleased, sleepy smile plastered all over his face as he kept rocking his body closer, pushing Jacob deeper. He was right about it feeling bloody kinky: Kit all tangled bare limbs, and the only places they were skin-to-skin were cock and arse and chest. Kit's cock rubbed against him with every press of his body, and Jacob held on to him, so bloody tight, arse and back, to keep him close, keep him moving.

Kit kneaded at his shoulders, legs squeezing at Jacob's ribs, his breathing still even. He moved, rocking lazily as if they had all the time in the world, but Jacob smugly noticed the flush spreading across Kit's chest and shoulders. His cock throbbed against Jacob's belly, and his lips drew back from his teeth, air hissing between them.

"Could have done this down at the station," Kit whispered, meeting Jacob's eyes. "On your desk. Anyone could have come in." He yelped when Jacob's hips stuttered against him, then grinned. "Ride you hard on that chair."

The images were enough to make Jacob pull him closer, harder, trying to kiss him to shut him up, because Christ, he didn't want to finish like a horny teenager on his first try. Kit tilted his head away, laughing out loud.

"Tell me you wouldn't want to," he challenged. "Bend me over the desk and bugger me with them right outside, knowing we were the ones to solve it."

"Kit," Jacob growled. His fingers dug into Kit's back, and he moved as sharply as Kit, both of them breathing harder now, grabbing at each other, the bed creaking beneath them.

Kit's mouth brushed his ear again, his voice a hot breath. "You did it, y'know. They had no idea. And you...the eye, the time travel, the suspect, the connection." He dragged his teeth down Jacob's ear, making hot fire burst through Jacob's body. "You're the one who solved this one." His fingers were tight on the back of Jacob's neck, like he knew, knew exactly what his words were doing. "You got your—"

Jacob grabbed Kit's hair in his fist, pulling his head back hard enough so he could kiss him, his ragged groan spilling into Kit's open mouth. His hips shuddered as he came, panting against Kit's lips, and he swallowed Kit's delighted laughter.

Kit didn't stop, still hard, still wanting more. Jacob tried to gather his wits, but every time Kit moved, a fresh blaze of pleasure surged, and that wasn't helping. His hand still had Kit's arse, though, and he remembered...

The smack of his palm against Kit's tightly bunched buttock sounded like a gunshot.

Kit squeaked, and Jacob laughed so hard it shook them both.

"Two can play," he panted.

Kit leaned in closer, sandwiching his dick between them, and kissed Jacob again, softer, teasing flutters of lips, tongue, and teeth. Jacob stroked his backside, and swatted again, playfully, lightly, enough to make his lover jolt against him.

It was sudden when it came, the urgency forgotten in slow lazy kisses and gentle pressure. Kit tightened his hands on Jacob's shoulders and opened his eyes, staring at him as his cock twitched and spattered cum between them.

Their lips met again, both of them catching their breath. Jacob tasted the salt of sweat on Kit's skin, and Kit nibbled his lower lip.

"I'm keeping you," Kit said suddenly, his arms tightening around Jacob's shoulders. "You know that, don't you?"

Jacob splayed his hand low on Kit's back. "Yeah?"

Kit brushed the tip of his nose against Jacob's. "Mm-hm. I like your bum."

Jacob snorted and tipped them both sideways, sprawling on the covers, Kit's legs and arms around him at all angles. "You're a tit," he said fondly, wiping at Kit's chest with his shirt. "And you ruined my good trousers."

Kit peered down between their bodies as Jacob got the condom off. "Joint effort there," he said, smiling as Jacob craned toward the side of the bed to drop it in the bin. "Looks like we'll have to get your clothes off after all."

Jacob laughed. "Ah, I see. Your cunning plan of jizzing all over me suddenly makes sense."

Kit tapped the side of his nose. "You're onto me."

Jacob smiled. Maybe his whole world had been turned on its head, but at least he had someone with him who knew about it, too, and could still help him to smile through it.

Together, they got rid of the stained clothes, and Kit draped himself over Jacob, nestling against him. He quieted, and with the lights low and the silence, Jacob wondered if he'd fallen asleep.

"Jacob?"

He tilted his head to peer at Kit. "Mm?"

"I'm serious." Kit's blue eyes were uncharacteristically solemn. "I...kind of like you. A lot."

Jacob curled his fingers into Kit's hair, drawing the younger man up to kiss him. "I know," he murmured. "I like you too."

In the half-light from the street outside, Kit beamed like a kid on Christmas.

Chapter Fifty

Sometimes, Kit thought ruefully, a new position and a keen lover were a bad combination.

Jacob left the hotel room before he did, and so far, no one had said anything as Kit walked into the police station, but his current wobbly stance bore a strong resemblance to a bowlegged cowboy, his arse aching like a bastard.

A group of people were in the lift when he got in, so he tucked himself as near the door as he could. He leaned against the wall, sipping his coffee and counting down from fifteen. The doors opened as he reached zero.

The main room was empty when he entered, so he avoided the amused looks as he waddled to his desk and gingerly sat. He was early— Jacob and his bloody seven o'clock wake-up jog—and as far as he knew, Temple had locked away everything he had access to.

He took another sip of his coffee, spinning the chair slowly around with one foot, and glanced up at the incident board.

He'd never paid much attention to it, not when he knew practically everything on it, and probably a few things that weren't. Something, though, caught his eye, and he set his coffee on a desk, then got up and approached the board.

He frowned, flicking through the images, and leaned closer, examining each one.

"What the hell are you doing?"

Kit yelped in alarm at the voice from behind him. He spun around to see Anton standing in the doorway. The detective didn't look pleased to see him. No shock there. Even with his discoveries in the eye, Kit could tell Anton didn't like him. "What are these meant to be?"

Anton raised his eyebrows. "I thought you were our technical wizard." He pulled off his overcoat and hung it on a stand by the door. "Those are what we call 'hard drives.'"

Kit looked at him impatiently. "Are you going to keep on being a tosser, or are you going to help me? These hard drives—are they the ones that were found with the girl? The ones she was meant to have stolen from Tom's place?"

"Yeah. We had the pieces digitally reconstructed."

Kit looked back up at the board and flicked through the images. "And there are exactly the right number that were stolen?"

"According to Mrs. Ashraf, there should have been six. We have the pieces of six." Anton approached him. "What are you seeing?"

Kit turned to look at the other man. "These weren't Tom's hard drives."

Anton frowned, staring at them. "You're sure."

"I know the machines Tom worked on." Kit flicked through them again. "They might have been compatible with the machines he used, but he wouldn't have upgraded to this model. When you do work like we do, you don't buy cheap shit."

Anton ran his hand over his eyes. "This is either really good or really bad."

Kit retreated to the nearest seat, perched on it. "You mean Tom's data is still somewhere out there?"

"That's the bad side," Anton agreed. "But this also means it's very unlikely she jumped. If she tried to top herself, why would she take the time to replace the hard drives with fakes and keep one memory drive in her pocket? This means someone put her there, and they didn't think we'd notice the hard drives were wrong."

"If someone still has the drives though—"

Anton looked at him. "I don't think there's any question of who the someone is."

Harper. It was a work of bloody and ruthless stupidity, especially for someone with no idea of the complexities of time travel. Somewhere in the future, Harper had access to a faulty gate loosely based off Tom's designs. That meant somewhere in the future, he knew enough about the origins of time travel to send someone back to steal the working design. If he had succeeded, and Tom hadn't been the creator, then somewhere in the future, Harper wouldn't have known about it to begin with.

Kit stared at the board. "Shit."

"What?"

Kit looked at the other man. "We're not going to find them."

"'Course we are. We need to find all the places he might have stashed—"

"No, no, no. I know we won't find them, because somewhere in the future, he uses them. He wanted to make sure no one else got to time travel before he did." Kit rose from the chair and tapped open the folder with the footage from the eye. He brought up one of the freeze-frames of the gate. "That's why his plan was bollocksed. He got someone to build it for him using Tom's old schematics."

Anton frowned again. "I don't follow."

"When Tom started out, he couldn't pinpoint the destination. He fixed the place first, but the time element didn't work. The first tests were hit or miss, sometimes by days, sometimes by years." Kit tapped the glowing image of Harper's gate. "This must have been based on his original designs. They must have assumed it would work. That's why they ended up in the wrong time."

Anton stared at the board. "Shit. Shit's right." He blew out a breath. "And it's not like we can charge him with it, either, can we? I mean, we can't let anyone know what they're going to do in the future, or we'll fuck up the future, right?"

"Welcome to the wacky world of time travel," Kit said morosely.

Anton rubbed at his jaw. "So we get him in the here and now. Nail him for what happened to that girl and get him locked up for a good long while."

Kit blinked. That would explain why it would take Harper over twenty years to get the gate built if he ended up in jail. The stupid bastard had screwed up his own life twice over: once in the future, and again in the present to unsuccessfully improve the future.

Still, it wasn't like he could confirm that for Anton.

"Yeah. Yeah, sounds like a good plan." Kit stepped back. "Can you get me the drive you have? Temple wanted me to keep working on it."

By the time Temple arrived, he was well into the decryption. Sanders had used one of the more complicated keys, and Kit looked up bleary-eyed when Temple tapped on the edge of his desk to catch his attention.

"Any luck?"

"Just about," he said, dry-mouthed. "It's running a last cycle. You?"

She sat on the edge of the desk. "One thing our friends forgot when they dropped the girl at the tracks—this country is infested with cameras. Maybe the ones at the station weren't working, but there are only so many roads they could have used to get there, and my people are thorough."

Kit stared at her. "You got it?"

A smile split Temple's face. "Got teams on the way to the last known location."

"So you've got him!"

She patted him on the shoulder. "Easy, tiger. We may have the pod, but we still need to make the connections between it and Harper himself."

"Oh. Right." He rubbed at his eyes. "Yeah. Should have thought of that." His slate chimed, and he looked back at it. "Huh."

"What?" Temple rose and stepped behind him, looking over his shoulder. Both of them stared at the screen and the screeds of data. "What is this? Is it some kind of code?"

Kit shook his head, frowning. "No." He looked up at her. "It looks like timestamps."

Temple turned suddenly and strode across to the incident board. She pulled up a folder and flicked several of the files toward him.

Kit opened them up. The masses of numbers made no sense, but suddenly, he realised what she had spotted. In the screeds of digits, the numbers from Sanders's drive appeared at intervals.

The more he stared, the more the other numbers started making sense.

He touched the desktop, illuminating the surface to give himself a wider workspace, and cascaded the files to spread across it. Temple spoke, but he wasn't listening now. He had an idea, and it was all falling into place with timestamps matched up to her files, and he pulled up the maps.

His fingers danced across the desk, dragging and matching what he could, trying to make sense of what he couldn't. It shouldn't have made sense. The information in Temple's files was at least a decade old, and there were a lot more numbers on her files than there were on Sanders's drive.

Dates cross-referenced with grid points matched up.

Nearly sixty percent of the numbers were on both sets of data.

Kit sat back, staring at the desk. "My God."

"What?" Temple demanded impatiently. "What's this all about?"

Kit shook his head in disbelief. "He wouldn't have. Not without all the research...he knew what a risk...Jesus Christ."

"Kit," Temple said sharply. "What the hell is this?"

He looked up at her. "That gate in his basement, it isn't something new. We all thought he had to be working on something new, but it isn't that." He touched the scrambled list of numbers in her file. "This must have been all the possible destinations from the first time they tried to use the gate, back when they started."

"And?"

Kit felt shaken. Sanders had always been so methodical in his actions. When Mariam had said he'd been trying to find his wife, he assumed Tom would have been mapping out details, working out the exact location, building the technology to take him back to the right time, but Tom hadn't been doing that at all.

"He was trying to find her," he said quietly. "His wife."

"We know that. He was—"

"No." Kit looked up at her. "He was literally trying to find her. Every date you have on this list, it's him trying to find her. He never tried to make a teleporter or something to go into the future or anything else. It was to take him back to try and find her."

"But I thought..." Temple shook her head. "You said he put rules in place. All that research. All those secrets. Why would he have those in place if he broke them anyway?"

Kit could only shrug helplessly. "I don't know."

Temple tapped her fingers on the back of his chair, then sighed. "All we can do is send it up the line. Maybe it's something your boss will be able to explain for them. Maybe not." She patted him on the shoulder again. "You did well."

"You already had the numbers," he said. "I just recognised what they were."

"And let us know Harper still has the drives, so we have more cause to keep looking into him. Not to mention giving us his connection to our two future victims." She smiled. "You're not very good at accepting compliments, are you?"

Kit shrugged. "When Harper's been charged and the case is tied up, we can try again. Right now—"

"Right now, you just found out your boss was more of a scheming bastard than anyone realised."

Kit looked down at his hands on the desk. "And Jacob's still out of a job because of it all."

"That old bugger'll be fine," she assured him. "Don't worry."

"Wish it were that easy."

Chapter Fifty-One

Jacob tapped his knuckle against his lower lip, studying the wall.

When he'd returned to the hotel after his jog, Kit had already left for the police station, so he'd showered, changed, and set out himself. Nagy answered the door of the home he shared with Schmidt, and he didn't look at all surprised.

They'd spent the previous day working together on the police files stolen from Jacob's slate, and now that he knew he wouldn't be arrested for it, Nagy was more than willing to let Jacob continue. He'd left Jacob to go through the files again, and retreated back up the stairs.

Without anyone around or any distractions, Jacob went through every bit of data he had at his disposal. He didn't think there was much left he could uncover, but it felt better to make the attempt than sitting on his hands and waiting.

He'd shifted his focus to the old man who had dispatched the two unfortunate time jumpers.

It had taken him a long time to figure out why the man seemed so familiar. Only when he pulled up a comparison headshot of Patrick Harper and overlaid it with the old man's face had everything slipped into place. Those pale eyes. That high, domed forehead.

Turned out, losing at least fifty percent of your body weight could do a number on a person's appearance.

And yet, as far as Jacob knew, they hadn't noticed the similarity down at the station. He sighed, opened out his quill, and sent a brief message on to Kit, advising him that he should compare the two images.

It might be unusable, but any piece of evidence of the part Harper had played in the whole affair had to help. It was another matter whether the DCIs—or whoever the hell had taken charge of it all—could use it as a means to keep Harper in custody until they found more contemporary evidence against him.

A message came back a moment later: *I thought you were having a break.*

Jacob smiled ruefully.

Another message followed: *wait. I forgot it's you.*

Kit had included a picture of himself pulling a face.

"Ass," Jacob murmured fondly. He switched the screen off, tucked the quill back in his pocket, and headed for the kitchen to put the kettle on.

The floorboards creaked quietly as someone moved around upstairs. It was strange to be in another old house, though nowhere near as old as the Sanders house. He had to wonder if people who worked with history liked choosing buildings that they could have visited the day they were built.

In Nagy's case, he could understand why, as Nagy hadn't been raised in purpose-built multistorey complexes. A house like this would probably have been a luxury for him in his own lifetime.

In Sanders's case, he couldn't begin to guess what had drawn Tom Sanders to such an old-fashioned building. Given the technology he used, it must have cost a fortune to have the whole place made fit for purpose.

Jacob poured water from the kettle into a mug, watching the coffee granules dissolve.

"Back again?"

Jacob turned, startled. He hadn't heard Schmidt coming down the stairs. "Sorry. I needed something to do."

Schmidt's lips twitched at one side. The day before, his makeup had been pristine; today, he was barefaced, his hair dishevelled. He hadn't put on anything more than a pair of shorts and a robe.

"If you want, there's a Workaholic mug in the cupboard over the sink," he said. "Janos is a weak fucker when it comes to novelty presents."

Jacob smiled crookedly. "I think I'll manage with this one. You want one?"

Schmidt studied him. Every time they'd been around each other, Nagy had always been present. Jacob had never seen Schmidt on his own before. "Go on, then. Jan's in the shower now. He'll be at least an hour." He laughed fondly. "You'd think hot water was a fucking miracle, the way he goes through it."

Jacob filled a second mug. "You mind if I ask you something?"

Schmidt canted one hip against the counter and shrugged. "Feel free."

Jacob stirred some milk into his coffee, then held the bottle over Schmidt's, raising an eyebrow. Schmidt shook his head and reached for his mug.

"I was wondering how he adapted," Jacob said, putting the lid back on the bottle. "I mean, to go from World War II to a computer programmer. They didn't even have computers back then."

Schmidt's expression softened. "Because he's a fucking genius, that's how." He took a sip from the mug. "Back then, he wanted to get an education, but he had to work the land for his family." He met Jacob's eyes. "Makes you wonder how many Einsteins we lost because they were poor or prisoners or killed or whatever, doesn't it?"

"Zero to computer hacker in three years is pretty impressive, even for a genius."

Schmidt started laughing. "Three years? You're underestimating him. He taught himself how to use a computer in two months in his third language. When I say he's a fucking genius, that's not even the tip of the iceberg."

Jacob looked at him in disbelief. "Seriously?"

"Mm." Schmidt's eyes were dancing over the rim of his mug. "Hot, brilliant, and a sarcastic shit on top of it all. I hit the fucking jackpot."

Jacob leaned back against the counter, wrapping both hands around the mug. "I get the feeling it's a good thing we're on the same side."

Schmidt glanced over his shoulder at the police files projected onto the wall of the living room. "I know he could get in trouble for all of this..."

Jacob straightened. "This didn't happen. No one knows about it. No one will know about it. Once this case is closed, all of this is destroyed. It's as simple as that."

"Is it? You were on the side of the law."

Jacob looked at him. "You've got the wording right—I was. Now, I'm not." He walked back through into the living room and looked up at Harper's face on the wall. "That son of a bitch got at least two people killed and orphaned a child in the name of profit. He would have blackmailed me into covering up for him. He fucked with peoples' lives. I have no qualms about doing what I have to, to ensure he gets what's coming to him."

A chair squeaked on the floor as Dieter pulled it out at the dining table behind him. "You got any idea what you're going to do now?" Schmidt inquired.

Jacob turned to face him. "Do?"

Schmidt had one arm propped on the back of the chair, something oddly feline about his stance. Jacob couldn't help feeling like prey. "Yeah. You said it yourself—he fucked up your life. You can't go back to the force, and no fucking way are you private security material."

Jacob snorted. "Thanks. I think." He sat at the end of the table and set the mug on one of the decorative wooden coasters. "I don't know. Hadn't thought beyond the end of the case."

Schmidt slid a coaster along the table toward him. "Mind if I ask you something?"

"If you like."

"You figured out what the TRI did. You never said how."

Jacob scratched at his cheek with his thumb. "Suppose it's like pieces of a puzzle. A lot of little things coming together. Sanders's potential for jumping forward, far too advanced technology, stuff Kit said, the Potiorek conspiracy, the man who died before he was born. With all that taken into account, only time travel could make sense."

"Even though you knew it sounded fucking mental?"

Jacob smiled. "I've been a copper for thirty years. You get used to seeing weird shit." Schmidt raised his pierced eyebrow. "Okay, maybe not quite as weird as this, but you sometimes have to take a leap of faith on it."

Schmidt sipped his coffee, then looked down into the cup. "You're good at making sense of evidence, Mr. Ofori."

"Jacob," he said quickly. "Mr. Ofori makes me feel old."

Schmidt raised his eyes back to him. "Jacob, then. You know what the TRI does. Things are up in the air now, but you and I both know there's no fucking way the TRI is being shut down. We'll be supervised. Monitored. Regulated. Whatever happens, they'll come up with some bullshit so we'll be able to keep on doing what we do."

Jacob nodded. Time travel was a valuable resource. People would want to use it.

Schmidt set his mug down on the table, his fingertips resting lightly on the rim. "What we do is investigate historical events. Put together the details we can and collect the information we don't have." He gazed at Jacob. "What we need is someone who is good at putting the pieces together."

Jacob stared at him. "Are—" He frowned. "Are you offering me a job?"

Schmidt shrugged. "You know what we do. You know what the complications are like. You wouldn't be coming into it because it's this new and exciting time-travel bullshit. You know exactly what kind of shit you'd be landing in." He sat forward, propping his arm on the table. "It's not an easy place to work. Never has been, but when it's good, it's fucking amazing."

Jacob felt that now-familiar sensation of the world shifting under his feet. "You can't be serious. You don't have the authority for—"

"Ask Mariam, then," Schmidt said. "You've already protected our interests. You've shown you're fucking good at what you do and you'll do what's necessary. We've lost a shitload of staff, and along comes a man who has all the skills we need who has been fucked over by the same bastard who fucked us over. Doesn't seem like a coincidence to me. She doesn't think so either."

Jacob picked up his mug, downed a mouthful of coffee. When he'd come around to work with Nagy's files again, he hadn't expected this result at all. "Does she know you're asking?"

Schmidt nodded. "Jan let her know you were here. She told me to ask."

"I'm guessing he's not really in the shower at all?"

"Not for an hour," Schmidt said. "He knew I was going to ask. He didn't want to be around to sway your decision either way." He leaned forward. "Look, I know this isn't how you saw your life going. This whole thing has been shit for everyone. But this is an opportunity for you. You can liaise with whoever ends up being responsible for this mess. They'll respect you for being the one who identified the TRI and brought it into the public domain."

Jacob got up. "I need some air."

Schmidt rose at once. "Take your time, but we're serious, Jacob. The salary might be a bit shit compared to what you're used to, but we could use someone like you."

Jacob only nodded and headed for the front door.

It had been raining, the grass shining and damp. He walked out across the lawn, to the edge of the garden where a swing dangled from one of the trees. He sat down on it, staring back at the house.

Fifteen minutes later, he hadn't moved until his quill buzzed in his pocket.

The screen illuminated. Kit calling.

Jacob hesitated, then answered. "Hey."

Kit's face filled the screen. "Thought you'd like to know they've traced the pod that took the girl to the station," he whispered. From the look of his surroundings, he was in the staff toilets.

It should have been a huge relief, a triumph, but Jacob's world was spinning off its axis. "That's—that's great."

Kit frowned. "Are you okay?"

"Yeah. Yeah, I'm—" He broke off, then laughed tightly. "I don't know. Everything's happening too fast. I feel like I'm slipping, and I've got nothing to hold on to."

Kit glanced away from the camera, then back. "I don't think they need me about anymore. Want to meet me at my place? To hell with the reporters. I'll run you a bath, get some food in, and see if Luke wants to come over."

Jacob's throat felt tight, and he nodded. "Yeah. Please."

Kit touched the screen. "Wish they made these so I could reach through. You'll be okay to get back?"

"Yeah." Jacob pushed himself up off the swing. "I'll see you there in a bit."

Kit kissed the tip of one finger and pressed it to the screen. "I'll have the bath waiting."

Jacob made his way back up the garden to the house. He didn't really want to, not knowing that Schmidt would be expecting an answer, but he couldn't walk out without letting them know he had to head back to town.

Nagy glanced up from the table when he came in, and Schmidt put down his slate.

"I'm going back to town," Jacob said before either of them could speak. "I need to think."

Schmidt nodded at once. "You know where to find us."

Nagy rose, lifted Jacob's jacket from the back of one of the chairs, and crossed the room to give it to him. "I told him you are not a man who likes big surprises." He offered Jacob a rueful smile. "But he wanted to ask quickly, before you find new job."

"I get it." Jacob pulled his coat on. "I do, and I'm grateful, but it's—"

"A big surprise." Nagy said. "Take all the time you need for this. It is a big decision."

Jacob turned away and stepped back out into the rain.

Chapter Fifty-Two

Pizza had been ordered, and Jacob had been left to simmer in the bath, with Luke due to arrive any time in the next half hour.

Kit walked in a circle in his living room. He'd already been over it twice, tidying up things that didn't really need to be tidied up, but it had been a long time since he'd had more than one guest visiting, and he didn't want to give Luke a bad impression.

Part of him wanted to nip into the bathroom and check on Jacob, but when Jacob had arrived, he'd looked so out of it Kit got the feeling it wasn't the time for damp cuddles. He'd herded Jacob into the bathroom, the room already full of steam and ambient light and music, and closed the door after him.

He sank onto the couch, opening out his quill. Given the choice of that or stress-hoovering again, calling home won.

A touch dialled his mum's number.

She answered at once. She always did, and unsurprisingly, she looked concerned. He hadn't been calling enough, not in the last few weeks, especially when the TRI news had broken. "Hello, love. Everything okay?"

He waved his fingers. "All right, Mum. How are you?"

She gave him that look that said she could see through him. "I don't think that's why you're calling."

He looked down sheepishly, then back at the screen. "Just needed someone to talk to."

"About work?"

He winced. Of course. She would have seen his job all over the news. "About that, Mum...I wanted to tell you, but—"

"Confidentiality." She smiled. "I'm not daft, kitten. Time travel, eh? Like *Back to the Future*?"

He tried to smile. "Sort of."

"So you'll be a bit busy to visit, then?"

He twisted his fingers together to keep himself from picking at his nails. "Mum, it's all a bit mental up here. I've been helping the police with stuff. Trying to find the person who hurt my boss."

She looked startled. "You can help them?"

His lips trembled. "Time-travel stuff," he said. "I can help them with that, and it's good because we might be able to find who's behind all of this and...and..." He breathed in and out hard, then blurted out, "I might have a boyfriend."

They stared at each other for a moment; then she laughed quietly. "And you didn't think you should lead with that?"

He ducked his head, praying he hadn't gone too red. "It's just—we're starting out. He's one of the policemen."

"*Ah.*"

"Whaddya mean 'ah'?"

She laughed and made air quotes with her fingers. "Helping the police."

"Mum!"

She grinned into the camera. "You take your time," she said, "but when you're less busy, I wouldn't mind having you pop in. If it's going well, bring him with you. It's been a long time since I've seen my little man."

A quiet laugh behind him made him whip around sharply to find Jacob standing an arm's length behind him in boxers and a T-shirt, still steaming gently from the bath. "Jacob!" Kit groped for his quill. "I was just ringing my mum."

"I noticed." Jacob approached the couch and braced his hands on the back. "Afternoon, Kit's mum."

Kit looked nervously back at his mother. She gave Jacob a quick once-over and nodded in approval. Kit buried his face in his hand.

"Afternoon," she said. "I'll leave you boys be." She winked at Kit, then cut the call off.

"Well...that's Mum." Kit flicked the screen away. "Sorry. I needed to...there's a lot of stuff going on, and she's good at listening, and I didn't know if you would mind if—"

Jacob stooped over the couch, catching the back of Kit's head in one hand, and kissed him. Kit made a soft sound of approval, rising on his knees, and wrapped an arm around Jacob, pulling him closer.

Both of them were breathing harder when they broke the kiss, and Jacob knocked his brow gently against Kit's. "You talk too much."

"It's been said." Kit kneaded at his back and kissed him again. "Feeling better?"

"Much." He curled his fingers in Kit's hair. "Thanks."

Kit smiled, sliding his hand under Jacob's T-shirt. "Glad I could help." He traced his fingers up the valley of Jacob's spine, admiring the way Jacob's eyes darkened. Without another word, he climbed onto the back of the couch and kissed his lover again.

The T-shirt had just hit the floor when someone pressed the door buzzer.

"Bugger it!" Kit groaned.

Jacob chuckled against his throat and unwrapped Kit's legs from around his waist. "We've got time for that later."

"Yeah?" Kit slid off the couch.

Jacob's smile was small but wicked. "We've got time and a lot of surfaces."

Kit beamed, then dashed for the door. Mercifully, the deliveryman had beaten Luke, which meant he had time to run to the bathroom and jump in a quick icy shower before Luke arrived. He could cope with having his boyfriend's son around, but definitely not meeting him at the front door with a stiffy.

By the time he came out, Luke had arrived and Jacob had spread the boxes of pizza out on the coffee table.

"D'you have a bottle opener?" Luke asked by way of greeting. "I brought beer."

Half an hour later, the pizzas were reduced to scraps of cheese and burnt crust, and the beer bottles were mostly empty.

Luke slouched back on the couch. "I could get used to this."

"You'd have a waist as thick as a tree trunk if you did," Jacob countered, kneeling up on the far side of the coffee table to close the boxes. He stacked them, then folded his arms on the tabletop. "Listen, something's come up."

Kit didn't know whether he or Luke sat up fastest.

"What is it?"

"Is something wrong?"

Jacob glanced between them and shook his head. "Nothing's wrong." He pulled his beer bottle closer, turning it on the spot in front of him. "You both know I'm finished with the police force." Kit mutely reached over to touch his forearm, earning a small smile. "I've had an offer of a job."

"Already?" Luke sounded pleased. "Knew you were too smart to be unemployed for long."

Jacob continued to turn the bottle between his hands. "It's complicated." He raised his eyes. "It's at the TRI."

Kit stared at him. "The TRI? My TRI?"

Jacob nodded. "They—" He sighed. "I don't know if it's a good idea. I mean, the reasons they gave me are good, but I don't know—" He took a swig of beer, then set it down. "I forced them to go public. I don't know whether it's a good idea to get involved."

Kit didn't know what to think. No one had mentioned it to him, but then they hardly ever did. And technically, it would be good to have Jacob working nearby. But then, it might make things weird if they were working together. And he really didn't have a say in it. It was Jacob's life after all.

"What kind of job is it?" Luke asked, arms braced on his knees.

"I'm not sure of the details," Jacob replied. "They said there's investigative work involved, solving historical problems and things like that."

"So basically, historical policeman?" Luke said. "I don't know about you, but to me, that sounds right up your street."

Jacob scratched his chin. "It's not that simple."

Kit picked at his fingernail. "Yeah, it is." He didn't look at Jacob. "Take me out of the equation. Take the case out of it. If you were offered this job, this chance to do that kind of investigative work and solve crimes no one has been able to solve for centuries, would you want to do it?"

Jacob frowned pensively; then one side of his mouth turned up. "Ultimate cold cases, eh?"

Kit lifted his eyes from his fingernails. "You should take it."

"It might make things...complicated."

Kit snorted.

"What I think your shag toy is trying to say by way of grunts," Luke said, ignoring Kit's yelp of indignation, "is that this situation is complicated anyway, but that's no reason to look a gift horse in the mouth, especially not doing a job you know you'd be bloody amazing at."

"I'm still the man who forced the TRI to go public."

Kit laid his hands on the table. "They knew it would happen eventually. You can't cover up something this big forever. If Mariam's asking you, you know it's coming from the top. They think you're the right person for this, Jacob." He looked at his lover. "And if it doesn't work out, you can walk away, and no one would blame you."

Jacob silently reached over and grasped his hand. Kit curled his fingers, squeezing Jacob's, and tried to smile.

"You really think I should do this?"

Kit watched the way their fingers were overlapping. "Yeah," he said quietly. "I think we need someone like you in there." He raised his eyes to Jacob's. "It's your decision. Do it because you want to, not because we think you should. It's your life."

Jacob furrowed his brow. "I've fucked things up before because I put work first. I don't want to do that again. If this is going to get in the way of us—"

"It won't," Kit interrupted. "It won't. I work in engineering. You wouldn't even see me. You'd be in with all the historical people. And if they say anything about it, I'll rig their chairs to catapult them out the window."

Jacob smiled that gorgeous smile of his, dimples deepening on his cheeks. "Yeah?"

"Engineer," Kit replied, smiling in return. "I do what I can."

A muffled sound from the couch made them turn. Luke had his elbows propped on his knees and his clasped hands pressed to his mouth. From the look of it, he was trying to hide a smile, and another muted squeak escaped him.

Jacob snorted, but he sounded happier. "Shut up."

"You like him," Luke singsonged, making Kit blush. "You liiiiike him."

Jacob laughed openly now, and hurled a pizza crust at his son's head. "Did I mention my son is a little shithead?" he inquired as Luke ducked, laughing, behind a cushion.

Kit could only smile. "Like father, like son?"

Jacob pulled on his hand, drawing Kit closer. "You have no idea."

Chapter Fifty-Three

It felt strange walking into the station.

Jacob stood at the reception desk, waiting for the desk sergeant to notice him. Instinct told him to swipe his pass, walk through the door, and get to work, but DCI Crawford had his pass, his badge, everything that had identified him as a policeman.

He hadn't really wanted to come to the station today, or at all for a while, all of it too recent, too raw, but Crawford had left a message for him, ordering him to come in. There were loose ends to be tied up, formalities to be dealt with, his office to clear out.

He wished he were back at Kit's place, still in bed with Kit sprawled over him, a warm thigh draped over his arse and his lover nuzzling at his shoulders. It was a hell of a lot better than standing in the place where he'd been forced to abandon his career.

The sergeant turned from checking a monitor and exclaimed in surprise. "DI Ofori!"

Jacob managed to force a smile onto his face, but it felt tight and strained. "Just Jacob, Sergeant," he demurred. "Can you let DCI Crawford know I'm here?"

Sergeant Benson nodded at once, reaching for the phone.

Five minutes later, DCI Crawford met him as he emerged from the lift. "Mr. Ofori."

"Ma'am."

She gestured sharply, and he fell into step behind her. She didn't say anything, and he knew asking questions while walking in the halls would be far from appropriate. It was only when they passed her office that he grew more confused.

"Ma'am, where are we going?"

She glanced over your shoulder. "You would do well to keep quiet, Mr. Ofori." She turned into the corridor that led to the interview rooms and opened a door adjacent to one of the rooms. The viewing chamber for one of the bigger interview rooms. "In."

He entered and turned to her. "Ma'am, I don't understand what—"

"No more questions, Ofori," she replied shortly. "This was your case. It's only right that you see us finishing it. Remain in here. Do not move. Do not let anyone know you are here. Am I understood?"

His heart leapt. "Understood, ma'am."

For a moment, her expression eased and she nodded, then withdrew, closing the door behind her.

Jacob sat on one of the seats, looking through the pane of mirrored glass into the interview room. If he'd taken her meaning, they'd found something to pin Harper to all of the crimes committed in the present.

If that was the case, if they had him...

Jacob took a deep breath, trying to steady himself. No. He couldn't believe it until charges were laid. He'd seen so many, too many, cases fall apart at the final stretch. He would watch, listen, and pray like hell that everything would come together, but until it was done, he wouldn't celebrate, not yet.

Fifteen minutes later, Crawford and Temple escorted Harper into the interview room. They were accompanied by a man in a suit. Harper's lawyer, Jacob assumed. Harper didn't look as polished as he had the last time Jacob had seen him, stubble on his face, his clothing rumpled and creased.

All of them sat, and Temple did the usual setup of the monitoring system.

"Since you have two hours before your seventy-two-hour holding period is up," the lawyer began, "I assume this is your last-ditch attempt to try and get some kind of confession out of my client."

Crawford leaned back in her chair, her hands casually folded on the edge of the desk. She let Temple take point, and Jacob was grateful for that. Temple had taken over the case, and she'd done it without any hesitation. She deserved the chance to break it.

"We have a few last questions for Mr. Harper," Temple said. "As we discussed in previous interviews, you were aware that we were looking for a young woman in connection with the disappearance of Thomas Sanders."

"And as my client has previously stated, the woman came to his offices and departed shortly thereafter. He did not see her after that."

Temple gazed at him, smiling placidly, and Jacob wanted to applaud. He'd taught her that move, being confident enough to unnerve, but not so overconfident as to make stupid mistakes. "Yes, I recall he mentioned she came to his offices and only spent five minutes there. As *you* will recall, we have physical evidence confirming this was a lie, so you can see why we might find it difficult to trust anything your client says."

The lawyer's expression remained carefully blank. "Unless you have proof that suggests they met again, I would be careful how you proceed, DI Temple."

She kept smiling. "You know we found the young woman."

"Yes, we are aware of her misfortune on the railway."

Jacob kept his eyes on Harper. The man looked like he hadn't slept, and when people were tired, they were more prone to give themselves away.

"Sadly, our mystery woman passed away during the night."

A moment, a split second of relief crossed Harper's face before he schooled his expression. *Got you, you bastard.*

"And since you have no further evidence of this particular crime, perhaps you would—"

"I didn't say I was finished, Mr. Dennis." Temple cut across him smoothly. "Miss Smith died of injuries inflicted by the train. However, we have evidence that indicates she was not alone when she did. Indeed, the evidence suggests she was murdered."

"Oh come now!" Dennis exclaimed. "My client helped this woman when she was lost and distressed, and now, you are accusing him of what exactly?"

"Exactly what I said, Mr. Dennis. Conspiracy to murder."

Harper's eyes flicked to his lawyer, then back to Temple. "This is ridiculous," he snapped. "I was in custody when she had her accident! And now, you have the gall to say I had some involvement with this?"

His lawyer caught him by the arm, trying to calm him. "What my client is saying is that your own closed-circuit surveillance will confirm he has a solid alibi for the time of the woman's accident."

"What our surveillance will show is your client talking to you, and then you making a call on your quill as you left the building," Temple replied evenly. She laid a folded paper on the desk. "And this warrant gives us the right to check your outbound calls on your quill, particularly for a call to a certain Nicholas Garrett."

Harper's whole body went tense, his hands clenching on the desk. Jacob smiled. The man was sweating, and from the look of things, his lawyer had no idea what his client had involved him in.

Dennis frowned. "The name isn't familiar."

"Perhaps not to you, but he certainly is to Mr. Harper." Temple slid the paper across the table. "Do you recognise this number?"

Dennis stared at it, then back at them. "I need to speak to my client for a moment."

"You have five minutes," Crawford said, rising. She held out an evidence bag. "Put your quill in there, please." Dennis hesitated, then did so, and Crawford sealed the bag. "Interview suspended for five minutes. DCI Crawford and DI Temple exiting the room. Temple, with me, if you please."

Temple switched off the recording, which unfortunately had the joint effect of turning off the microphones that connected to the observation room. Still, Jacob could observe Dennis talking angrily at Harper, and Harper raising his hands to placate him.

The door of the observation room opened behind Jacob, and he glanced back.

"How's it looking?" Temple asked, coming over to lean on the back of his chair.

Jacob grinned. "Seems there's something he forgot to mention to his lawyer, doesn't it?"

Temple laughed. "We thought that might be the case."

"You have something on this Garrett, then?"

Temple squeezed his shoulder. "Just wait and see."

"You're doing well in there." He reached up to squeeze her hand. "Harper looks like he's about to have a heart attack."

"Thanks, chief." She studied him for a moment, then said, "That Rafferty's a good kid, you dirty old pervert."

Turning around to face her properly, unable to hide a smile, he warned, "Don't you start. Luke's bad enough."

She raised her eyebrows. "He's already met the family? It's that serious?"

Jacob shrugged. "Could well be."

"I'm glad then." The door opened again, and both of them glanced over. DCI Crawford jerked her head. Temple nodded, stepping back. "Once this is over with, we'll talk, all right?"

Jacob nodded. "Yeah."

He returned his attention to the glass as the two women re-entered the interview room. The lawyer looked on edge, Harper pale and tense—the kind of combination every officer liked to see in a suspect.

Temple restarted the recording. "Interview resumed at 11:47. DCI Crawford and DI Temple present." She propped her forearms on the desk and folded her hands together in front of her. "So, Mr. Dennis. We showed you a number on the warrant. Do you recognise the number?"

"Yes." Dennis set his jaw. "My client asked me to telephone that number. I was advised it pertained to a business meeting he needed to cancel, on account of being held in custody."

"A business meeting." Temple tapped the balls of her thumbs together. "I'm afraid Mr. Garrett said it was about another matter entirely."

Harper's breath rasped, the sweat rolling off him in thick ropes.

Dennis swallowed hard. "My client has no comment."

Temple smiled without showing any teeth. "Your client's silence speaks volumes." She leaned forward. "Your assumption, Mr. Dennis, was incorrect. We did not bring your client in here as a last-ditch attempt to delay any proceedings. We brought your client in here to give him a last opportunity to give us the truth of the situation. He has not done this, and the record will show this when his case is taken to trial."

"On what charges?" All the fight had gone out of Dennis.

"Where to begin— We have perverting the course of justice, attempted blackmail, aiding and abetting a fugitive, conspiracy to commit theft, theft, conspiracy to commit murder..."

"There's no evidence for half those charges," Harper rasped. He looked pasty and ill. "No evidence."

"On the contrary." Temple unfolded her hand and touched the desk, illuminating it. Jacob couldn't see the image from his angle. "This is the pod that carried Miss Smith to the train station."

"I don't see how—"

"It appears Miss Smith knew she was in danger," Temple interrupted smoothly. "We found trace evidence under her nails that matched the fibres of the seats, and scratches on the seat. There were also fingerprints that identified your Mr. Garrett, thanks to his previous misdemeanours." She touched the desk again, changing the image. "He tried to burn the interior, and if he had succeeded, he would have destroyed any evidence, but he made the mistake of closing the doors once he set the fire." She folded her hands and smiled. "I hope you understand science well enough to see his error."

Jacob clapped. Yes, yes, *yes*!

"Shit." Harper's voice was a wheezing breath.

Temple's smile widened. "We picked Mr. Garrett up this morning. He does not want to be held solely accountable for a crime of your making. He informed us of your instructions to conceal the girl at one of your unlisted properties until the furore died down. We have the address of that property now, and a team will be examining it thoroughly. He also informed us that when it became clear we were shifting our investigation in your direction, she was to be dealt with."

She rose from her chair, and Jacob grinned from ear to ear. She knew every trick he had, using them like a professional.

"We have one last question for you, Mr. Harper, and consider carefully before you answer. The young woman had a box of hard drives. Mr. Garrett confirmed he substituted the hard drives while your guest slept." She leaned down, bracing her hands on the edge of the desk. "Where are those hard drives now?"

Harper stared at his plump fists.

They had him on so many charges. He was going to be put away for a long time, if justice was served. He hadn't been honest at any time through the whole case, and it came as no shock at all when the man lifted his head.

"I have no idea," he spat.

Temple's smile turned a little harder. "So you say, but if we do find them, believe me when I say I'll find some new charges to bring against you." She tapped the monitor controls on the side of the table. "Interview terminated 11:56."

She strode out of the room. DCI Crawford followed, and Jacob was off his chair and waiting by the door when it opened.

He and Temple stared at each other, and then he grabbed her around the waist and spun around, swinging her off her feet. She hugged his shoulders tightly, laughing.

"We did it! We got the bastard!"

He set her down. "I could kiss you on the mouth right now, Abby."

"Eurgh, no!" She laughed, swatting at him. "I don't know where that thing's been."

"I bet you can take a pretty good guess," he countered, grinning. He looked over at Crawford, standing beside the door. "Ma'am, thank you for letting me be here to see the end of it. I know you didn't have to—"

The DCI stepped forward. "Don't get sentimental on me, Ofori," she said and held out a hand. "You did a damned good job on this case. We couldn't have closed it without you."

He shook her hand. "Thank you, ma'am."

She smiled. "Now, get your arse out of here and go up and clear out your office before anyone wonders what you're doing in the building."

He nodded at once and strode past her.

"And, Ofori..."

"Ma'am?"

She leaned out into the hall to look at him. "Try not to look too excited until Temple comes up and makes the announcement."

He tried to school his expression into a more serious one. "Yes, ma'am."

Chapter Fifty-Four

They didn't have a proper funeral.

You couldn't really have a proper funeral without a body or a grave.

Instead, the TRI held a memorial service in the garden where a stone had been laid for Olivia Sanders years before. Tom's name had been added to the stone, and people stepped forward in turn to offer their memories of him.

Kit stood close to the back of the crowd of mourners, Jacob's hand around his a silent comfort. On the periphery of his vision, the bloody reporters lurked with their cameras, held in place by the police cordon.

"You okay?" Jacob asked quietly as yet another person stepped forward to speak.

Kit shook his head. "This is all wrong. None of this should have happened." He felt raw, all the memories and horrific thoughts of the last few weeks flooding back.

"It shouldn't." Jacob pulled on his hand. "You don't need to stay. Come on."

They weren't the only ones to drift away from the group. Mariam sat on a bench a hundred meters away with Ben beside her, clinging to her, crying. Kit's heart ached for the boy. Both parents killed in action, no bodies in their graves, no family to go to.

The gravel crunched underfoot, and Ben lifted his head, startled.

Jacob's hand tensed against Kit's.

Fat tears rolled down Ben's pale face. "You said you'd find him. You said."

Jacob released Kit's hand to crouch by the bench. "I know," he said, so gently. "I tried my best, Ben, but I was too late. I'm so sorry I couldn't bring him back."

"But you said." Ben's voice broke.

Jacob lowered his head. "I know. I was wrong."

Mariam put her arm around Ben's shoulder. "Mr. Ofori found the man who did all of this," she said softly. "He won't hurt anybody else."

Ben whimpered, then slid down off the bench and wrapped his arms around Jacob, hugging him tightly. Jacob fell onto his knees and hugged the boy, Ben's shaking sobs muffled against his shoulder.

Kit met Mariam's eyes. She smiled sadly as she got to her feet.

It had been a rough few weeks since the TRI had gone public with decisions still to be made. Their business was being debated across the globe. As the new head, Mariam had become the focus of attention, expected to answer all questions. It couldn't be easy, raising her own family, taking in Ben, and doing everything else on top of it.

"If you need some help," Kit offered, "Ben can come and stay with us for a bit. We have plenty of rooms in the flat."

He didn't know quite when the flat had gone from being his flat to their flat. Jacob didn't stay every night, but more often than not, they woke up together, and it felt right when Kit came home from work and found him on the couch.

They tried not to meet up at work. Jacob had laid that ground rule because he knew how he'd be viewed. He was right as well. Many people gave him a wide berth, but things were getting better. Janos would regularly join him for meals, which seemed to give the green light to others. The TRI had started to accept him, and that was all Kit needed to know.

Work was work. What they had together, they kept for outside.

Mariam looked down at Jacob, rubbing his hand in circles on Ben's back. "Maybe," she agreed. "I'll talk to him about it." She touched Ben's shoulder. "Ben, do you want to go home now?"

Ben straightened up, nodding. He rubbed at his eyes with his fist and said unsteadily, "Thank you for catching the bad man."

Jacob only nodded, lowering his head. Kit reached down to squeeze his shoulder as Ben and Mariam took each other's hands and walked away along the path.

"You okay?" Kit asked quietly.

Jacob shook his head as he got back to his feet.

Kit pulled him around gently and stepped closer, wrapping his arms around Jacob. "I'm here." Jacob's breath came hot and rapid against Kit's throat, and he held on to Kit tightly. Kit stroked the back of his neck and rubbed his back, trying to offer what comfort he could. "You did everything you could. You caught Harper. You know you did all you could."

"Yeah."

Kit drew back to look at him. "That doesn't help, does it?"

"Not when he's left without his parents." Jacob looked in the direction of the retreating figures of Mariam and Ben. "She'll take good care of him, I know, but it's not the same. Not when he loved his dad so much."

So much was going unsaid, and Kit couldn't help remembering everything Jacob had told him about his own family. He took Jacob's hand. "Want to go home?"

Jacob nodded, wiping at his cheek. "Yeah."

The gravel crunched as they walked.

"Maybe you can call Luke," Kit suggested quietly.

Jacob didn't look at him, but he held Kit's hand a little tighter. "I think," he murmured, "it's the right time for me to call my parents."

Kit glanced at him. "You want to?"

Jacob nodded and smiled sadly at him. "Yeah. At least I still have the chance."

Kit stepped closer to kiss him. "And no matter what happens, I'll be right there with you."

Jacob nodded, and this time when he smiled, it reached his eyes.

Acknowledgements

Six years after I first finished a novel, now I have the whole series all in one place and I'm thrilled to bits. Many thanks to NineStar for taking a chance on a series already halfway through. I could not be happier with how these novels have been honed and polished. And to my usual gang, it's over! We're done! You never have to hear me flailing about paradoxes again! Cake for everyone!

About the Author

C.B. Lewis has been writing and telling stories as far back as she can recall. It's a great delight for her to have all of the Out of Time series completed together. Onward, to the next adventure!

Facebook: www.facebook.com/cblewisauthor

Tumblr: www.tumblr.com/blog/cb-lewis

Website: www.cblewis.co.uk

Other books by this author

Out of Time Series

Time Waits

Time Taken

Time Turns

Out of Time

Also Available from NineStar Press

Connect with NineStar Press

Website: NineStarPress.com

Facebook: NineStarPress

Facebook Reader Group: NineStarNiche

Twitter: @ninestarpress

Tumblr: NineStarPress

www.ingramcontent.com/pod-product-compliance
Lightning Source LLC
Chambersburg PA
CBHW051602100726
47898CB00001B/191